SINCERELY Yours

A NOVELLA COLLECTION

SINCERELY YOURS

Jane Kirkpatrick, Amanda Cabot,
Laurie Alice Eakes, *and* Ann Shorey

Revell

a division of Baker Publishing Group
Grand Rapids, Michigan

A Moonlight Promise © 2014 by Laurie Alice Eakes
Lessons in Love © 2014 by Ann Shorey
One Little Word © 2014 by Amanda Cabot
A Saving Grace © 2014 by Jane Kirkpatrick

Published by Revell
a division of Baker Publishing Group
P.O. Box 6287, Grand Rapids, MI 49516-6287
www.revellbooks.com

Printed in the United States of America

Library of Congress Cataloging-in-Publication Data
Sincerely Yours : a novella collection / Jane Kirkpatrick, Amanda Cabot, Laurie Alice Eakes, and Ann Shorey.
    pages cm
    ISBN 978-0-8007-2204-3 (pbk.)
    1. Christian fiction, American. I. Kirkpatrick, Jane, 1946– author. II. Cabot, Amanda, 1948– author. III. Eakes, Laurie Alice, author. IV. Shorey, Ann Kirk, 1942– author.
PS648.C43S56 2014
813'.01083823—dc23   2013040885

Most Scripture used in this book, whether quoted or paraphrased by the characters, is taken from the King James Version of the Bible.

Scripture quotation on page 318 is taken from the New American Standard Bible®, copyright © 1960, 1962, 1963, 1968, 1971, 1972, 1973, 1975, 1977, 1995 by The Lockman Foundation. Used by permission.

14 15 16 17 18 19 20   7 6 5 4 3 2 1

Contents

A Moonlight Promise

Laurie Alice Eakes

To my high school friend Camilla S. C.

Since I was fifteen, I've thought your name,
as lovely as you are, would be wonderful
for a heroine.

And he said unto me, My grace is sufficient for thee: for my strength is made perfect in weakness. Most gladly therefore will I rather glory in my infirmities, that the power of Christ may rest upon me.

2 Corinthians 12:9

Prologue

New York City
May 23, 1825

Dearest Camilla,

The London newspapers to which my husband subscribes informed me that your brother, too, has left us. My deepest sympathies. Before I chide you for this news coming from a newspaper and not your fair hand, allow me to offer you some relief for the difficulties I expect you now face.

In October, the 26th day to be exact, my husband and I shall depart for the Great Lakes via the Erie Canal, which will open on that day. Because we will begin this new adventure of our lives in a land that is little more than wilderness, I would love some civilized companionship. No one I know is more civilized and genteel than you, my girlhood friend.

Do, I beg you, join us here in New York, or, if you do not arrive in America soon enough, come up the river to Albany, from which we will depart. Dozens of steamboats leave for the north daily. The harbor master can advise you as to which captains in port are reliable.

I do hope you will say yes and understand if you do not.

Sincerely yours,
Joanna

ONE

"Wait. Wait." Camilla Renfrew raced down Barclay Street, waving her umbrella at the lone figure at the dockside of the last steamboat moored along that section of the East River. "Please, do not leave."

The man who had been pointed out to her as Captain Nathaniel Black glanced toward her and said something inaudible above the chugging of the boat's engine, the patter of the rain against Camilla's umbrella, and the clatter of her hard leather soles on the wooden planks of the wharf. She did not need to hear what he said. His turned back and feet heading up the gangway, his dark hair lifting like mourning kerchiefs waving farewell in the icy wind blowing off the Atlantic, spoke a trumpet blast of a message—he would not wait for her. Emphasizing his rejection, a bell clanged from the upper deck.

Camilla kept running toward the solitary boat and broad, indifferent back. "Oh, no, please, just another moment." Heedlessly sacrificing her last bonnet to the rain, she collapsed her umbrella and tucked it under her arm so she could gather up her skirt with one hand and run unimpeded by layers of fabric.

She hit the edge of the dock just as the gangway began to rise.

13

A bell clanged, and the paddle wheel began a languid *shug, shug, shug*.

She glanced at the growing gap between wharf and gangway, took a deep breath, and leaped onto the latter.

The gangway rocked beneath her, swaying like a tree branch in a gale. Men shouted. Two left the tarpaulin they were tying over some barrels and surged toward her. Captain Black motioned them back with a gesture so forceful he may as well have shoved them, and charged toward Camilla. "What do you think you're doing?"

"Coming . . . aboard." Running, sliding, gasping for breath, she closed the distance between herself and the captain.

The boat heeled beneath the onslaught of an incoming wave, and Camilla landed on the planks at his feet. She gripped his arm. Beneath her gloved fingers, his arm stiffened to something akin to an iron railing.

She glanced up at its owner and could not move. Eyes the pale green of spring grass back home in Gloucestershire pierced into hers like ivory knitting needles. For all their sharpness, those were young eyes. He could not be more than two or three years beyond her own twenty-five.

"What," he asked in a frosty tone, "possessed you to do something so dangerous? If you'd fallen into the river, the current would have pushed you right into the wheel."

Camilla gulped. Her stomach churned like the paddle wheel towering at the stern of the boat. Even in the gloom of the rain-soaked afternoon, the blades flashed in lethal grace. If she had gotten caught, those paddles would have pounded her like a piece of hide in the hands of a tanner.

She clutched Black's arm more tightly, though her fingers slipped on his wet leather coat, and swallowed three times before she managed to speak. "I insist."

In response, Black extricated his arm from her grasping fingers and stepped away from her. His face turned stony, emphasizing every chiseled angle. "I can't help you."

Behind him, the now mostly idle crew watched with expressions varying from dismay to amusement.

Their curiosity lent Camilla some courage to press her suit. "But you must help me." She firmed her chin to keep it from quivering, and her voice emerged so sharply she feared she sounded shrewish. "All the other boats have left, and I must reach Albany before October twenty-sixth."

"You're not the only one." He turned half away. "This is not a passenger boat. There'll be more of those tomorrow."

"But I cannot—"

She could not stay in the city another night. She could not tell him that, however. Of everything else she had lost over the past six months, no one could remove her pride.

She hefted her reticule. The beaded and embroidered velvet bag hung limp with its sad complement of some English and American pennies and a five-dollar gold piece she doubted would last her another day in the city.

Her chin quivered despite her efforts. "Please."

"As soon as we can get turned back, I'll put you ashore again." He walked away from her, past a black tower belching smoke and radiating blessed heat, and up a stairway.

Camilla followed. "You do not understand, sir. It is vital I reach Albany immediately."

He paused at the top of the steps. "And it is vital I'm not delayed any longer." He strode along the upper deck to another set of steps leading to a structure that did not appear to provide much shelter from the rain beyond a roof and boards no more than a yard high on three sides.

Camilla cast a longing look at the row of cabins toward the stern and followed the man. Beneath the roof, a man stood to one side of a wheel as tall as his shoulder, a good five and a half feet.

With one hand, he gripped a pin protruding from the side of the wheel, and with the other, he reached up to pull one of several rings dangling from the ceiling. With a screech of gears from the machinery below, the boat ceased backing. Another pull on the rope, and the vessel lurched forward.

Camilla lost her balance and dropped her valise to catch hold of the wooden side.

"Sit down before you fall down." Black gestured to a bench bolted to the floor, then turned back to the pilot. "How's visibility?"

"All right if this don't turn into fog." The man pulled another lever, and a long, deep whistle blasted low and harsh.

The vessel swung into the stream, the flagpole at the center of the bow pointing the way. Camilla dropped onto the bench and hugged her arms across her middle. She gritted her teeth to keep them from chattering. Heat radiated through the floor of the wheel-house, but not enough to combat the blast of wet wind funneling through the open front of the structure.

She glanced at the captain, pleading with her eyes for him to reconsider taking her upriver. He did not even glance her way. He and his crewman kept their faces turned toward the bow of the boat and the river beyond, an endless stretch of churning dark water with wharves and warehouses and growing cities along its banks, sailing ships and steamboats and ferries traversing its surface. Bells and whistles sounded in an endless chorus, and smoke from hundreds of boilers fogged the air.

Her heart ached for the clean, crisp air of the Cotswolds, and the home she would never see again because it belonged to someone else.

She swallowed. "How long until you can turn back?" Her voice emerged with the social lightness she had been trained to use in company. With these two hulking men in front of her, her tone sounded weak, barely above the river cacophony.

"With this traffic and rain, ten minutes, maybe twenty," came the captain's laconic response.

"I could perhaps perform some task to make myself useful on the journey."

"Can you cook?" the pilot asked.

Camilla grimaced. "Ladies are not taught to cook."

Black snorted.

The crewman glanced at her with disgust, though he sported a missing eyetooth and scarred lip above it. "You're English, aren't you?"

"Yes, I am. I just arrived here two days ago. I was to meet a friend here in New York, but my voyage was delayed. My friend has already gone on upriver." She spoke quickly to get everything out before she lost the men's attention, what of it she garnered anyway. "And if I do not reach Albany before the canal opens, she and her husband will head west without me."

And she would be destitute in a strange land.

"I . . . must not be left behind," she finished rather lamely.

"Other boats will be leaving early tomorrow morning," Black said.

Camilla shook her head. "Nothing can possibly travel that far that swiftly."

The two men gave her amused glances.

"Any riverboat captain with half a paddle wheel can get to Albany in a day or a little more," Black said.

"It is the little more that concerns me." Camilla stared down at her reticule.

If only she had not spent every last farthing on running, hiding, sailing across the Atlantic.

Another chill racked her body. "Please." She gulped and fixed her gaze on Captain Black, a broad back that looked about as movable as the shaft of wood holding the giant wheel in place. "The harbor master said you were reliable and trustworthy, which does not seem to be the situation with most . . . riverboat men."

Not a good choice of words. She was so unpracticed at begging for help she forgot to keep her opinions to herself.

17

Neither man responded. They spoke to one another about depths and directions, the best way to skirt an oncoming vessel, and something about the cargo and hot coffee. She preferred tea, but hot coffee sounded heavenly.

She ran her tongue over her dry lips and tried one more time. "Why do you have cabins if you do not take passengers?"

"The boat came with them."

"What if I simply take a portion of deck rather than a cabin. It would be a rather small portion."

"Let me explain this, Miss—"

"Ren—"

"I don't care to know your name." He held up one hand for emphasis before reaching for one of the ropes hanging from the roof and giving it a tug. "I am not going to have a solitary female unprotected on my boat."

"I crossed the Atlantic unprotected and was perfectly all right."

Black did not respond. He appeared to concentrate on his ropes and the wheel and the river traffic.

She tucked her chin into the collar of her cloak and hugged her arms across her middle. "Why are you so opposed to having one passenger for the next day?"

The man shrugged.

"Captain Black, that is scarcely—"

The thud of boots on the steps stopped her from lecturing him like a schoolmistress. The crewman appeared with tin cups and a dented pot from whose spout coffee-scented steam spewed. "This should warm us, Nathaniel."

"Serve her ladyship first," Black said.

"I am not titled. I am merely the daughter of—" Camilla closed her eyes and her mouth. Her cheeks grew warm for the first time in days, as she realized the man was insulting her, not paying her a courtesy. "I would appreciate some coffee, thank you."

"Anything for a pretty girl." The crewman set pot and cups on the bench beside Camilla and poured hers. "It ain't a lady's drink the way we make it, but it's hot."

Hot and thick as oil. She drank the coffee. It tasted like sludge and smelled like burned stockings, but in its heat lay comfort. In the wheelhouse lay a few moments' respite from the tumult of the city.

She glanced ahead and saw another wharf growing closer, another unfamiliar place in this strange land where nothing seemed to matter but money. She had departed from her boardinghouse to find her friend, her new employer, and returned to discover the landlady had rented out the room.

"Couldn't be sure you was coming back," had been the explanation.

Camilla gripped the tankard so hard she feared she would crush the thick tin. She set the cup on the bench and tucked her hands inside her cloak before they grew cold again.

"You drank that?" Black glanced from where he was once again allowing the crewman to pilot the boat, to Camilla huddled like an old woman in the London stews. "You must be stronger than you look."

"It was hot. I was cold."

The boat deck rose, fell, heeled to port beneath her feet. The coffee burned her stomach and up to her throat. A lump formed in its wake, and she could scarcely breathe.

Black glanced her way again. "We dock at Washington Street. I believe there's a woman there who rents rooms to respectable females."

"I fear I do not look particularly respectable."

The captain swept his gaze from her drooping hat, to her wrinkled black dress, to her muddy half boots. He shook his head, ruffling his thick, dark, and overly long hair. "You don't."

Nor was she now, the sister of a disgraced and deceased peer.

Lord, you said you would provide all our needs.

Except he hadn't been doing that for her of late.

"Signal the engine room for less speed, Billy." Black's baritone voice rumbled through the wheelhouse in counterpoint to the engine. "We'll be docking—" He broke off and muttered something that sounded rude.

Camilla followed his gaze and murmured a prayer of thanks. God had listened to her pleas. He had sent another boat. As long as it was headed upriver also and not on its way home, as long as it had enough room for her, as long as she had enough money to pay for passage . . .

She hugged herself, then crossed the wheelhouse to the steps. She need not lower herself to begging and pleading with this indifferent captain. Another boat waited at the dock as though summoned just for her.

She tossed Captain Nathaniel Black a triumphant smile. "Apparently I need not beg you to keep me aboard."

"No," he said through gritted teeth, "you don't." Then he turned to his crewman. "Let's take her out again. I'm not getting anywhere near Riley Lancaster."

· · · ⦿ TWO ⦿ · · ·

The *Marianne* underway once more, placing as much distance as possible between his boat and that of the man bent on destroying all Nathaniel had worked for since the age of fourteen, he returned his attention to the English lady. She stood at the wheelhouse steps, her valise clutched in one hand and a ridiculously beaded and stitched-up bag swinging from her other wrist. She looked soaked to the skin, bedraggled and waiflike, engendering sympathy he didn't want to feel. Her poor excuse for a hat drooped on one side and her golden-brown hair curled out of its pins to frame a face too sharp for beauty, yet compelling enough to draw more of his attention than he should give her.

This female, especially, had already proven herself troublesome, leaping aboard like some kind of acrobat. If she had fallen into the river . . .

A shudder ran through Nathaniel. "Not all the elements on the river are trustworthy, Miss—" He compressed his lips to stop himself from asking her what her name was.

She glanced over her shoulder at him. "Renfrew. I am a Renfrew of Gloucestershire."

Of course. Nothing plain and simple like Miss Smith or Jones from Nowhere would match her demeanor. Against his will, he wondered what her Christian name might be. Theodosia or Zabrina perhaps?

"Miss Renfrew," he tried again, "I'm taking you to Albany. Never you mind why."

"Thank you." She set down her valise and raised a hand to her hat. "Do I warrant a cabin?"

Nathaniel sighed. "You warrant a cabin. The last one on the left. It won't be warm, but it's dry."

If she didn't look so pathetic beneath the sodden hat, he wouldn't feel so compelled to take care of her. He might find something else to do with her, like put her ashore in Brooklyn Heights, a far better place for a solitary female than Manhattan.

"Thank you." She brushed the edge of her cloak across her rain-wet face. "I need to see if I can salvage my hat."

"It looks beyond salvaging to me."

"I must try." That luxurious lower lip might have quivered. "It is my only hat."

He must have been mistaken about that moment of weakness with the lower lip. One as full and soft as her mouth would always appear to tremble with sadness, with joy, with an invitation to be kissed.

He snapped his eyes over her head, observing Riley Lancaster's boat heading into the river right after them, a bad sign. A very bad sign.

"Now if you'll excuse me, I have work to do." He started to walk away from her, then the part his mother had raised to be a gentleman sent him to lift her valise. "I'll take this down for you first." He led the way down the pilothouse steps to the cabin deck. "You'll be right in front of the paddle wheel."

Right in front of the paddle wheel? Her tip-tilted nose wrinkled.

Nathaniel nodded. "Yes, and above the engine."

"Is that not rather loud?"

"Yes, it is, and it's also the safest cabin."

She stared up at him. "Safest, how?"

He smiled. "You have a chance at survival if the boilers blow up."

Her eyes widened and darkened, and this time he did not mistake her trembling lower lip. "Th-that does not happen often, does it?"

"No." Relenting, he touched the back of her hand. "Not often enough to scare us off of the river. Now get inside where it's dry, if not warm." He opened the door to the last cabin. A rush of stale, dank air puffed out, as no one had traveled in there since the eldest and best of Nathaniel's business partners died two months earlier.

He dropped Miss Renfrew's case on the floor and swung away. "Stay out of everyone's way. This needs to be a fast run. I'll put you on a proper passenger boat as soon as we reach a town with one docked."

"I was willing to go on that other one if it was going north." She gave him a quizzical glance from beneath the brim of that pathetic hat.

"I don't think you'd have been safe coming off of this boat and going onto that one."

"Enemies, Captain Black?"

"Not by choice." Wanting no more questions from her, he turned on his heel with the intention of walking away.

"So what is in the other cabins?" she asked.

He didn't look back.

"That is, what is more valuable than people?"

Almost anything.

Figuring she wouldn't like that kind of response, he glanced over his shoulder and gave her the truth, not that it was any of her concern. "The first cabin to starboard is mine. Six other ones contain sugar, molasses, other spices like cinnamon and nutmeg and black peppercorns, and other things I prefer to keep out of the elements as much as possible. They bring a far higher profit transporting them upriver than do people."

"Where does your crew sleep?" she asked.

Nathaniel shrugged. "Wherever they can find space."

"They do not have quarters?" Her incredulity rang in her voice.

"They have work and the opportunity to make a profit. What more matters?"

Her nostrils pinched as though he smelled bad, though he didn't think he did. "I am surprised you have left this cabin empty."

"Be as surprised as you like. It belonged—" He closed his mouth. She didn't need to know about Ralph and Marianne Spraig, how they were more parents to him than his own had been.

She looked away. "I apologize. That was inappropriate for me to say."

It was, and her admission knocked away any irritation her remark might have caused.

"I am not without a care for friends," he said gently. He tucked his hands into the pockets of his coat. "Make yourself comfortable. Someone will bring you supper."

She watched him all the way down the passageway between the two rows of cabins. At least he figured she did, as she didn't close her door until he reached the steps up to the wheelhouse.

"Get her settled in?" Billy asked.

Nathaniel nodded. "As much as she can be."

"She's either a brave or stupid little thing."

"I suspect the latter."

"Uh-huh, that's why you kept her aboard."

Nathaniel glanced aft. "I'll get rid of her as soon as we're rid of Lancaster's shadow. But I see he's still there."

"Has been since he spotted us passing the Washington Street wharf." Billy pulled the line to the whistle, signaling a slower vessel they were passing. "Why wouldn't you just let her go aboard? Never heard of Lancaster being anything but gentlemanly with females."

"Do you think he would be fair to a lady he saw coming off of the *Marianne*?"

Billy's silence was answer enough. That morning after the meeting of the partnership in the lawyers' offices, Riley Lancaster had made clear he would stop at nothing to ensure the partnership ended in a month. Nathaniel's boat would no longer be his boat if the partnership dissolved.

But it wouldn't. If he had to go without sleep for the next thirty days, he would in order to buy Spraig and Lancaster's shares.

He should sleep now. Billy could manage the piloting during daylight. With one or two hours of sleep, Nathaniel could manage to steer their way north all night.

He descended to the lower deck and the engine. It sounded a little rougher than he liked, and he wanted to pinpoint the problem so he could fix it at the next stop. He needed to keep a lookout for Lancaster trying to cause trouble on the river once they left the crowded waters around the city. He needed sleep.

He went to his cabin and dropped onto the chair before his desk. The ledgers lay open with their tale of needing more profitable runs than one boat could accomplish. He needed a miracle to save his company, his future, his very reason for existence.

His conscience prickled over caring so much about profits and accumulating money for the future. But he would not be the failure his father and brother called him when he chose to leave home. He would prove them wrong.

Unable to rest, he left his cabin. On the cargo deck, he ate what he could of the tasteless mush the only crewman who dared attempt cooking called stew. Night having fallen, Nathaniel climbed to the wheelhouse. Billy didn't have the piloting experience to navigate at night.

Nathaniel knew every pull and rope hanging from the pilothouse roof, every bend of the river by heart. He might have only captained his own boat for two years, but he had been on the river for fifteen, a pilot for ten.

As if the *Marianne* were his. Indeed, he only owned a quarter of the vessel. He had saved and prayed, invested and prayed some more for eight years to come up with enough money to make it and his skill as a pilot, not to mention his ability to make the crankiest of engines run, appealing to investors. He had found them—Spraig, Harriman, and Lancaster—and thought, at last, his days of being nothing but another man's lackey were at an end. Soon his father and older brother, growing rich and fat selling horses to those bargemen trading through the Erie Canal, could no longer sneer and taunt and mock him for his passion for steam engines and the water. He would be an independent man in a couple more years, able to buy out his partners, able to build a house in Albany and start looking for a wife.

Then Ralph Spraig suffered an apoplexy and died. Now Nathaniel's dreams looked about to explode like an overheated boiler.

"Lord, you said you would provide all my needs, and maybe this isn't a need in your eyes, but please provide anyway." He grimaced at his prayer. It sounded selfish and grasping. "But it really isn't."

Mrs. Spraig couldn't afford for the partnership to dissolve either. Her husband had sunk a great deal of their life savings, the capital on which they needed to live, into the venture. The *Marianne* had made a comfortable profit for them to live on, but if the partnership dissolved, what the assets brought would not provide for Mrs. Spraig's future. It would not provide Nathaniel with enough money to invest in another steamboat. He would return to piloting for other men. His thirtieth birthday approached faster than he liked. Before he reached that milestone in a year and a half, he hoped for a home, a family, a wife to greet him with open arms when he finished a run.

An image of Miss Renfrew, her tilted eyes, her tilted nose, her quivering lower lip, danced before his eyes, interfering with his concentration on the watery road before him. He shook his head and another image of the English lady appeared—the lady with her hair tumbling around her face, softening her sharp features, thick, shining locks inviting a man's hands to lift it from her neck and—

26

Nathaniel grinned at his own foolishness. He would get the lady to Albany for whatever was so urgent she had risked her life jumping aboard his boat, and then he would forget about her. He didn't have time for females until Lancaster cooperated and agreed to continue the partnership. And if Lancaster decided to see it dissolved, Nathaniel could forget females until his hair was gray and his hands gnarled with rheumatism from the constant damp aboard a boat.

He sighed. His stomach growled in response. At the same time the pilothouse steps creaked.

Billy strode into the wheelhouse, a paper-wrapped loaf of bread tucked under one arm. "Thought you could use a bite, Nate."

"Where did you get that?" Nathaniel tried not to snatch the bread from his lifelong friend and stuff it into his mouth.

"Bought it in the city and kept it hid." Billy opened one end of the parcel and tore off a chunk of the loaf. "A pity that gal you brought can't cook."

"I didn't bring her aboard. She jumped. Remember?"

"How will any of us forget? I think we're all older for watching her." Billy handed Nathaniel the loaf so he could pull off his own hunk of bread. "Think Lancaster will try to stop us?"

"He knows if I don't get to Albany by Wednesday, this run won't be nearly profitable enough to buy both my and Spraig's partnership shares." Though he chewed the bread, he had lost his appetite. "Mind you, making enough of a profit in time for the deadline won't be impossible, just unlikely."

"If we could unload and reload cargo more efficiently, we could maybe get another run in every ten days. Right now, we're taking fifty-two hours between the trip itself and the lading."

"Hmm." Nathaniel signaled to the engineer to slow for a bend in the river, then he sounded the bell as a warning to any vessels lurking around the curve.

The *clang, clang, clang* echoed off the surrounding hills. No other bells or whistles responded. The river rolled on like a black ribbon beneath a thin layer of clouds glowing from a nearly full moon above.

One more run per ten days would give them three more profitable runs between now and the 25th of November when they either had to buy Spraig's and now Lancaster's shares to continue the partnership, or see the assets sold at auction and the partnership dissolved.

"Any ideas on how to speed up loading and unloading?" Nathaniel asked.

"I was thinking two gangways, or hire extra crew."

Nathaniel shook his head. "We'll never get the dock space for a second gangway and extra crew will be impossible with the canal opening. But let's keep—" Movement below the wheelhouse stopped him, a shadowy figure too small to be one of the crew. "Miss Renfrew?"

"Yes." She reached the bottom step to the wheelhouse. "I-I'm sorry. I woke up and couldn't get back to sleep." She climbed halfway up the steps. "Is it possible—" She gave out a little cough. "Could I have something hot to drink?"

Had she asked in a manner that suggested a demand, Nathaniel would have given her a flat-out no, even though coffee was always available. But that hesitancy, that nervous cough, slammed into his heart, softening it toward her far more than the vulnerability her tumbled hair had demonstrated.

"Come on up and sit. Billy will fetch you some coffee."

Billy cast him a glance with eyebrows raised. "Her ladyship might prefer that stash of tea you have in your cabin."

"I would." Her hair tied back at the nape of her neck with some kind of bow, she reached the pilothouse, a fragile silhouette against a light on the lower deck. "But I am not a lady. That is, I am only the daughter of a viscount, so am merely Miss Renfrew." She inclined her head. "That is, I was the daughter of a viscount."

"We don't understand the niceties of British titles here." Nathaniel fought the urge to reach out and draw her forward to stand beside him—only to give her protection and warmth, not because he wanted to touch her, of course.

"But we do understand you prefer tea to coffee," Billy added.

"Especially to our coffee." Nathaniel smiled.

Miss Renfrew's teeth flashed in the near darkness of the pilothouse. "It is rather awful, you surely know."

"We do, but we drink it anyway." Billy slipped past her and headed down the steps, calling back, "We have sugar, but no milk. No cows this run."

Miss Renfrew started. "You carry cows?"

"Quite often, but only when going downriver." Nathaniel focused more fully on the river. Night travel was too risky to let a female distract him. "Grain and fruit and livestock go downriver, cloth and spices and other manufactured goods go upriver."

"Is the food always such as we had tonight?" Behind him, fabric rustled, and the scent of lavender drifted over the sting of woodsmoke. "It does not seem like men would be inclined to work for you with those sorts of viands to look forward to."

"We stop along the route once or twice to deliver goods and get a good meal then."

"But does that not waste your travel time?" The backboards of the pilothouse, raised to block out light from below, rattled as though she had seated herself on the bench and leaned back.

Suddenly wishing he could sit too and rest his back against something, preferably something more comfortable than the sliding wood partition, Nathaniel admitted she was right. "It probably wastes an hour every time we stop, rounding the men up and all," he added.

"If you had a cook, they would not leave the vessel at all."

"It's occurred to me." He stared into the night, concentrating on the water, the sky, the direction the prow was pointing, anything but the musical lilt of the woman's voice behind him.

He could not even think of a female until he owned this boat free and clear. So much he yearned for a home to return to, a woman at his side aboard and on land, every moment around an attractive lady reminded him of what he could not have if he did indeed fail.

She stirred on the bench. "Forgive me if I overstep. I am simply anxious to reach my destination."

"What's for you in Albany, Miss Renfrew?" he asked softly.

"Work." She laughed, a light tinkling trill that managed to still not sound amused. "My ancestor signed the Magna Carta, and I am having to become a housekeeper for the daughter of a *cit*, who married an American adventurer."

"Most of us work, Miss Renfrew. There's no shame in it." Nathaniel hesitated a moment, then asked, "What is a *cit*?"

"A city merchant, a member of the middle class."

The softness he'd felt toward her froze in place at her offhand condescension toward those who didn't inherit their money. "And beneath your royal highness, except her money is good when it comes your way."

At the top of the pilothouse steps, Billy caught his breath. On the bench, Miss Renfrew said nothing. She didn't even move.

"I have some tea for you, Miss Renfrew," Billy announced. "You didn't say if you wanted sugar, but I put some in it anyway."

"That is quite all right, thank you." She spoke as though addressing an underling.

Or maybe she was simply overly gracious and he wasn't used to it.

"Shall I, um, leave?" Billy asked.

"I could use an extra pair of eyes," Nathaniel said. "We're getting into the Highlands and may encounter fog between the mountains."

"How far have we come?" Miss Renfrew asked.

Nathaniel drew a watch from his coat pocket and squinted to see the time in the faint light. "About forty miles. We made good time when we had daylight. It's midnight now, so we're going slower."

"Midnight. We have traveled eight hours then?" A hint of excitement had come into her voice. "Then we should have no difficulty reaching Albany, if we can continue going this quickly."

"No, we shouldn't," Nathaniel said.

"If we don't stop too long in West Point," Billy added.

The back boards rattled in their frame, as though Miss Renfrew jumped. "Stop? In the middle of the night?"

"We have an order of fine china for someone at the academy." Nathaniel calculated who to send to ensure the china was located before landing. "They take delivery when we get to their destination. Sometimes that's in the middle of the night."

"And if we're in the Lord's good graces," Billy said, "the inn will still be open enough to provide us with some edible food."

"But . . . but that sounds like a terrible delay." Again, panic, uncertainty, vulnerability tinged her tone.

A number of responses ran through Nathaniel's mind, none of them particularly polite. So he said nothing and concentrated on watching for the lights of West Point and the wharf. The town glowed with a soft radiance against the mist over the river, and the wharf did lie nearly empty. Nathaniel pulled the signal to slow the boat, nuzzled the prow against the dock, and hit the pedal at his feet to signal stop in the engine room. The paddle wheel slowed, then ceased altogether. The engine quieted to a gentle rumble, and steam hissed from the boilers like a sigh of relief.

"I should return to my cabin." Miss Renfrew had risen. She headed for the steps to the cabin deck.

A little guilty over his churlish behavior, Nathaniel caught hold of her hand. "I'll bring you back something better to eat than that stew, if you like."

"Yes, I—" She glanced down to where that silly bag had hung earlier. "I have some money in my reticule in the cabin. Shall I fetch it? I, um, still owe you for my passage."

The hesitation, the uncertainty in that single "um," was curious, interspersed with her hauteur the rest of the time. A hesitation over money.

"Exactly how much money do you have in your purse?" A rude question, but he wanted to know.

For a heartbeat, her shoulders drooped, and she looked away. "I have enough for passage, if that concerns you."

"Passage is two dollars. Food, whether you eat only aboard here or in towns along the way, is extra, though, of course, the food aboard is cheaper, and someone is likely to charge me with robbery for asking for even a penny for a bowl of that."

She gave him a half smile for his attempt at humor. "Distasteful as it is, I had better eat aboard."

"If my conscience will let you do that."

If he was generous with one of the Lord's lost and vulnerable creatures, surely the Lord would be generous with him.

"I'll walk you down," he said, and offered her his arm.

Her hand was small, tucked into the crook of his elbow. Small and cold. The iciness of her fingers seeped through his coat and shirtsleeves. If he knew her just a bit better, he would have covered her fingers with his other hand, warmed them—

He brought his thoughts up short and halted at the head of the cabin passage. "I will see you soon. Perhaps an hour or so."

"I will pay you for my passage then." She inclined her head, then spun and glided down the passageway, her hair flowing down her back in ripples and waves like a wind-ruffled river, a temptation.

He left the deck and descended to the cargo bay. Billy was shouting at two crewmen about the crates of china. The men stared at him with identical vacant gazes.

Billy bellowed. "If you don't find the right crates in five minutes, you can't go ashore to eat a decent meal."

"Maybe we could remember better if we had a decent meal," one of the men muttered.

"And maybe you can stay ashore." Nathaniel entered the cargo deck ahead of the engine. "Find the china. Billy and I will see it gets delivered so you can go eat straight off."

Grumbling, but complying with this compromise, the men located the correct crates in two minutes. The four of them lugged the boxes onto the wharf, and the crewmen vanished into the sleepy, but not entirely asleep, town.

"We need a wagon." Billy glowered at a crate.

More time wasted. They woke a liveryman and acquired a wagon in which to deliver the crates. At the officer's home, they waited awhile to wake a servant, who had to wake his employer to authorize the delivery and the payment. An hour had passed before they reached the inn, but the landlord, used to their odd hours, provided them with thick, savory soup, nearly fresh bread rolls, and fresher apple pie. By the time they finished eating and collected a basket for Miss Renfrew, nearly two hours had passed and another steamboat had docked beside theirs.

Riley Lancaster had found them again.

ᴄᴛʜʀᴇᴇ

amilla paced the cargo deck, too restless to sleep, too cold to stand still. The men took far too long in unloading the boat. The fact they could not find cargo was a problem easily solved. But not in time to help her if they endured many more stops this long between West Point and Albany.

But the Lord had provided her with transport, so surely he intended for her to reach Joanna in time to procure the position as her companion, in time to keep her out of the hands of Marcus's moneylender now that her brother was beyond their reach.

Meanwhile, she didn't want to be in debt to Captain Black. For a man who hadn't wanted to take her aboard, he was certainly proving to be kind.

Camilla began to tour the cargo area, taking note of the random towers of boxes and crates, barrels and rolled bundles. No wonder the crew could find nothing. From what was marked on the sides of the containers, nothing appeared to be in any particular order. If the storage rooms beneath Renfrew Hall had been so disorganized, back when those rooms had held plentiful goods, the servants would have spent most of the day hunting out needed ingredients.

Unable to learn from a crewman anything about how the cargo was organized, or where they stopped next, Camilla retreated to her cabin. It was cold and dark and still smelled of the revolting stew she had eaten only because she was hungry. These men needed a cook. They would save time not eating on shore if they had one.

Time. Time. Time. It dragged like heavy boots across her spine. Surely God would not provide transport only to deny her ultimate goal.

Oh, yes, he would. He had been taking from her since Father died and Marcus began to run through the family fortune. Yet her notion that the Lord only provided in half measures wasn't right, according to what she'd been taught. God provided in full measure, shaken down and spilling over.

"So where are those blessings, Lord?"

Camilla returned to the deck in time to see a stocky, well-dressed man walking away from the *Marianne*'s gangway toward the boat carrying Lancaster. One of the *Marianne*'s crew glanced around, then scurried back aboard. Lancaster's boat began to back from the pier, as Captain Black headed up the gangway.

One of his men had been talking to Lancaster.

Black glanced up at her. "Miss Renfrew, I brought you food."

The aroma reached out to her as he climbed the steps. She stood with her arms folded across her middle to stop her stomach from growling and her hands from grabbing the box he carried.

"Come into the wheelhouse to eat. The boilers keep it warmer than your cabin." He preceded her up the second flight of steps and set the box on the bench.

"My cabin is not too cold. It is warm enough that my hat dried."

"But you're not wearing it."

"I thought I looked better without it."

"You do. We can see your pretty hair."

Her pretty hair? She shoved her fingers into the tangled mass of waves and ringlets barely confined in a grosgrain ribbon. "I, um, well—" Her mouth went suddenly dry. She should thank him. That was the proper response to a compliment, but the words stuck.

The captain let out a low laugh. "So Miss Renfrew isn't always self-possessed." He touched one of her hands still tucked into the warmth of her hair. "Sit down and eat. We need to be underway before Lancaster gets ahead of us." He turned to the massive wheel.

Camilla dropped onto the bench. Hands, face, and her entire person warmer than they had been in days, she reached for the carton of food. Fresh bread rolls. Butter. Apple tart. It was food she would have scorned as common not six months ago. Now she considered this a feast, a feast her hands shook too much for her to pick up.

A ridiculous state, to have a simple touch of fingertips against her hand leave her so dazed. During her three disastrous London seasons, she had been touched many times, had received numerous compliments on her hair, her eyes, her smooth complexion, even a few bold ones on her figure. They all rang false from men who wanted the Renfrew connection and what, at that time, had been her dowry.

She was nothing to Captain Black but a nuisance. And he seemed completely unaffected by that contact of hands. All his concentration directed toward his boat, maneuvering it away from the dock, shouting something to Billy about not letting Lancaster get ahead.

But Lancaster was ahead, ahead and crawling up the river through a light, misting rain.

"We could row faster than this," Black grumbled, then pulled the line that set off the blast of the throaty whistle.

"Is something wrong with him?" Camilla's voice returned.

"Yes, he wants to slow me down." Black let off two blasts on the whistle and started to steer around.

Lancaster's boat turned across their path.

Camilla shot to her feet. "What is he doing?"

"Playing a dangerous game." Black's foot stomped on one of the levers on the floor.

A moment later, the boat jerked to a halt.

36

Lancaster's boat pulled ahead, chugging, chugging, chugging faster and faster, its side paddle kicking up white foam in its wake and surely a roar of male laughter rising above the rumble of the engines.

"Why would he do that?" Camilla asked, returning to the bench.

"He wants me to fail to make a profit this trip, and a few more." Black pulled one of the handles hanging from the ceiling, and the *Marianne* began to get underway again. "He wants to dissolve the partnership, but if I get enough money together, I can buy out Ralph Spraig's shares instead."

Camilla selected a bread roll from the box and managed to butter it in the near darkness without too much difficulty. "I beg your pardon, and I am afraid I do not understand."

Black shrugged. "It's not particularly interesting."

"It is if you're being kept from your goal." Camilla bit into the roll and closed her eyes to savor it for a moment before adding, "Especially since this concerns me, if he is trying to keep you from reaching Albany by Wednesday. Besides, I have nothing else to do but listen."

Black said nothing for so long, she thought he wouldn't, then he shook his head and shot her a smile. "I haven't talked to a female much since I last visited Mrs. Spraig."

"And who is Mrs. Spraig?"

"The widow of one of our partners. Ralph Spraig died a few months ago. According to the partnership agreement, we three other partners have to either buy out his shares by the end of November, or the partnership will dissolve and the assets will be sold."

Camilla straightened. "Including your boat?"

"Including the *Marianne*."

"What will you do without her?"

He shrugged. "Pilot for someone else. Try to start again."

"That is quite awful." Camilla knew all about selling everything one owned and cherished, or seeing it go to others, the cousin who inherited upon Marcus's death. "Why wouldn't Mr. Lancaster want to buy out Mr. Spraig's shares?"

"I suspect he doesn't have the money or means of procuring it. He gambles."

Camilla shuddered. "A curse on the world."

"Indeed."

"But if he needs money, why can you not buy his shares?"

"The other partner and I are trying to collect that much money, but Lancaster needs the money from the sale of assets, so is trying to prevent us from getting it."

"By delaying our journey north?"

"By delaying our journey north."

"So that little game back there was not all he will do?"

"I'm afraid not. He'll try something else if we don't get ahead of him."

"What—" Camilla swallowed renewed dryness in her throat. "What else can he do?"

"There's a jar of fresh cider in that box if you're thirsty." Black leaned forward as though trying harder to see the nearly invisible water ahead. "It hasn't gone hard yet."

"Thank you." She reached for the earthenware jar and pulled out the cork top.

The cider slid over her parched lips and tongue with cool, sweet tartness. A shiver of pleasure ran through her.

"This was very thoughtful of you, Captain Black. I am quite certain I owe you a fortune."

He shrugged one shoulder. "Not quite." He pulled another rope overhead.

"What do all those do?" Camilla asked.

"They signal the engine room."

"There's someone down there all the time?"

"When the engine is running, yes." He began to point them out, though Camilla only knew they were there because she had seen them in daylight. "Slow, faster, back, forward. And these"—he tapped the floor—"signal to stop."

"Fascinating." She rose and carried the jug to him. "Would you like some of this?"

He flashed her a quick glance. "I would, thanks." Surprise rang in his tone.

"There is no cup, I am afraid, so perhaps you would prefer not to drink after me."

"I don't see why not." He took the flask from her and raised it to his lips.

Warmth from the boilers radiated into the wheelhouse above them, but not enough to account for suddenly feeling as though her cloak and gown were too heavy and hot.

He handed back the cider jug. "Thank you. It's one of the good things of fall."

"Fall?" She sipped at the refreshing liquid, too conscious of his lips having been on the same rim. "What is falling?"

"Leaves, rain, snow." He laughed. "Autumn."

"Oh, how ridiculous of me. I love autumn. The harvest, the smell of the air, anticipating the hunt. Riding to hounds, that is, not that Mama approved of me doing that, but Father said it was all right, and I so enjoyed riding."

"You like horses?" He sounded appalled.

"I do. I had a lovely little mare . . ." A lump formed in her throat. The mare, like everything dear to her, was now gone. "Do you not like horses?"

He gave his head one emphatic shake. "My father and brothers are making a fortune raising and selling horses for the canal boats. It's all they talk about and all they care—" He broke off and lifted one hand. "Did you hear that?"

She leaned forward, brushing her shoulder against his arm. "I hear another engine ahead is all."

"I thought I heard something hit the—"

She heard it that time, a thud like wood striking wood.

"Is it something bad?"

"It can be." He pulled one of the overhead lines. "Will you run down and fetch Billy for me? He should be asleep near the foot of the steps."

"You—" The bottle of cider in her hand reminded her she shouldn't care that he was sending her on an errand like one of the crew.

She set the cider flask in the box and sped down the steps to the cabin deck and then the lower deck. "Mr. Billy?" She didn't know the man's surname. "Captain Black wishes—"

"On my way." Voice sleep roughened, Billy pushed past her and charged up the steps. "Heard it, Nate."

Along the cargo deck, men stirred from rolls of blankets and began to mill about, murmuring, going perilously close to the edges that did not boast a railing to prevent men from toppling overboard.

Men or women. Camilla held fast to the stair railing, listening to the men, listening to the thuds against the hull, listening to the engine's rods slow, slow, slow, and just before the great paddle wheel stopped altogether, a screeching, crackling sound, as though the legs were being pulled off a giant's chair.

"What was that?" Camilla picked up her skirt and ran up the steps, dashed across the upper deck, and up the pilothouse stairs.

Charging past her, Billy nearly knocked her down. She flattened herself against the wall, already not needing an answer. Billy's actions shouted aloud, "Disaster."

Still, Camilla continued into the wheelhouse and asked again, "What has happened?"

"It seems," Captain Black said with a ferocity that pinned Camilla at the head of the steps, "that a number of unexplained objects have found their way into the river and damaged the paddle wheel."

$\mathcal{F}$OUR

Nathaniel stretched out along the upper deck and leaned as far down to the now motionless paddle wheel as he could without plunging headfirst into the blades. Two crewmen lay beside him, holding lanterns down to light the scene of destruction.

Two of the paddles, rather than resembling shallow buckets, now looked like nothing so much as kindling. Whatever had hit them had been more than the normal debris floating in the river. This was the sort of log that plagued rivermen after heavy storms, mostly in the spring when the river ran high from mountain snow runoff. Even with the rain of that day—no, the previous day now—no logs should have gotten free enough to float down the river and smash his blades.

"How do things look?" Billy asked from behind Nathaniel.

"Bad." He began to clear the rubbish away from the steel frame. "Two blades gone." He slid a little farther forward, and heard a feminine gasp.

The princess should be in her cabin, not out in the chill and mist watching him dangle upside down over a paddle wheel. Even with his guts feeling as splintered as the blades, a thread of heat at her presence traced through his middle. Maybe she wasn't as self-absorbed as he thought she was.

Likable.

But unattainable, like his future.

He yanked a sliver the size of his forearm out of its pin as though he could so easily remove thoughts of Miss Renfrew and her glorious hair from his mind. "Once I clear this away and we're not sending splinters flying around like shrapnel, we'll have to limp back to Cold Spring and make repairs." He slammed the broken wood onto the deck and grabbed the next piece of splintered wood so hard, an edge tore through his glove and into his palm. He hissed through his teeth at the pain and kept working to clear the frame of what remained of his precious paddles.

He carried replacement paddles with him. Accidents happened. This could be an accident. He couldn't prove otherwise. But accidents like this were rare in the fall with the river low, with the amount of traffic that had gone before him, and Lancaster's boat so close ahead.

Close enough ahead to have tossed something off his vessel and straight into the *Marianne*'s path. Not a sure way to cripple a boat. Nathaniel might have seen the debris even in the dark, but more than one thud had sounded against the deck. Lancaster had made as certain as he could to cause damage.

Nathaniel removed the last of the mangled blades and pushed himself back onto the deck. "All right, let's get underway again and go back to Cold Spring."

Billy gave him a questioning look. "Shouldn't we go ahead—"

"Moving downstream with two missing buckets will be easier than continuing up." Nathaniel made no attempt to disguise his impatience.

Miss Renfrew's face paled in the yellowish glow of the lanterns. "Was that village not an hour and a half ago?"

"Yes, about six miles back." Nathaniel gave her the brutal truth. "We've been traveling slower than usual as it is, and now we'll lose more time, as we'll have to wait for morning to make repairs."

"Of course that is necessary." Her accent sounded even more precise and clipped than usual. "But you have injured your hand. You should take care of it."

"No time." His palm throbbed, but they needed to get out of their anchorage in the middle of the river before another boat came along and caused an accident.

"But, Captain Black—"

"Excuse me, Miss Renfrew, I have work to do." He took a step toward her.

She stepped aside. "Well then, I suppose I may as well get to my cabin and rest." Her chin a little too high and firm, she spun on her heel and marched away.

Billy grinned. "Upset her ladyship. She don't like not getting her way."

"No." Nathaniel gazed after her. A tightness settled over his chest that had nothing to do with the sabotage to his boat and too much to do with the female who had vanished into her cabin.

"Let's get underway." Nathaniel spoke too harshly, as though everyone dawdled after receiving orders.

He strode off to the wheelhouse steps and took them two at a time. He wouldn't trust anyone else with the piloting in this maneuver. Even before the engine commenced with its thumping, hissing rumble and the paddles began to turn, he gripped the wheel. Pain shot through his right hand. Probably splinters of wood left in the gash. No time to concern himself with it now. He couldn't remove fragments without light. No light aboard now. He needed all the night vision he could conjure.

Slow, slow, slowly they backed. The paddle frame rattled. Nathaniel gritted his teeth and peered into the mist. The jackstaff swung to starboard, its canted tip pointed at an ancient oak towering above its neighboring trees on the hillside. If he kept that in sight, used it like a compass apex . . .

Heat rose up through his boot soles. Too much heat. Someone

had overstoked the boilers for these speeds. Miss Renfrew might appreciate it if some of the heat reached her cabin, but not if they all exploded. Must not think of her and her big, bright eyes, a little too bright in the lantern light. She was too cool, too self-possessed to cry over a delay. She was—

The current caught the boat, shoving it starboard, yanking Nathaniel's thoughts away from the princess to his boat, the true love of his life.

For another month if Lancaster had his way.

Lord, I've done a good deed taking this female aboard against my will, surely you will honor that.

Maybe. Maybe not. God didn't seem inclined to favor him of late.

If getting them to Cold Spring without further damage to the boat was evidence of God's favor, then he was paying attention. Once facing downstream, the *Marianne* limped back to Cold Spring. They moored at the dock and shut down the engine and boilers. Enough heat would remain in the latter to keep the crew warm, though a few decided to seek lodging on shore where they could sleep in real beds.

Nathaniel headed for his own cabin. He hadn't slept for nearly twenty-four hours, and the strain of the day weighed down his limbs like anchors. But Miss Renfrew's door stood open, and a light glowed from within. He continued down the passageway until he stood in the doorway.

"Miss Renfrew?"

She glanced up from the book on the table before her, then rose, divesting herself of a quilt wrapped around her shoulders, all in one graceful motion. "Captain Black, I was waiting to ensure you had seen to your hand."

"That's . . . kind of you." He gazed into her sleep-shadowed eyes, and felt as though the boat moved a mile beneath his feet. "It's just a scratch. You didn't need to sit up waiting for me."

"I could not sleep." She pursed her lips a moment and looked away. "The delay concerns me. If I do not reach Albany in time—" She shifted her shoulders in a motion too fluid to be called a shrug, and smiled at him. "So I may as well take a look at your hand." She held out hers.

Nathaniel laid his hand in hers. His palm was at least twice as broad as hers, his fingers more than an inch longer. Her skin felt as smooth as the finest China silk he had ever carried. His must feel like emery grit in comparison. Yet she held his hand steady, lifting it closer to her lantern.

"You have splinters, I think. It is difficult to see with the blood." Blood that didn't make a princess squeamish.

Her hand beneath his, the hint of lavender around her, her very calm when faced with the sort of gash that most females squealed and backed away from, set his insides vibrating like the deck beneath the engine.

"Shall I wash it for you?" She glanced up at him, her gaze as cool as the temperature inside the cabin, completely unmoved by their nearness. Except that her hand trembled ever so slightly beneath his.

He drew away. "I'll go wash it myself. No sense in you getting your basin dirty."

He wished that basin were forty miles away rather than forty feet. Distance between himself and this unflappable female, who left him feeling anything but levelheaded, was a good idea.

"Lord, I shouldn't have brought her aboard," he muttered to himself, as he poured icy water from his pitcher into the basin and sponged the blood away from his gash. Contact with the wound sent air hissing through his clenched teeth. Splinters in there for sure. He should pull them out himself.

He would have done so. He would have stayed away from her ladyship, if he had cut his left hand. But his left didn't have the dexterity he needed.

He returned to find her waiting for him with a metal object that looked like something out of a torture chamber—small metal pincers.

"What," he asked, "is that?" He indicated the metal claws.

She laughed, a genuine trill of amusement. "Tweezers." She touched one finger to her perfectly arched eyebrows. "You do not believe these grow like this, do you?"

"Now that I notice, I suppose not," he couldn't resist saying.

Her cheeks turned pink, and she laughed again. "I suppose that puts me in my place, does it not?" She seized his hand with surprising strength, showing a little more than necessary. "Shall I get to work?"

"If I tell you you have pretty eyes, will you promise to not cause me too much pain in your doctoring?"

"No need. You have already complimented my hair."

He had. The truth. With her head bent over his hand, her hair shone in the lantern light like a waterfall of honey. He raised his left hand. If she had not chosen that moment to swoop in with those tweezer things and pluck a splinter from his palm, he might have reached out and touched one of those glossy tresses.

He shoved his free hand into his coat pocket. "So why is it that you can doctor, but you can't cook?"

"The lady of the manor is expected to play apothecary, but cooking is beneath her." The slightest hint of sarcasm tinged her tone.

Nathaniel grimaced. "Are you a lady of the manor?"

"Obviously not, or I would not be here." She drew another, longer splinter out.

He flinched.

"Terribly sorry. Just one more, I think."

A pity.

No, he must be worn to a nub to have just thought having the final splinter pulled out of his palm a pity. It wasn't the doctoring; it was having an attractive female holding his hand with gentle

46

competence and kindness. It was the notion that a competent, gentle, and attractive female was the sort of wife he needed.

She probed at the cut with those tweezers. He welcomed the prickle of pain. It distracted him from stupid notions.

"You were raised to be lady of the manor?" he asked.

"And endured the dubious pleasure of three London seasons."

"London—gentle there, if you please. I need my hand intact. Now what—what is a London season?"

"Where I got trotted out like a mare for the highest-ranked bidder." She replaced the tweezers with her fingertips, light, gentle, probing. "The marriage market."

He flinched. "You're a widow then?"

"No, I did not take. Then my father died, so I missed the next season, and then my mother died, and after that, I was quite on the shelf with no dowry to make up for my lack of looks."

She delivered the speech with such coolness, Nathaniel suspected a great deal of pain and disappointment lay beneath the surface of her tale. He considered telling her that her looks were more than passable. No, she wasn't pretty in a conventional way, but with her beautiful eyes and soft lips, she caught a body's attention.

But maybe compliments weren't a good idea. They were far too alone for words that steered close to flirtatious.

"Are you alone in the world now?" he asked.

"I have relatives. A cousin inherited the title and land, but staying around was unwise. My mother, my father, my brother are all—gone." She released his hand so abruptly it fell as though not attached to his arm. "That should do it." She kept her head bent as though still examining his wound. "It should be bandaged, but I expect you need the use of that hand, so just keep it as clean as you can."

Dismissed like the lady of the manor sending a servant back to his duties.

Half a day ago, he would have wanted to leave her in Cold

Spring to find her own way to Albany. At that moment, he sought for words of comfort.

"Any lady who has the courage to jump over open water onto a boat to get where she wants to go is going to get on in the world just fine."

"Courage?" She flashed a smile at him. "Do you not mean stupidity?"

"Well, there's that too." He grinned at her.

She blinked, and tears glinted on her long eyelashes. "Now let us hope that risk was not in vain. Do you—" Her lower lip quivered. "Do you think we will have any more disasters?"

"This wasn't a disaster, just a minor inconvenience. We should still reach Albany by Wednesday."

"Then I shall pray we have no more inconveniences, minor or catastrophic."

"You do that, and so will I."

If not for the loss of revenue, he wouldn't in the least be bothered if their journey took many extra days so he could spend more time with this lady.

And in the morning, he realized he would obtain his wish and that he had spoken incorrectly when saying the broken paddles were only an inconvenience. They were a disaster, for his replacement buckets were no longer in their storage compartment.

$\mathcal{F}$IVE

amilla woke to an odd sensation she spent several moments identifying as warmth. For the first time in days, she didn't feel as though someone had stuffed her into a larder like a crock of butter needing to be kept cold. Sunlight poured through the porthole in a flood of celestial fire. For several luxurious minutes, she lay motionless, savoring the sun's heat, rocking gently as the river current tugged at the boat's hull, and remembering those moments in the cabin earlier that morning, when she had held Captain Nathaniel Black's hand, while he told her she had pretty eyes.

"You are a fool, missy," she heard her old governess say, as she had when, at seventeen, Camilla decided to toss her cap over the windmill for the curate. "He has no future."

And neither did Nathaniel Black. Without some kind of divine intervention, he would lose his boat, all he had worked for, and like that young curate, be nothing more than another man's tool.

Yet she would have been better off with the curate. He now was doing well for himself, drawing in parishioners to hear God's Word. And she was stranded on a riverboat somewhere between New York City and Albany, her future slipping away into emptiness like the water flowing beneath the hull. No man had so much as pretended to pay court to her for nearly five years.

Nathaniel Black thought she had pretty hair.

She curled her fingers as though still holding his hand, scarred and calloused and beautiful in its capable strength. If her hands were half as useful as his, she could build a future for herself as he had, as he would again even if his partnership disintegrated around him. But she only knew how to plan and organize and direct servants, and carry on intelligent conversation, skills Joanna needed, even if her letter hadn't quite said so.

Nathaniel Black was repairing his boat with calm resignation. Each word tugged on her to rise and follow that voice to its source, watch him perilously hanging over the end of the deck, his fingers deft, his hair lifting in the breeze as though ruffled by an affectionate gesture . . .

She was a fool. She knew nothing of him except he flirted with her despite her disheveled appearance. She was such an old spinster to have her head turned that easily. If he knew the debt that literally followed her, he would put her ashore there in Cold Spring and leave her far behind.

She rolled off the side of the bunk and divested herself of her blanket and quilt. Beneath, her muslin gown was hopelessly crumpled. What she would give for an iron, or a washtub, her newly acquired skills since she could no longer employ a maid. Her cloak, left hanging over a chair to dry, looked worse than her gown.

After brushing and braiding her hair, she left the cloak flung over the chair and pulled a shawl out of her valise. An elderly woman on the voyage across the Atlantic had taught Camilla how to knit. The stitches were uneven, but she had improved as she went along, acquiring another skill and a warm garment that was crimson rather than black.

She wrapped it around her shoulders, pinned it into place with a bow-shaped brooch in plain cut steel, and left her cabin. About to step onto the deck, she stopped and clapped a hand to her head. Going about the boat at night without a hat didn't feel odd. She had attended evening parties without hats. But this was daylight. Her hair and skin were never fully exposed to the light.

Nathaniel Black thought she had pretty hair.

That thought stuck in her head, a smile pasted onto her lips, she sauntered onto the deck, where the captain lay prone on the boards, hanging so far down he looked about to plunge headfirst into the river. He didn't notice Camilla. If the other men did, they said nothing to her. No one offered to fetch her coffee or a chair or an explanation as to how the repairs got on. She may as well have been invisible.

She may as well get used to it. Companion or housekeeper or whatever Joanna intended to call her, she would be invisible to others.

And if she had married the curate, she would have been too much on display once she was a vicar's wife.

She didn't want either. She wanted . . . something in the middle. A comfortable life perhaps. Children. A husband who loved her as Father had loved Mama.

Unlikely in the northern wilderness.

Deciding to go find her own coffee, or at the least something for breakfast, Camilla traversed the cabin deck to the pilothouse steps. Her box of viands from the night before, barely touched, still waited upon the bench. She ate another roll with butter and drank some cider, then wandered over to the wheel. She wanted to look at it now that she stood there alone. Its size astounded her, at least as tall as her five feet three inches, and disappearing into the floor. She grasped a pin on the side. What strength must be needed to twist such a massive wheel. What skill to turn a boat the length of a Navy frigate. She half closed her eyes to block out the sight of the town to her left and pretended she guided the boat up the river. She smelled the woodsmoke of the boilers being stoked, heard the rumble of the engine. Amazing power to drive a vessel against the current. Who needed to gamble when one could go on adventures like—

"Are you enjoying yourself?"

Camilla jumped away from the wheel, tripped on a brake pedal, and careened backward into Captain Black's chest.

He caught her beneath the elbows and steadied her. "You looked like you were."

"Yes, I was rather." The sun warmed her cheeks. "I hope I did nothing wrong."

"No, nothing." He released her and she faced him.

"I was thinking this would be a pleasure to pilot."

"I love the river. It's always changing." He heaved a sigh and looked over her head. "But I won't be piloting today."

"What?" Her gaze flew up to his. "What's wrong?"

"I usually carry extra paddles in the event of damage." His hands fisted against his thighs. "But they have mysteriously disappeared."

Camilla's hand flew to her lips. She began to shake. "How? I mean who—?"

"Since one of my crew disappeared in the night, I suspect he did it." His eyes were chips of green ice.

Camilla shivered. "Why?"

"Money, I expect. But we don't need to know who. Somehow Lancaster got to him."

"When—?" She stopped, the breath leaving her lungs in a rush as though she'd been punched. She clasped her hands against her middle, nearly choking on her next words. "I saw them. I mean, I didn't see them talking, but I saw a gentleman walking back to Lancaster's boat at the same time one of your crew came back aboard. I should have told you. I didn't see them talk, and you came back right after, so I thought nothing of it, but—" She flung out a hand, intending to grasp the wheel for support.

Black caught her hand instead, held it tight, steadying her. "It's all right. You couldn't have known. I should have guessed Lancaster would do something like this."

"What will we do?" She spoke in a whisper.

"Wait until another boat comes along with paddles we can buy."

"They have none here?"

"They should, but this has been an unusually busy season with the canal opening."

"Tomorrow." Her lower lip quivered against her will, and the sunshine and blue sky blurred before her eyes. "We won't be there, will we?"

"I . . . don't know. We can put you on another boat maybe."

"That is what you wished for all along." The clawing fear in her belly lent her tone more asperity than she intended. "I am sorry." She blinked hard to hold back tears.

"I'm sorry too." He brushed a tear off her cheek with his thumb. "Sometimes I'm wrong." He released her hand. "Would you like to go ashore? There are some shops. You could buy a new hat."

She couldn't, not if she wouldn't have work after all. She wouldn't have a home or food or—

"I need to go to my cabin."

She was going to be sick or scream or both.

The captain still gripped her hand, bringing her up short. "Miss Renfrew, wait."

"I can't. I can't. I—" A sob broke into her words. Tears gushed out of her eyes.

Black muttered something that sounded like, "Lancaster will pay for this," and drew her against him.

SIX

No one had comforted Camilla like this since Papa died and Mama had held her while she wept. Marcus had been off losing his fortune when Mama gave up on life without Papa. But this sometimes brusque and always kind stranger, whose coat smelled of leather, woodsmoke, and some of those spices he carried, whose speech was common and whose livelihood bore no resemblance to the gentility of the sort of persons with whom she had always associated, curved his big hand around the back of her neck, his arm around her shoulders, and held her. He held her until she managed to get her bout of weakness under control. He held her even after the sobs subsided and her breathing returned to normal. He held her when she wanted to run and hide from the sheer mortification of him holding her. Wanted to, but remained motionless, preferring the comfort of being cared for by another person.

Then the creak of the pilothouse steps drew her attention to the silence of the boat with the engine shut down, the paddle wheel still. Everyone on board must have heard her sobs. Anyone around could see her in Captain Black's arms.

Perhaps she could crawl into the space that housed the rest of the wheel and hide there for about fifty years. Her mortification might subside by then.

She drew away and pulled a corner of her shawl over her face. "I am so sorry. I do not know what came over me."

"Don't you?" Black tucked his hand under her chin and tipped her face up. The kindness in his eyes nearly set her off again. "You set your heart on getting to Albany, and now it doesn't look like that will happen."

"It is more than my heart." She glanced at the steps in time to see Billy backing down the steps. "It's my future. Even after my brother started running through the family wealth, Mama kept saying the Lord would provide. But it seems like he's taken more than he's given, and my faith is wearing thin."

He pulled a strand of now damp hair off her cheek and smoothed it behind her ear. "I wish I could say I didn't understand, but I do. This little trick of Lancaster's may have scuttled both our plans."

"Then what does a body do? I mean, I wasn't raised to take care of myself, to be honest."

He smiled. "Seems to me like you're doing all right at it. Or are English ladies of the manor taught to leap onto moving boats to get their way?"

"Walking into Almack's was worse, believe me."

"Almack's?"

"The highest-priced market for wives in my . . . er . . . former social sphere."

"But you survived, and you will. You don't know that your friend won't be in Albany, or that another boat won't come this way in time to get you to Albany by tomorrow."

"Won't that need to be soon?"

"Within the next three to six hours, I expect." A cloud dimmed the bright green of his eyes. "And if one doesn't, we have to keep believing even when our faith turns as thin as river mist."

"Why, Captain, that is downright poetic."

He grinned, though a faint flush rose under his sun-darkened skin. "I, uh, might have left home at fourteen, but I do still read.

Sometimes there's not much to do aboard a boat. And speaking of not much to do, I think I should take you ashore."

"Will we not miss a boat if it comes?"

"We'll hear its whistle and get back in time."

"I look rather disreputable."

"Go wash your face, and you'll do just fine."

She wouldn't. She didn't need to see her reflection to know her eyes were puffy, her gown hopeless, and that uncovered head. But she washed her face and donned the crumpled cloak so she could pull the hood up in lieu of a hat.

She never should have worn her hat in the rain, but her valise was full to bursting, and she simply could not go about without something on her head. It was her last vestige of a claim to being a lady.

And now it was gone along with her social standing. She was going ashore with a riverboat captain as her escort, and looking forward to doing so. "You need not accompany me. I am quite certain you have work to do."

"And I'm just as certain that I don't." His voice was tight, a little hard. "I can't repair my boat without the right parts. My paperwork is complete. And if I stay here, I just might think up ways to scuttle Riley Lancaster." They reached the lower deck and he took her arm. "In short, Miss Renfrew, I need a distraction." Suddenly, he laughed.

Two crewmen, who looked as though they were standing watch, turned and stared, mouths agape as though hearing their captain laugh was unusual.

Camilla glanced up at him. "May I be in on the jest?"

"I didn't want you aboard because women are too much of a distraction. They cause trouble."

"Do we now?" She stuck her nose in the air.

"Indeed." He guided her down the shaky gangway to the wharf. "You've seen that missing tooth of Billy's? He got it because of a female passenger. She was a flirt and teased the men mercilessly until she provoked a fight between two of them. Billy's now scarred for life, and I lost a good crewman."

"D-dead?"

"No, he left the boat with the female and I was an engineer short that trip."

She tilted her head and shot him a glance from the corner of her eye. "I do not flirt with crewmen."

Perhaps not crewmen, but she was flirting with the captain, a skill she had learned from watching a hundred other ladies. She hadn't intended to practice it now. It slipped out, warm, teasing, a little too intimate for such a short acquaintance.

But then, after weeping all over his chest, she felt rather closer to him than such a short acquaintance should make them.

He caught her gaze and held it just a moment too long, then tucked her hand into the crook of his elbow and led her ashore. Once they skirted a row of warehouses, he paused and frowned down at her. "You don't need to play games to get me to help you, Miss—" He sighed. "What's your Christian name?"

"Ca-Camilla." She swallowed against sudden dryness in her throat and tried again without the stammer. "Camilla Renfrew."

"Of course. You wouldn't have a nice normal name like Jane or Mary."

"What's wrong with Camilla?"

"Nothing. It's just right for you."

They reached the town with its inns and shops and neat houses before Camilla said, "Now who's flirting with whom?"

"I don't flirt with females." He paused before the display window of a bakeshop exhibiting tender-looking pastries. "The last thing I need is a female thinking I'm interested in her."

"Isn't it about time you were married?" She caught her breath. "I am sorry. It is none of my concern."

"No, it's not, but I was hoping to be married by the time I turn thirty. But I won't marry anyone while I have no choice but to be on the river twenty-five days out of thirty. I don't think that's fair to a wife or family."

"Unless your wife traveled with you. Are you going to go in that shop or stand here staring at its goods?"

For response, he opened the door. The aroma of sugar and cinnamon, butter and apples wafted out like ambrosia. Camilla's head spun.

"Captain Black, haven't seen you in a while." A matronly woman bustled out to stand behind the counter. "And you have a passenger?"

"More like a stowaway." He rumbled the response, but his smile belied the severity of the words. "How fresh are your apple fritters?"

"You'd burn your mouth if you ate them right now. Shall I wrap some up?"

"Please, and a flask of coffee."

The woman wrapped some round pastries in twists of paper, all the while casting glances at Camilla. The captain didn't enlighten her. Camilla merely gazed back with the impassive stare she had perfected once she realized she didn't want to marry any of her choices and discovered indifference sent them packing faster than words.

Black asked the woman about a few boats, if she had seen them recently. She had—days before. Everyone was going upriver, few coming down yet. Many were continuing on up to Troy. And still the woman stared at Camilla. Still Camilla folded her arms across her front and stared right back.

The instant the order was complete, Black paid the reckoning, scooped up the food from the counter, and bade goodbye. Camilla preceded him out of the shop, holding the door. She did not take his arm again once they reached the street.

"What," she asked, "was that all about?"

"She's never seen me with a female other than Marianne Spraig, who is older than my mother."

"Your mother's alive and you still left home?"

He smiled down at her. "Come. Let's go eat these in Mrs. Spraig's garden."

"She will not mind?"

"She's in Albany visiting her sister. The house is empty."

It wasn't merely empty; it was abandoned with the windows boarded up on the ground floor and the garden barren of vegetation beneath the autumn sun. The garden might have been pretty even a week ago with colorful foliage on the trees. Now the trees stretched nearly naked branches to the pale blue sky, a carpet of soggy leaves at their base.

Camilla sank onto the top step, the stones providing warmth, and spread her wide skirts out like a fan, like a protective barrier, forcing the captain to sit on the step at her feet.

"How appropriate," he murmured, as he lowered himself to the bottom tread. "Do you expect men to abase themselves at your feet?"

Only her brother had the day he made his horrible confession, the last day she saw him.

"Do you think I would be here if I did?" She shoved back her hood so the sun could warm her head.

Black handed her one of the still warm pastries. "Careful when you bite into this. It's full of apples."

"We fill our fritters with mushrooms."

He gave her a look of disgust. "I prefer apples."

She took a bite and had to agree.

"So tell me, Miss Camilla Renfrew," Black asked her while her mouth was full, "what are you doing here?"

She swallowed, then cleared her throat. "I told you. Taking a position because my brother—"

"Yes, and you said no one wanted to marry an impoverished princess with only passable looks. But why isn't that cousin you mentioned taking care of you?"

"Why is your family not helping you buy your partnership shares if they are doing so well selling horses to the canalers?"

"Good riposte." He handed her the flask of coffee.

She savored the smooth coffee to which hot milk had been added.

"I may be only passably pretty and twenty-five, but he is not yet wed and I could scarcely stay under the same roof without a chaperone he was unwilling to pay for."

"You're traveling with me without a chaperone." He kept his gaze on her face as he drank from the same flask, seemingly unselfconscious at the intimacy of sharing.

She shrugged to feign indifference at watching his mouth touch the silvery rim. "I am a lady in England. I am a nothing here."

"You may be a number of things, Miss Renfrew." He spoke in a rather husky voice. "A stowaway, a servant, an adventure-seeker . . . But you will never be a nothing."

She certainly felt like something at that moment—either a hawk ready to take flight to the top of the nearest oak, or a rabbit ready to flee for the nearest warren.

He could not make her feel this way. They barely knew one another. Yet she had already spent more time with him than she had with either of the men who had come up to scratch and offered for her. Yet those were men whose pedigrees she had known before they met—their pedigrees and their rumored flaws, bad enough to have her father turn them down. This man had no pedigree.

As though hers had done her any good.

"I think," she said, "I need a walk."

"I think—"

The blast of a steam whistle cut off what he thought.

Camilla sprang to her feet. "A boat. If they have room for me and are going upriver, I might reach Albany in time."

And escape these weird notions running through her head and squeezing at her heart.

She hastened from the garden, her hood forgotten, her skirts swinging. She retraced their steps at an unladylike speed. No matter. She wasn't a lady. Not like she had been raised in the privileged sense. The notion was suddenly freeing, not a burden of loss. She could still conduct herself with the moral code drilled into her since birth and be honorable, without having to walk sedately no matter what the emergency.

A steamboat moored alongside the *Marianne*, dwarfing it with gleaming white paint and three flags fluttering from the jackstaff.

And a deck crammed with passengers with both two and four feet. Men, women, children, and a number of domesticated animals from a cat to a cow filled every inch of space on both decks.

Even before she found the captain hauling crates of something out of a warehouse, she knew what his answer would be.

"Sorry, miss." He shook his grizzled head. "Not an inch to spare."

"Do you have any buckets to spare?" Captain Black had come up behind Camilla.

"I saw your paddle wheel was damaged. What happened?"

"Deliberate debris in the river." Black's tone was curt. "Do you have any?"

"No, but Todd's right behind me. He might."

The man and his crewmen carrying crates trundled off toward the boat. Moments later, it backed from the wharf and into the midstream of the river.

Camilla pressed her hand to her lips as she watched.

"I can see that lower lip quivering through your fingers." The captain drew her hand away from her face and held her fingers clasped in the shelter of his. "There will be other work if you miss your friend, you know."

Work that would take her out of reach of the man who claimed she had borrowed ten thousand pounds from him and vowed he would stop at nothing to get it back?

She couldn't confide that to Black. He would likely leave her behind for fear of getting tangled in her morass.

"Let's go aboard the *Marianne* and wait for the next boat." Still holding on to her hand, Black led her back to his boat. "I have some books in my cabin, if you'd like."

"I would. I only brought a Bible and a volume of Shakespeare with me, and nearly have the Gospels and Mr. Shakespeare's sonnets memorized."

The crewmen left aboard to keep watch gave them knowing grins, then quickly turned away. Black ignored them and continued to his cabin.

The space, only a little larger than Camilla's, sported a desk as well as the table. Above the former, a shelf held a row of well-worn books, beginning with a Bible and ending with a ragged copy of Samuel Johnson's dictionary.

"Where did you get that?" She reached across the metal grille holding the books in place and plucked up the book.

He shrugged. "I found it in a shop of secondhand things a long time ago. As for the rest of the books? Much the same way."

"And you have read them all?"

"Many times." He plucked up a copy of *Castle of Otranto*, Horace Walpole's gothic novel. "This one might be my favorite."

"I liked it too, though it has been many years."

He placed it in her hands. "You're welcome to it." He hesitated in the doorway a moment, then glanced toward her cabin. "May I read your Shakespeare? I've, um, never read Shakespeare."

He had never read Shakespeare. A knot twisted inside Camilla's chest, grief for a boy allowed to go out on his own too young yet struggling to get an education.

"Of course you may borrow it." She retrieved the book and, by the time she returned to him, had made up her mind. "Poetry should be read aloud, though."

Something like panic flashed in his eyes. "I've never read aloud."

"And your accent's all wrong." She grinned. "I will read to you."

Only when they were settled in the pilothouse and the book fell open in her lap did she think about the nature of most of the bard's poems.

·· · $EVEN ·· ·

A man could listen to that voice all day. Mellow and well-modulated, the tones rose and fell with a cadence oddly intense yet soothing. After a while, she grew a little hoarse, and he left the wheelhouse, where they sat for the sake of the sunshine and propriety, to make her tea from the stores he had always kept for Mr. Spraig, who abhorred coffee. She thanked him with a smile that melted something inside him he hadn't realized was frozen, and continued to read the tender, mocking, and passionate verses.

Not until his stomach growled and the warmth of the day began to leach from the air did he realize how much time had passed—time without any sign of James Todd's boat.

"I think," he said when she paused to take a sip of tea, "we should go find some dinner."

"It is rather late." Her gaze flicked from the setting sun, to the empty river, and that vulnerable lower lip quivered. "The other boat hasn't come."

"No."

"Why?" She slapped the book closed and flung it onto the bench. "Why? Why is God doing this to me—to us? I am certain you must be losing money on this, and Joanna will not wait for me forever."

"I don't know. I'm trying not to ask myself the same thing."

63

He rose and went to the wheel, staring out at the river shimmering and dark in the falling light. "I can't say I chose an easy way of life on the river, but believing God was with me, taking care of me, loving me as my earthly father never did, hasn't been hard. Until Ralph Spraig died. Since then, I can't seem to succeed in any of my plans. First I had to find the money to buy out Spraig's shares, then Lancaster decided the partnership should go. He said he'd get his way, but I never thought he would until now. The river would never be this empty except everyone is waiting in Albany for the canal to be officially opened all the way to Lake Erie. And I'm sitting here like a bird with a broken wing, while everything I've worked for disappears." He gripped the wheel so hard the healing cut on his right hand opened and a trickle of blood ran warm over his fingers.

"And I have not worked for anything in my life." She was there beside him, taking his hand in both of hers and pressing a lacy handkerchief, probably one of the few she owned, against his injured palm. She gazed up at him, her eyes luminous in the dusk. "I had everything and did not appreciate it. I thought it my due for being born a Renfrew. And now I have nothing. Worse than nothing, for if I lose the belief that God is in control of my life, I—well, what else is there in life?"

"We keep believing then, no matter what." Her gentle touch, her honest words, calmed him, set a light, small but bright, glowing inside him. He raised his other hand to her cheek, marveled at its smoothness. "Thank you."

"If I had not delayed you, you would not have encountered Lancaster and this would not have happened."

"Maybe. Maybe not. I suspect he was lying in wait for me, and his boat is a side-wheeler. They go a bit faster through turns than this one can. Besides, I'm not sure I regret you being aboard."

Her hands tightened on his. Her eyes widened, her lips parted. That lower lip so full, so soft, so kissable looking, puffed out in invitation.

He looked away and clasped his hands behind his back. "Let's go get some supper."

"I think perhaps we should."

In silence, they descended to the cargo deck and back into town. In silence they found themselves at an inn where hot venison stew and crusty bread was served on long tables full of other people. They sat across from one another and avoided one another's eyes. When they both reached for bread at the same time, their eyes met and held, and Nathaniel admitted to himself that he hoped she was forced to find work in Albany, not in the western territories. He could see her then, court her properly.

And torture himself with the fact he had no future to offer a female if the partnership died.

He returned to food that tasted like charcoal. He finished it because he needed the nourishment. Across from him, Miss Renfrew seemed to be doing the same thing—choking down her last bite. He rose and removed her cloak from a hook on the wall. Ralph Spraig had always held his wife's cloak for her. Nathaniel did the same for the sort of woman he would have chosen for a wife and allowed his hands to rest on her thin shoulders for just a moment longer than necessary.

She tilted her head back and smiled at him. "Thank you."

If they had been alone in that moment, he would have done something really stupid like kiss her. Instead, he released her and strode away, waiting only long enough to hold the door for her. He didn't offer her his arm on the way back to the boat. On the cabin deck, he wished her a brusque "Good night," and closed his cabin door before she reached her own.

He leaned against it, his fingers shoved into his hair. What was God doing to him? Giving or taking? He had known the lady for little more than a day, yes, a twenty-four-hour period in which they had spent more time in one another's company than not, but still, too short to feel this longing to turn twenty-four hours into twenty-four days and twenty-four months and—

The blast of a steam whistle was beautiful music to his ears. He charged to the cargo deck in time to see a boat docking nearby. In moments, he was at the other gangway, one thought in his head—get the paddles replaced so he could be on his way and rid himself of foolish dreams that could never be.

His adage remained true—females were nothing but trouble aboard.

A crewman directed him to the boat's captain, not a man he knew. "How are things upriver?"

"Too crowded for me. Can't get a mooring to save your life."

They talked over coffee and negotiated the price for one paddle. "All I can spare."

"It's a start."

Despite a nearly full moon, he couldn't work on the wheel in the dark, so he returned to his cabin, noted a light under Miss Renfrew's door, but forced himself to close his own. He had enjoyed less than two hours of sleep in the past forty hours and needed to rest while he could. Sleep would clear his head of ridiculous heart notions.

But in the morning, when he came face-to-face with the lady, he knew the sleep had done nothing but emphasize his attraction to her, especially when she gave him a tremulous smile and peeked at him from beneath her lashes.

"Did the boat that came in last night have any paddles?" she asked.

"Just one. I'll get to work on it as soon as I get some breakfast. Have you eaten?"

"Billy made me some tea."

"He's more of a gentleman than I sometimes. Shall we?" He held out his hand without thinking.

She took it and he tucked her fingers into the crook of his arm. "So Albany is overcrowded with boats, I learned. I expect by to-morrow, the river will be teeming with boats coming down while we're still heading up."

"I wonder where Mr. Lancaster is." Her fingers were tense on his arm.

"Causing more trouble, no doubt."

"Do we have to make more stops along the way?"

Too much he liked her use of "we."

"Just one. Poughkeepsie." They reached the inn, and he held the door open for her. "I've cargo to unlade and fuel to take on."

For a female who had been brought up to dine in the finest houses in England, she slid onto the bench as though she had done that all her life. "Why fuel?"

"It's cheaper than buying it in the city, and I can carry more cargo if I don't take all the fuel I need at once."

"Well, then, how can we make this go faster? If you have the Poughkeepsie cargo—that's a rather odd name, you know—if that cargo is sorted ahead of time—"

So while he, Billy, and two other crewmen worked on replacing the paddle called a bucket for its scoop shape, she directed two other crewmen in organizing the cargo. Though he concentrated on the precarious work of affixing a new paddle securely to the frame, part of him listened for her voice, commanding without being strident, insistent without being shrewish, calling to him, calling, calling, calling.

They finished installing the paddle. Nathaniel cleaned up, donning a fresh shirt, and went to find her. He found her nearly upside down trying to read the label on a crate someone had set down facing inward.

"You should get the men to move that for you."

She jumped, banging her head on another box. "Ow." She dropped to her knees on the deck and pressed her hand to the top of her head.

"Are you all right? Let me see." He crouched before her and tugged her hand away from the injury. "Looks like you're going to have a goose egg, but no skin's broken." He tilted her chin up. "Can you see one or two of me?"

"Just one."

"No concussion then. But maybe you should go lie down."

"No, I am all right. It just hurts some."

He leaned forward and kissed the swelling bruise, then started back as though burned.

She gazed up at him with her big cat eyes full of confusion.

He wished he were confused. He wished too clearly he didn't realize that if one could fall head over heels in love in two days, he had done just that.

··· ℰIGHT ···

amilla scrambled to her feet. "I, um, should move this crate so we can get all the cargo organized. You know, if you do this ahead of time, you will save yourself even a quarter hour each stop. That adds up, you know. And if you had a cook aboard, you all would have no need to go on shore for so long to find meals—"

"Shh." He laid a finger across her lips. "If I made my boat go as fast as you're talking, my boiler would blow."

She thought something inside her would explode if she didn't get away from him, or perhaps fling herself against him and hold on tight. She didn't know which she wanted. She feared the latter. She remained motionless save for her hands twisting together the edges of her cloak.

"Let's go for a walk." He held out his hand to her. "There's nothing more to do aboard here except to wait, and that can drive a body mad."

Perhaps that was what was wrong with her. She liked moving, riding when she still owned a horse, walking after that, even digging in the garden when they had to let the gardeners go.

She took his hand. This time, he did not tuck her fingers into the crook of his elbow, but laced his fingers with hers as though he were courting her. And perhaps he was in his untutored way. He had given her that kiss she couldn't take as playful, such as when a mother kissed the bruise of a child. The deepening of the green of his eyes when he looked at her afterward told her he wasn't feeling in the least playful.

They passed through the town this time and entered a wooded area with more leaves on the ground than on the trees. The carpet of vegetation silenced their footfalls. With most of the birds having flown south and the wind calm, quiet surrounded them—the kind of place where she expected God's voice could be heard.

Suddenly the trees parted and the land sloped down to a natural inlet at the mouth of a stream. "The Dutch who settled here called these streams 'kills.' I don't know why. But someday I want to build a house here. It's close enough to town to hear the boats coming in, but far enough away to give a body peace."

"Peace indeed." Below them, the river slipped past in an endless pewter ribbon touched with the gold of sunlight. "It's fascinating how the water flows down to the sea, but we build machines to help us go against that current."

He grinned. "That's how I've lived my life—going against the current of what is expected of me. I was supposed to raise horses with the family, but I don't really like horses much, not enough to make them my life. But the river!" He turned to her, his face alight. "Have you ever been certain you know what your life's purpose is?"

"I did not have to. It was mapped out for me before I was born. And now—" Her heart yawned empty to experience the kind of joy he showed.

"I was eleven years old when Robert Fulton made his first voyage up the Hudson in a steamboat. I stood on the shore and watched him go against the current at four miles an hour. It was a miracle, and I wanted to be a part of it. Steam is the future." He shook his head and some of the light died. "I want to have a place to come home to, though."

If he lost his boat, he also lost his home.

Heart aching for him, Camilla sought for words to comfort him. The rumble of an engine and *shug, shug, shug* of a paddle wheel closed her need for speech. A steamboat was chugging down the river, drawing them back to town and the harbor.

That boat didn't have the right size paddle to spare. Camilla and Black returned to town with Billy and other crewmen to find some dinner. They were finishing what was becoming a ubiquitous apple pie when another boat docked. They had a paddle with which they could part. "We can install this in the morning and be on our way," Black promised.

"How long?" Camilla asked.

"About seventeen more hours. Now get some rest."

She wrapped up in two quilts to keep warm, but sat at the table, her Bible open and unread before her, the lamp lending light, if not warmth. She kept thinking how they could save time. One more stop. They could unload cargo quickly now that she had moved that to the front, but the men going ashore for food was another matter. If they had something edible onboard, they wouldn't need to go ashore. How difficult could it be to add flavor to the stew and to not cook the vegetables all at once with the meat so they became nothing but tasteless gray mush? Surely the captain would be willing to spare a few spices from his cargo.

She was about to go ask him when he knocked on the door. "I saw your light and thought you might like to come sit by the stove and have some hot cider."

"I would." Her heart leaped and skipped and acted altogether foolishly at the sight of him standing in the doorway, a warning she should stay put.

She rose and followed him to the cargo deck, where the stove used for cooking radiated heat to the half-dozen men who gathered around it. They were telling stories of the river and travel. One man had been up the Mississippi. Another had nearly died when the boiler of his boat exploded. Camilla listened with fascination, with awe, with the knowledge they probably exaggerated a bit for her benefit. She laughed and applauded, and felt right at home. When one by one the men decided to find beds for the night, Camilla rose slowly from her crate chair, thinking her empty cabin would feel lonely.

She bade everyone good night and started for the steps.

"Miss Renfrew." Captain Black caught up with her. "May I show you something?"

Of course he could.

She said nothing, simply stepped aside so he could precede her up the steps to the pilothouse.

"Just this" was all he said.

He didn't need to say more. The town was dark. The boats were dark. Moonlight blazed cold and bright in the sky, turning the river to a rippling silver ribbon and the frost on the trees to shimmering jewels.

She caught her breath and hugged herself against outward cold and inward warmth. "I see why you love the river."

"Unfortunately, cold means our work will come to an end for the winter."

She glanced up at him. "What do you do then?"

"I go to a boardinghouse somewhere. I've thought about going down to the southern states where a body can work all year, but I don't know those rivers as well, so I couldn't pilot."

"Taking orders is difficult after you are used to giving them." She rubbed her arms.

He slipped his arm around her shoulders and tucked her head against his chest. "Better?"

"Much." Warmth stole through her. The town and boats and river lay in such stillness she heard his heart, beating as hard as her own.

"Miss Renfrew . . . ? Camilla?"

"Yes?" Startled at the use of her Christian name, she glanced up.

And he kissed her. She was twenty-five and had never been kissed. This meeting of lips tasting of cider and cinnamon was worth every year of waiting. No wine-soaked roué who had dragged her onto terraces during balls could hold a candle to this man, no matter how large their fortunes or elevated their titles. She leaned against him, she buried her fingers in his unkempt thick hair. She returned his kiss until she couldn't breathe.

Then she drew away only long enough to inhale a lungful of frosty air before burying her face against his chest again.

"Camilla." He murmured her name. He stroked her hair. "I was thinking. I can winter in Albany, if you stay. I'm sure you can find work there. Court you proper. We probably don't know each other well enough for me to have just kissed you, but I've wanted to since I met you, and the short time just didn't seem to matter."

"Not to me either."

The specter of Frederick Conover and his threats rose between her and Nathaniel, and she drew away. "I promised Joanna I would go with her to Michigan."

He kept his arm around her. "And if she didn't wait?"

"I will find a way to follow."

Anything to make finding her too difficult for Conover to bother collecting the money he thought she owed him—or worse.

She felt rather than heard his sigh. "And I have no right to suggest I'll find a way to make you stay, if I have nothing to offer you in the way of a future. I should let you go now. I should send you back to your cabin and tell you to stay away from me until we land."

Instead of all those things, he kissed her again. Then he released her. "Now go. It'll be an early morning."

He didn't walk her even as far as the cabin deck. She made her way down with her hand to her lips, cherishing the sensation of their lips clinging together. Her legs felt boneless, her insides the consistency of an overbaked apple, and her heart sang, stuttered to a halt, raised its voice again.

By the time she crawled onto her bunk, the heart singing had ceased beneath the weight of what she was keeping from Nathaniel. He would forget about courting her if he knew the burden from which she fled. She would tell him once they reached Albany. Except what if Joanna hadn't waited and Camilla couldn't find a way to follow? She would need work and she was good at so little, just organizing.

The following morning, watching the men rearrange her carefully arranged cargo for no obvious reason, as Nathaniel worked on the paddle wheel, an idea struck Camilla's head. As soon as the captain returned to the pilothouse, she ran up to talk to him, needing to get his attention while the boilers fired up and the engine got enough steam to drive the great wheel.

"Natha—Captain?" She was breathless as she reached the wheelhouse.

He turned and smiled at her. "Did you sleep well?"

"I, um—" She blinked to break the spell of his green eyes gazing at her with enough warmth to turn the blustery autumn day into deep summer. "I think so."

"Good. We should be underway soon, provided those repairs hold."

"That is wonderful."

"You'll only be two days late. Considering how much downriver traffic there is, we might even get a mooring near the city."

"That would be even better."

Suddenly, he reached out and clasped her hands. "Once we're underway and I'm sure those buckets will hold, I'll turn the wheel over to Billy so we can talk some more."

"I thought I'd try to make the stew today so we don't have to stop so long in that town."

"Poughkeepsie?"

She nodded.

"If it tastes halfway decent, I'll consider you a miracle worker.

Now I've got to get to work. You can sit here, but it's much warmer down by the boilers."

She sat in the cold and damp of the open pilothouse, watching his unhurried movements, listening to him talk with Billy, wondering how she would tell him she was, in essence, a woman with a price on her head. And as she sat on the hard bench bolted to the floor of the wheelhouse, an idea took root in her mind. But she couldn't share that with Nathaniel either.

At noon, she descended to the cargo deck and tiny galley in time to stop a crewman from dumping potatoes, carrots, and some kind of gourd into the pot along with chunks of dried beef. "Do you have any salt or peppercorns?"

She didn't know how to cook, but she knew how well-prepared food tasted. Perhaps going backward from how she knew something should look or taste would prove useful.

Shortly after she began to add salt and ground peppercorns and taste the results, Nathaniel joined her. With the crewmen nearby, they said little and looked at one another a great deal. When his gaze dropped to her lips, her cheeks heated from more than the stove, and a thrill ran up her spine.

A thrill followed by an ache, an emptiness, an understanding of a future having known at least the beginning of love and cast away because she had trusted an untrustworthy brother. She could only savor the moment—if that was fair to Captain Black.

Cold despite the heat of the stove, she wrapped her arms across her front and began to pace through the stacks of barrels and crates on the cargo deck. The motion didn't help her think.

The passageways were too narrow for Nathaniel to fall into step beside her. Instead, he circumvented a stack and met her face-to-face in one of the narrow corridors. "What's troubling you, sweetheart?"

The endearment brought tears to her eyes. "I am fretting about what is ahead for me. How long can I hold on to this gossamer thread of faith?"

"The faith of a mustard seed moves mountains, remember?" He smiled, but it didn't reach his eyes.

"You're worrying too." She touched his cheek, felt the rasp of a day's growth of whiskers.

He took her hand in his and kissed her fingers. "I am, and for two reasons now. I'm not sure how I'll manage if I lose both the boat and you."

Tell him. Tell him. Tell him.

"Captain—?"

"You kissed me back, Camilla. I think you can call me Nathaniel."

"We English never use first names. At least not in my—" She laughed with an edge to it. "My social rank indeed. Yes, I think I can call you Nathaniel, especially—"

The great bell began to clang. Nathaniel dropped a kiss onto her lips, then bolted for the pilothouse.

Camilla followed at a more sedate pace, considered hiding out in her cabin so she didn't have to tell him the truth, see the rejection in his beautiful eyes. The sight of lights on shore marked their arrival in Poughkeepsie, so she hid out on the cargo deck instead, organizing what crew were available to haul the crates meant for the town closer to the gangway. A pity they didn't have a handcart. It would make moving heavy boxes so much easier and safer. The cargo moved, she retreated to the galley to taste her stew. To her surprise, it was rather flavorful. The carrots and potatoes were still too hard, but by the time the men unloaded and loaded, those would surely be soft.

"Tell the men to eat here," she said to Nathaniel when the *Marianne* was moored. "It will save time."

"You're amazing" was all he said.

She wasn't certain he would comply, but once the cargo was unloaded and a load of wood hauled aboard, the men all followed, one bearing a pile of fresh bread and a crock of butter.

The men ate in shifts, as they were needed on boilers and in the engine room. Nathaniel didn't appear at all. He was busy taking the boat back into the river. Camilla was wondering how he would manage to eat, when Billy strode into the galley, his face grim.

"Nate wants to see you."

"Can't you take the wheel so he can come down to eat?" She reached for a bowl anyway.

Billy shook his head. "No, he's not interested in food, just seeing you."

Her belly aquiver, Camilla climbed to the pilothouse, where Nathaniel stood in the open darkness, his right hand gripping the pin of the wheel.

"Is your hand healing well?" she greeted him.

"It's doing all right." He pulled one of the overhead handles, and the boat increased speed. "Sit down, Camilla, I need to ask you something."

The quivering turning to nausea, Camilla chose to stand beside him at the wheel. "What is it?"

"Lancaster tried to cause us trouble in Poughkeepsie." He kept his gaze focused on the river ahead. "We weren't supposed to have fuel available, but it took us so long to get the paddle fixed, more fuel had been brought in."

"That is fortunate."

And had nothing to do with her.

"And while I was hearing about the wood," Nathaniel continued as though she hadn't spoken, "I learned something else."

Camilla pressed her hands to her middle. "What is that?"

"It seems a man named Frederick Conover is looking for you. Something about you being a thief?"

NINE

She recoiled as though he'd struck her. Instinct prompted Nathaniel to reach out and draw her to his side, shelter her, protect her. But the gaping wound inside his heart, the fear of betrayal, since learning of Conover's claim, kept both his hands on the wheel and his gaze fixed on the endless road of water before him, a bleak and empty road in the night, as his future too easily could become.

Trust the Lord's plan.

Not easy with the woman he was more than a little certain he loved standing beside him white-faced in the moonlight, her hands pressed to her middle as though she were about to be sick. Worst of all, she remained silent. She didn't deny the accusation.

How far could a gossamer thread of faith fray?

His right hand throbbed as he gripped the pin to signal the engine room to slow the boat once again, and fixed one eye on Camilla. "So there's truth in it?"

"N-no. That is . . ." She covered her face with her hands. "Yes, it's true, but it wasn't on purpose. I did not know . . . I did not realize . . . This is why I needed to ensure I got onto that boat west."

"Because you're running from the law."

"No, not the law." Her head shot up and she glared at him. "I would rather end up in the Marshalsea Prison for debt than what Conover has in mind for me."

"And what is that?"

"He threatened to sell me for debt."

He may as well have been standing over a cold boiler in a blizzard for all the warmth he felt in his limbs at that moment. "So you're the one in debt? Are you the one with the gambling habit, not your brother?"

"No, I have never gambled in my life, except for coming to America. It was my brother." She held out her hands palms up. "When he ran out of money and unentailed property to game away, he began to borrow from a cent per center."

"A what?"

"A moneylender with usurious interest."

"Conover."

She took a shuddering breath. "He—my brother—told Conover I needed the money and put up my mother's jewelry as collateral. But when Ashby—my brother, Marcus Lord Ashby—fled for the continent, Conover came after me for the jewels."

"And you fled with them instead of paying the debt?"

"No, I turned them over to him."

"So how could he claim you were a thief?"

She pressed one hand to her lips. "They were counterfeit, paste replicas. He found a London jeweler who claimed a female fitting my description, probably someone my brother found, had them copied."

"Was it you?" He hated to ask. He would have hated himself if he had not.

She gasped. "You can ask me that?"

"I just did."

"You do not believe me?"

"I—" He wanted to. Every fiber of his being ached to say yes. His sense of betrayal that she hadn't told him in the days, in all the hours they had spent together, warned him her silence meant she had something to hide, especially since she chose to run away to the west rather than stay and face down her accuser. "I don't know if I should."

Her shoulders straightened, stiffened. "Then I need say no more. I shall remain in my cabin until we reach Albany, and you may turn me over to Conover there."

"To be sold as a-a—" He couldn't say the word in front of a lady.

"It won't matter to me if you think me a liar."

"I don't want to." He pounded his fist on the wheel. "But you are running away like a thief."

"And how can I prove my innocence to a greedy moneylender, when you, who have paid court to me, who shares my Christian faith, however fragile it is right now, won't believe me?"

He flinched. "I want to believe you, but why didn't you trust me with the truth?"

"Because I was afraid you would turn away from me." She drew in an audible breath. "And you have. I understand. What man who is trying to save his boat wants a woman with that kind of a burden on her head? It's why I will stop at little to go west even if Joanna did not wait for me. I have no choice, especially now that Conover has come after me."

"Shouldn't he be going after your brother?"

"My brother is dead."

"You couldn't tell me that?" He was too angry to give her sympathy. "Something so important in your life? I feel, Miss Renfrew, like maybe you have just been using me to get north, and you don't care about anything between us at all."

"I do."

"But not enough to tell me the truth."

"Too much to burden you with my disgrace." She laid her cool, smooth fingers against his cheek. "I had no business getting close to you, but I couldn't help it. You were . . . You are the most amazing

80

man I have ever met. If I were to let myself love anyone . . ." She stepped back. "But I am not. I am sorry I let this go too far." With that, she turned and walked away from him.

He gripped the wheel, feeling he could rip all eight feet of it from its moorings in the deck and run the boat aground. At that moment, he didn't care if he went aground. What was two hundred tons of wood and steel in comparison to losing the lady of his heart?

"That's it, isn't it, Lord?" He stared into the night, oddly light-headed and lighthearted, the burden of years slipping from his shoulders.

He understood now. He had been valuing the wrong things. Bent on proving his father and brother wrong about him being a failure as a steamboat pilot and then part owner, he had placed his faith in making money rather than serving the Lord. He had been so angry with Camilla because he knew her debt came between them. As much as he claimed to care about her, in his heart, he didn't want a female burdened with debt for which he might end up responsible. His accusations rejected her, pushed her away. Like the way his father and brother let their success and scorn of his ambitions come between family, he was allowing money to come between him and the lady he didn't want to live without.

By the time he reached Albany, he knew what he must do.

The boat had ceased moving. Camilla lay on her bunk, gray light from the porthole washing over her, unable to believe she had finally fallen asleep and awakened to no more *shug, shug, shug* of the paddle wheel. Unless something had gone wrong, they had reached Albany. Today, she would learn her fate.

If only she had a decently ironed gown and hat to wear when she made her appearance at Joanna's house.

If only the idea of leaving the *Marianne* didn't break her heart in a hundred pieces.

If only she could grasp harder to the filament of faith she still possessed, that God had a perfect plan for her life and all would be right in the end. But was not the unknowing yet still believing what faith was? Trusting in the Lord. Not something she was good at since she learned of Marcus's treachery—trust. She hadn't trusted Nathaniel, and he believed her capable of having the jewels copied. If she had, would she be going upriver in crumpled gowns and a straw hat good for nothing beyond lining a bird's nest?

Her hair felt like that bird's nest, tangled from her restless night tamping down tears, forcing down a desire to run up to the pilot-house and tell him she loved him. As though he would believe her.

Heavy eyed and heavier limbed, she donned her best dress, only a little creased from lying at the bottom of her valise, and combed and braided her hair into submission. Valise in one hand, reticule in the other, she exited the cabin for the last time and descended to the cargo deck in search of the captain.

Billy stood at the head of the gangway directing the unlading of the cargo. He gave her a cold look and shouted orders to two more crewmen before giving her his attention. "What do you want?"

"Captain Black." She held out her five-dollar gold piece. "I never paid him for my passage or meals."

"He doesn't want it. He told me to tell you to keep your money."

Nathaniel hadn't even waited to collect the money she owed him, he so much didn't want to see her.

She shoved the coin back into her reticule. "I'll be on my way then."

Billy didn't so much as glance at her.

Her valise feeling as though it weighed more than her entire body, she descended the gangway and headed along the wharf, still crowded with vessels and their crews, cargo, and passengers. She had written Joanna's Albany address on the back of the letter inviting her to come to America. The third person Camilla asked knew where to find Niblo's hotel on Broad Street. The walk was long and her bag heavy. Her heart weighed heavier, paining with each step away from the steamboat landing, away from Nathaniel.

Through a rain of tiny ice crystals against her face, she trudged past brick houses and lovely trees. The town spoke of prosperity and newness, a place to start life again.

Like the rest of the area, Niblo's looked like a fine place, if one had the money to stay. Cold and wet, Camilla knew her bedraggled appearance wouldn't garner her a warm reception in the lobby.

The man at the desk inside gave her a frosty glare. "We are not hiring at present."

"I am not seeking work." Realizing she just might be shortly, she hastened to add, "I am seeking Mrs. Arnaud."

"Indeed?" The man gave her a sweeping glance that would have made any English peer's butler proud. "Who is asking?"

Hope flared. "Is she still here? Please tell her Camilla Renfrew has arrived."

"Mrs. Arnaud," the supercilious clerk said, "has departed for Michigan." He shuddered as though saying so pained him, then lowered his nose enough to add, "But she left Miss Renfrew a letter."

Camilla's heart began to pound. She couldn't breathe. Everything would be fine. Joanna had made provision for Camilla to follow. She understood the hesitancy to come, the delay . . .

The clerk gave her a letter. Hand shaking, Camilla slit the seal with her thumbnail and unfolded the heavy vellum and read. Then she read it again. The precise handwriting began to swim and blur before her eyes until only one paragraph stood out . . .

We'll have gone by the time you read this. You didn't respond for so long I presumed you weren't coming and hired someone else. I am praying for you and have full confidence you will find work here in Albany . . .

The letter crumpled in her hand, the lobby darkening before her eyes, Camilla spun on her heel and stumbled to the door.

"Miss, your bag," the clerk called after her.

"Air. Need air." Camilla flung open the door to the freezing rain.

And tumbled into the arms of Frederick Conover.

$\mathcal{T}$EN

I couldn't do this without talking to you about it first." Nathaniel stood in the middle of the parlor belonging to Mrs. Marianne Spraig's sister, holding one of Mrs. Spraig's soft and wrinkled hands between both of his. "I couldn't make you suffer for the sake of my heart." His face heated as he spoke the last words.

Mrs. Spraig smiled up at him. "I'm quite all right, Nathaniel. My sister wants me to keep living with her, so the sale of the Cold Spring house will leave me a tidy sum to live on, even if you can't raise the funds to buy out Ralph and Riley's shares. But it's a lot to risk for your sake, if she doesn't wait for you."

"I know." Nathaniel shoved his hands into his pockets and strode to the parlor window and the scene of icy rain beyond. "But I have to do this regardless. Without her, I never would have realized how I've been letting my desire to prove something to my father interfere with letting the Lord direct my life. And I can hope that once she knows she's free of debt, she can stay here or come back."

"I'd say getting your heart right with the Lord is worth ten thousand pounds." Mrs. Spraig's voice was gentle. "Will you still sacrifice everything if she doesn't care for you the same way?"

Nathaniel's breath steamed the window before him. He wrote Camilla's name on the glass and smiled. "Yes."

"You haven't known her for long."

"I've spent more time with her than do many who plan a future together." Nathaniel faced the old lady. "I have to do this for her to make sure she's free to choose me if she wants."

Mrs. Spraig wiped her eyes on a lace handkerchief. "Then she doesn't deserve you if she rejects you." She rose on tiptoes and kissed his cheek. "Now you run along to your boat before this weather gets any worse and don't worry about me. Whatever happens, I'll do just fine."

He hoped she was right, though from the look of the brick house on Broad Street, Mrs. Spraig's sister wanted for nothing. And Mrs. Spraig supported his decision, the revelation that had come to him in the night—to pay off Camilla's debt. He could find work if Lancaster persisted in breaking up the partnership. Nathaniel's share of the boat sale would give him a foundation to start again, even after they ensured all creditors were paid. And if Camilla stayed in Albany, he could court her every time he was in the city, solidify the budding love he knew they shared, and plan for that house on the river near Cold Spring.

He stepped into the rain and headed to his boat, back to tell Camilla what he intended to do. With patches of ice forming on the pavement, going proved treacherous for pedestrians and vehicles. One carriage sped past too quickly for safety. It hit a pile of wet leaves on the road, slewed sideways, rocked as though about to topple to one side, then righted itself, and sped on to the docks.

Camilla would be cold in her cabin, though maybe she had gone to sit by the galley fire. Either way, the notion of seeing her again, asking her forgiveness for how he had acted the night before, telling her with his actions how much he cared, yes, how much he loved her, compelled him to take risks like the speeding carriage and break into a trot.

The carriage must have gotten slowed somewhere along the way, as it was just pulling up to the gangway of a boat that had docked since Nathaniel left for the bank and to visit Mrs. Spraig.

It was Riley Lancaster's boat.

He waited for the usual surge of rage tensing his guts. It didn't come. Peace from the knowledge that the Lord would manage the future stole through Nathaniel instead.

Then Billy's footfalls thundered down the gangway. "Nate, they've got her."

Nathaniel blinked rain from his eyes. "Who has who?"

"That man from Poughkeepsie, Cono something, has Miss Renfrew. A boy just delivered this." Billy produced a grimy piece of paper from inside his coat.

Nathaniel snatched it and raced up the gangway to the covered portion of the cargo deck for fear of smearing the ink.

It was written in pencil and already smudged nearly beyond recognition as letters. Enough remained to send Nathaniel shouting orders to get the *Marianne* prepared to set out, then charging onto the wharf—too late. That reckless carriage was already driving away in one direction and Lancaster's boat pulling away in another. No sign of Camilla on the deck.

It might not be true. This could be another trick to destroy Nathaniel's boat or chances of continuing his work until the weather stopped voyages on the river for the season. He couldn't risk calling Lancaster's bluff in the event it was no bluff.

"Camilla, why didn't you wait for me?" The words emerged aloud on a groan from his heart.

Lancaster's boat drew away from the dock, and Nathaniel sprinted back to his. They were too far behind, taking too long to build up the steam needed to drive the engine. Lancaster would be two miles ahead of them at the least. Thirty minutes unless Nathaniel took the risk of exploding his boilers to go faster. But then, Lancaster might try the same once he knew Nathaniel chased him.

Nathaniel started to take the steps to the pilothouse two at a time. Halfway up, he paused, fixed his gaze on the trail of smoke from

Lancaster's boat, and prayed for Camilla's safety. Then he proceeded at a more dignified pace and found Billy poised by the wheel.

"Why wasn't she onboard?" he demanded of his lifelong friend.

"She wanted to find her friend." Billy pursed his lips and stared at the diminishing plume of smoke from Lancaster's boat.

Nathaniel gripped the wheel hard enough to split open the cut on his hand again. "Even though you told her to wait for me?"

Billy avoided his eyes and shrugged.

Stomach sinking below the pilothouse floor like the wheel, Nathaniel leaned toward Billy. "You did tell her I wanted to talk to her before she went to find her friend, didn't you?"

"I, uh—" Billy sighed. "Nope."

If the engine room hadn't rung the bell to indicate the engine was ready to go, Nathaniel might have knocked Billy down to the cargo deck. The need to concentrate on backing from the dock and turning the *Marianne* downstream calmed him enough to ask in a civilized fashion. "Why?"

"I couldn't watch you prove your father right over a female who happily walked away from you."

Nathaniel gritted his teeth, knowing Billy meant well in the name of friendship, knowing he was the one suffering the consequences of Camilla leaving the safety of the boat. "Did she look happy when she left?"

"She, uh, looked like she wanted to cry." Billy spoke slowly, reluctantly. "But I couldn't let you wreck your future over a female who might not care about you. We've all worked too hard."

"And we can continue to work hard. It's a risk I was willing to take. Except I took too long to think of it and now this has happened." Nathaniel gestured to the smoke now barely visible in the leaden sky. "I can't live with riches knowing she was living in fear of her freedom through no fault of her own."

"So she says," Billy muttered.

Nathaniel shot him a glare. "Regardless of whether or not you believe her tale, even if she chooses to go west, I can't live a comfortable life knowing she is in fear."

The smoke disappeared ahead, Lancaster too far away.

Nathaniel signaled the engine for more speed. Black smoke belched from his smokestack, and the *Marianne* leaped forward. Still Nathaniel could see neither smoke nor wake from Lancaster's boat. He knew he was being followed. The note said he intended to be followed, taunting Nathaniel with the knowledge he had met up with Conover and partnered with him to take away Nathaniel's lady along with his livelihood.

I told you to let the partnership go, Lancaster had concluded.

Greed. Money. Camilla's brother gambling with his inheritance. Lancaster gambling with his partnership shares. It all led to this, a chase at risky speeds on the Hudson River with a lady's life in the balance.

"Lord, please don't let that gossamer thread of her faith break under this." Nathaniel said the prayer aloud, then signaled for more speed.

"Nate, we can't."

The deck was already growing hot beneath their feet.

"We must." Nathaniel leaned over the wheel, seeking the merest hint of Lancaster's boat.

He caught it, the suggestion of a light flashing through rain and billows of smoke.

"They're in sight. Faster." Nathaniel reached for the line to signal more speed.

Billy knocked his hand away. "I won't let you blow us all up." He softened his tone. "Nor her. The faster we go, the faster they go."

Billy was right. Against all his instincts to chase down Lancaster's boat at any cost, Nathaniel pulled the line to signal decreased speed.

The light ahead faded into the gloom, reappeared, vanished like a taunting will-o'-the-wisp. Lancaster's boat slowed, sped up, slowed again. Nathaniel's hand twitched, aching to pull the handle to indicate greater speed. Steady. Steady. Steady. Lancaster could go for only so long before traffic or the need for fuel forced him to stop.

His hand twitched again. "A little more speed. We can manage a little—"

Light flashed ahead, bigger, brighter than any lantern. Moments later, the boom struck their ears, rattled the signal line handles together in an amelodic clang.

"Their boilers blew." Only the wheel held Nathaniel upright. He knew he must take action, knew what those actions were, but his head felt as numb as hands left too long in cold water.

Cold water. The river. Camilla thrown into the swift current of the Hudson.

The wave from the blast struck the hull. Nathaniel staggered, and the paralysis left him.

"Take the wheel, Billy. Take her slow." Nathaniel skimmed down the steps to the main deck. "Light. We need light up here. Look for survivors."

They saw the debris first, chunks of twisted metal from the wheel frame and engine. Wood chunks bobbed past, bounced harmlessly off the sides of the slow-moving *Marianne*. Already stuck in the mud along the bank, a cabin, nearly intact, rested as though taking up residence.

A cabin. Camilla. They'd have put her in a cabin.

But she wasn't in that one. She wasn't in the river. No one was in the river. At least no one's head bobbed above the surface, clinging to a plank.

Nathaniel would not believe no one survived. Men and women survived steamboat explosions. More often than not people were blown free of boiling water and fire. They didn't always drown.

"If I had a rowing boat or canoe, I could search better." Nathaniel leaned so far over the edge of the deck, he risked toppling into the water.

That water was so cold no one could survive in it for long. A woman in full skirts would never be able to fight the current.

"Oh, Camilla." His heart felt as though it would explode like the boiler.

"Captain." A crewman gestured to a plank to which clung a lone figure, a man with thinning dark hair—Riley Lancaster.

"Throw him a line." Nathaniel kept hunting, seeking with his eyes, praying with his entire being.

One more figure, two, half a dozen bobbed near the *Marianne*, clinging to a bench, a door, one of the paddles. The boat's crew drew them all aboard, wrapped them in blankets, and gave them hot coffee.

Neither Camilla nor Conover appeared.

The bulk of the wreckage passed, Nathaniel stalked back to the galley stove and confronted Lancaster, his hands on his hips. "Where is she?"

Lancaster grinned despite a black eye and bruised jaw. "Back in Albany, I expect, or maybe heading down the Erie Canal."

"Why?" Nathaniel pressed his fists together behind his back. Faces wary, the others moved away, leaving him alone with Lancaster. "Why did you do it?"

"I told you Monday," Lancaster said, "I need the money. I can't put money into the partnership anymore. I need to get out of it what I can, especially now my boat's gone." He cast his uninjured eye toward the last of the debris. "My future hope of regaining my wealth."

"I don't care about your boat. It was insured, wasn't it?"

Lancaster shook his head, winced, looked down. "Didn't pay up."

Nathaniel tamped down any notion of pitying the man. He had chosen his own path. Except that path had led to this disaster, no hope of Lancaster changing his mind about the partnership, and Camilla disappearing.

"Your money problems don't matter to me." Nathaniel took a

step closer to Lancaster. "I want to know what you did with my lady."

Lancaster shrugged, but took a step backward. "I don't know what Conover did with her. I was just supposed to get you out of Albany."

"Why?"

"Conover wants to marry her. Seems her family is something special in England, even if her brother was a ne'er-do-well and the new viscount a prig."

Vaguely, Nathaniel realized that Billy was turning the boat back upriver to Albany. Nathaniel kept his attention focused on Lancaster, trusting him a lot less farther than he could throw the man, since he figured he could throw him clear to Poughkeepsie at that moment.

"What did he pay you?" Nathaniel asked the question through his teeth.

"I don't see why I should tell you." Lancaster said nothing more but dropped onto a stool as though his legs no longer supported him.

Nathaniel crouched before the older man. "Whatever he's paying you to help him, I will pay you more."

"Can you pay me more than this?" Lancaster drew a chain from beneath his shirt. A gold pendant hung from the heavy links, a pendant set with a red stone whose heart glowed with the depth surely no paste imitation could produce.

"Is that one of the Renfrew jewels?" Nathaniel asked as though his heart weren't threatening to beat a hole through his chest.

Lancaster grinned, albeit lopsidedly. "So she told you about those."

"She said they were all copies and that's why Conover came after her for the money."

"Then Conover lied to her. I took this to a jeweler. This is genuine."

Which meant that, quite possibly, the rest of Camilla's jewels were too.

His insides feeling like the wound-up spring on a watch, Nathaniel caught hold of the ruby pendant and tugged Lancaster forward so he half slid off the stool. The heavy links of the chain held. Lancaster clawed at Nathaniel's hand, but he held on. "This is proof you are abetting abduction and theft. If you don't tell me what Conover has done with my lady, I will do all I can to make certain you never see the outside of a jail."

"And if I do help you?" Lancaster's curled upper lip suggested he thought Nathaniel could never meet his price.

Nathaniel thought of the money saved in the bank, then pictured himself going south to work on boats for the winter to stay alive until the season opened up on the Hudson again, starting over with nothing, adding years to when he could court Camilla or any lady. Yet if he didn't do it, he would never have peace in his heart, nor so much as a breath of hope of Camilla in his life.

He took a deep breath. "I have twenty thousand in the bank. You can have that plus my share of the sale of the partnership assets."

"And I can keep the ruby?"

Nathaniel gritted his teeth against epithets less kind than calling the man a vulture. "That is Miss Renfrew's decision to make, not mine. But the rest I'll put in writing, if you like."

Lancaster's brows shot toward his hairline. "Why would you do that for a woman?"

"Because my pursuit of wealth has interfered with my relationship with the Lord, and I want that right in my heart before I make a lady my wife." He tugged on the ruby again, and this time the chain snapped. "Do we have a deal?"

ELEVEN

Camilla could barely breathe. Conover had wound her up in her own cloak like some kind of Egyptian mummy, and the heavy, damp wool choked her with each inhalation of air.

But she was still on land. Conover hadn't taken her aboard a steamboat. She could escape on land. She didn't know how, with her arms bound and her vision obscured, but she would manage. Though he had removed her shoes, he hadn't tied her ankles. She could walk, even if she walked into the path of traffic.

She could not, however, open doors with her hands bound, and Conover half carried, half pushed her out of the carriage and into a structure whose door slammed behind them with a solid thud. The floor was wooden beneath her stockinged feet—wooden and icy cold. Her toes grew more numb with each step into the frigid building. Conover's footfalls echoed as though the rooms were empty of furnishings.

Camilla's heart pounded. She tried to picture a gossamer thread shining against a clear blue sky. All she needed was that thread, a mustard seed of faith to build a mountain.

Or escape a man who had spent the half hour in the carriage explaining that she could pay her debt by being sold into a house of ill repute, or by marrying him.

"I have a great deal of money. Now I need a wife to add consequence to my name. Why else do you think I lent your dissolute brother more money?"

Camilla hadn't tried to speak through the suffocating folds of wool.

"I knew that loan wasn't in your name, but a body can't put a peer in debtor's prison, more's the pity." Conover prattled on as though she had asked for more details. "But a pretty sister left destitute was easy to manage." His tone grew sulky like that of a small child. "Didn't expect you to leave for America."

I never would have wed you, she screamed inside her head.

Given the choice between marriage and the other life he suggested, she probably would have married him. There in America, who knew what Conover could do. For all she knew, the Americans didn't have laws that prevented a man from forcing a woman to wed him.

She would escape before that happened. She would escape and find a way west to Joanna. No, to the river to find Nathaniel. No, she couldn't rely on others to save her. Neither Joanna nor Nathaniel wanted her. Joanna only considered her a convenience easily replaceable. Nathaniel said he loved her, but believed her capable of deception she hadn't practiced except in what she hadn't told him.

She needed to survive on her own, cling to that thread of faith until it was stronger. She must draw her strength from the Lord, not others. Relying on others, relying solely on herself, had only gotten her where she was now—dumped onto a cold, hard floor like a disused carpet.

I don't know how to have faith in you. She may as well be honest with the Lord. *I am clinging to what I have.*

She began to drum her heels on the wooden floor. It sounded like the drums of an approaching army.

"Stop that," Conover commanded. "No one is coming to get you. Lancaster has led Black on a merry chase down the river."

Camilla lay still, seeing that, indeed, she was on her own. Joanna gone west and Nathaniel gone east. God had placed her where she could only rely on him. Perhaps it was a good place to be in the end. At the moment, the helplessness made her want to draw her knees to her chest and howl like an infant in need of feeding.

An involuntary whimper escaped.

"Don't worry," Conover said. "We will only be here until dark, then we'll take a barge down the canal. At the first town, we'll stop and marry."

Camilla swallowed bile at the idea.

"No protest? Good. You see sense. I thought you would." Conover moved.

A rasp and crackle suggested he started a fire. In moments, blessed heat reached out to her.

"I'm going to unwind you," Conover said. "One attempt to escape, though, and I'll stick a gag in your mouth. If you do escape, I'll harm that young riverboat captain."

Harm coming to Nathaniel, even if he didn't truly care for her, was a worse threat than the gag.

After he untied and unwound the cloak and freed her arms, Camilla remained motionless, allowing the heat to wash over her frozen limbs, breathing the air of fresh-cut lumber, as though the building in which they waited was still being constructed. She needn't fight or take foolish risks. God would show her a way to escape. Suddenly, it wasn't just lip service to the notion. The peace of surety settled over her, and she pushed herself upright.

"May I have something to drink?"

He made her tea. He produced bread, cheese, and apples. He kept the fire going.

"When you're my wife, I will treat you like a queen. I will cover you in jewels." He drew a pouch from his coat pocket and spilled its contents onto the hearth.

Diamonds, sapphires, and pearls the size of quail eggs shimmered and glowed and gathered the light of the fire.

"The Renfrew jewels," Camilla whispered.

"Not all of them, alas." Conover sighed. "Your brother did sell most of them, but these are left, less the ruby I gave Lancaster. He wanted it instead of money."

Camilla's mouth felt drier than the hard cheese she'd eaten. "You lied to me." The words were barely audible to herself. Then a surge of power shot through her, and she shot to her feet. "You lied to me. I don't owe you anything, you-you—" She snatched up the gems and flung the lot into his face.

And then she ran.

Nathaniel sprinted from the *Marianne*, leaving his crew behind to guard Lancaster at all cost. Billy protested. He didn't want Nathaniel to go alone.

"Stay with the boat. That's an order."

He departed, expecting to be obeyed. He must travel nearly two miles to the outer edge of the city before darkness fell and Conover took Camilla onto the canal. Nathaniel proceeded on foot. Finding a horse would take too much time. If Conover got onto the canal, Nathaniel might never catch them. Too many settlements had risen along the waterway where Conover could take her. Nathaniel could waste days seeking her in each one.

Already darkness was descending, helped by the leaden sky. Twice he slipped on black ice invisible in the gloom. So he slowed. He couldn't afford to break a limb. He couldn't afford the slower pace. Darkness taunted him with every stride, gathering beneath the trees, creating the sort of shadows into which Conover and Camilla could vanish.

Nathaniel didn't know this part of town. The houses grew farther apart and the trees thicker, taller. When he thought he must have passed the house Lancaster mentioned, Nathaniel caught a hint of woodsmoke. He increased his speed heedless of more patches of ice forming as night fell. This must be the house ahead, dark, but the smoke growing stronger. Camilla was closer. Camilla was—

A shadow darted between the trees, rustling leaves, breathing in rasping gasps. Nathaniel swerved from the pavement and ran toward it, caught the swirl of a skirt as the runner spun to dart into the woods.

"Camilla, stop."

She did. She turned. "Nathaniel?" Then she was in his arms, clinging to him, laughing, sobbing, pushing him toward the trees. "Run. Conover is—"

"Right here." The click of a cocking pistol blasted in the quiet woods. "I told you I'd hurt him if you ran."

"Run, Nathaniel."

Camilla took her own advice. She ran toward Conover and his gun. Nathaniel lunged after her. He caught her. They slipped on slushy wet leaves and landed against Conover's legs, knocking him flat. The pistol blasted, the flame from the barrel shooting toward the sky.

"Don't move." Nathaniel surged to his feet and planted a boot on Conover's chest.

Shouting obscenities, the older man flailed at Nathaniel's legs with the pistol. Nathaniel kicked it out of his hands.

"Do you have a sash, Camilla?" Nathaniel asked. "I think we can tie him up."

"Of course we can." Her calm efficiency again told Nathaniel why he had fallen for this lady so quickly, why she was the right female to be his wife.

They dragged the moneylender back to the house and the fire. With the reasoning that Nathaniel was better suited to watch over Conover than she was, Camilla donned her cloak and shoes and ventured forth to find the authorities. Nathaniel settled beside the man now trussed with his own coat, expecting a long wait.

It wasn't. Within minutes, two marshal service deputies appeared to take Conover away. Billy had sent them in pursuit.

"You'll need to come make a statement," Captain Troy, the older of the deputies, said. "But take care of the young lady first."

They stood alone before the fire, and all Nathaniel could think to say was, "I want to take care of you. That is, I was a fool last night."

"My determination to rely on myself didn't help. I could have told you the truth straightaway. I should have." She started to hold her hands out toward him, then clasped them against her waist. "But you let me go this morning."

"No, you weren't supposed to go. Billy was supposed to ask you to stay until I got back." His mouth went dry. "I went to the bank to arrange to pay your debts."

Her gaze flew to his. Her lips formed a very kissable O.

So he kissed her. She drew his head down and kissed him back. For several peaceful moments, they abandoned thought of everything that lay behind and before them.

Then Nathaniel pulled away. "I promised Lancaster all my savings and my portion of the sale of the partnership assets to tell me where to find you. That leaves me where I was ten years ago—nearly penniless. As much as I love you and want to build a future with you, I can't do it empty-handed. That is—" His ears went hot. "Even if it is something you might want after how I didn't trust you."

"And if I'd trusted you, none of this might have happened." Her beautiful gold-green eyes smiled into his. "But it was good for me to lose all hope of a future with you or Joanna. It left me with only the Lord to rely on, and he showed me a way." She shoved her hands into the pockets of her cloak and gave him a flirtatious sideways glance. "If you were to ask me, I would be willing to work on building that future with you."

"Camilla, I have nothing."

"Nathaniel, we have everything." She rested her head against his chest, trusting and close to his heart. "My faith is stronger than that fragile thread now. And you—you were willing to give up everything for my sake."

He wrapped his arms around her. "I'd rather work for another man all my life than see you married to another man—or worse. But if you can't wait for me to earn enough to support a family, I understand. I don't like it, but I won't hold you to any promises."

"Was that a proposal?"

"For a future, uncertain date, yes."

"Then I say yes with a proposal of my own." She pulled out of his arms, took one of his hands, and set a heavy velvet pouch in his palm. "The Renfrew jewels. I don't know for certain, but I expect their sale will more than pay for Spraig and Lancaster's shares, especially along with the ruby Lancaster doesn't des—Why are you shaking your head?"

"I can't take these. It's too much. It's-it's—"

"My dowry. Or, if you prefer—" She laughed. "My purchase of two partnerships—in business and in marriage. Deal?"

"Deal. I can't think of a wiser partner to join me."

He let the jewels fall to the floor at their feet so he could draw her to him again and kiss her very kissable lips.

DEAR READER,

In 1807, a strange beast belching smoke and fire and creating a racket loud enough to wake the dead crawled up the Hudson River to Albany at a shockingly speedy four miles an hour. The beast was Robert Fulton's steamboat. His contraption cut the time of travel from the harbor at New York City to the docks at Albany down to a quarter of the hours sailing had previously taken.

A new era had begun.

For the first few decades of the steamboats' life, they were not the luxurious works of art we later associate with the Mississippi and Mark Twain. These were little more than layered platforms fitted with an engine, boilers, and a paddle wheel or two, atop which a few primitive cabins perched. Suspended even higher was the wheelhouse without glass and only wooden partitions to protect the pilot from the worst of the elements.

If a passenger could procure a cabin, he enjoyed no amenities like a dining room. Most of the time, passengers camped on one of the decks along with cargo, baggage, and livestock. They risked sunburn, frostbite, and the danger of an overzealous engineer blowing up the boilers and thus the vessel. Yet steamboats thrived on America's rivers because they were fast, compared to sailing.

The opening of the Erie Canal from Albany to Lake Erie in 1825 expanded westward travel and shipping further. The industrious could and did make a fortune.

As a lover of all boats and the water, I could not resist exploring this age of steam travel. As a lover of romance, when I discovered the moon was full during the dates of my story . . . Well, it was all too promising to resist.

Sincerely yours,

Laurie Alice Eakes

Laurie Alice Eakes used to lie in bed as a child telling herself stories so she didn't wake anyone else up. Sometimes she shared her stories with others, so when she decided to be a writer, she surprised no one. *Family Guardian*, her first book, won the National Readers Choice Award for Best Regency in 2007. Since then, she has sold over twenty books to publishers such as Revell, Zondervan, Barbour, and Harlequin Love Inspired.

Eight of her books have been picked up by Thorndike Press for large-print publication, and *Lady in the Mist*, her first book with Revell, was chosen for hardcover publication by Crossings Book Club.

Laurie Alice teaches online writing courses and enjoys a speaking ministry that takes her from the Gulf Coast to the East Coast. She has recently relocated to Houston, Texas, with her husband and pets and is learning how to live in a big city again.

Lessons in Love

Ann Shorey

For friend and fellow author, Amanda Cabot—

Thank you for suggesting me as one of the authors
in this novella collection.
This has been the most fun I've ever had
with a writing project.

Now there are diversities of gifts, but the same Spirit. And there are differences of administrations, but the same Lord. And there are diversities of operations, but it is the same God which worketh all in all.

1 Corinthians 12:4–6

✺ONE ✺

Chicago
July 1858

At the sound of light footsteps in the hall outside her aunt's study, Merrie Bentley paused in the act of dipping her pen into an inkwell. She groaned to herself. Another interruption. She'd promised the editor of *Kipler's Home Weekly* an article by next week, but at this rate she'd never fulfill her agreement.

"Miss Merrie." The housekeeper's voice carried into the book-lined room. In another moment, the door swung open and Mrs. Wagner dashed in, her ruffled cap askew. "Did you forget your piano lesson? Mr. Thackery has been waiting in the music room for ten minutes."

"Why didn't you tell me he'd arrived?" Merrie dropped a paper-weight over her manuscript and scrambled to her feet.

"I reminded you this morning at breakfast. He's here at three every Thursday." Arms akimbo, Mrs. Wagner frowned. "You're twenty years old—I expect you to keep your own appointments."

"I apologize. You did remind me." She slipped her arm around the shoulders of her aunt's diminutive housekeeper. "I don't know what I'd do without you to look after me."

"I don't know either, and that's a fact. Once you shut yourself away with your writing, lightning could strike and you wouldn't notice."

She opened her mouth to argue, then closed it. Nothing captured her attention as thoroughly as writing her articles. Not even Mr. Thackery's dark eyes and shy smile. She glanced down at her emerald-sprigged muslin skirt and brushed at wrinkles.

"I wish I had time to change to a better dress."

"Just go on. Your aunt pays him whether you're learning anything or not. Don't waste her money."

She chafed at the reminder. One of these days, she'd earn enough from her writing to take care of herself. "I'm not wasting her money. I enjoy the piano. Mr. Thackery is a good teacher." She left the study and directed her steps toward the music room off the reception hall of her aunt's spacious home.

"Wait. I forgot to give you this." Mrs. Wagner held out an envelope. "Peters brought it for you when he came back from town." She shook her head. "Don't know why they can't get your name right."

When Merrie read the address—"Mr. M. M. Bentley"—her heartbeat quickened. Payment from *Kipler's Home Weekly* for her most recent article.

"Thank you," she called after the housekeeper's retreating back.

Mrs. Wagner waved her hand and continued toward the kitchen.

As soon as she was out of sight, Merrie paused beneath a lighted sconce in the hall and used her forefinger to slit open the missive. She'd submitted a longer piece last time, with several references, and hoped for a larger sum in payment. Her conscience pricked at not correcting the editor when he assumed she was a man, but she knew she had a better chance of being published as *Mr.* M. M. Bentley.

Her eyes widened when she saw the amount of the bank draft, then narrowed with concern when she noticed a folded sheet of paper remaining in the envelope. Most unusual. Mr. Kipler seldom sent messages with her payment. She glanced toward the music room where Mr. Thackery waited, knowing she should wait to read the letter until after her instructor departed. But another minute or two wouldn't hurt. She unfolded the page and scanned the contents, then drew a sharp breath and read the message again.

✉

Colin Thackery paced across the Persian rug to stand in front of the grand piano that filled one corner of the music room. Miss Bentley was late again. Her hour would be over before they had time to review last week's lesson. His fingers itched to touch the keys, to stroke one of Chopin's nocturnes from the beautiful instrument.

He folded his arms and turned away. He couldn't presume to use the piano for his own enjoyment. He was hired to teach Miss Bentley the musical skills expected of a young lady of her social standing. His personal time at the keyboard would have to wait until he returned home, where he could use the upright in the church his father pastored.

The latch on the glass-paned door clicked downward, and Miss Bentley flew into the room. A few coppery-brown curls corkscrewed loose above her ears. Her cheeks were bright pink and worry lines wrinkled her forehead. She looked prettier every time he saw her.

He made a point of glancing at the ornate case clock against the rear wall. "We've lost more than fifteen minutes. I hope you're prepared to learn a new piece this week." He cringed at the sternness in his tone. She must think him a dry stick.

Instead of going to the piano bench, she sank onto a tapestry-covered settee facing the window. "I'm sorry I'm late." She folded her arms across her middle. One slippered foot tapped the floor.

"Being a few minutes late isn't that serious. Please don't be upset."

"That's not why I'm upset." She waved a sheet of paper at him. "I just received this letter, and I'm trying to think what to do."

"Bad news?"

"The very worst."

"Nothing has happened to your parents, I hope." He knew they had left her with her aunt while they devoted their attention to business interests back East.

"No. The last I heard, they're both well." She rubbed one side of her head, dislodging more curls.

Seeing her in distress called forth his protective instincts. He dragged the piano bench across the room and sat facing her. "I'm a good listener. Would you care to tell me what's happened?"

A moment of silence passed between them while she surveyed his face.

He rubbed moist palms on his trouser legs, praying she couldn't see past his surface platonic concern to the attraction he felt toward her. If she believed him to be over-familiar, she could have him dismissed.

Apparently she decided to trust him, because she exhaled a long breath and leaned forward. "Mrs. Wagner is the only person who knows about this." She folded the letter into a square and rubbed her fingers against the paper. "I've been writing articles about marriage for *Kipler's Home Weekly* for several months now."

"Marriage?" His amazement echoed in his voice.

She drilled him with a stern look. "You don't actually have to be married to know what the Lord expects."

He decided to let her statement pass. From what he'd seen of his father's ministry, being married was a prerequisite to possessing an intelligent opinion of matrimony.

"How did you . . . why did they . . . ?"

"I read a notice in the magazine requesting submissions on the subject. So I sent a sample, and to my delight Mr. Kipler agreed to publish my thoughts. He pays me by sending a draft, which is what I thought this letter was about."

He stared at her dumbfounded, any thoughts of a closer relationship dissolving. She was not only part of a higher social class, she was an ambitious woman.

"You want to be a writer, like Mrs. Hale?"

"She's far more accomplished than I—look how popular *Godey's Lady's Book* has become. But later on, who knows?" Miss Bentley spread her hands. "For now, I'm just thankful to see my words in print."

He rose and crossed to the piano. "Then why are you upset over the letter? Didn't he send payment?"

"He did. But the message that accompanied the draft . . ." She unfolded the paper, then held it out to him.

When he read the salutation, his jaw dropped. "Dear *Mr.* Bentley?"

"Read the rest."

I've heard from a number of my subscribers regarding the quality of your matrimonial advice. May I suggest a meeting in my office on Monday, the 19th, at ten o'clock in the morning, with the object of discussing your future with our publication?

Sincerely yours,
Horatio Kipler

···•·ᴄᴵwo ···•··

Merrie took the letter from Mr. Thackery's outstretched fingers. The expression on his face had slipped from stunned to disapproving. She swallowed her embarrassment at what he must think of her. The question now was what to do about Mr. Kipler's request. She tilted her head and studied Mr. Thackery's square-chinned profile. Hmm. Considering his patrician features, he looked like a Bentley.

"I'm open to any ideas you may suggest." She tried for an airy tone.

He shook his head. "Why did you pass yourself off as a man? If you'd told the truth in the first place, you wouldn't have this dilemma."

"I didn't lie. I've always signed my name as 'M. M. Bentley.' It's easier than writing 'Marigold Montgomery Bentley.' Mr. Kipler just assumed the signature was that of a man."

"Marigold Montgomery?" A smile flitted across his face. "I'd probably use initials too."

"I'm glad you're finding this so humorous. This letter is a serious matter to me."

He carried the bench across the room, placing the polished seat in front of the piano. "Let's try to redeem some of your lesson time.

You have almost two weeks to respond. By then I'm sure someone as resourceful as you are will arrive at a solution."

She stalked to the instrument and ran through the scales with a staccato touch. "I already have a solution." She relaxed her fingers, stroked the opening bars of "Listen to the Mockingbird" from the keyboard, then swung around on the bench to face him.

"If you will accompany me on the call to Mr. Kipler's office, you can pretend to be Mr. Bentley, and I'll be your wife. That way I can hear what he has to say without revealing I'm the author of the articles."

He jerked his head back as though she'd slapped him. "I can't be a party to something like that. My father would be appalled if he knew of your request—not to mention what Mrs. Daintree would say."

"My aunt is currently in Springfield trying to persuade members of the legislature to allow women's rights. She's too busy with her own concerns to bother with me." Inside, she quaked at the thought of what Aunt Isabella might say. Merrie's parents had left her in Chicago with the hope she'd make a good match among society's elite. They had no knowledge of her ambition to be a writer, nor did her aunt.

"You're presuming, Miss Bentley. I'm here to help you master the piano, not to make you the next editress of *Godey's*. Aside from the hour we spend together each week, we hardly know one another." He swallowed hard. "I can't risk losing my position here. I teach students all over the city—if word got out that someone of your aunt's stature in society dismissed me, my reputation would be ruined."

From the agonized expression on his face, she knew his admission had embarrassed him. His unlined skin and shining black hair indicated he could be only a few years her senior. He'd undoubtedly worked hard to be so well-regarded for his skill at the piano. She dipped her head with sudden shame.

"Please forgive me. I was so caught up in my own concerns that I failed to consider yours." She rose, her hands clasped in front of her waist. "I'll think of something. The meeting with Mr. Kipler is only for this one time. Maybe Mr. Peters . . ."

His eyebrows shot up. "Your coachman?"

"I'm not asking him to marry me." She shot him an indignant glance. "Just to pretend for an hour or so."

"Nevertheless, who'd believe a man his age would be your husband?"

"Mr. Thackery. Since you won't help me, please allow me to make my own decisions." She turned to the keyboard, her chin thrust upward. "We have a few minutes remaining. Please show me the piece you want me to learn next."

His color high, he settled on the piano bench. "From what I heard of your rendition of 'Mockingbird,' we need to spend more time on the current lesson. Please watch my hands as I play the opening notes."

She moved closer to stand behind him as his long fingers traveled over the keys. Something stirred in her chest as she watched. He'd said he had students all over the city. She wondered how many of them were girls of marriageable age.

She shook her head to remove the thought. At the moment, she needed to focus on finding a temporary husband, instead of being distracted by her handsome piano teacher.

After the lesson ended, Colin walked toward the stables behind Mrs. Daintree's mansion. He paused at the sight of Mr. Peters resting in the shade of a wisteria-covered trellis. The coachman's trouser legs were tucked into muck-splashed boots, and he wore a collarless shirt open at the neck. A pipe was clenched between his teeth.

He jumped to his feet when he saw Colin.

"I'll have yer horse out to ye in just a shake." He loped toward the stable.

How Miss Bentley thought she could pass the coachman off as her husband was a mystery. Even if she found suitable clothing for him, there was nothing about Mr. Peters that fitted with her dainty beauty. Not to mention that once the man opened his mouth the masquerade would be over.

He considered her request again. An hour or so together away from her aunt's home wasn't so much to ask. If only the prospect of being her husband were really possible . . .

"Here ye be." Mr. Peters led the bay gelding toward the mounting block.

Colin took the reins and swung onto the saddle. "Thank you."

"Pleasure, sir." He doffed his cap, revealing sweaty strands of gray hair.

The horse's hooves clattered against the stones that paved Mrs. Daintree's curved drive. Once he reached the street, Colin traveled the remainder of the distance to his home on quieter, but dusty, roads. Miss Bentley's answer to her dilemma rode with him.

In the long run, what would it hurt if he offered to help her? He pondered how he could get around the introductions without actually referring to himself as Mr. Bentley. Perhaps the editor would assume that's who he was, and he wouldn't have to say a word. He wiped the sweat that gathered on his forehead. Maybe by next week, a better solution would present itself.

After Mr. Thackery left, Merrie took the letter and walked through the house to the back garden, where she sought a bench in the shelter of an oak tree. A manicured lawn surrounded by formal flower beds stretched to the wrought-iron fence at the boundary of her aunt's property. At the edge of the brick pathway, a few dandelions dared to grow amid the landscaped perfection. The sight made her smile. No matter how her aunt tried to bend nature to her will, some rebel plants went their own way.

After unfolding the letter and reading again, a new thought struck her. What if Mr. Kipler's phrase *"the object of discussing your future with our publication"* meant she had no future? Perhaps this was his way of telling her they no longer wanted her articles. She hadn't thought so at first, but on closer perusal, he hadn't said he liked the articles, merely that he wanted to discuss her future with the magazine.

Anxiety clutched her throat. Instead of worrying about whom she'd ask to pretend to be Mr. Bentley, she should have considered the possibility that after the nineteenth, no pretense would be necessary.

Perhaps Mrs. Wagner could offer a solution. Merrie rose and hurried toward the kitchen, careful not to tread on the dandelions.

She slipped into the light-filled room where the housekeeper sat at a worktable with her hands cradling a cup of tea. She looked up, smiling. "Just having a bit of a rest. Sit with me a minute, lovey. Something's on your mind, isn't it?"

"How did you know?"

"That pretty face of yours gives you away." She blew on her tea and took a sip. "Well?"

"This letter from *Kipler's* magazine . . . he wants to meet with me at his office the week after next. I'm afraid he'll tell me he doesn't want me to write for him anymore."

Mrs. Wagner held out her hand. "Let me see." She read slowly, her lips moving, then placed the message next to her cup. "He doesn't say any such thing."

"He doesn't say he likes my writing, either." Merrie stood and paced between the stove and the table. "I don't know what I'll do if I can't write for his magazine. I like not having to ask Aunt Isabella or my parents for money when I want to buy books or paper."

"Most young ladies are content to ask. It's the way of the world."

"It's not my way. My mother helps Father with his business—she earns as much as he does."

"Your mother is . . . different."

"Then maybe I am too." She plopped on the chair she'd vacated a moment earlier. "What do you think I should do about the letter?"

"Go. If he tells you to quit writing for him, the least you can do is listen to his reasons."

"I plan to. But there's another problem." Merrie lowered her voice. "He didn't make a mistake on the envelope. He truly believes I'm a mister."

"Oh, my." The laugh lines around Mrs. Wagner's eyes deepened when she smiled. "You've really done it this time. What will you wear? Trousers?"

"Of course not. I have a better idea."

Before returning to her room, Merrie slipped out the carriage entrance and feigned a casual stroll along the drive toward the stable. In spite of Mr. Thackery's opinion, she didn't see why her aunt's coachman couldn't serve as an escort. When they met with Mr. Kipler, she'd inform the editor that she needed to speak for her husband, since the poor man suffered from laryngitis. All Mr. Peters would have to do would be to nod at appropriate times.

"Miss Bentley. You needing to go somewhere?" Carrying a pitchfork, Mr. Peters stepped out from the stables. The odor of manure followed him like an affectionate dog.

She drew a shallow breath while studying him. Creases seamed his affable face. Strands of gray hair poked out from under his cap, straggling down his neck to rest on the grimy shirt he wore. Her shoulders sagged. Her aunt provided him with a smart uniform to wear when he drove her carriage, but by no means would he be believable as Mr. Bentley.

"No, thank you, Mr. Peters. I just came out to get some air."

"Stable ain't the best place for that, miss." His mouth curved up at his own humor.

"Indeed not." She smiled back at him, then turned toward the house. Her mind circled around the few young men she'd met since coming to live with her aunt. She hadn't liked any of them. Taking one into her confidence was out of the question.

Merrie set her jaw in a firm line. As long as Aunt Isabella remained in Springfield, she'd never learn of Mr. Thackery's pretense. Somehow, there had to be a way to convince him. She could hardly wait for next week's lesson.

*T*HREE

On the following Thursday afternoon, Merrie raced down the stairs when she heard Mr. Thackery's voice in the reception hall. She'd dressed in her favorite dotted pink gown, and confined her flyaway curls to braids at the crown of her head.

Mrs. Wagner stood at the door of the music room, a surprised expression on her face. "Right on time for once. Good." She patted Merrie on the shoulder. "Enjoy your lesson."

"Indeed I shall." She smiled up at Mr. Thackery. "I've been practicing all week."

"You've been on my mind—that is, your lesson has—all week as well." He nodded toward the open door. "Shall we begin?"

Once inside, she settled on the piano bench and ran her fingers over the scales. The best way to win his attention would be to show she took her lessons to heart. Then she'd present her arguments. "Do you want me to play the opening of 'Listen to the Mockingbird'?"

"Certainly. That's why I'm here."

She dropped her gaze to the keyboard. Why must he always be so serious? Huffing out a breath, she arranged the music on the stand and played through the first verse of the popular song. Tilting her head, she glanced up for his approval and caught him staring at her with a distracted expression on his face.

"Well?"

He started. "Forgive me. My mind was elsewhere. Would you please run through the piece once more?"

She bit back a sharp retort. Last week he lamented the waste of practice time. Now he paid no attention to her. While she played, she wondered which of his other students had captured his thoughts.

When the last notes faded, he smiled and placed a new sheet of music in front of her. "Excellent. Perhaps you're ready for something more advanced."

She blinked at the title. "'Wedding March'? I'll never learn this. It's too complicated."

"Nonsense. Since you write about marriage, I thought you'd enjoy playing the music Queen Victoria's daughter chose for her ceremony." His eyes sparkled with mischief.

So he had a sense of humor after all. She played the first few notes. They sounded more tentative than triumphant.

"Show me." She rose and pointed at the bench.

He took his seat. Mendelssohn's "March" throbbed in the air as his hands flew over the keys. When he finished, she shook her head.

"How beautiful. I wish I could play like that."

"Someday you will."

Taking heart from his relaxed expression, she clasped her hands together and drew a breath. She'd ask him again. Now.

"Mr. Thackery, I've spent this past week thinking about my appointment with Mr. Kipler. Have you considered—"

"Your appointment has been on my mind also. It seems to me—"

"Please, let me finish. As long as my aunt remains in Springfield, she'll never know you escorted—"

"About your aunt—"

She jammed her hands on her hips. "Will you please listen? I've thought about this all week, and if you'll agree to act as Mr. Bentley, I promise I'll never say a word to my aunt."

He sent her the widest smile she'd ever seen on his face. "I've been trying to tell you, I've decided to help. We can work out a way to introduce me. I don't want to speak an untruth."

She closed her eyes as waves of relief washed over her. Even if Mr. Kipler said he didn't want her articles any longer, at least she'd have someone with her when she heard the news.

"Thank you, Mr. Thackery. You have no idea how much this means to me."

"Please, call me Colin. If we're going to be a married couple, you should use my first name."

The look he sent her tingled all the way to her toes.

Merrie rose early on the morning of the nineteenth. The gown she'd chosen to wear, a light brown carriage dress striped with black, hung pressed and ready inside her dressing room. Suppressing a flutter of nerves, she brushed and braided her hair, then fastened her stays and stepped into her cage crinoline, tying the hooped underpinning at her waist. Her hands shook as she fastened the jet buttons on her bodice.

She pinned her pearl-colored bonnet over her braids, fluffing the fan of black lace and feathers attached to the crown. A final glance in the mirror assured her that she looked the part of a demure spouse.

The idea to have Mr. Thackery—Colin—pretend to be her husband no longer seemed brilliant. So much could go wrong. She peeked out the window at the stables behind the house. Mr. Peters had the team and buggy waiting, but she hadn't heard Colin arrive. Surely he hadn't changed his mind without telling her.

Her pulse hammered in her throat as she descended the stairs. If he didn't appear, there wasn't time to make other plans.

Mrs. Wagner met her in the reception hall. "Time's wasting. You should've been on your way by now."

"I know. Colin's normally very prompt."

"'Colin,' is it?"

Merrie felt a blush rising in her cheeks. "He invited me to call him by his given name. I don't see the harm." She heard the defensive note in her voice.

"No harm, lovey. Your aunt wouldn't have hired him if he wasn't a decent fellow."

A shadow crossed the leaded glass windows beside the entrance. In a moment, the knocker echoed in the hall.

"He's here!" Merrie flung the door open to reveal Colin standing on the porch. "I was afraid you'd changed your mind."

"I apologize for my tardiness. My father was in an unusually talkative mood this morning. Since I couldn't confide my reason for leaving, I stayed and listened." He lifted his shoulders in a shrug. "We have plenty of time. I asked Mr. Peters to bring the buggy to the carriage entrance when I left my horse in the stable."

She swept her gaze over his well-fitted black frock coat and iron-gray trousers, and on down to his shining boots. For a moment, she wished he were calling on her for social reasons. "I expect to return by noon," she said to Mrs. Wagner.

"Good luck—to both of you."

"There's no such thing as luck," Merrie said. "But thank you. I pray all goes well." She pushed down a prickle of conscience at using prayer to cover deceit.

Mr. Peters stopped the carriage in front of a three-story stone building on Lake Street. When Merrie looked up, she read KIPLER'S PUBLICATION OFFICES painted beneath the roofline over the main entrance. A chill shivered over her in spite of the warmth of the morning.

As though sensing her disquiet, Colin patted her gloved hand. "This will take only a short while. Try to be calm." He stepped to the boardwalk and helped her from the vehicle.

Sending him a wobbly smile, she took his arm. "Calm isn't the word that comes to mind."

"Not to mine, either." He guided her past tall front windows to the entrance. Inside, the hall area formed a tee, with offices on both sides, as well as others lining a facing wall. Brass plaques next to the doors identified activities carried on within.

She tipped her head toward the first plaque on their right. "Horatio Kipler, editor. Shall we—"

The door opened and a short man with side-parted russet hair and a bushy chinstrap beard beamed at them. "Mr. Bentley. You're very prompt. Please come in." He nodded a greeting at Merrie, then stepped to one side to allow them to pass.

They entered a small anteroom furnished with a few plain wooden chairs and a table piled with copies of *Kipler's Home Weekly*. Wall sconces fought a battle with the dimness of the space. Mr. Kipler gestured toward a doorway behind him.

"My office is in there. Time is limited this morning. If you'll please follow me, Mr. Bentley." He turned to Merrie. "We won't be long, ma'am. Feel free to browse through our back issues while you wait."

She gasped. "I . . . I'd rather not stay out here alone." She hoped he didn't hear the panic in her voice.

"Nonsense. You're perfectly safe. If you wish, you may seat yourself in one of the chairs near my door, so we can hear you if you call out."

"But, I—"

"There, there. I know it's the nature of ladies to take fright, but I assure you no one has ever come to harm in this building. Chicago's best policemen patrol this street at all times."

Colin cast a wide-eyed glance in her direction as Mr. Kipler closed the door behind them.

Her heart thumping, Merrie stared at the solid barrier between her and whatever the editor had planned to say. She tiptoed close, but could hear nothing more than the murmur of male voices.

She prayed Colin possessed a good memory.

After a lengthy wait, the door opened and the two men returned to the anteroom. Merrie jumped to her feet.

Mr. Kipler clapped Colin on the shoulder. "Good talking with you. I trust you'll put my suggestions to work in future articles." He nodded in Merrie's direction. "Thank you for your patience. I can see where your husband gets his excellent ideas on the role of women in the home."

Speechless, she stared at Colin. He lifted one shoulder in a nearly imperceptible shrug. She lowered her eyes. Mrs. Wagner claimed Merrie's feelings showed on her face, and it wouldn't do for Mr. Kipler to see how she felt at that moment.

"Shall we go, my dear?" Colin extended his elbow.

She took his arm and allowed him to lead her out to the waiting carriage. As soon as she believed they were beyond earshot, she rounded on him. "I hope you memorized every word he said to you."

"I'm pretty sure I got the gist."

She rubbed the side of her head, not caring that she loosened her tight braids. "The gist?" She groaned. "As soon as we return to my aunt's home, would you please tell me his suggestions? I'll write everything down before you forget."

"Certainly." He helped her into the buggy.

Once they settled onto the seat, Mr. Peters flicked the reins and headed for the outskirts of town.

Merrie rode with her arms folded across her chest, mind racing. "Did he tell you how many articles he wanted?"

"Not exactly. He did say he enjoyed my—your—writing, and wanted to feature me—you—in several future issues." His voice softened. "I'm sorry you had to wait outside. I know how important this is to you. If you wish, I'll call on you an extra day every week to read over your articles before you submit them."

"Thank you. I'd like that."

"Which day would you prefer?"

"Monday, if that's agreeable to you. I send them by post on Fridays."

"Monday it is."

She suppressed a quiver at the caring in the depths of his eyes. With Colin's assistance, she felt sure she could meet Mr. Kipler's expectations. And spending more time with Colin would be a bonus in itself.

The buggy approached the fence surrounding the city block that comprised her aunt's estate. Mr. Peters slowed the team, guiding them through the gates and up the drive to the carriage entrance.

"Here ye be. Careful getting down, now."

"Thank you. We had a pleasant ride." Merrie scooted over on the seat and waited for Colin to help her to the ground.

"Where have you been? I was forced to hire a cab from the station."

At the sound of the familiar voice, Merrie gaped at the figure beyond Colin's shoulder.

"Aunt Isabella!"

· · · ﬀOUR · · ·

Merrie ran to her aunt and threw her arms around the stout, red-haired woman. Until this moment, she hadn't realized how much she'd missed her father's sister. "I'm so glad you're home. The house is too quiet when you're away."

Aunt Isabella kissed her cheek, then put her hands on Merrie's shoulders and stepped back. Her gaze surveyed her niece's attire. "You're dressed like a little wren today. Don't you have any prettier frocks?"

"Of course I do—you've provided several lovely gowns." Her mind raced for an explanation of her decision to wear her plainest dress. "But it seems a shame to neglect this one just because I have others."

"Hmm. While I'm home, I'll send for my dressmaker. If you insist on wearing brown, she can create something with ruffles and flounces."

"While you're home? Are you leaving again?"

"Yes, fairly soon." Aunt Isabella looked up at the coachman. "Please don't unhitch the team, Peters. You need to go to the station and collect my trunks. The baggage master is holding them."

He touched his cap. "Yes, ma'am. Right away." Wheels squeaked as he turned the carriage in the drive and headed in the direction of the Illinois Central Railroad Depot.

She turned to Colin, who stood a few feet away holding his hat at his side. "Mr. Thackery. How unusual to see you someplace other than the music room. You and my niece were out for a buggy ride?" Her tone challenged.

Merrie held her breath, wondering how he'd respond.

"It's a fine morning, Mrs. Daintree. When Miss Bentley suggested I accompany her, I was happy to oblige."

"And didn't we set Thursday afternoon as your appointed lesson time?"

Color rose in his face. "I volunteered to add an extra day when necessary."

"I see." She put her fingers to her lips, suppressing a smile. "I'm sure we've kept you long enough. You probably have other students waiting."

Alarmed, Merrie placed her hand on Aunt Isabella's arm. "Mr. Thackery and I have a few things to discuss before he leaves." She cast a frantic glance at Colin.

"Nonsense, dear. He'll return on Thursday. In the meantime, Mrs. Wagner has prepared a lovely tea. I'm eager to hear all about your activities. Please excuse us, Mr. Thackery."

"Certainly." He bowed in their direction and strode toward the stables.

Biting her lip, Merrie watched him go. By Thursday, he might forget everything Mr. Kipler had told him.

Aunt Isabella's return couldn't have come at a more inopportune time.

Merrie followed her aunt into the drawing room, where an elegantly appointed tea awaited them. A tray laden with frosted cake slices, tiny sandwiches, and a bowl of ruby-red cherries graced the center of the table. A silver teapot, surrounded by delicate china cups, sat to one side.

She recognized the cake as one Mrs. Wagner had planned for their evening supper.

The woman was a marvel. Aunt Isabella hadn't been home more than a couple of hours, yet the housekeeper had produced a light meal worthy of prestigious guests.

Her aunt settled on one of the chairs and helped herself to generous quantities of everything. While she ate, she regaled Merrie with anecdotes about her meetings with legislators in Springfield.

Merrie's concerns about Colin and Mr. Kipler stole her appetite. She listened to her aunt while she pushed a half-eaten serving of almond cake around on her plate. Then she lifted her tea cup and sipped the fragrant brew, waiting. Sooner or later, her aunt would get around to asking about her whereabouts that morning.

Aunt Isabella finished the last few crumbs of her cake and leaned back in her chair, arms folded across her ample bosom.

Merrie braced herself.

Her aunt patted her lips with her napkin. "Do you and Mr. Thackery often go riding together?" She voiced the question as though it were a casual comment, but Merrie heard the steel beneath the sweet smile.

"Today was the first time, and probably the last, although he is pleasant company. I didn't believe you minded how I spent my days, as long as I progressed in musical skills." She matched her aunt's tone.

"Music isn't the only area where your father is hoping to see progress. I'm supposed to introduce you to Chicago society so you can make a suitable match." A smile lifted a corner of her mouth, making her look younger than her fifty-some years. "Not that I always do what my brother asks, but I feel I should at least make an effort."

Merrie reached across the table and clasped her aunt's hand. "You've been wonderful to me. It's a blessing to live in your home rather than moving from pillar to post with my parents."

"I treasure your affection, but you do need to meet with other young ladies and gentlemen of your station. Have you considered the Hyde Park Literary Club? I mentioned the group to you last spring."

"I went once." She swallowed, staring at her lap. "It was . . . painful. You know how shy I am with strangers. Almost no one spoke to me."

"You didn't act shy with Mr. Thackery." Her aunt's eyes held a mischievous glint.

"He's not a stranger anymore. When he first began my lessons, I could hardly lift my eyes from the keyboard. But he's very kind and patient—sometimes he even displays a sense of humor. I'm glad you hired him." As she said the words, she realized how true they were. Aside from moments she could steal to spend writing, Colin's visits were the high points of her weeks.

Aunt Isabella folded her napkin and laid it beside her empty plate. "Nevertheless, I believe we should pay a call on another of my friends, Mrs. Bunting. Her husband is in the Social Register, and they have an unmarried son a few years older than you are. Elliott, I believe his name is. He recently returned from a trip abroad."

Merrie blinked back tears. She hated being paraded in front of eligible bachelors as though she were merchandise on display. Even worse, she sensed bachelors disliked the practice as much as she did. If she could be left alone to write, with weekly visits from Colin, her life would be perfect.

Colin rode toward the parsonage. As he left Merrie's aunt's home on Ashland Avenue, the houses became noticeably less pretentious until he reached his own neighborhood, where they were downright humble. He led his horse to the stable behind the simple frame house near his father's church.

The contrast between his home and the estate where Merrie lived seemed sharper today than usual. A girl with her advantages could never be interested in someone like him.

After watering his horse and seeing to it the animal had fresh hay, he walked along the side of the house to the kitchen entrance, screened from the street by a vine-covered lattice. As soon as he stepped inside, his father called a greeting from the parlor.

Colin winced. He'd hoped to have a few quiet moments to write down Mr. Kipler's instructions. Merrie was depending on him—not that she needed to worry. He had an excellent memory.

"I wonder if you have some free time to accompany me on a house call," Jeremiah Thackery asked as he entered the kitchen with his coat over one arm. "One of my widowed parishioners is in need of counsel. Or so she says. It's the third time this month she's sent her servant to summon me." His brown eyes crinkled at the corners when he smiled. "I think she's more interested in finding a husband than receiving advice."

He studied his father. With his tall, slender build and the distinguished gray streaks in his dark hair, he could see why widows in his congregation had been after him since Colin's mother died several years ago. So far, none had caught his interest.

"Could this wait for an hour or so? I need to write some notes."

"Her housemaid came by right after you left this morning. Best if we go now and get it over with."

He grinned at his father. "Why don't you marry one of these ladies? That way the rest of them could settle down and pay attention to your sermons instead of your manly good looks."

"Hmm. Never thought of that. Do you think it might hurt attendance if I'm off the market?" He chuckled and rested his hand on Colin's shoulder. "In the meantime, are you coming with me or not?"

"All right, I'll go."

"Good. While we walk, you can tell me why you went to see the bashful Miss Bentley on a Monday."

"She was bashful only at first. Once she got to know me, she relaxed."

His father raised an eyebrow. "No need to be defensive. I meant no disrespect toward the young lady." His voice gentled. "It won't do for you to forget your station. You're her music teacher, not her suitor."

The reminder stung. For a few moments that morning, he'd come close to imagining there were no such barriers between them.

Merrie sat at the writing desk in her room, where she'd taken her papers following her aunt's return. She stared at a blank sheet, wishing she knew what Mr. Kipler had told Colin. The blank sheet stared back, but instead of seeing ivory-colored paper, she saw the tender expression on Colin's face as he'd escorted her from Mr. Kipler's office. What a good actor. If she didn't know better, she'd think he cared for her.

Sighing, she pushed to her feet. He'd be here Thursday with his notes on the meeting. With that cheering thought in mind, she stepped to her wardrobe to select a dress for this afternoon's call on Mrs. Bunting and her son, Elliott.

Aunt Isabella tapped on the doorframe and poked her head into the room. "Peters will have the coach at the door in ten minutes." She surveyed Merrie's simple muslin frock. "Surely you're not wearing that?"

"No." She draped a white muslin day dress sprigged with pink and green flowers over her arm. "I'll be dressed in a moment."

Her aunt nodded approval. "That garment enhances the coppery tints in your hair. You're sure to make a good impression on the Buntings."

Merrie's stomach felt like she'd swallowed a stone. The last thing she wanted was to be on display before yet another bachelor, but she'd keep her objections to herself. As soon as the women's rights movement beckoned, Aunt Isabella would be off again, and Merrie could resume her peaceful routine of music lessons and writing. Much as she loved her aunt, she could hardly wait for her to leave.

FIVE

Mrs. Bunting answered the door at their knock. Her face broke into a wide smile when she recognized her caller. "Isabella! What a treat to see you." She tilted her head at Merrie. "And this must be the niece you've told me so much about."

Merrie flushed.

The woman swung the door wide. "Please, do come in. My son is eager to meet you both."

Inside the dark-paneled entry, curved archways led to a drawing room on the right and what appeared to be a library on the left. A center hall led to the rear of the house.

Mrs. Bunting escorted them into the drawing room. She gestured toward an overstuffed sofa piled with brocade pillows. "Make yourselves comfortable. I'll tell my son you're here. Tea will be served in a moment." She slipped out of the room.

"What did you tell her about me?" Merrie whispered.

"Nothing untrue. I said you were charming, talented, and accomplished on the piano." Aunt Isabella fidgeted a bit, then cleared her throat. "I may have mentioned your father left it up to me to find a suitable husband for you."

Heat swept over Merrie. "You didn't!"

"That's the way these things are done, dear. You don't just wander about willy-nilly hoping to find a mate."

"I don't want—"

Mrs. Bunting stepped into the room, her hand on the elbow of a stout young man who resembled his mother. His ash-blond hair was combed into a high wave over his forehead. His skin glowed pink, as if he'd been interrupted in the midst of strenuous exercise. "My son, Elliott." She beamed at Merrie. "This is my dear friend Isabella's niece, Miss Bentley."

He tucked a bow in her direction. "Pleased."

Merrie nodded, forcing herself to meet his gaze. He didn't look at all pleased. Her palms moistened inside her tight gloves. She tried to think of something to say, but failed.

Mrs. Bunting broke the silence. "I wonder what's keeping the maid. Our tea should be here by now. If you'll excuse me . . ."

Aunt Isabella looked at Elliott. "Your mother tells me you've recently returned from Europe. Did you have a pleasant tour?"

"Yes. Thank you." He set his lips in a straight line.

"She also told me you had some lovely garden statuary shipped home. Perhaps you might show them to my niece. She enjoys gardens."

Merrie's mouth dropped open.

Elliott gave her an indifferent glance. "Of course. If you'll come with me, Miss Bentley." He extended his elbow.

"I . . . I'm sure my aunt would like to see the garden too. Wouldn't you, Aunt Isabella?" She pinned her aunt with a daggerlike gaze.

"Not at all, my dear. You two go ahead. I'll enjoy a chat with his mother while you're gone."

Merrie took his proffered elbow, knowing her face must be as red as the Persian carpet beneath her feet. Without speaking, Elliott moved along the hall to a sunroom at the rear of the house, then opened glass-paneled doors to the garden. He waved his hand at a pair of stone lions guarding the graveled path winding through the flower displays.

"Mother always fancied lions, so I sent these to her. Over there, that stone pedestal will hold an urn once she decides which one she wants." He paused and studied her face. "You're not the least bit interested, are you?"

"Truthfully, I'm mortified that my aunt so blatantly pushed me at you." Her voice trembled. She hoped she wouldn't cry.

His shoulders relaxed. "So this wasn't your idea?"

She swallowed and shook her head.

"There's a bench over there by the birdbath. Why don't we sit for a few minutes before we rejoin those two schemers?" He took her elbow again and guided her to a stone bench.

"Thank you."

He plopped down beside her, resting his hands on his plump thighs. After a moment, he cleared his throat. "You need to know, I plan to return to Europe before the end of the year. To Berlin, specifically. I met a young lady there during my travels, and we plan to marry."

"How nice," she murmured, wondering why he confided in her.

"Mother is aghast at the thought of me marrying a foreigner, so she's dragging all her friends' daughters over here to meet me, hoping I'll find someone appealing. It hasn't happened."

Even though she wasn't the smallest bit attracted to him, the remark stung. Merrie twisted her hands together, wishing the visit were over. She dragged her gaze from her lap to his eyes.

"I pray you'll have a happy life." The beginnings of a headache pushed at her temples. Without waiting for his response, she rose and hurried toward the house. Regardless of what her father and aunt wished, she would not go through this again.

Merrie sat stiffly beside her aunt as their carriage bore them home. The heat of the afternoon added to the waves of humiliation that cascaded over her. Words from someone like Elliott shouldn't matter, but they did. Colin would never speak to her in such a haughty tone.

"The visit went well, don't you think?" Aunt Isabella patted her arm. "Elliott looked disappointed when we left."

"If anything disappointed him, it was probably the empty cookie plate. He knew you and his mother were presenting me for his approval, and he wasn't interested. He told me he's already met someone he wishes to marry." She drew a deep breath. "No more arranged meetings, please. You can write Father and tell him I plan to be a spinster."

"Surely not!"

"Well, no. But I want to wait for butterflies and tingles. And someone who'll love me for who I am, not because I'm your niece."

Her aunt shook her head. "I won't write your father just yet. I'm not ready to admit defeat."

In spite of herself, Merrie chuckled. How like her aunt to turn this into a personal mission. She leaned over until their shoulders touched.

"Neither am I."

On Thursday afternoon, Merrie paced the music room awaiting Colin's arrival. Fortunately, her aunt was out paying calls. She hoped another matchmaking attempt wasn't in the offing.

She placed sheets of paper on a table beneath the front window and arranged two straight-backed chairs on either side. An inkwell and pen sat next to the blank pages. She'd transcribe his notes first, then they'd review her progress on the "Wedding March."

As soon as she saw him climb the steps to the porch, she ran to open the door before he had time to knock.

"I thought today would never get here," she said, then felt her cheeks warm. "That is, I'm dying to know what Mr. Kipler told you."

His lean face creased in a smile. "If you'll allow me to enter, I'll tell you."

She flushed again and stepped away from the entrance. "I have everything ready in the music room. Did you bring your notes?"

"Such as they are." He followed her across the hall. "I had some unexpected interruptions when I left here Monday, so several hours passed before I had time to write things down."

Apprehension prickled through her. "But you did remember everything, didn't you?"

"I have an excellent memory." He walked to the table and drew out a chair for her. "Shall we begin?"

"By all means." She dipped the pen in the inkwell and held the instrument poised over the paper. "To begin with, how many articles does he want, and when is the first one due?"

"Hmm. He didn't exactly say how many."

"Then when does he want the first one?"

"Next week, then once a week thereafter."

Her apprehension grew. With her aunt at home, she'd have less time to focus on writing. She hoped the topics would be simple ones. She dipped the pen in the inkwell a second time, although the nib was still damp. "I'll need to start right away. Please, what themes did he request?"

Colin whipped a small piece of paper from his coat pocket. "Goals, gifts, speech, home, children, love, faith—things like that."

She scribbled down his words while he was speaking, then paused. "What do you mean, 'things like that'?" She jammed the pen in its holder and stared at him. "He must have given you more details. What are they?"

"He did talk a bit about what he wanted, but I had a hard time following every word. The man talks faster than an auctioneer at a farm sale. Why don't you start on one of the topics, and Monday we can review the piece together? Once I see what you've said, I can tell you whether you're going in the right direction."

For a moment, Merrie feared she might faint. He thought she could write on a vague subject and trust him to make proper corrections? She tipped her head back and closed her eyes. The whole masquerade had been for naught.

"Merrie?" His voice sounded closer.

She opened her eyes to find him bending over her, concern shadowing his handsome features.

"We can do it. You'll see. I'll be here on Monday morning for our first collaboration." He gave her hand a reassuring pat.

A tingle ran up her arm. "I'll be ready."

After Colin left, Merrie sped up the stairs to her room, carrying paper in one hand and the inkwell in the other. Her first article would be about godly homes. After living in a variety of places with her parents, often hotels or rented rooms, she cherished the home Aunt Isabella shared with her. Even when her aunt traveled, Merrie had Mrs. Wagner, who was more family member than servant.

Merrie reached for her Bible. She knew the Scriptures she wanted to use—the pages were already bookmarked. Humming, she turned to the verse that stated a place was prepared for her in heaven. A prepared place meant one that was clean and well-ordered, with dependable routines.

She wrote as fast as she could, thoughts tumbling through her mind, until she reached a stopping point. As she read over her words, she wondered what Colin would think when he read them. Somehow when she'd been writing, his face had been the one she visualized as sharing her perfect home.

"Your aunt sent me to fetch you. She's waiting at the dinner table." Mrs. Wagner stood in the doorway, an amused expression on her face. She gestured at the papers scattered across Merrie's writing desk. "Lost in your words again, eh?"

She scrambled to her feet. "My goodness. The time got away from me." She returned her pen to its holder and flipped the filled pages over, then rested her Bible on top. "Please tell her I'm on my way."

Mrs. Wagner moved across the room and cradled Merrie's right hand in her own callused palm. She tapped an ink stain on Merrie's middle finger. "First, come to the kitchen with me and clean this off, so your aunt doesn't wonder what you've been up to."

"But she's waiting."

"Another minute or two won't hurt." She nodded toward the back stairs at the far end of the hallway.

Merrie followed her down the narrow steps. When they reached the kitchen, the aroma of curried chicken and fresh-baked rolls surrounded her. She noticed a white-frosted cake waiting on the worktable. "Mmm. You must be the best cook in Chicago."

Mrs. Wagner beamed. "Go on with you." She filled a basin with warm water and placed it next to a towel on the counter, then cut a lemon and set it to one side. "This should do the trick. Rub the juice on the ink, then rinse your hands in the water. I'll tell your aunt you'll be there directly."

She hurried to comply, thankful for Mrs. Wagner's attention to detail. While Aunt Isabella was away, she hadn't needed to be careful to keep ink stains from her fingers, since no one noticed her hands. Unless Colin paid attention to her hands while she played . . .

Did he? She paused in her scrubbing and tried to remember. She studied her smooth, white skin and rounded nails, running her fingers along an imaginary keyboard to see how they looked in motion. Just in case he noticed, she'd be sure to remove any stains before her next lesson.

Mrs. Wagner bustled into the kitchen and sent her a pointed look. She grabbed a basket of rolls from the warming shelf over the stove, then dashed back to the dining room.

Seizing the towel, Merrie dried her hands and pushed through the swinging door after the housekeeper. Aunt Isabella sat in her usual place at the head of the table. She gave a slight huff when she saw Merrie, then made a show of spreading her napkin over her lap.

"You've put Mrs. Wagner to a great deal of trouble keeping our meal warm. I suppose you had your nose in a book again."

"Not so much trouble, ma'am." The housekeeper placed the rolls near a lighted candelabrum on the gleaming mahogany table.

"I apologize. The afternoon seemed to slip away." She took a chair to her aunt's right. "I apologize to you too, Mrs. Wagner."

"You're forgiven, lovey." She patted Merrie's shoulder and returned to the kitchen.

Aunt Isabella shook her head, smiling. "Well, if she's not upset, then neither am I. Tell me, how are your piano lessons progressing? Mr. Thackery was here today, was he not?"

"Yes. He's given me a difficult . . . assignment to master, but I'm doing my best. Fortunately, he's offered to call here on Monday to provide extra help." She drew in a breath, wondering how her aunt would react.

"Two days each week wasn't our agreement. I imagine he'll expect double wages."

"Oh, no. That is, he didn't mention charging more." Surely Colin wouldn't ask her aunt to pay him for spending additional time with her.

· · · SIX · · ·

The following Monday, Colin arrived at Mrs. Daintree's home a few minutes ahead of his expected time. He'd awakened early, eager to spend the additional hour with Merrie, and once he'd shaved and dressed he couldn't think of a reason to wait any longer to see her.

Mrs. Wagner escorted him to the music room. "If you'll wait a moment, she'll be right down." She cocked her head and studied him for a moment. "Does this extra visit have anything to do with 'Mr.' Bentley?"

His mind raced. Merrie told him the housekeeper knew of her writing for *Kipler's Home Weekly*, but he didn't know whether the woman was aware of the depth of his involvement. He tugged at his tie. "You mean Miss Bentley's father?"

"Hardly." She took a step closer. "I notice you're not carrying your music portfolio."

If she hadn't been watching, he'd have slapped his forehead. How could he pretend to be here for lessons without his music? He met her gaze, determined not to add another lie to the deception. "You already know I agreed to play the part of Mr. Bentley. She didn't tell you what happened?"

She shook her head. "What with her aunt's return and all, I've been busy." Curiosity lit her eyes. "So, did he believe you're the one who did the writing?"

"We fooled him too well. He took me into his office and left Merrie in the reception room. Then he spelled out what he'd like to see in her next several pieces."

"And you told her what he said."

"Not right away." He squirmed inwardly at her incredulous expression. "We went over the assignment when we met on Thursday, but I'm not sure I gave her a clear idea what Mr. Kipler wants. I promised I'd help by looking over the articles as she writes them."

Chuckling, she said, "That girl has a way with her, doesn't she?"

"She does." He thought of her brilliant blue eyes and compelling smile. He'd given in and pretended to be Mr. Bentley, even though he knew he should have refused to be part of a lie. Now he was being drawn further into the conspiracy.

"Just so you know, Mrs. Daintree is expecting you to present a bill for adding another day to your schedule."

"I don't want money. I told Merrie I'd help her, and I will."

Mrs. Wagner's expression softened. She put her index finger to her lips. "In that case, your secret is safe with me. I'll let you explain these visits to Mrs. Daintree yourself. Remember, she doesn't know Merrie wants to be a writer—*is* a writer."

He swallowed. "I'll remember." One deception led to another, like stacking uneven stones to build a wall. Sooner or later, the whole thing would collapse.

At that moment, Merrie appeared on the stairs carrying a sheaf of paper and an inkwell. When she saw him, her lips lifted in her beautiful smile. Then a shadow crossed her brow and the smile faded. "You're very prompt."

"I'm eager to see what you wrote."

"Shh. Aunt Isabella's in her study. She may hear us. Would you mind if I sit on the piano bench while we talk?" Without waiting for his answer, she preceded him into the room and arranged her pages on the music rack above the keyboard, placing the ink and a pen to one side.

He closed the door. Once she settled on the bench, he stepped behind her. A few tendrils of hair had escaped from her braids and curled against the back of her neck. He jammed his hands into his pockets so he wouldn't give in to the temptation to run one of the silky-looking strands between his fingers.

She tilted her head up, a serious expression on her face. "I'll play 'Mockingbird' while you read over my shoulder. If you see that I've missed what Mr. Kipler wanted, tap the page and tell me where I went wrong."

"Fine."

Her hands struck the opening chords, and he bent forward to read.

Heaven's Plan for a Godly Home

Happy is the wife who follows the example set out in the Gospel According to St. John, which tells us that our Lord went ahead to prepare a place for us. Clearly, this message is for wives. Ladies, be faithful in keeping your homes prepared for your husband. Whether the house be grand or humble, it should be clean and welcoming.

When your husband returns home at the end of his busy workday, he should find the children quiet and occupied, and a lovely supper waiting on the stove. Be sure you are wearing a clean apron, and your hair is freshly arranged. All of these actions will communicate your love for him. Love in the home is the chief happiness of all who dwell within. . . .

His lips twitched at the image of his mother at the end of a day made up of pastoral calls, cleaning, cooking, and chasing after him and his older sister. Apparently Mama hadn't quite mastered the technique of appearing unruffled. Yet love had been the chief happiness of his childhood.

While Merrie played the tune, he read to the end of her article, trying to recall precisely what Mr. Kipler had specified in his request for a piece about the home. Try as he might, he couldn't come up with the man's exact words.

He tapped the page after the final period.

She dropped her hands in her lap. Without turning around, she said, "Do you think he'll approve this?"

"I certainly do. What man wouldn't?"

She slid to the end of the piano bench and faced him.

"Really? You're sure I don't need to make changes?"

"I think it's perfect." He gazed at Merrie, picturing her in a clean apron, greeting him at the end of the day. He shoved the image from his mind. She hadn't written the article for his benefit—he was merely an unacknowledged collaborator.

"Which topic shall I choose next?"

Mr. Kipler's suggestions fled from his memory when he gazed into her eyes. He tried to think. "Hmm. Why don't you pick one and surprise me? You can tell me your choice when I come on Thursday."

"Will you be back next Monday as well?"

"Absolutely. That reminds me, I need to speak to your aunt. Would she mind an interruption?"

Her expression turned stony. "I'm sure she won't. I'll take you to her." An unmistakable chill iced her tone.

Bewildered at the change in her attitude, he followed her to her aunt's study at the end of the hall. The door stood ajar. Merrie tapped on the frame and then stepped across the threshold.

"If you have a moment, Mr. Thackery wishes to speak to you."

Mrs. Daintree laid the newspaper she was reading to one side of her desk. "Of course. I was expecting him to see me today." She glanced at Colin and gestured toward an armchair. "Come in, young man. Merrie, would you please close the door when you leave?"

Merrie lifted her chin and obeyed without looking at him. He couldn't understand what he'd done to bring about the sudden chill. Following Mrs. Daintree's request, he sank onto the soft brocade upholstery and faced her.

"I hope it's not inconvenient to your household to have me here on Mondays as well as Thursdays. I had no other appointments, so I'm happy to help."

"Not inconvenient at all. Our schedule isn't crowded. However, it would have been better if you'd stated your terms ahead of time." She bent to one side and lifted a small box, which she placed on the desktop. "I'm going to assume your fee for Monday lessons will be the same as you're receiving for your Thursdays?" A metallic click accompanied the opening of the lid.

She must think him greedy, or even worse, opportunistic. He sprang to his feet. "No, ma'am. It isn't."

"A discount, then?"

"No! No fee at all." He leaned forward, resting his palms on her desk. "If you don't mind my presence, we'll just consider the Monday hour part of the lesson, not an addition."

She folded her arms over her waist and regarded him with a half smile. The look on her face reminded him of his mother, when she suspected there was something he wasn't telling her.

Mrs. Daintree closed the metal box. "You came highly recommended, and from what I hear of my niece's playing, she's progressing well. If you don't mind donating another hour of your time, I have no objection."

Colin relaxed and turned toward the door. "Thank you."

"One more thing."

He stopped.

"I've tried to get her to participate in outside activities, but her shyness keeps her at home. Perhaps you could encourage her to develop interests other than music to fill her days."

"I'll do what I can, ma'am. I'm sure we'll arrive at something."

He smiled inwardly at the thought of Merrie's articles for

Kipler's Home Weekly. Her days were already filled. The next time they were alone, he'd ask why she hadn't confided in her aunt.

After she closed the door behind Colin and Aunt Isabella, Merrie hurried back toward the music room. Colin was asking for more money—for spending an extra hour with her. Her face felt hot. Somehow she'd believed he offered so they could have more time together. Obviously, she'd misjudged him.

She dashed over to the piano and removed her papers and ink from the top of the instrument. Perhaps after Mr. Kipler approved one or two of the new articles, she'd be able to conclude her assignment without Colin's participation. She hoped so. Why should he profit from his own error? If he'd paid better attention to Mr. Kipler, there'd be no need for a Monday "lesson" at all.

Merrie heard the door to her aunt's study click open. She scurried from the music room and hastened up the main stairway before Colin emerged. She'd look over the pages one final time to be sure there were no errors, then give the article to the coachman to post.

Half an hour later, she descended the back stairs to the kitchen carrying a sealed envelope. When Mrs. Wagner saw Merrie, she stopped buffing the silver bowl she held and laid her cleaning cloth next to a container of whiting powder. After a glance at the envelope, she asked, "You seeking Peters?"

"Yes. He's here, I hope?"

"Busy with the horses, I'm sure. Your aunt told him to be ready with the carriage at noon. She's off to lunch with one of her women's rights ladies."

"Then I just have time to give this to him."

She stepped out onto the paved drive leading to the stable. Fragrance from honeysuckle vines wrapped around an arbor perfumed the humid July air. She took a deep breath and held it for a moment, preparing herself to enter the anything-but-perfumed stable.

148

Before she took more than a dozen steps in that direction, the carriage approached, Mr. Peters on the driver's seat. He wore his full uniform, including a top hat. Perspiration dotted his forehead.

"Ye going w' Mrs. Daintree?"

"No." She held the envelope up.

"Ye'll be wanting me to post this, then?"

"Please. Perhaps you could arrange to do so while she's with her friend?"

He tipped his hat. "Be glad to." Sending her a conspiratorial grin, he leaned down from the driver's seat. "That young feller was looking for ye awhile ago. Said he wanted to have a few words with ye before he left."

She straightened her shoulders. "Why would he look for me in the stable, of all places?"

"He weren't in the stable." Peters pointed with the whip. "He walked about in the garden, said he thought you might be there."

"Did he tell you what he wanted?"

"No, miss." He shook the reins and guided the horses to the carriage entrance.

How curious. Since Colin was here only because he needed extra money, she couldn't think of anything he'd have to say that couldn't wait until he returned on Thursday.

She hurried back to the kitchen before her aunt could come outside and invite Merrie to join her for a luncheon with a boring women's rights supporter. Or worse yet, ask her why she needed to speak to the coachman.

On Thursday, Merrie's fingers coaxed the closing notes of Mendelssohn's "Wedding March" from the keyboard. Her shoulders slumped and she blew out a long breath. "I'll never be able to play this well. I've practiced and practiced."

"Nonsense. You're improving all the time." Colin folded his

arms and beamed down at her. "Play the opening section again. Listen to yourself. You're progressing nicely."

If she didn't know his true motives, she'd think he was enjoying her company.

He encouraged her through several more repetitions, until she dropped her hands in her lap. "No more, please."

"You're tired. Why don't we walk in the garden for a few minutes? You'll feel better if you get some fresh air."

His face wore a caring expression, one she supposed he'd learned from his father. She knew Colin was assuming a role. Still, she felt herself responding to the comfort he offered. Between struggling to master Mendelssohn and working her way through her latest article for Mr. Kipler, a stroll around the garden sounded like a few moments of heaven.

"What a good idea. It's a beautiful day." She rose from the piano bench. "Please give me a moment to fetch my parasol. We'll leave by the carriage entrance—it's closer."

Colin kept his hands clasped behind his back as they walked together along the paved drive and passed through the wrought-iron archway leading to the formal gardens. Colorful buntings flitted among the branches of a redbud growing to one side of the curving brick pathway.

Merrie paused next to a sundial set on a pedestal in the center of a riot of purple coneflowers. The shadow across the face told her the hour was near four.

"Your time is almost up. Perhaps we'd better postpone our walk."

He moved close to her side. "I'm in no hurry. There's no place I'd rather be than here."

At the tone of his voice, butterflies tickled in her throat. She shooed them away, reminding herself again that Aunt Isabella paid him to spend time with her. She'd treat him with the same politeness she used with her aunt's friends.

"It is pleasant, isn't it?" She stepped onto the brick path. While they strolled, she pointed to a shady area at the far side of the lawn. "This path will take us around the flower beds. We'll end up under that oak tree over there. By then I expect we'll have had enough sun."

They walked in silence for a minute or two. When they reached a carved bench at the far end of the garden, he turned and gazed back at the house. "Your aunt has one of the finest homes in Chicago. I expect you know that. Coming here is a treat for me."

Her heart softened at the sincerity in his tone. She gave him a half smile. "My parents brought me for visits often when I was growing up. It's a treat for me to be here, too. If only Aunt Isabella—"

"You'd like her to understand about your goal to be a writer."

"How did you know?"

He leaned closer and she inhaled the sweet, woody fragrance of the oil he used on his dark hair. "Because she seems determined to get you out into society. She said as much when I met with her on Monday. I've considered her words since, and obviously she has no idea of the amount of time you need to spend writing in order to succeed."

Merrie stiffened. "You were discussing me? I thought the two of you were talking about your wages."

"We did talk about wages. She expected to pay me for coming an extra day."

"I know. I trust her terms were satisfactory." Ice coated her words.

"Not at all."

Her eyes widened. "You asked for more?"

"I can't accept pay for something that's my idea. I told you we'd work together, and we will."

She walked to the bench and sank down, tipping her parasol forward to hide her flushed cheeks. He really did want to spend time with her. The butterflies were back.

$\cdot \cdot \cdot$ SEVEN $\cdot \cdot \cdot$

M errie sat at her desk, penning her third article for Mr. Kipler. She wondered if the post had deposited her previous submissions into an abyss. They were almost halfway through August without a response from the magazine. If she had some idea whether he approved of her subjects, she'd feel more confident in proceeding.

Colin would be here for her music lesson tomorrow. She needed to finish the article so he could review her words. She read through what she had written thus far.

Godly Communication in the Home
The wife of the home should at all times strive to keep her speech soft and gentle. Through such means, many lessons are agreeably taught to her youngsters. The husband, as well, will be at all times eager to listen to his wife if she will avoid shrill, grating tones.

When tested, both husband and wife would do well to heed the words of the First Epistle General of Peter: "Be of one mind, having compassion one of another . . . not rendering railing for railing; but contrariwise, blessing."

In her memory, she heard her mother and father arguing in the room adjoining her bedroom. She knew they loved one another, yet her mother tended to be forceful in her opinions. She was right more often than not. But rather than argue, Merrie's father would slam out of the house, vowing never to return.

Remembering, Merrie's stomach clenched with the same fear of losing her parent that she'd experienced as a child. She prayed for wives who might read her words, that they would think twice before upsetting the children in their care.

Assuming they read her words.

Perhaps Colin's excellent memory had failed him, or Mr. Kipler had meant something entirely different when he requested topics for his magazine. She wished she knew.

She huffed a frustrated breath and replaced her pen in the holder. Horses' hooves clopped beneath her window, signaling Mr. Peters's return from his daily trip downtown. Maybe today there'd be a letter from Mr. Kipler. In haste, she tucked her manuscript pages in the top drawer of her desk and sped down the main staircase.

She slipped out the carriage entrance, hoping to intercept the coachman before her aunt had an opportunity to go through the post. Merrie would never be able to explain a letter from *Kipler's Home Weekly.*

Mr. Peters stood in front of the stable, unfastening carriage traces from the team. When he saw her coming, he paused in his task and wrapped the reins around one hand. "Something ye need, Miss Merrie?"

"I came to see if you'd like me to collect the post and take it to my aunt."

"Well, now. That's kind of ye, but Mrs. Wagner saved ye the trouble today." He flicked a drop of perspiration from the tip of his nose. "Likely she'll be in the kitchen w' it right now."

"Thank you." She turned away, praying her aunt wasn't also in the kitchen at that moment.

Her hopes dropped when she entered the stuffy room at the rear of the house. Aunt Isabella stood at Mrs. Wagner's worktable. Several unopened letters lay in front of her.

"Ah, Merrie, there you are." She reached down and selected a cream-colored envelope. "This is addressed to you. I notice it's from the Buntings." A pleased smile crossed her face. "You must have made a better impression than you realized."

She bit the inside of her lip. She could have sworn she'd made no impression whatsoever on Mrs. Bunting, let alone her son.

"Well?" her aunt asked. "Aren't you going to open it?"

Mrs. Wagner stepped to her side and offered a small penknife. "Use this, lovey."

After slitting the envelope, Merrie removed an embossed card. She read through the message with a growing sense of doom. "I'm invited to a ball in Elliott's honor next Saturday, the twenty-first."

"That's wonderful." Her aunt's eyes shone with delight.

"No, it's not. Being part of a crowd where I don't know a soul will be torment. I don't want to go."

"Mrs. Bunting is one of my dearest friends. Of course you'll go. I'll have my dressmaker sew a new gown for you."

The room was really too hot. Merrie felt as if she might faint. "Aunt Isabella, please. You know how I hate being with strangers."

"The only way to overcome fear is to face it head-on. By the time the ball arrives, you'll be prepared."

"No—"

Mrs. Wagner slipped her arm around Merrie's waist and turned to her aunt. "She's looking a bit peaked. This heat would put anyone on edge. Why don't I help her upstairs for a nap?" She glanced up at Merrie. "You'll feel better after you rest, I'm sure."

"You know best," Aunt Isabella said. "We can discuss this tonight at dinner."

Merrie leaned against the housekeeper as they climbed the stairs. "Thank you," she whispered.

"Glad to help. Your aunt's a fine woman, but stubborn. Perhaps she'll change her mind." At the top of the stairs, they turned left into Merrie's bedroom. Mrs. Wagner drew a folded magazine from

154

her apron pocket. "Here's something for you to read while you're resting." She winked and closed the door.

Merrie stared down at an issue of *Kipler's Home Weekly.* The edge of an envelope protruded from the front cover.

She dropped the magazine on top of her desk, glanced at the return address to confirm the missive came from Mr. Kipler, then slit open the flap. Her heart bumped when she drew out a letter, but no bank draft. She unfolded the paper slowly, postponing his response as long as possible.

August 10, 1858

Dear Mr. Bentley,

I am in receipt of your submissions of July 26th and August 6th. Your interpretation of my guidelines has me puzzled. I thought myself perfectly clear when we met last month, but apparently that was not the case.

Nevertheless, we will publish your first two articles in our upcoming issues, and wait to gauge reader response. Please try to recall the specifics of my request before sending future submissions.

A draft in payment for "Heaven's Plan for a Godly Home" and "Rearing Godly Children" will be forthcoming upon publication.

> *Sincerely,*
> *Horatio Kipler*

Merrie sank onto the chair in front of her desk and rested her head in her hands. Tears threatened. With her eyes closed, she took several deep breaths. The whole thing was Colin's fault. If he'd done as he promised and written everything down right away, this wouldn't be happening. When he arrived tomorrow, she'd tell him so.

A verse she'd learned in Sunday school slipped into her consciousness. *Lying lips are abomination to the Lord, but they that deal truly are his delight.* Perspiration trickled along her temples. She shouldn't blame Colin for something that was her doing. The first time Mr. Kipler mistook her for a man, she should have corrected him.

Standing, she stared unseeing out the open window. She couldn't say anything now. The deception had gone too far.

On Thursday morning, Colin sat at the table in their kitchen while his father stood at the stove stirring a skillet filled with eggs. The smoky aroma of bacon rose from a platter on Colin's right. He slid his hand toward one of the crispy strips.

"Hold your horses. Eggs are about ready." After a few more brisk stirs, his father scooped two servings onto plates and set them on the table. He blessed the meal and then turned to Colin.

"Are you coming with me on my calls today? Or are you going to the church to practice on the piano?"

"Neither one." He chewed a bite of bacon. "Today's Miss Bentley's music lesson."

"You were just there Monday. This is getting to be a regular thing."

Colin wished he could tell his father why he needed to spend the additional day every week with Merrie. The articles she'd produced filled him with admiration. She'd make some fortunate man a wonderful wife. What a pity all her attention seemed to be focused on advancing her career as a successful writer, even to the extent of deceiving her editor.

"I don't think she'll need extra help for too much longer." Once she received confirmation from Mr. Kipler, she'd be on her way. True, he'd continue to see her on Thursdays, but he'd be denied the pleasure of working through her articles together.

He felt a stab of regret. The hours spent with Merrie had become the highlight of his week.

"You look disappointed." A worried frown creased his father's forehead. "It won't do to become too attached to the young lady. You know that."

"She's one of my students. Nothing more." He forked up some scrambled eggs, wishing he meant what he said.

Merrie met Colin at the door when he arrived that afternoon. A few curls had worked loose from her braids and fluffed around her face. Distress clouded her features.

"Thank heavens you're here. I thought three o'clock would never come. Mr. Kipler sent me another letter."

He stepped into the reception area with his portfolio tucked under one arm, then glanced behind her down the hall. "Shh. Lower your voice, so your aunt doesn't hear."

"She's gone to one of her women's rights meetings."

Merrie took his free hand and tugged him toward the music room. He drew a breath when he felt the softness of her palm against his. His father's admonition rang in his ears.

The warning had come too late.

Once they were inside she released him and crossed to the table in front of the window. Scattered sheets of paper covered its surface. She lifted a creased page and held it out to him.

After depositing his portfolio on the piano bench, he took the paper from her grasp. He scanned the contents once, then read through the message again, his spirits sinking. *Please try to recall the specifics of my request before sending future submissions.*

No wonder she was upset. He'd bungled his assignment, and now she was suffering for his carelessness.

He reached toward her, then let his hand drop. "I'm sorry, Merrie. I don't know what to say. We went over your articles together. To the best of my memory, you fulfilled his requirements."

She dropped onto one of the chairs beside the table. One side of her mouth lifted in a crooked smile. "Obviously, your memory failed you."

"Apparently so."

A moment of silence passed between them. Colin settled in the chair facing her and glanced at the pages on the tabletop. "Is this your next article? 'Godly Communication in the Home'?"

"Yes. Would you mind looking through it? Something might spark a recollection."

He raised his eyebrows. "Why would you trust me?" He tapped Mr. Kipler's letter. "This is my fault."

She leaned toward him, sending the fragrance of rose water drifting in his direction. "I thought so at first, but I must be honest with myself. If I hadn't continued the 'Mr. Bentley' deception, things would never have come to such a pass."

"It's not too late." He stood and faced her. "Don't you see? If he doesn't like what you've written, this would be a perfect time to tell him the truth. Explain why you couldn't recall the specifics of his request."

Her face paled. "Then he'd never print anything of mine again."

"You don't know that. He asked to meet you because he liked what you wrote." He held his breath, hoping she'd agree.

"I don't want to take the chance."

"You can't base your ambitions on untruths. Sooner or later—"

"Can't I wait until later? Please? Let's go over this article together and see what we can change." She gazed up at him, her blue eyes pleading.

Colin gazed back at her, his heart a leaden lump in his chest. True, her station in life was a hurdle between them. But her ambition was an insurmountable barrier.

His jaw tightened. He'd promised to help her, and help her he would. Resuming his seat at the table, he gathered the manuscript pages in his hand and began reading.

EIGHT

Mrs. Wagner met Merrie in the hall after Colin departed. "I didn't hear a note of music being played this afternoon."

Merrie's senses were still humming from spending the past hour shoulder to shoulder with Colin. The occasional moments when their fingers brushed while exchanging pages left her wishing he'd clasp her hand, slip an arm around her, tip her chin up for a kiss. She shook her head to dislodge the thoughts. However much she might wish their social positions were different, he'd never step beyond the bounds of propriety. No doubt that's why Aunt Isabella had hired him.

She forced her attention back to Mrs. Wagner. "We were too busy working on my most recent submission for *Kipler's Home Weekly*. Thank goodness my aunt wasn't home."

"You'll miss her when she leaves."

"Of course I will, but she'll be here for quite a while, won't she?" Mentally, she calculated how many free hours she'd have to write, between accompanying her aunt to lectures and joining her for morning and afternoon tea.

Mrs. Wagner followed her up the stairs. "First part of September, she's going to New York City to join the committee planning the next convention."

"So soon?"

A shadow of loneliness brushed over Merrie. As challenging as it was to keep her writing secret, she didn't look forward to eating her meals alone in the capacious dining room. Mrs. Wagner refused to join her and didn't feel it was proper to allow Merrie to eat with her and Mr. Peters in the kitchen.

When they reached the upper floor, the housekeeper stopped at the threshold of Merrie's room. "Miss Gordon will be here any minute now. When you put your papers away, you can wait for her in the parlor."

"I forgot the dressmaker was coming today!" She rubbed the side of her head. "I don't need a new ball gown."

"Your aunt thinks you do."

Her shoulders sagged. "Elliott Bunting isn't interested in me at all. I can't imagine why I was invited."

Visions of a long evening spent sitting in a chair at the edge of the dance floor curdled her stomach. The time could be better spent writing. She could always think of the right thing to say on the page—and if she didn't like the words, she could change them. Unlike social events, when she'd spend the following days going over what she should have said.

Mrs. Wagner gave her a sympathetic glance. "Meeting rich folks isn't a punishment. When the right gentleman learns you're from this fine home, you'll catch his interest—your aunt will make sure of it."

"This is Aunt Isabella's house, not mine. I've been told my mother's family didn't have a fancy home, and my father married her anyway."

A faraway look crossed the housekeeper's face. "That he did." She sighed. "Romantic, it was. Sometimes I think your aunt—"

"What?"

"I'm talking out of turn. You put your papers away now. I'll show Miss Gordon to the parlor soon as she arrives."

Merrie tucked her manuscript into a drawer, wondering what Mrs. Wagner had intended to say about her aunt—and her parents. All she knew of their marriage was the little she'd been told about their elopement. From all accounts, her father had given New York society something to talk about for months afterward. Since then, the two of them, and eventually Merrie, had lived up and down the East Coast while her father attended to his import business.

She rested her forefinger on her lips. She had questions to ask before Aunt Isabella left for New York City.

Merrie perched on a velvet-upholstered settee in the parlor, surrounded by *Godey's* and *Peterson's* magazines.

Miss Gordon fanned swatches of silk across a tufted ottoman at her feet. A woman beyond middle age, she was dressed in a smart day dress of stone-colored peau de soie. Around her neck, she wore spectacles suspended on a chain, which she lifted to her eyes each time she spoke to Merrie.

"For a late summer ball, I'd suggest a light color. Perhaps a soft green or lemon yellow. Then as an underdress, what do you think of white? And of course, over your hair, matching flowers." She pointed to an illustration of a ball gown in *Godey's* and held up a square of pale green silk. "This shade would look stunning on you."

The fabric rippled like water over the woman's fingers. Merrie studied the picture, then the silk. "It is beautiful." She heard the yearning in her voice.

"You would like me to create this one?" Behind the round lenses, Miss Gordon's eyes brightened. "I can have the basting finished within a week. Your aunt instructed me to follow your wishes exactly."

Merrie dipped her head, overwhelmed by her aunt's generosity. Since Aunt Isabella was willing to go to such lengths to assure that she wouldn't feel out of place, the least she could do was act properly grateful. Shame for her childish refusal to attend the ball heated her cheeks. When she saw her aunt tonight at dinner, she'd apologize. After all, what could one evening at the Buntings' hurt?

"Thank you, Miss Gordon. I'd love to have this gown. I'll be ready for a fitting next Thursday."

As she left the parlor, the image of herself in a billow of sea green and white silk gliding over the dance floor clouded when she contemplated her only partner would likely be Elliott Bunting. If only Colin could be there . . .

On the evening of the ball, Merrie stood in front of the mirror in her room while Mrs. Wagner helped her into her dress. The ruffled underskirt frothed over the toes of her satin slippers as the housekeeper fastened the buttons up the back of the green silk gown.

Aunt Isabella beamed at them from a chair next to the writing desk. "That dress is nothing less than a confection. You're sure to turn heads tonight."

"You'll be the belle of the ball, for certain." Mrs. Wagner fluffed the lace trim around the shoulders.

Merrie didn't recognize the girl in the mirror. She'd never worn such wide skirts. With ribbons and flowers woven through the ringlets in her hair, she looked like an illustration in a ladies' magazine. She stroked the fabric with her fingers.

"This is the prettiest gown I've ever had. Thank you." She bent and kissed her aunt's cheek. "I just pray someone asks me to dance." Her insides quivered at the thought of sitting on the sidelines throughout the evening.

"Nonsense, child. Your card will be full." She patted Merrie's hand, then stood, gathering her robe around her. "We'll leave once Mrs. Wagner helps me with my dress."

The housekeeper hurried to join her in the hallway.

"She'll be a success tonight, don't you think?" At the sound of her aunt's voice, Merrie turned from the mirror. The toe of one of her slippers caught on the ruffled underskirt and she paused, taking a step backward to untangle herself.

"You know she doesn't really want to go. She's not comfortable among so many strangers," Mrs. Wagner said.

"Well, the apple doesn't fall far from the tree, does it?"

Her ears perked up. Was Aunt Isabella referring to Merrie's mother? She slipped closer to the open door, knowing she shouldn't eavesdrop, but unable to resist.

"You mean Mrs. Bentley."

"Yes. Madeline was decidedly uncomfortable when my brother, Wallace, brought her to meet our family at our Christmas ball. I felt sorry for the poor girl—one moment she's working in a millinery shop, and the next she's rubbing elbows with New York's elite."

Her aunt's voice faded as they moved along the hallway. Merrie inched closer to the threshold.

"It rattled my mother's sensibilities when I took Madeline under my wing, but the years have proved me right. She's been the strength behind Wallace's business. I doubt he would be where he is today without her keen mind."

"Be that as it may, Mrs. Bentley still avoids society."

"Which is why Wallace asked me to find a good match for Merrie. I'll do what I can, but if she—" Aunt Isabella's bedroom door closed.

Heart pounding, Merrie sank onto the chair next to her desk. Her mother had worked in a shop—as a milliner. Her father defied his family and married her anyway. Answers to questions from the past fell into place. As Mrs. Wagner had said, their story *was* romantic.

An idea for a new article formed in her mind. The title would be "Foundation for a Godly Marriage." As far as she knew, Scripture said nothing about social standing as a prerequisite for matrimony. As soon as she returned from church tomorrow, she'd excuse herself and begin writing.

Her father had made his own match. Once this evening's ball was past, she'd do the same.

A manservant carrying an umbrella greeted Merrie and her aunt when their carriage stopped at the portico in front of the Buntings' home. He helped them down, holding the umbrella high over their heads.

"Have a care, ladies. The paving stones are slippery tonight."

"Thank you." Merrie gathered her skirts above the tips of the slippers. She and her aunt stepped through the rain to the shelter of the entrance. Once they were safely under cover, the servant returned to his post near the drive.

Another servant took their evening cloaks and escorted them through an archway at one side of the reception hall into the transformed drawing room. Parlor chairs lined the walls. A refreshment table stood at the far end, with a cut crystal punch bowl as a centerpiece. Hidden behind potted palms, a pianist, accompanied by violins, played a waltz tune as dancers swirled around the polished floor. Music and snatches of conversation greeted them when they entered.

She pressed her hand to her lips. "We're late," she whispered. "Everyone's staring at us."

"If anyone stares, it's because you look enchanting." Her aunt took her arm. "Smile."

Mrs. Bunting swept into view. "Isabella. Miss Merrie. I'm so pleased to see you." She glanced over her shoulder. "Elliott has been most anxious for your arrival."

At that moment Elliott made his way along the edge of the dance floor and bowed in front of her.

"Miss Bentley. I'd hoped the rain wouldn't keep you away this evening."

He looked the picture of elegance wearing a black tailcoat and matching trousers. A spotless white cravat rode beneath the blond goatee on his plump chin. He nodded at Aunt Isabella. "So good of you both to come."

"We've been looking forward to this evening, haven't we, Merrie?"

She swallowed a tangle of nerves. "My aunt has spoken of nothing else since we received the invitation."

For a moment, she thought she saw a flash of understanding in his eyes as he bowed again in her direction.

"If you'll excuse us, Mrs. Daintree, I'd like to request the honor of your niece as a dancing partner."

"Most certainly. I'm eager for a chat with your mother."

He led Merrie to the dance floor, placed his right hand on her shoulder blade, then took her free hand in his. They moved into the circle of dancers. Although her wide skirt kept him at arm's length, she smelled rum punch on his breath.

"Don't know what I would have done if you hadn't come." He stumbled slightly, then righted himself. "Mother invited every one of her friends and their daughters tonight. I'm counting on you to help me keep them at bay."

A flush climbed up her neck. All her aunt's expense for this beautiful gown, just so Elliott could deceive his mother?

"I don't see what I can do. Aside from you, I know no one here."

"You can act as if we're—" He bumped into another couple. "'Scuse me."

Merrie tipped her head back and studied his reddened face. "Perhaps we'd better leave the floor."

"Nonsense. The waltz hasn't ended." He tightened his pressure on her back and guided her through a turn.

When they circled past the musicians, she glanced over her shoulder, then stared. Elliott spun her away, but not before the pianist met her gaze.

Colin.

NINE

Merrie breathed a relieved sigh when Elliott led her back to her aunt.

"I trust you'll save the next waltz for me." He touched his lips to her gloved hand before releasing her.

Merrie rested her fingertips on her temple. "I . . . I'd like to sit for a bit. It's quite warm in here."

"I'll bring you a cup of punch."

Unable to think of a gracious way to refuse, she nodded. "Thank you." A crowd of dancers waited at the punch bowl. Perhaps by the time he was served, his mother would have brought another young woman to meet him. She hoped so.

As soon as he was out of earshot, Aunt Isabella leaned toward her. "He seems quite attentive."

"He's not interested in me." She kept her voice low. "I was invited so that his mother would stop her matchmaking."

"Why, that's shameful. Making you a part of his deception."

"I have no intention of allowing the pretense to continue."

"I should hope not."

Merrie felt a twinge of guilt at her words. Elliott's maneuvering felt too much like her own efforts to hide her writing from her aunt.

Across the room, the musicians left their instruments and moved toward a door almost hidden by the potted palms. If she hurried, she could visit with Colin for a moment. She excused herself and hastened across the empty dance floor.

"Colin."

He turned when she spoke his name. "Miss Bentley. I'm surprised to see you here—although I shouldn't be. This is your world, after all."

She waited to respond until the violinists departed. "You can call me Merrie now. No one's listening."

"It's not proper for you to be talking to me in these surroundings. I'm hired to be here—you're a guest."

"I'm not worried about proper. We're friends."

He took a step closer and bent his head toward her ear. "Not here. I don't want to ruin your chances in society."

"But, Colin—"

"Here's your punch, Miss Bentley." Elliott swayed beside her, the ruby liquid dangerously close to spilling on the pale green silk of her gown. "I can't imagine what you'd have to say to the entertainers this evening. The order of the dances is already listed on your card."

She took the cup from his hand, holding it away from her skirt. "Mr. Thackery and I are acquainted. I was merely saying hello."

"Well, now that you've greeted him, shall we join the party and let him enjoy refreshments with his companions?" He gave Colin a brusque nod. "Fine music, Thackery. Carry on."

"Thank you, Mr. Bunting," he said, his face a mask of politeness. Turning abruptly, he strode through the doorway his companions had used a moment earlier.

Merrie stared after him, then rounded on Elliott. The pulse pounding in her throat threatened to choke her. "Mr. Thackery is a pianist, not a . . . a . . . chimney sweep. You didn't need to speak to him in that manner."

He gripped her elbow and steered her toward her aunt. "Right now he's in our employ. I'll speak to him however I wish."

She felt the gazes of other guests as he propelled her across the floor. When Aunt Isabella noticed them coming in her direction, she stood. "Are you quite all right, Merrie? You look flushed."

She set the untasted cup of punch on a small table. "I'm feeling quite ill. Would you mind if we left early?" She shook her arm free of Elliott's grasp.

"Of course not. Elliott, would you please ask one of your servants to have our carriage brought around?"

He gave her aunt a forced smile. "Right away, Mrs. Daintree." On his way out of the room, he turned and scowled at Merrie.

She watched him go, thankful his charade had come to an end.

Within minutes a maidservant appeared. "Your carriage is waitin' out front, ladies." She helped them don their cloaks, then opened the door.

"Thank you," Aunt Isabella said. "Please give our regrets to Mrs. Bunting, and tell her I'll call on her next week."

"Yes, ma'am."

When Merrie saw Mr. Peters smiling at her beside their carriage, she dashed toward him, heedless of the rain. This evening couldn't end soon enough. Halfway to his side her slipper caught in the ruffles around her skirt. Stumbling forward, she put out her hand to break her fall and landed on her knees in a puddle.

A burning pain shot up her right arm.

"Miss Merrie!" Mr. Peters took her by the shoulders and lifted her to her feet. "Are ye hurt?"

She cupped her throbbing wrist with her left hand. "No. Just embarrassed. Please, let's leave."

The coachman helped her into the covered carriage, then assisted Aunt Isabella. Once they were headed toward home, she leaned against her aunt. "I'm so sorry. There's mud all over the front of this lovely dress."

"Mud can be cleaned. Your well-being is more important. After watching Elliott this evening, I'm thankful he's not the one for you."

"I'm thankful too," she said, thinking of the frozen expression on Colin's face when he turned away from her. Somehow she'd have to make amends for the insult he received because of her actions.

By the time they reached home, Merrie's wrist felt hot. Without thinking, she extended her right hand to Mr. Peters to help her from their conveyance, then sucked in a sharp breath when he clasped her palm.

Flickering light from the lamps in the carriage entrance illuminated his stricken features. "Forgive me, miss. Did I hurt ye?"

"A little." She tucked her injured wrist against her body. "Would you mind lifting me down?"

"O' course." His strong hands clasped her waist. As soon as her feet touched the ground, Aunt Isabella hastened to her side.

"Let's get you indoors." She turned to the coachman. "Peters, please fetch Dr. Goodrich."

Merrie shook her head. "I hate to disturb the doctor this late. I'll be fine until morning."

"I don't want to take the chance."

Her aunt nodded at Mr. Peters, who returned to the driver's bench and directed the coach toward town. She slipped her hand under Merrie's left elbow as soon as the horses were in motion. Once inside, they stopped under one of the lighted sconces in the reception hall.

"Please, let me look at your arm. Do you want me to help you remove your glove?"

"I can do it." Merrie slipped her left thumb under the cuff and slid the elbow-length glove as far as her wrist. Wincing, she stopped and stared. The light revealed puffy, reddened skin. She gritted her teeth and pulled her hand free. The effort left her trembling.

Aunt Isabella hovered next to her. "Merciful heavens! That looks dreadful." Hesitating, she glanced down the hallway, then put her arm around Merrie's waist. "We won't awaken Mrs. Wagner. Come upstairs with me. I'll help you out of your dress before Dr. Goodrich arrives."

The doctor strode into Merrie's bedroom, his gold-rimmed spectacles gleaming in the yellow lamplight. From his well-tailored black coat to his polished boots, he looked as if he'd been waiting by his door for a patient to call him out.

"Well, well, Miss Bentley. Your aunt tells me you took a nasty spill." He placed a small leather satchel on top of her bureau. "Let's have a look at that arm."

Merrie shifted in her chair and pushed the sleeve of her dressing gown above her elbow. Dr. Goodrich bent over her. Placing his hand under her wrist, he raised her arm almost level with her shoulder.

"Hmm. Hot. Swollen. Can you move your fingers?"

She wiggled them, blinking back quick tears of pain.

His thumb probed against the bones of her wrist, causing fresh tears. "Doesn't feel broken. More like a severe sprain."

Relief flooded through her. "So I can use my hand? That's wonderful news."

"Not so fast." He turned to Aunt Isabella, who stood in the doorway. "Would you be so good as to bring me a basin of cold water, ma'am?"

When her aunt left, the doctor opened his satchel and removed a narrow roll of white cloth. Facing Merrie, he said, "As soon as your aunt fetches the water, I'm going to soak these bandages and wrap your hand and arm. For tonight, keep the wrist cold and wet. The longer you can tolerate the moisture, the better."

She gazed at her bed with its fluffy down-filled quilts. "But . . . how will I sleep?"

"You must keep your arm atop the covers. You might try resting it on a serving tray."

The image of her arm looking like a poached salmon on a platter brought a weak smile to her face. "Then tomorrow I'll be better?"

He shook his head. "You'll need to rest the injury for at least a week—probably more. Your aunt can fashion a sling for you. You must not use that hand."

"But I—" She bit off the rest of the sentence. The doctor wasn't interested in her concerns, and she couldn't ask Aunt Isabella to help her write her articles. Thankfully, Colin would be here on Monday. She'd ask him.

While the guests at the ball enjoyed a midnight supper at the Buntings', Colin left by a side door leading from the kitchen. Once the dancing ended for the evening, he had no reason to linger.

Seeing Merrie with young Mr. Bunting left a sour feeling in the pit of his stomach. She looked like an angel in her elaborate gown. And like an angel, she was out of his reach.

With his cloak slung over his shoulders against the early morning chill, he held the reins in a loose grip as his horse plodded over muddy streets toward home. Broken clouds allowed sufficient moonlight to illuminate his route.

He'd been a fool to think Merrie could ever be interested in him. His parents had made a happy life together with very little, but Merrie had always known the best of everything. Compared with the impressive houses he passed on his way to the parsonage, he had nothing to offer. The least painful thing would be to stop seeing her.

He straightened in the saddle and resolved to make his next visit his last. Mrs. Daintree would find another piano teacher. Once he left her employ, he hoped he'd be able to forget Merrie's brilliant blue eyes and fetching smile.

On Monday morning, the memory of Mr. Bunting's faultlessly tailored evening attire spurred Colin to take special care as he dressed. He stropped his razor to a fine edge and shaved his dark whiskers as close to his skin as possible. After donning a clean shirt and pressed trousers, he fastened his necktie in a wide bow and draped his black frock coat over his arm.

His father's eyebrows shot up when Colin arrived at the breakfast table. "What's the occasion?"

"Nothing special." He strove to keep his tone casual. "I'm going to Miss Bentley's this morning."

"Does she expect you to be dressed in your finest?"

He shook his head. He'd never been able to pretend one thing while doing another. His father had a way of cutting through the fat to reach the meat of a subject.

"No. I don't believe she pays much attention to what I wear." As he spoke, he realized the statement was true. Merrie focused on him as a person.

"If you set the standard too high, she'll expect this every time," his father said, with a teasing grin.

"I plan to tell her I won't return after today." His stomach twisted into a knot. Saturday night he believed he had a good idea, but Monday morning's light cast shadows over his intentions. Not to see Merrie again? He quailed at the prospect.

"And why is that?" His sharp gaze drilled into Colin.

"She lives in a different world. You should have seen how beautiful she looked at the ball. Like an angel. The hostess's son paid special attention to her. And who am I? A lowly piano teacher."

"You're the same person you were a week ago. She liked you then, didn't she?" His expression softened and he rested his hand on Colin's shoulder. "I know I've cautioned you against becoming attached to Miss Bentley, but perhaps I should have remained silent. Let her decide whether she no longer wants your company."

"I've already decided. This will be best for both of us."

$\mathcal{T}$EN

The sling Merrie wore rubbed the back of her neck. She rolled her shoulders, trying to shift the weight of her right arm to a more comfortable position. After a moment, she gave up. She had more important things to do this morning. Aunt Isabella and Mrs. Wagner had hovered over her all day Sunday, but today her aunt left to make calls and the housekeeper was busy with laundry.

Eyeing the paper and ink she'd smuggled into the music room, she decided to start on her "Foundation for a Godly Marriage" article before Colin arrived. By jotting down a few thoughts now, she'd be better able to guide him through the piece. She leaned over the table and closed her fingers around the pen. The motion shot pain through her hand and up her bruised arm. Merrie gritted her teeth, then dipped the nib in the inkwell. The doctor said she should rest her hand, but using a pen shouldn't hurt anything. After all, writing wasn't as taxing as arranging her hair or buttoning her dress—she'd allowed Mrs. Wagner to help her with those necessities.

She centered the paper with her left hand and wrote, "Foun—" before gasping and dropping the pen.

Colin would be here any moment. She'd wait.

Blowing out a frustrated sigh, Merrie left the room and stepped onto the covered porch in anticipation of his arrival. The morning air hung heavy with humidity. Blue jays squabbled among the branches of a hackberry tree, sounding as cross as she felt.

Within a few minutes, Colin rode into view. Instead of passing down the drive toward the stable, he tied his horse to a hitching post beside the front walk and dismounted. How odd. Normally he let Mr. Peters care for his horse.

Her heart did a little hop at the sight of him. He looked especially handsome in his black coat and gray trousers. When he approached the porch, she smiled and hurried forward.

Before she could utter a word, his gaze landed on her sling, then met her eyes. "You're hurt. What happened?" He reached for her as if to grasp her shoulder, then let his hand drop.

She looked down at the purple and red bruise that enveloped part of her hand and forearm. "I sprained my wrist Saturday evening."

"At the ball?" His voice rose to a higher pitch. "How could that be?"

"I slipped as we were leaving. Thankfully, no one noticed save my aunt and our coachman." She held out her left hand. "I'm so glad you're here. I've been waiting to apologize for the way Elliott Bunting spoke to you on Saturday evening."

"You're not responsible for Mr. Bunting's manners."

"True, but—"

"Saturday evening made me see the differences between us, Merrie."

"There's not as much difference as you might think. Please, let's not stand here on the porch. We can talk in the music room."

He shook his head. "No, thank you. I think it's best if I don't come here again. Rather than send a message, I rode over this morning to tell you face-to-face." Stepping to one side, he asked, "Is your aunt at home? I have a letter of resignation for her."

"No. She went to a meeting." Tears burned her eyelids and threatened to overflow. She dashed them away with her forefinger.

How could she have been so mistaken about his feelings? Drawing a shuddering breath, she raised her right arm so he could get a closer look at her wrist.

"I need your help, Colin. I can't write with this hand. Please, if I tell you what to say, will you write for me? As soon as I'm better, you're free to leave for good." She'd never begged for anything in her life, but she was begging now.

An agonized expression crossed his face. Turning away, he glanced at his horse, as if trying to decide whether to stay or flee. When he looked at her again, she thought she saw caring reflected in his eyes before his features tightened. He took several steps toward the driveway, then stopped and faced her.

"I'll stay on for a couple of weeks, no longer. You should be able to use your hand by then."

She felt she might collapse with relief. Matching his impersonal tone, she said, "I appreciate your willingness. Please come inside and we'll begin."

Colin sat opposite Merrie at the table in the music room. Heaven help him, he couldn't resist the tears he'd seen swimming in her blue eyes. Two more weeks. He hoped he'd be able to hold to his resolve to leave when the time was up. He didn't know how much longer he'd be able to be close to her without revealing his feelings.

She pushed the inkwell toward him, along with a fresh sheet of paper, then rested her injured wrist in her lap. "I think it would be best if you'd print. That way the differences in our handwriting won't be apparent. The title will be 'Foundation for a Godly Marriage.'"

He printed the heading in the center of the page. In spite of himself, he felt intrigued by her choice of subject. The society girls to whom he'd given piano lessons were interested only in finding wealthy husbands. Godly choices didn't seem to enter into their thinking.

She rubbed the side of her head with her left hand. "Are you ready?"

"Yes." More than ready. He was curious.

"A godly home cannot exist without the Lord's blessing on the union of marriage. Scripture is silent on whom one should marry, but—"

"Slow down, please." He wrote until he caught up with her words, then nodded at her.

She continued, "—but the Second Epistle to the Corinthians warns both men and women not to be unequally yoked with unbelievers. Beyond that, one is free to make one's own choices." She leveled her gaze on him when she paused.

As he scribbled her words on the page, a glimmer of what she was implying flashed through his mind. Choice outweighed convention. He wished he knew whom she'd chosen, himself or Mr. Bunting.

He wrote at her dictation until the case clock in the hallway struck eleven. When he replaced the pen in its holder, Merrie lifted the pages and read over what he'd written. A little smile flitted over her lips at certain portions of the manuscript.

"Thank you. When you're here on Thursday, we'll finish this and send it to Mr. Kipler."

Her formal tone shook him, then he remembered he'd only promised to help for two weeks. She had no way of knowing his heart.

He stopped on his way to the door. "I have a question for you."

"Yes?"

"How do your writing pursuits fit into your view of a godly wife?"

Closing her eyes, she bowed her head for a moment. Then she gazed up at him through her lashes. "A godly wife is subject to her husband in all things. I believe she would look with care before she marries to be sure she found someone worthy of her trust."

Her words remained in his thoughts as he rode away. From the way he'd seen Mr. Bunting treat her, the man wasn't worthy of her trust. He'd likely force his will upon whoever crossed his path.

Colin drew a breath. Perhaps he'd been hasty in giving notice. Too late now. His letter rested on Mrs. Daintree's desk.

Merrie sat at the desk in her room, jaw clenched as she formed each letter of the heading for a new article. She penned "Shared Gifts in a Godly Marriage," then stopped to wait for the pain in her wrist to subside. She leaned back in her chair, feeling perspiration break out across her forehead. Colin's two weeks would be up in a couple of days. She had to be able to write unaided.

Sorrow that had nothing to do with composing her articles swept over her. At some point during their time together, her feelings toward him had changed from friendship to love. There must be a way to let him know how much she cared before it was too late. An idea tumbled into her head. Perhaps if she began this article with an example of a piano teacher married to a writer . . .

She dipped the pen in the inkwell and wrote a sentence before resting her wrist. At this rate, it would take her all day to compose a page. So be it. She wrote a second sentence.

"Miss Merrie, Peters brought a letter for you." Mrs. Wagner entered the room and placed an envelope next to the inkwell.

A message from Mr. Kipler. Now she'd learn what his readers thought of her articles. She bit her lower lip, afraid of what she'd read when she opened the letter.

"Thank you. Did my aunt see this?"

"No. I tucked it in my pocket before I gave her the mail." She cleared her throat. "It's not my place to say, but I'm thinking you should tell her what you're doing. I doubt she'll be upset."

"She wants me to make a good match. My sitting here writing isn't what she had in mind."

Mrs. Wagner patted Merrie's shoulder. "Maybe. Maybe not." She bustled out of the room, her footsteps receding down the hall.

Merrie stared at the letter for several moments before summoning the courage to open the envelope. Her heart lifted when she saw a bank draft enclosed with the message from the editor, thankful that the past articles had been good enough to warrant compensation.

She unfolded the crisp paper and read,

September 3, 1858

Dear Mr. Bentley,

I'm delighted to inform you that your recent submissions on Godly Marriage have met with an enthusiastic response from our readers. Kipler's Home Weekly *has received an unprecedented number of letters requesting more of these articles. Accordingly, we would like to offer you a weekly column through the end of this year, subject to renewal at that time.*

She dropped the letter into her lap and drew an excited breath. Such an offer far exceeded anything she'd dared hope. She couldn't wait to tell Colin when he arrived on Monday. Without his collaboration, this would never have happened.

In the next moment, she remembered that after Monday she'd no longer have his help—or his companionship. Some of the luster faded from Mr. Kipler's message.

Picking up the paper, she continued reading.

To express our appreciation for your contribution to the success of our magazine, Kipler's Home Weekly *requests the honor of your presence at dinner in the Orion Hotel on Saturday, September 11. I will personally meet you at the door at eight o'clock on the evening of the event.*

Sincerely,
Horatio Kipler

She gasped. This couldn't be happening.

Her thoughts spun in frantic circles. She had one week to come up with a plan that didn't involve Colin.

ELEVEN

When Mrs. Wagner ushered Colin into the music room on Monday morning, Merrie greeted him with a strained smile. She seemed lovelier than ever, wearing the dotted pink dress that made her look like a flower. Perhaps the knowledge that he wouldn't see her after today was affecting his judgment. He doubted that was the case.

He glanced at the table in front of the window. Hoping to lighten his somber mood, he asked, "Are those papers my assignment for today?"

"In a moment." She opened a slim drawer beneath the tabletop and withdrew a folded page. "I think you'll be interested in the letter I received from Mr. Kipler on Saturday."

As she read the editor's words aloud, Colin's eyebrows rose.

Merrie concluded with, "'Accordingly, we would like to offer you a weekly column through the end of this year, subject to renewal at that time.'"

She refolded the page and dropped the letter on a corner of the table, but not before he noticed that the message filled the entire sheet. She hadn't disclosed the full contents. He wondered what else the editor had to say—not that it was any longer his concern.

Her left hand brushed his arm, a butterfly touch. "I couldn't have accomplished this without your help. I hope you know how grateful I am."

A weekly column. She'd achieved her goal.

A door closed between them.

"Merrie, I—" He tightened his jaw. "No need for gratitude. You did the work." He tried to ignore a twist of pain at the thought of saying a permanent goodbye at the end of the morning's session.

She looked down at her hands. "We worked together." Her voice was barely a whisper. Then she lifted her chin and pushed filled manuscript pages across the tabletop.

"As you can see, I'm able to write now. Here's one last article for you to review, then you're free."

He glanced at her right wrist. Her bruises had faded from deep purple to a yellowish hue. Anything that unsightly had to hurt. "Are you sure? I'd be willing to stay on longer if you need me."

She tucked her arm in her lap, hiding her injury. "No, thank you. I'm quite recovered."

"Well, then, let's see what you have this week." Her views on matrimony often surprised, and always pleased, him. If only they'd met under different circumstances . . .

He pulled a chair next to the table and noticed the title, "Shared Gifts in a Godly Marriage." Intriguing. Wondering how she'd weave spiritual gifts into the estate of matrimony, he perused the opening paragraphs, sensing her gaze on him as he read.

A section at the top of the second page stopped him.

As an example, there is a lady of my acquaintance who is gifted in the use of words. Pursuing her interest brings her great delight. This lady has been supremely blessed to possess a husband who not only indulges her interests, he encourages them. This husband spends much of his own time perfecting the gift of music, with which he has been blessed. The two of them share a most happy existence.

If at all possible, I would encourage any young lady contemplating marriage to look beyond social standing and strive to learn her would-be husband's attitude toward the encouragement of her special talents—or gifts, if you will.

Startled, he looked up at Merrie. "Are you saying—?"

Her cheeks flamed. "I never should have written that. I don't know what came over me." She snatched the pages from the tabletop. "I'll change it later. In fact, I'll rewrite the whole thing. You don't have to read the rest."

"I don't mind. I'm interested." He reached for the manuscript, but she held it behind her.

"Since this is your final visit, you needn't concern yourself." She backed toward the entrance. "My aunt has written a letter of recommendation for you. Please excuse me a moment. I'll bring it right away." She hastened through the open doorway and dashed down the hall, the pages fluttering in her hand.

Colin started after her, then stopped at the door. He felt sure she'd intended the example for him to read. What had changed her mind?

Shoving his hands in his pockets, he paced back to the table and glanced down. The letter from Mr. Kipler rested beside an inkwell. He cocked his head, eyeing the folded paper. Should he?

Certainly not.

But maybe the contents would throw some light on Merrie's behavior.

He reached out and unfolded the page while listening for her returning footsteps.

Now or never. Be quick.

He scanned the final paragraph.

To express our appreciation for your contribution to the success of our magazine, Kipler's Home Weekly *requests the honor of your presence at dinner in the Orion Hotel on Saturday, September 11. I will personally meet you at the door at eight o'clock on the evening of the event.*

Sympathy coursed through him. On the one hand, Mr. Kipler promised her the success she sought, then with the other snatched it away. Mr. Bentley didn't exist. Colin wondered how Merrie would manage to decline the invitation without losing the promise of a weekly column.

The sound of heels tapping across the reception hall startled him from his thoughts. He dropped the letter and turned as she entered the music room, an envelope in her hand.

"This is for you. My aunt and I . . ." She swallowed. "We're sorry you're leaving."

The regret he felt lodged in his throat. "Thank you. My time here has been a pleasure." His voice emerged cold and formal. He wished he could go back to the day he'd told her he couldn't stay and take back the words. He felt sure Mr. Kipler's letter had defeated her hopes, and he wouldn't be here to help her this time.

She gave him a ragged smile. "Yes. It's been a pleasure for me too." Holding up her right hand, she continued, "I'd hoped to master the 'Wedding March' by now, but this got in the way."

He tried for a grin. "Ah, well, you've perfected the left hand accompaniment." His throat tightened. If he didn't leave soon, he'd embarrass himself. Men didn't allow tears to show. "When the time is right, you'll be able to play the entire piece flawlessly." He tucked the envelope containing Mrs. Daintree's recommendation into his breast pocket. "Goodbye, Merrie."

Merrie stood at the window as Colin rode away. Her limbs felt heavy, as if she'd walked a long distance.

She wished she'd never given him the article to read. From the stunned expression on his face when he turned to the second page, she knew he'd never pictured the two of them as man and wife. Of all the ill-thought-out plans she'd ever had, this one was the worst.

Mr. Kipler's letter lay where she'd left it on a corner of the table.

In any case, without Colin to masquerade as Mr. Bentley she couldn't be sure she'd have the opportunity to continue writing for *Kipler's Home Weekly*. A goal that meant so much to her a month or two ago no longer seemed important.

With Colin out of her life, nothing seemed important.

She jammed the letter in her pocket and walked through the house toward the back garden, her steps dragging. Skirting the sundial, she followed the path between flower beds to the bench under the oak tree. Her favorite thinking spot.

Bees worked among the white blossoms on a summersweet shrub growing nearby. She leaned back on the shaded seat, inhaling the flowers' spicy perfume. House wrens trilled in the branches over her head.

She released a weary sigh. Much as she'd like to, she couldn't ignore Mr. Kipler's letter. A proper response must be sent by tomorrow at the latest. She chewed her lower lip. She had two choices. Invent a reason to decline the invitation, or accept and be prepared to explain Mr. Bentley's absence.

She made her decision, then rose and stepped into the hot September sunshine.

TWELVE

Aunt Isabella, may I speak to you for a moment?" Merrie hesitated in the doorway of her aunt's study. Her palms moistened at the thought of what she was about to say.

"Of course. You never have to ask." Her aunt walked around the desk and patted the tufted upholstery on an ornate carved settee. "Come over here and tell me what's bothering you." She squeezed Merrie's hand. "It's Mr. Thackery, isn't it? You've grown attached to him."

"Would that be so bad?"

"Not in my eyes."

For a moment, Merrie's heart lifted. "I never dreamed . . . I thought you wanted to match me with a society gentleman."

"That's what your father wants. I've watched you all summer—and especially at the ball—and I've come to believe you're more suited to someone quiet. Social life doesn't agree with you."

Merrie closed her eyes and took a long breath. If only she'd known. But would the knowledge have made a difference? Colin's decision to leave was out of her hands. "I've been trying to tell you that all along," she said in a small voice. "Now it's too late. He's gone."

Her aunt drew her against her pillowy bosom. "If he cares for you at all, he'll be back." She patted Merrie's shoulder. "You wait and see."

As she snuggled into the comfort of her aunt's embrace, she wished she shared her conviction. Aunt Isabella hadn't seen the expression on Colin's face when he read the example she'd used in her article. He couldn't wait to leave.

After a moment, Merrie leaned away and pressed her hands together in her lap. "Mr. Thackery isn't the reason I interrupted your morning." She swallowed. "I came to ask whether Mr. Peters could drive me to the Orion Hotel on Saturday evening."

"Whatever for?" Her aunt couldn't have appeared more astonished if Merrie had announced she wanted to audition for the stage.

She straightened her shoulders. The time had come. "There's something I've been keeping from you." Heart pounding, she relayed her deception about writing for *Kipler's Home Weekly*, including her involvement of Colin.

"So now I learn the real reason for the Monday visits."

Merrie nodded, feeling her cheeks burn. "I never meant things to go this far. Mr. Kipler has invited me—or rather, Mr. Bentley—to a dinner at the hotel on Saturday."

Aunt Isabella surveyed Merrie with one eyebrow raised. A half smile lifted a corner of her mouth. "How will you explain Mr. Bentley's absence?"

"I don't know yet. I'll think of something."

"You're determined to go?"

"Yes." She took courage from the interest in her aunt's voice.

"I can't permit it. A young woman alone—it isn't safe."

Her courage deflated. "Mr. Peters will be with me." She hoped she sounded more confident than she felt.

"Peters will be with the carriage. No telling what might happen to you in the hotel."

Merrie stood and moved toward the door, her thoughts mired in a pool of despair. Before she reached the threshold, her aunt spoke again.

"There's no help for it. I'll go with you as chaperone."

She turned and met her aunt's sparkling gaze. "You will?"

"I wouldn't miss it. The evening promises to be more entertaining than writing an agenda for a women's rights meeting."

Merrie flew across the room and hugged her. "Thank you. I'll run upstairs right now and write an acceptance letter."

Her steps slowed after she left the study. Composing a letter would be the easy part.

She wished she knew what she'd say when she met with Mr. Kipler.

The remainder of the week dragged by. When Saturday came, Merrie found herself sitting in the garden missing Colin. Everything about the upcoming meeting with her editor reminded her of the day they'd traveled to town together, except now she no longer had him as her companion. Although Aunt Isabella meant well, Merrie intended to meet with Mr. Kipler alone. She'd gotten herself into this predicament, and she'd get herself out.

A cup of tea with Mrs. Wagner would help. She walked toward the house, noticing as she passed that the dandelion heads at the edge of the lawn had disappeared. Their lighter-than-air seeds had scattered to plant themselves in new gardens. When Merrie entered the kitchen, Mrs. Wagner stood in front of the open oven holding a baking sheet in her towel-wrapped hand. She turned and smiled.

"What perfect timing. I just took your favorite treat out of the oven—almond cookies."

"They smell wonderful. Thank you." She settled on a chair next to the worktable. "I came for some cheering up. Cookies and tea will certainly help."

"Are you worried about tonight?" Mrs. Wagner placed the cookies beneath an open window to cool, then lifted a teapot from the warming shelf over the stove and filled two cups. "I'm proud of you for telling your aunt about your writing. She's all atwitter about this meeting."

"So am I, but probably for a different reason. I feel like Daniel, walking into the lion's den."

"The Lord was with Daniel. He's with you too, lovey."

"I know that, but I can't help worrying how badly I'll be bitten before I escape." Merrie stepped over to the window and lifted a cookie from the pan. The warm pastry melted on her tongue. "Mmm."

Mrs. Wagner leaned against the table, her arms folded over her middle. "What are you going to tell Mr. Kipler? Your husband's sick? Ran away? Dead?"

Merrie stared out at the driveway, picturing her aunt's carriage awaiting them in two more hours. She shook her head.

"None of those things."

Merrie removed her brown-and-black-striped carriage dress from her wardrobe—the same dress she'd worn when Colin accompanied her to meet Mr. Kipler. After slipping the garment over her hoops, she fastened the jet buttons on the bodice and then opened a hatbox and withdrew a plain black straw bonnet trimmed with a single velvet feather. For what she planned to do, she didn't want to look frilly or overly feminine.

Aunt Isabella stood in the doorway, watching while she pinned her hat over her coiled braids.

"You'd look prettier if you pulled a few curls loose." Her eyes twinkled. "Maybe you can charm him into listening to you."

"After he hears what I have to say, I doubt he'll find me charming." She followed her aunt out to the carriage entrance, where Mr. Peters waited with the brougham.

They sat in silence during the ride to town. Merrie kept her gloved hands folded in her lap, postponing until the last minute telling her aunt that she intended to meet Mr. Kipler alone.

When the carriage turned onto Dearborn Street, she saw the

four-story Orion Hotel with its columned entryway on her right. Although it was past sunset, streetlamps illuminated Mr. Kipler's stocky frame and ginger-colored beard as he waited outside the double doors.

Merrie's insides turned to jelly.

Her aunt took her hand. "Is that the man?" She pointed at the editor.

"Yes." Her voice squeaked.

"He doesn't look so fearsome."

The carriage jounced as Mr. Peters descended from the driver's perch. When he opened the passenger door, Merrie slid forward to take his hand.

"I should go first," Aunt Isabella said. "I want to tell your editor a thing or two about his policies. Women should have the same rights as men when it comes to writing for his magazine."

Merrie leaned toward the door, blocking her aunt's way. "I'm going by myself. Please wait with the carriage." She scrambled to the paved walk and hurried to Mr. Kipler's side.

"Merrie, come back here!"

Ignoring Aunt Isabella's command, she slipped her hand under the startled man's elbow, then tugged him past the doorman and into the crowded lobby.

THIRTEEN

Knowing she might have but a few moments before her aunt caught up with her, Merrie forged past the groups of well-dressed patrons toward one of the alcoves along the sides of the high-ceilinged lobby. Her grip on Mr. Kipler's elbow remained firm. Years of living in hotels with her parents gave her confidence that she was leading him to an area where they could talk without interruption.

"Mrs. Bentley. This is most irregular. I told your husband I'd be waiting at the door. He'll never find me in here." He waved his hand to encompass the plush sitting area where she'd paused.

Her heart thudded. She glanced over her shoulder to be sure her aunt wasn't following. When she didn't spot a round woman dressed in black silk, she released her hold on the editor's arm. Digging into her reticule, she withdrew his most recent letter and handed the missive to him.

After scanning the words, he frowned at her. "This is addressed to your husband. He's the person I invited to dine with me tonight."

"You offered a weekly column with the magazine, isn't that correct?" Merrie held her breath.

"Of course."

"And you're happy about the reception the articles have received?"

He assumed a haughty expression. "Yes! Now if you'll excuse me, I'll return to the entrance and hope I haven't missed your husband's arrival."

She reached into her reticule again and passed him a handful of pages. "Please look these over."

With the air of one indulging a child, he unfolded the papers and read the top sheet, then turned to the next page. His eyes flicked from side to side as he read her latest article. After a moment, he met her gaze. "Fine work. Your husband has a way of reaching out to the ladies. I'll be happy to take this with me and save him the trouble of using the post."

She clenched her fingers together and summoned all the courage she possessed. With her chin high, she said, "I don't have a husband."

"Nonsense. I met him in July." A flicker of worry crossed his face. "Are you . . . quite all right, young lady? Would you like me to summon a doctor?" He took a step toward the bustling lobby.

"Thank you, no. There's nothing wrong with me." She met his gaze without flinching. "I wrote that, Mr. Kipler. I've written everything that you've published by Mr. Bentley."

She walked to a round table that held a bouquet of silken plumes. Producing a pencil and a scrap of paper from her reticule, she wrote "Shared Gifts in a Godly Marriage" on the page, then handed the article's title to him. "Compare the handwriting, if you wish. You'll see they're identical."

He stared at her. Sounds of laughter and conversation from the lobby rolled over the silence in the alcove. After a moment, the scrap of paper fluttered to the floor.

"By thunder. Tricked by a slip of a girl." He tugged at his beard. "Why didn't you come right out and say who you were at the beginning?"

She wished she'd taken her aunt's advice to soften her appearance. If she ever needed charm, it was now.

"I didn't set out to deceive you, sir. I always sign my name 'M. M. Bentley.' When you assumed I was a man, I was afraid you wouldn't accept my work if you knew the truth." She rubbed the side of her head, heedless of the hairpins that loosened under her touch. "I'm truly sorry. I never dreamed the pretense would go this far. If you don't wish to publish any more articles on marriage from an unmarried lady, I'll understand."

A smile cracked his frozen features. "Nonsense, I—"

"Am I late, dear?" Colin dashed into the alcove, dressed in a black frock coat and gray striped trousers. A starched black cravat was tied in a fashionable bow beneath the high collar of his white shirt.

Merrie's heart threatened to stop beating. She took several steps backward and dropped onto a velvet-upholstered settee. "What are you doing in this hotel?"

"Keeping my appointment with Mr. Kipler. It was good of you to entertain him while he waited."

He'd come here. To help her.

Mr. Kipler looked thunderstruck. "Mr. . . . Bentley?" He glanced at Merrie. "But she—"

She rose, laying her hand on Colin's arm. "I told Mr. Kipler the truth. There is no Mr. Bentley." Turning, she included the editor in her gaze. "This is Mr. Thackery, sir. He's not to blame for any of this. I persuaded him to masquerade as my husband against his better judgment."

Colin slipped his arm around her waist. "I'd like to end the masquerade my way, Miss Marigold Montgomery Bentley. Would you be good enough to excuse us, Mr. Kipler?"

"Certainly." She heard the editor murmur, "Marigold Montgomery? No wonder . . ." as he slipped into the lobby.

After he left, Colin led her to the settee, then sat beside her. "You told him the truth." His eyes shone with an emotion she couldn't identify. "I'm proud of you."

"Thank you, but I confessed so I could be proud of myself."

His nearness sent tingles of warmth coursing over her. "How . . . how did you know about this meeting?"

His cheeks flushed. "I have a confession to make also. I read Mr. Kipler's letter when you left the music room on Monday." He clasped her hand in both of his. "I love you, Merrie. I couldn't let you face him alone."

Now she recognized the emotion in his eyes. Love. Colin loved her.

"In spite of our differences?" She held her breath while she waited for his answer.

"Choice outweighs convention—isn't that what you implied in your 'Foundation for a Godly Marriage' article?"

"So you paid attention." She quirked her lips in a teasing smile.

"To every word. It just took me awhile to believe you meant what you said."

"I always mean what I say."

"Then answer this." He drew her to her feet and pulled her close. "Will you be my wife?"

Nestling into his arms, she whispered, "Yes."

He lifted her chin with his thumb. "Fortissimo, please."

"Yes!"

He dipped his handsome face toward her as she lifted her lips to meet his. After a long, pulse-pounding kiss, she leaned back in his arms.

"After someone else plays the 'Wedding March' for us, will you give me more lessons?"

"For a lifetime. If you don't mind practicing in humbler surroundings."

"Humble surroundings don't matter. I love *you*. I'll be happy wherever we live." With a blissful sigh, she snuggled closer and pulled his head down for another kiss.

DEAR READER,

One of the things I like best about writing historical fiction is illustrating the contrast between women's lives today and what their expectations were in the past. For instance, early in *Dandelion Wishes*, Colin asks Merrie if she wants to be a writer, "like Mrs. Hale."

Although Merrie and Colin are fictitious characters, Sarah Josepha Hale was a real person, and a remarkable one at that. Widowed in 1822 shortly before the birth of her fifth child, Sarah was faced with the dilemma of finding a means to support herself and her family. With few options open to women, she tried millinery and writing poems before writing a novel, *Northwood*, which was quite successful in its day.

The success of her novel led to an offer to act as editor for a periodical called *Ladies Magazine,* which later became *Godey's Lady's Book.* During the time my fictitious Merrie was sending her articles to the equally fictitious *Kipler's Home Weekly,* Sarah had already been editor of *Godey's* for over twenty years.

Today we think of *Godey's* fashion prints as defining the magazine, but back in her day, Sarah used her pulpit as editor to influence civic values, literature, intellectual life, homemaking, and women's rights and responsibilities. It was as a result of Sarah's unceasing efforts that President Lincoln declared Thanksgiving a national holiday in 1863.

Interestingly enough, although Sarah continued in her career as *Godey's* editor for forty years, she encouraged her female readership to stay at home and shape their worlds through their influence as wives and mothers.

Today, with our twenty-four-hour news coverage and the bombardment of emails, tweets, and other media shouts, it's difficult to imagine a time when magazines dominated women's attention.

As you think back over Merrie's commitment to her writing, imagine yourself in her shoes. Having her words published would have made her part of a very small group of successful women.

An inspiring goal, indeed.

Sincerely yours,

ANN SHOREY

Ann Shorey has been a story collector for most of her life and has been a full-time writer for over twenty years. Her writing has appeared in *Chicken Soup for the Grandma's Soul* and in the *Cup of Comfort* series. She made her fiction debut with *The Edge of Light*, book 1 in the At Home in Beldon Grove series, which released in January 2009. The final book in the series, *The Dawn of a Dream*, released in April 2011. Her latest, the Sisters at Heart series, debuted in January 2012, with *Where Wildflowers Bloom*. The third book in that series, *Love's Sweet Beginning*, released in February 2014. She's tempted to thank Peet's coffee and Dove chocolates when she writes the acknowledgments for her books.

When she's not writing, she teaches classes on historical research, story arc, and other fiction fundamentals at regional conferences. She lives with her husband in southern Oregon.

Ann loves to hear from her readers and may be contacted through her website, www.annshorey.com, which also contains her blog, http://annshorey.blogspot.com/, or find her on Facebook at http://www.facebook.com/AnnShorey.

One Little Word

Amanda Cabot

For everyone at Revell
who was involved in turning this book from
a dream into reality—

I'm absolutely delighted to be part of
your first novella collection.

I will instruct thee and teach thee in the way which thou shalt go: I will guide thee with mine eye.

Psalm 32:8

$\mathcal{O}$NE

"What else can you do?"

Lorraine Caldwell tried not to wince. It wasn't as if she hadn't asked herself the same question dozens of times.

Though it was only an hour since breakfast, Uncle Ambrose leaned forward to take another of the frosted pastries he'd had delivered when Lorraine entered his office. "I don't want to sound cruel, my dear, but you need to be realistic. You were trained to be the wife of a wealthy man. Just because you can play the piano, paint a watercolor, or arrange a party doesn't mean you could survive on your own. No one is willing to pay for those talents." Lorraine's uncle took a bite of pastry, washing it down with a gulp of coffee before he said, "As I see it, you have no choice. You need to marry Robert Sims by the fourteenth of September unless you want your cousin to receive your inheritance."

Neither was a palatable alternative. Robert loved the thought of her parents' estate far more than he would ever love her, and Cousin Alan would only squander the Caldwell fortune. There had to be another way. The problem was, though Lorraine had thought of little else for the past few weeks, she was no closer to a solution than she'd been a year ago.

Show me the path you have prepared for me, Lord. Please. It was the same prayer she'd offered dozens of times. There'd been no answers before. There would be none today.

But less than an hour later, a maid knocked on the door to Lorraine's sitting room.

"You have a letter, Miss Lorraine."

Where was he? Lorraine stared out the window as the train screeched to a stop. The small station bearing the name Plato Falls was the correct one. Mike's letter had been clear about that. The two years without a message, wondering where he was and if he was still alive, were over. The brother she loved so dearly was alive, he was happy, and soon they'd be reunited. That was why Lorraine had been counting the hours, then the minutes until the train would reach its destination. Now the train had arrived, but he wasn't there.

The excitement that had buoyed her on the journey from New York dissipated as she descended from the train. Following Mike's instructions, she had sent him a telegram, announcing her schedule. But as the porter unloaded her trunk and set it next to her traveling bag, Lorraine scanned the platform for the tenth time. Not only was Mike not there, but no one was. With a resigned sigh, she headed for the station. Surely the attendant could arrange transportation to Lilac Hall. Her hand on the station door, Lorraine turned for one last look, and as she did, she noticed a wagon approaching from the east.

It was an ordinary wagon, the type she'd seen farmers use to transport goods to and from town. The only thing that distinguished it from those wagons was its color. This one was painted purple. Not simply purple, but lilac. That could not be a coincidence. Admittedly, it was not the kind of conveyance she had expected, but at least Mike was on his way.

Lorraine's heart soared before plummeting a second later when it became obvious that the driver was not Mike. This man's hair was darker than Mike's, and he appeared to be a few inches taller, a bit leaner than Mike. Whoever he was, this man was not her brother.

Though the driver was not her brother, there was no question that the wagon belonged to the inn where Mike was staying, for its sides proclaimed Lilac Hall in large black letters. The man climbed down, and as he did, Lorraine blinked. What kind of resort sent someone dressed like that? Instead of a tailored uniform, this man wore a paint-spattered jacket that hung loosely from surprisingly broad shoulders, and paint smears decorated one side of his pants. Instead of a cap, his brown hair was uncovered. And though gloves covered his hands, they were a mismatched pair. *Oh, Mike, what have you gotten into?*

"You must be Miss Caldwell." The driver's voice, oddly cultured for a laborer, bore a strong English accent.

"Yes, I am," she replied, her voice the cool, impersonal tone Mother had taught her to use when addressing servants. Lorraine swallowed deeply, trying to tamp back the realization that this crudely dressed man was the most handsome creature she had ever seen, with perfectly sculpted features and a face that appeared almost aristocratic. Even Robert Sims, with generations of breeding and the finest of schools behind him, didn't exude the same sense of entitlement. "I was expecting my brother."

The driver shrugged. "Mike asked me to come in his stead."

"You mean Mr. Caldwell." There were some things no lady overlooked, and impertinence was one of them.

The man appeared amused. "Mike," he said, emphasizing the name, "is busy right now. But you needn't worry, Miss Caldwell. I'm perfectly capable of driving you back to Lilac Hall."

"I'm certain you are, Mr. . . ." She let her voice trail off, inviting him to tell her his name.

"Mann, but you might as well call me Jonah. Everyone else does."

"Certainly, Jonah." Lorraine gestured toward the two satchels at her feet. "These bags and the trunk are mine."

With what seemed a mere flick, he loaded the trunk into the back of the wagon before helping Lorraine onto the seat. It wasn't the first time a man had placed his hands on her waist. It wasn't the first time a man had lifted her off the ground. But it was the first time that simple gesture had sent waves of heat rushing through her veins. Robert, the man her uncle expected her to marry, hadn't caused that flutter of excitement.

"How far is it to Lilac Hall?" Lorraine asked, trying to mask her discomfort with an ordinary question.

Jonah's look said he had noticed the flush in her cheeks. How embarrassing! "It's about a ten-minute ride. The countryside between here and there is pretty. Unfortunately, the lilacs aren't in bloom yet, but if you stay another three or four weeks, you'll see them in their glory." There was nothing exceptional about the words he'd pronounced. It was only the tone and the glance he gave her that were inappropriate. Jonah Mann was treating her as if she were an equal, when it was clear that he was a servant.

"I don't expect to be here that long." Lorraine kept her voice clipped and cool, refusing to expand her explanation. The truth was, she planned to remain in Plato Falls just long enough to convince Mike to return to New York.

Jonah's lips curved into a smile. "You might change your mind. Mike did. He saw the place, thought he'd spend a week or so, but weeks turned into months. He's been there for a year and a half now."

And no one knew. All the while Lorraine had been worrying about her brother, wondering where he was and how he was faring, he'd been only a few hours from home. "I don't understand why he'd stay at a hotel for so long." She hadn't meant to speak her thoughts, but somehow they slipped out.

"Perhaps he found what he was looking for here."

That made no sense. "Mike had everything he needed at home."

"Are you sure about that, Lorraine?"

She turned, planning to rebuke Jonah Mann for his informality, but his cocky grin told her he would slough off the reprimand as easily as he'd lifted her trunk, and so she said nothing, merely stared straight ahead, as if the scenery were fascinating. In the meantime, she would ignore this impertinent man who had obviously missed the classes that taught servants proper deportment.

It was perhaps ten minutes later when he turned off the main road onto a long, curving drive. Though the countryside had been more intriguing than she had expected, with gently rolling hills and trees that were just now leafing out, Lorraine found herself staring at the row of shrubs lining the driveway. Their heart-shaped leaves left no doubt that these were lilacs, and it took little imagination to picture them in full bloom. She inhaled deeply, wishing she could savor their fragrance. It was foolish, of course, for she would not be here when they bloomed. Instead, she'd have Jenkins purchase a bouquet at the flower market.

The road curved, then formed a Y, with a narrower lane on the left. Jonah continued on the main road, guiding the horse around a final corner. And there it was. After seeing the shabby condition of Jonah's clothing, Lorraine had expected a ramshackle building, not this magnificent Greek Revival mansion. Constructed of what appeared to be white marble, it was one of the most beautiful buildings she had ever seen. Six two-story-high ionic columns supported the massive pediment and framed the long windows that looked out onto a broad porch. It would have been beautiful in any setting, but surrounded as it was by expansive lawns and still more lilac hedges, it could only be described as glorious.

And standing on the front steps, waving his hand, was her brother. Lorraine's eyes widened as the details registered. Mike was a bit thinner than she recalled, his hair a bit longer. But what surprised her most was the fact that her normally impeccably dressed brother wore clothing that resembled her family's chef's uniform and that he had his arm around a tall blonde dressed like Lorraine's laundress. What on earth had Mike done with his inheritance that he had to work as a chef, and what was he doing with a laundress?

"Lorraine!" Her brother grabbed the woman's hand, dragging her with him as he sprinted toward the wagon. "I'm so glad you came." He reached up and pulled Lorraine from the wagon, holding her close for a second, and in that second Lorraine knew that, no matter what had brought him here, no matter what changes his absence had wrought, Mike was still her brother, the man she'd adored her whole life.

She tilted her head so she could look into his eyes and laughed. "How could you think I wouldn't come? You made sure I would when you wrote that last word, didn't you?" She had carried Mike's letter in her reticule, and even though she had memorized the few sentences, she had withdrawn it several times on the train ride, savoring the sight of his careful script.

"I hoped you would," he admitted. Slinging his arm around the blonde, he drew her to his side. "Let me introduce you to the reason I wanted you to come to Lilac Hall." His smile was radiant as he looked at the woman. "This is Betty Freeman. We're getting married tomorrow afternoon."

·‥·TWO·‥·

He hadn't expected her to be so beautiful. Jonah frowned as he unlocked the door to the building that had served as his workshop for the past year. Knowing that she was one of what some would call "the" New York Caldwells, he'd expected Lorraine to be proud and spoiled. She appeared to be both. What he had not expected was beauty, and yet the woman who bore little resemblance to Mike was breathtakingly beautiful. Jonah had never been attracted to dark brown hair and eyes the color of rich chocolate; he'd never cared for women who reached only to his chest; he'd never even wanted to make the acquaintance of a New York socialite. That's why it made no sense that he couldn't dismiss thoughts of Lorraine Caldwell.

He lit lamps as he made his way to his workbench. Picking up the block of wood, Jonah smiled. This was why he was here. The eight pieces of basswood that he'd glued and clamped were now ready for his gouge and chisel. In a few hours, he would have finished carving the last leg for the most important horse on his carousel.

His carousel! The thought turned Jonah's frown into a grin. So what if Lorraine Caldwell had looked at him as if he were dirt beneath those tiny feet. So what if she'd raised those perfectly groomed eyebrows in obvious disgust when she'd seen the paint spatters on his clothing. None of that mattered. What was important was that he was here, turning his lifelong dream into reality.

Positioning the mallet over the chisel, Jonah made the first cut. He had no reason to be thinking about Lorraine. It wasn't as if she were someone he'd see again. She'd leave as soon as Mike and Betty were wed, and then she would be out of Jonah's life. That was what he wanted. In the meantime, he hoped that Mike wouldn't regret having invited his sister. While Mike fit into Lilac Hall as smoothly as if he'd been born here, Lorraine did not.

Jonah took a step back, studying the wood before he made the next cut. He suspected few people here knew that Mike was the son of Frederick and Adelaide Caldwell, members of New York's high society who'd been killed in a carriage accident a few years earlier. Though there were times when Jonah wondered what had brought Mike to the small inn, he wouldn't ask. More than most, Jonah understood the need to escape family obligations. After all, he'd been doing exactly that for the past four years and ten months. Now only two months remained before he would return to Traywood and begin the life his ancestors had destined for him. But first, he had a carousel to finish.

Smiling as he smoothed the edge of the leg, Jonah reflected that even if he never saw America again, his painted ponies would continue to bring pleasure to Lilac Hall's visitors. His smile faded as he envisioned Lorraine Caldwell riding one of those horses. Absurd! There was no reason for his thoughts to return to Mike's little sister. She'd made her opinion of him clear. Crystal clear. In her eyes, Jonah was a servant, unworthy of her attention.

What she thought of him was of little import, although Jonah had to admit it would be amusing to see her expression if she learned that the man she found beneath contempt was actually Jonah Manderley, the future viscount of Traywood, a man who could trace his ancestors back to the time of Charlemagne. That didn't matter. What was important was that the woman with the elaborately monogrammed luggage did not ruin Mike and Betty's wedding day.

In the meantime, Jonah had a horse to finish carving. Turning his attention to the leg that was taking shape, he tried to dismiss the niggling question that lingered at the back of his consciousness. LMC. For some reason, he couldn't dismiss the memory of that monogrammed luggage. There was no doubt about the first and last initials, yet he found himself wondering what the *M* stood for. Mary, Martha, Margaret, or something else? It shouldn't matter, and yet somehow it did.

"I don't understand." Lorraine settled onto the surprisingly comfortable chair in what Mike had told her was the servants' sitting room. There were many things she didn't understand, including why Mike had made a reservation for her in the smallest of the guest rooms, when the resort was practically empty, and why he had told no one other than Betty and Jonah that she was his sister. Those questions, however, paled compared to the one that had haunted her for two years.

"Why did you leave me?"

Mike shook his head slowly, a lock of hair tumbling onto his forehead as he said, "I didn't leave you, Lorraine. I left a life I no longer wanted to live. It was bad enough when Mother and Father were alive, but after they died and Uncle Ambrose moved into the house . . ." He let his words trail off, reminding Lorraine that her brother and their uncle had been at each other's throats more often than not. Fortunately for him, Mike had already received his inheritance before the carriage accident took their parents' lives, so their uncle had no hold over him.

Impatiently, Mike brushed his hair back. "I didn't want to be part of a society that wouldn't see anything beyond the fact that

Betty's a laundress. Everyone Mother and Father considered friends would have reacted the way you did." Before Lorraine could protest, Mike continued. "Don't deny it. I saw your expression when you met her."

"I was surprised. Shocked, actually."

"Don't try to sugarcoat it. You were horrified."

Lorraine hadn't realized that her feelings had been so evident. "I'm sorry. Truly, I am." She would never willingly have hurt her brother. "I was upset by that impertinent Jonah Mann."

"Jonah's a good man. He's one of the reasons I stayed here."

Good man was not how Lorraine would have described him. Arrogant, condescending, unfairly handsome. She sighed at the realization that Jonah Mann was occupying far more of her thoughts than he deserved. "The man doesn't know his place, but let's not talk about him. I don't understand you, Mike. You could have continued working at the bank and become president one day, and you could have married any one of a dozen women."

Her brother shook his head, his blue eyes serious. "I never wanted to be a banker. From the time I was a boy, all I wanted was to be a chef. Don't you remember how I used to sneak into the kitchen and watch Cook?"

Lorraine nodded, recalling the times Mike had brought her cookies, proudly announcing that he'd helped make them but that Mother was not to know.

"I like to cook," he continued, "and I'm good at it. I really believe it's what God intended me to do, just as he intended me to marry Betty." Mike's lips curved into a smile unlike any Lorraine had seen. "Betty's ancestors may not have come over on the Mayflower, but she makes me happier than any of those society girls Mother and Father thought I should marry." There was no doubting either Mike's sincerity or the change that came over him when he spoke of the woman he planned to marry.

"I'm sorry I acted like such a snob," Lorraine said, contrition washing over her like waves over the shore at Coney Island. "You deserve to be happy, big brother."

"So do you, little sister." Mike grinned at the names they'd given each other so many years before. His smile faded as he said, "I imagine Uncle Ambrose expects you to marry Robert Sims."

Nodding, Lorraine confirmed his suspicion. "That's one of the reasons I'm here. I'm trying to figure out what I want to do with my life." Lorraine felt tears well in her eyes as she looked at her brother. "I'm not as lucky as you, Mike. I'm not sure what God intends for me. All I know is that my life has to have more purpose than marrying a man who values me only because I can pay off his family's debts. I want to be loved."

"And you should be." Mike was silent for a moment. "Maybe you need a change of scenery. Have you thought about going to England? You could track down our ancestors and see if there's any truth to Mother's story that the one named Maxwell was an aristocrat."

Lorraine knew her brother wanted to help, but that was not the solution. "It was Mother's dream that I'd marry an earl or a duke or some other title. I don't care about that."

"Then why don't you stay here? We can talk again when Betty and I return from our honeymoon."

A flicker of hope ignited deep inside Lorraine. Perhaps that was what she needed, different surroundings and time to reflect.

"All right. I'll stay."

·····ϾHREE ·····

Lorraine slipped the shawl around her shoulders. The rich burgundy and gold paisley pattern always boosted her spirits, and tonight she needed that, along with the additional warmth the soft wool would provide. Supper had been delicious, proving that Mike was right in claiming to be a good chef. He was more than that; he was a great chef. Some might consider fish chowder, freshly baked bread, and rhubarb pie simple fare, but the perfect preparation elevated them to extraordinary.

The food had been superb, the service impeccable, the dining room's décor exquisite, and yet as she was savoring Mike's culinary masterpieces, Lorraine had felt as if something were missing. Perhaps it was because there were so few guests at the resort. In addition to herself, there were only three couples, and the four parties had been seated in the four corners of the dining room. While the arrangement provided privacy, eliminating the chance of overhearing other guests' conversation, to Lorraine, it seemed lonely. That feeling of isolation continued when the meal ended. Mike had invited her to spend the evening with him and Betty, but Lorraine hadn't wanted to intrude. That was why she had wrapped the shawl around herself and was descending the stairs. Perhaps a little fresh air would clear her head.

The sun had set, and though a few stars twinkled through gaps in the clouds, no moon was visible. Still, the evening felt far different from nights in New York. Quieter. More peaceful, and oddly, not lonely. Though she'd been bothered by being alone in the dining room, when she stepped outside, Lorraine felt a burst of energy and found herself eager to explore the grounds of the place Mike had called home for over a year.

She already knew that the area to the right of the house contained a tennis court and a spot dedicated to croquet. Stables were hidden behind the inn. It was the building on the left, a medium-sized octagonal structure, that had caught Lorraine's attention when she'd strolled the length of the front porch before supper. Unlike the main house, the octagon boasted no marble. It was a simple wooden building, depending on its shape to draw a visitor's eye. Seven of the sides held windows, while the remaining one contained a Dutch door. Though the windows were boarded and the door closed, light seeped around the edges of each opening, telling Lorraine someone was inside.

Curious, she pushed the door open, then gasped. Though she'd thought it might be some kind of workshop, she had not expected this. More than half a dozen of the most beautiful wooden horses she'd ever seen leaned against the walls. That was astonishing enough, but it was the sight of the man at the worktable that caused Lorraine's heart to skip a beat.

"Come on in," Jonah said, his smile making her wonder whether he had recognized her confusion. When she'd seen his worn and paint-spattered clothing, she'd thought him an ordinary workman, never dreaming he was someone who could create such beauty. Lorraine had no doubt that the man holding a mallet and chisel was the one responsible for those spectacular painted ponies.

Jonah's smile broadened as her eyes moved from the finished animals to the one on his table. "You obviously realize these are part of a merry-go-round. Everyone at Lilac Hall knows what

I'm doing here, but guests aren't supposed to see the horses until they're finished and the carousel is assembled. Mr. Parker—he's the owner—agreed to that."

Jonah looked at her, as if trying to understand why she'd come to the carousel pavilion. He probably thought it was boredom, and there had been a bit of that, but it was primarily curiosity that had propelled Lorraine here.

"I'll make an exception for Mike's sister. You're welcome to stay as long as you don't touch anything."

That was generous of him, especially considering the way she'd treated him earlier. Lorraine gestured toward the horses. "I owe you an apology. I had no idea that's what you painted."

"And carved." Jonah held up a piece of wood obviously meant to be a leg, and as he did, Lorraine noticed how long and slender his fingers were, and how scarred. It appeared that carousel carving was more dangerous than she'd realized.

"This is incredible."

Jonah shrugged, as if what he'd accomplished was trivial. "They're supposed to be fantastic. You know that if you've seen a carousel before."

"I have. Mike and I rode one every summer when our parents took us to Coney Island."

Tapping the mallet on the chisel, Jonah removed a sliver of wood from the horse's leg. "That was probably Charles Looff's carousel."

"I never heard it called by a name. I just knew it was the most wonderful thing imaginable to ride one of those horses. With their fancy paint, they looked even more beautiful than real horses."

"It must have been Looff's merry-go-round. He's the one who taught me to carve."

Lorraine walked to one of the finished horses, admiring the golden mane and the jeweled bridle. Today had been filled with surprises—first discovering that her brother was working as a chef and was about to marry a laundress, then learning that the man she had believed to be a simple handyman created such exquisite horses. "Yours are more beautiful."

Shaking his head, Jonah said, "Just different from Mr. Looff's. I've added more decoration."

Mindful of Jonah's admonition, Lorraine did not touch them, but she walked slowly around the room, admiring each horse. "Some of them are smaller than the others," she said.

Jonah looked up from his carving. "That's because they'll be part of the second row. The platform is smaller there than on the perimeter. If the inner row horses were the same size, they'd be out of proportion." His attention once more focused on the block of wood that was rapidly taking shape, Jonah continued his explanation. "This is going to be a small merry-go-round—only twelve horses—but I wanted it to have two rows. Some people like to ride together."

Lorraine wrinkled her nose at the memory of her trips to Coney Island. "Mike never wanted to ride with me."

"Why would he? You're his sister. A man wants to ride with his sweetheart."

Though she tried to picture herself mounted on a carousel horse, Robert Sims at her side, Lorraine failed. Instead, unbidden, the image of herself next to Jonah planted itself firmly in her brain. How silly!

Determined to push such foolish thoughts aside, she moved back toward the workbench. "What made you want to create carousels?" she asked. She had never known anyone with the desire, much less the ability, to design and carve such beautiful animals.

"I saw one at home."

"You mean England?" His accent was more pronounced tonight, leaving no doubt about his birthplace.

Jonah nodded. "There are none in Traywood, where I live, but I rode one in Bath and couldn't forget it. My parents thought I'd forget. Unfortunately for them, I didn't, and it became close to an obsession. Finally we all agreed I should come to America and study with a master."

Jonah's explanation raised as many questions as it answered. Father had said that once people from Europe came to the States, they rarely returned to the land of their birth, but Jonah still referred to Traywood as his home and appeared to be planning to go back. Then, too, he'd acted as if he'd needed his parents' permission to come to America. Lorraine guessed him to be a couple years older than she. Surely he no longer needed their approval.

She looked at the leg Jonah had resumed carving and imagined it painted and attached to the body she saw on a smaller table. "I can't wait to see the finished carousel."

Jonah looked up, his hazel eyes faintly amused. "You can. I promised Mr. Parker I'd have it ready by June 1, so unless you rush back to your empty life in New York, you can be here for the unveiling."

Lorraine took a deep breath, trying to control her annoyance at Jonah's words. Once again he was the presumptuous man who'd met her at the train station. "What do you know about my life in New York?"

"More than you realize." He paused to chisel a tiny piece of wood from the fetlock. When he gazed at her again, all traces of amusement were gone. "I know you'll think I'm out of line for saying this, but I will, anyway. Regardless of how you feel about the match, I hope you won't do anything to spoil Mike and Betty's wedding."

Jonah's words were still echoing through Lorraine's brain the next morning. He was wrong. She wouldn't hurt Mike. Not knowingly. But the niggling thought remained that perhaps she had already caused her brother pain by not welcoming Betty to the family. She could—and she would—make amends.

Half an hour later, Lorraine knocked on the door to the room

Betty shared with two other servants. As she entered, the other women scurried away, leaving Lorraine with the future Mrs. Michael Caldwell. Mike's bride was wearing a pale blue dress that, though obviously not new, was freshly washed and ironed, and her pale golden hair was dressed in the newly fashionable pompadour. In Lorraine's experience, brides wore fancy gowns with long trains, elaborate veils, and an ostentatious display of jewelry. Betty had none of those, and yet the sparkle in her eyes and the glow on her cheeks left no doubt that she was a bride.

"Good morning, ma'am."

Lorraine shook her head. "Please call me Lorraine. After all, we're going to be sisters by marriage."

"Thank you, ma'am . . . er . . . Lorraine." Unlike Jonah Mann, Betty would never be presumptuous. She gestured toward a chair, waiting until Lorraine was seated before she perched on the edge of a stool. Clasping her hands together, she leaned toward Lorraine. "I want you to know that I never dreamt a man like Mike would love me. He's more than I ever hoped for. Mike is the kindest, most wonderful man in the world." Betty's eyes radiated sincerity, and her lips curved in a smile as she said, "The first time I saw him, my heart pounded so hard I could hardly breathe. He still makes me feel that way."

"I'm happy for both of you." Though the words could have been perfunctory, they were not. Looking at Betty's face and hearing her declaration told Lorraine that, though their parents would have disapproved of the match, Mike and his bride-to-be shared what she longed for: a deep and abiding love. They might not have much money—and once again Lorraine wondered how Mike had spent his inheritance—but neither one seemed to mind.

Clearing her throat to dislodge the lump that had inexplicably taken residence there, Lorraine reached into her pocket and withdrew a small velvet pouch. "I hoped you might want to wear these today."

When a pair of diamond earrings spilled onto her palm, Betty gasped. "I couldn't. Those are real diamonds, aren't they?" She touched one of the stones as gingerly as if she expected it to crumble.

Lorraine nodded. "They were my grandmother's. My grandfather gave them to her as a wedding gift." Each dangling earring consisted of a trio of diamonds linked together with tiny chains. "He said that the diamonds represented her, himself, and the children they would have."

Though Lorraine had always found the explanation sweet, Betty's reaction was different. What little blood remained in her face drained. "What if I lost them?"

"That's unlikely to happen." Lorraine picked up one of the earrings and held it next to Betty's face, then turned her so she could see her reflection in the mirror. "It's your decision, Betty, but I really would like you to wear them."

"They're so pretty." Betty held up the other earring. A smile began to blossom. "I already have something new and something blue," she said. "These could finish the poem. They'd be my something borrowed and my something old."

Delighted that Betty appeared on the verge of agreeing, Lorraine smiled as she shook her head. "I'm afraid you'll have to borrow something else. I want you to keep the earrings. They're my gift to you."

Her eyes wide with astonishment, Betty protested. "I can't . . ."

"Yes, you can. I insist."

·· · $\mathcal{F}$OUR ·· ·

As she breathed in the morning air, Lorraine smiled. Though her taffeta petticoats swished as she walked, her feet made little noise on the soft grass, and the birds that twittered in the trees seemed unaffected by her presence. It was a glorious morning, a time to enjoy the sights and scents of the country, and for the first time she could recall, Lorraine felt free. Here there were no expectations, no servants waiting for her commands, no friends wanting her to make afternoon calls with them. While it was true that her hair was not as well coiffed as if Annie had arranged it, Lorraine didn't mind. Life at Lilac Hall was more relaxed than at home.

Besides, there was no one she needed to impress here. The few guests who frequented the inn were not part of the same social circle as Lorraine and her uncle. That was, she suspected, part of the reason Mike had chosen this for his home. There was little danger of anyone recognizing him and reporting back to Uncle Ambrose.

And now Mike was married. The thought continued to amaze Lorraine. The wedding had been lovely but small, attended only by the staff of Lilac Hall and Lorraine. She doubted anyone else had noticed how frequently the bride touched her ears, assuring herself that she had not lost her new earrings. Lorraine found the gesture endearing, almost as endearing as the obvious love that shone from Betty's eyes whenever she looked at Mike.

After they had cut the cake, Mike and Betty had left for their honeymoon and the staff had returned to their normal duties. Only Lorraine had had nothing to do. Following an evening meal that could not compare to Mike's, she had retired to her room, determined that she would not bother Jonah Mann again. There was no doubt that his wooden horses were beautiful, but there was also no doubt that he did not approve of her. That didn't matter, Lorraine told herself. She would simply keep her distance.

Once breakfast was complete, she set out from the house, determined that wherever she went, it would not be to the octagonal building where Jonah created those incredible painted ponies.

And so she walked, not caring that the morning mist was dampening her shoes and skirt. As she wandered among the lilac bushes, Lorraine found herself filled with an unexpected sense of anticipation. By remaining here for another month, she could see the lilacs blooming, she could ride the finished carousel, and—most of all—she could talk to Mike again. Maybe by then she would have discovered God's plan for her life.

When she had told Mr. Parker that she wanted to extend her stay until at least the beginning of June, he'd nodded as if he'd expected her request and said he hoped she'd enjoy her visit. Lorraine planned to. That was why she was exploring the grounds.

She stopped, frowning when she recognized the building directly in front of her. Somehow her feet had carried her to the carousel workshop, even though that was the last place she wanted to be. She'd turn around. Of course she would. Instead, her hand rose and knocked on the door.

"C'mon in, Lorraine." Jonah's voice was warm, his smile welcoming. Perhaps it wasn't a mistake to have come, for this Jonah bore no resemblance to either the arrogant man who'd spoken of her empty life or the one who'd kept his eyes fixed on her throughout Mike and Betty's wedding ceremony, as if he'd expected Lorraine to disrupt it. This man was charming.

He looked up from the wooden leg he was sanding. "I had hoped to see you."

He had? Lorraine blinked in surprise as Jonah continued. "I wanted to tell you it was a nice gesture, giving Betty those earrings. It's all anybody could talk about at supper last night." He chuckled. "That helped take our minds off the fact that with Mike on his honeymoon, Cheryl's stretched so thin that our meals are pretty basic. She seems to think that porridge is a good supper."

Lorraine had never eaten porridge for supper, but that wasn't what caught her attention. It was one of Jonah's words. "The earrings weren't meant to be a gesture," she told him, her voice sharper than she'd intended. Though she couldn't explain it, something about this man set her on edge. If another man had pronounced the same words, she would have ignored them, but Jonah made her want to respond, to ensure that he understood. "I don't know Betty very well, but what I do know tells me she'll make Mike happy. I wanted to thank her for that and welcome her to the family." It was the same explanation she'd given Mike when he'd commented on the earrings.

Jonah ran his hand along the wood, nodding as he said, "Whatever the reason, you made Betty happy. To quote Corneille, 'The manner of giving is worth more than the gift.'"

The man was filled with surprises today. First he'd welcomed her, and now this. "You've read Corneille?"

Jonah shrugged as if it were of little import and picked up a different piece of sandpaper. "*Le Menteur* isn't my favorite of his plays, but I've seen it performed."

He'd seen a French play. Interesting.

"What brings you here today?" he asked. "Boredom?"

Lorraine wouldn't admit that she had had no intention of visiting him again, not now when she was discovering new facets to Jonah Mann, discoveries that made her realize it might be pleasant to spend more time with him. "Your horses are irresistible."

"And I'm not." He made it a statement rather than a question.

"You're intriguing," she acknowledged. "You appear to be a common craftsman, but your accent is cultured, and you're obviously well-educated."

"I've been fortunate," he said. "I've had a variety of experiences and have been able to visit a number of places." His right hand moved slowly along the carved leg, sanding the wood until it appeared as smooth as silk. When he reached the bottom of the hoof, Jonah looked up again. "If you had to pick a favorite place anywhere in the world, what would it be?"

"That's easy. Battery Park." Lorraine felt her lips curve in a smile. "I never tire of looking at the Statue of Liberty. When the arm and torch were displayed at Madison Square Park years before the statue was finished, I used to go there every week."

"A pilgrimage?"

She shrugged as she touched the leg he'd laid down on the table. It was as smooth as she'd expected. "I never thought of it that way. I was simply fascinated with the idea of the statue. Now when I look at it, I try to imagine how it appears to immigrants."

"I can't speak for everyone, but for me, it was a symbol of hope, of freedom, and of second chances."

Lorraine wondered whether Jonah had been running away from something in England and that was the reason he sought a second chance. She didn't know him well enough to pose such a question. Instead, she asked, "What's your favorite spot?"

"Chester." Jonah picked up another piece of wood and reached for a chisel and gouge. "You may not have heard of it, but it still has its original Roman wall circling the town. When I walk on it, I imagine what life was like when it was built."

"They didn't have carousels, did they?"

He shook his head.

"Then I wouldn't have wanted to live then." Lorraine walked to the unpainted horse's head on the table behind Jonah. "This one seems more elaborate than the others." There were flowers entwined in its mane, and the mane itself was longer and more detailed than the finished horses'.

"That's because it's for the lead horse," Jonah explained. "If you study a carousel, you'll see that one horse is usually fancier than the others. Carvers use that one to showcase their best work, and operators use it to count the number of revolutions so that all the rides are the same length."

Lorraine had never noticed the lead horse and wondered what else she had missed when she'd ridden the merry-go-round at Coney Island. "Do you sign your horses the way an artist does a painting?"

"Not often, but you might find a carver's initials almost hidden in some decoration on the lead horse."

The way Jonah spoke made Lorraine think he intended to do that, and so she asked him.

"Probably," he agreed, "but not on the romance side."

"The romance side?" It was a morning for learning new terms.

"That's what we call the side of the horse that faces the edge of the platform. It's more elaborate than the inside. Look." Jonah moved to one of the completed horses. Touching its right side, he said, "Notice how all the details are carved. If you look at the other side, you'll see that many are painted."

Lorraine watched as Jonah pulled the horse toward him so she could view the other side. Though the mane and saddle were carved, the flowers were painted rather than being carved. "It makes sense, since fewer people will see it."

"It also saves a lot of time. Sometimes we let apprentices do the painting. That's why that side is called the apprentice side."

Lorraine felt a surge of excitement. This wasn't the answer for the rest of her life, but it might be something to do while she waited for Mike's return. "I could paint it. I'm fairly competent with watercolors."

Though she had thought Jonah would welcome the assistance, he wrinkled his nose. "Oil's not the same."

"I could learn." The more she thought about it, the more Lorraine liked the idea of working on the carousel.

"Maybe, maybe not." Jonah picked up the mallet and chisel and returned to shaping the horse's leg. "Skill is important, but I'm also worried about what I'd do if you got bored and left me with a half-finished horse. The apprentice side isn't as important as the romance, but it still needs to be done properly, and that means being painted by one person."

"I could do it. I *would* do it."

Without raising his eyes from his carving, Jonah dashed her hopes. "I'm sorry, Lorraine, but I've seen your type before."

The pungent smell of sawdust filled the air, but Lorraine ignored it, focusing on the man whose moods seemed almost mercurial. "What type would that be?" she demanded, her voice tight with anger.

"Dilettantes. You start things, but you don't always follow through." Jonah laid the mallet down for a second and met Lorraine's gaze. "I don't mean that as a criticism. It's a simple observation. You were raised to be an ornament. I doubt you've done a useful thing in your whole life."

Lorraine stared at him for a long moment, trying to bite back the frustration that bubbled inside her. "You're a snob, Jonah Mann," she said at last. "For some reason, you think anyone who's born to privilege is useless. You're wrong."

"Am I? Then prove it."

"Are you certain you want to do this?" Mr. Parker ran a hand through his graying blond hair. When she'd left the carousel pavilion, Lorraine had returned to the lilac hedge, determined to get her temper under control, and as she'd walked, she had devised a plan. All it needed was the innkeeper's approval.

"Yes, I'm certain," she insisted. "I want to be useful." *And prove Jonah wrong.* "I know you're short-handed with Mike and Betty gone. I'd like to take over Mike's responsibilities." Jonah obviously respected Mike. If Lorraine demonstrated that she was able to prepare a meal, he would be forced to admit that he'd been wrong in calling her an ornament. An ornament! The mere word made her fume.

The owner of Lilac Hall gave Lorraine an appraising look. "Pardon my asking, Miss Caldwell, but do you have any experience as a chef?"

She wouldn't lie. "No, but I've watched our cook." Admittedly not as often as Mike had, and she'd never actually assisted Cook, but surely it wouldn't be difficult to prepare a simple meal. "Besides, Cheryl will be there if I need help."

Mr. Parker was silent for a moment. "It's true that there's too much work for Cheryl. All right, Miss Caldwell. You may help her prepare the servants' meals."

"Thank you, Mr. Parker. You won't regret this."

Three hours later, Lorraine wasn't as confident. She had burned her hand putting the roast into the oven. She'd proven inept at separating eggs. Now her arms ached from kneading bread. It would improve, though. Once she got the bread into the oven, all that was left was to peel the potatoes and make the pudding.

"Why did you want to do this?" Cheryl had been less than enthusiastic when Lorraine had appeared in the kitchen. Now the dark-haired woman whom Lorraine guessed to be in her mid-thirties looked frazzled, as if Lorraine's presence was hindering rather than helping. "There's no need to cook all this food. I was planning to make hash with leftovers from the guests' dinner."

But hash would be almost as bad as porridge. Lorraine was determined to serve a real meal. "I wanted to prove that I could do it."

Her face stern with disapproval, Cheryl looked at the pile of potatoes in front of Lorraine. "What you're proving right now is that you've never before peeled potatoes."

"What do you mean?" Though it was true, Lorraine saw no need to admit that. "I got the peelings off."

"Along with half the potato. Peelings are supposed to be thin." With a resigned sigh, Cheryl took the knife and potato from Lorraine and demonstrated the technique. It was true that far less potato clung to Cheryl's peeling.

Lorraine picked up another potato and attempted to emulate Cheryl but succeeded only in nicking her hand. "Ouch!"

"Why don't you give up?"

"Never! I've got to prove that I can do this. I will not fail."

But when she served the meal, Lorraine knew she had failed. The roast was overcooked and dry, the bread tough, the pudding too sweet. Only the mashed potatoes were edible; unfortunately, there were too few of them to satisfy the staff's appetites.

"I am truly sorry, Mr. Parker." Lorraine blinked back tears of frustration as she told the owner of her attempts. "I did my best, but it wasn't good enough. Tomorrow will be better."

The tall, thin man shook his head. "I too am sorry, Miss Caldwell, but there will be no second chances. No matter how much I owe your brother, you cannot go back to the kitchen."

Lorraine dashed an errant tear from her cheek. It was bad enough that she'd failed, but to have failed so spectacularly was humiliating. Trying not to think of the disaster she'd called supper, she focused on one of Mr. Parker's phrases. "What do you owe Mike?"

The innkeeper didn't bother to hide his surprise. "You mean he didn't tell you?"

"Tell me what?" This was beginning to feel like a riddle.

"Lilac Hall was barely surviving when Mike arrived. I knew it was only a matter of months before I'd have to close it, but he convinced me that if we made some improvements and added fancy meals, we'd be able to attract more guests. He was right."

That sounded like Mike. He was always giving advice, and that advice was often valuable. "So Mike's cooking changed things."

The innkeeper's lips curved into a lopsided smile. "That and his money. Your brother poured his inheritance into this place. He's part owner of Lilac Hall."

····· ꟻIVE ·····

Would you like to take a walk?" Though he doubted she
would admit it, Jonah suspected that Lorraine needed
a break after the mess she'd made of supper. He wasn't surprised
by the abysmal meal, but some of the comments had been cruel.
His co-workers might not have realized it, since she hadn't eaten
with them, but when the door had swung open, he'd seen Lorraine in the kitchen. She had undoubtedly overheard Sam declaring that even day-old porridge was better than what they'd been
served and Cheryl announcing that Lorraine couldn't possibly
be Mike's sister.

Jonah had stopped them before they could say anything more,
but the damage had been done. He could tell that from the slump
of Lorraine's shoulders as she sat on the porch, slowly rocking.

She looked up, a slightly bemused expression on her face. "I
thought you worked every evening." The tremor in her voice confirmed her distress.

"I can make an exception."

Straightening her shoulders, Lorraine was once more the perfectly poised woman he'd seen the day she arrived. "If you came
to gloat," she said, her tone as smooth as Lilac Hall's pond on a
calm day, "you're premature. It's true that I failed at cooking, but

I'm not done." Though her voice no longer betrayed agitation, Lorraine began to rock more quickly, wincing when she gripped the chair arms. She might deny it, but it appeared that more than Lorraine's pride had been hurt.

If there was anything Jonah hated, it was to witness another person's pain. He crouched at Lorraine's side. "Let me see your hands."

But she didn't move them. Instead, her eyes widened, making him wonder whether she was more surprised that he'd noticed her distress or that he wanted to do something about it. "Why?" she asked.

"Because you've obviously injured yourself." When Lorraine refused to remove her hands from the chair arms, Jonah peeled the right one from the wood and turned it over. No wonder she had winced. Two fingers bore large blisters, while a third had a newly formed scab from what appeared to be a knife cut. "Those must hurt."

She shrugged one shoulder. "I'm sure Mike had the same problems when he started."

"Maybe so, but there's no reason to suffer. Cold water will help those hands, and I know just where to get that."

He rose, extending his hand to help her out of the chair. This time she did not resist. When Lorraine was standing, Jonah crooked his arm and placed her hand on it, then descended the four steps to the ground.

"The kitchen is the opposite direction," she said as he led the way past the house.

"I know, but we're not going to the kitchen." There was no need to remind her of her failure by returning to the place it had occurred. "Where we're going is better."

"Is it far?" Lorraine's voice was stronger now, the tremor gone. "I hate to sound like Cinderella at the ball, but I can't stay out too long. I have a busy day tomorrow."

"What will you be doing?" Not cooking, he hoped. The staff didn't need another meal like tonight's.

"Laundry."

Despite himself, Jonah was impressed. Lorraine was far more determined than he'd expected. But laundry? He winced as he pictured a woman with blistered and cut hands washing clothes. "Are you sure you want to do that?"

Lorraine's nod was vigorous. "I may not be able to take Mike's place, but I can do what Betty did."

Nothing would be gained by pointing out that Betty was a larger, more muscular woman than Lorraine, and so Jonah said only, "No one expects you to take Betty's place."

Lorraine stopped and looked up at him, her eyes filled with something that appeared to be amusement. "Not even you? If that's true, what did you mean when you told me to prove that I wasn't a useless ornament?"

Regret washed over Jonah at the realization that he was at least partially to blame for her blisters. "I'm sorry, Lorraine. I didn't expect you to take that seriously. The truth is, I wasn't being completely honest with you. When you asked to help paint the horses, I needed an excuse, and that was the first one that came to mind."

"An excuse for what? I assure you, my painting skills are far superior to my cooking."

Jonah smiled at her feigned indignation. "I don't doubt that. The problem is, I don't want anyone else to work on the horses. I want them to be a hundred percent mine."

"Even if it means working eighteen hours a day?"

"That sounds a little foolish, doesn't it?" They'd passed the end of the mowed lawn and were now following a path between two rows of lilacs. In less than a minute, they would reach their destination. "This carousel is my only chance." And that was something Jonah didn't want to think about, much less discuss. Instead, he pointed toward the pond in the center of the clearing. "Now, isn't this better than a bucket?"

"It's prettier," Lorraine admitted.

It was indeed. That was one of the reasons he'd brought her here, wanting to share one of his favorite parts of Lilac Hall with her. The sight of the moon and stars reflecting on the smooth surface of the water never failed to bring him peace. He hoped it would have the same effect on Lorraine. But he wouldn't say that. Instead, Jonah kept his voice matter-of-fact as he said, "The pond is cool at this time of the year. You can soak your hands in it."

They must have hurt more than she wanted to admit, for Lorraine did not protest. She knelt at the side of the water and leaned forward to submerge one hand. "Cool?" she sputtered as she yanked it out. "This is frigid."

Jonah sat on the ground next to her, hoping to encourage her to remain. "It will soothe your burns."

"Only because my hands will turn to blocks of ice and I won't be able to feel the blisters."

He noticed that although she complained, Lorraine dipped both hands into the water. "Think about something else," he advised.

She turned to look at him. "You said this was your only chance to carve a carousel. Why?"

Why had she chosen one of the subjects he did not want to discuss? Jonah took a deep breath, exhaling slowly. "I have responsibilities in England," he told her, hoping she wouldn't ask for details of those responsibilities. One of the things he'd decided when he came to America was that no one would know his true identity. He had heard that some Americans were enamored of titles, practically fawning over anyone who possessed one, while others held them in contempt. Jonah had no time for either group. He was here to learn to carve, and he wanted nothing to interfere with that.

Lorraine's expression said she was waiting for the rest of his explanation. "I've been fortunate. I've had five years to experience my dream. Now those five years are almost over."

"What will you do when you return to England?"

"Start to take over the family business."

"And that is . . ." She let her voice trail off, expecting him to complete the sentence.

Jonah chose his words carefully. "Taking care of the land." And all the people who lived on it.

Lorraine pulled her hands from the water, shaking them as if to restore the feeling. "Will that make you happier than carving horses?"

Jonah shook his head. "It doesn't matter. It's what I have to do."

Lorraine wrung out the last of the towels, placing it in the larger of the two tubs that Alice had shown her. This was the final step, soaking the linens in bluing to make them appear a brighter white. It was fortunate that laundry required less concentration than cooking, because Lorraine found her mind whirling, alternating between what she'd learned about Mike and the conversation she and Jonah had shared last night.

Though at first she'd been surprised to discover that Mike was an owner of Lilac Hall, the more Lorraine thought about it, the happier it made her. It might not be the life their parents would have chosen for their son, but at least he was living his dream. And, unlike Jonah, that wasn't temporary.

After listening to Jonah, Lorraine had realized that her seeming inability to find a purpose for her life might be a blessing in disguise. How much worse it must be for him, having discovered the thing that brought him joy and being forced to turn his back on it.

She pulled a towel from the tub and squeezed it as dry as she could, trying to ignore the pain from her blisters. There were times when she questioned her parents' decisions, especially when she thought about the terms of their will, but never had she doubted their love. Jonah's family seemed different. Perhaps it was unfair to judge them without knowing all the facts, but even though many farmers developed a deep attachment to the land and sought to pass it on to their children, it seemed cruel for Jonah's parents to insist he return to England when he'd found happiness here.

Laying the towel in the basket, Lorraine repeated the squeezing process until they were all done. Once she'd hung everything on the line, she would begin her next task: ironing pillowcases.

Five minutes later, Lorraine spread the first pillowcase on the ironing board, then pulled the flatiron from the stove and laid it on the linen. There was no question about it: laundry was easier than cooking. It was true that her hands were chapped from being in so much hot water and that her blisters hurt while she was wringing towels, but aside from that discomfort, this was something she could do.

"What happened to all the starch?"

Lorraine swiveled her head to look at Alice, the head laundress. "What do you mean?"

"There was a whole tub of it. Now it's half gone."

"But I didn't starch anything." Perturbed by the problem, Lorraine hurried to the other side of the laundry room, where Alice was pointing at the two tubs she'd filled earlier that morning. The one that was still full had a distinctly blue cast to it. The half empty one did not.

Oh, no! "I must have soaked the towels in the wrong one."

Alice fisted her hands on her hips, her expression leaving no doubt of her opinion of Lorraine's action. "Cheryl was right. You're more trouble than you're worth. Starched towels." She snorted in indignation. "They'll have to be washed again. Get them off . . ." Alice stopped in midsentence and sniffed. "What's that?"

As the odor of scorched linen reached Lorraine, she raced toward the ironing board and grabbed the flatiron. It was too late. The pillowcase was ruined.

Lorraine tried not to sigh. It wasn't even midmorning, and her career as a laundress had ended.

SIX

Half an hour later as she descended the stairs from her room, Lorraine knew there was no reason to ask Mr. Parker if she could try something else. No matter how much he owed Mike, the innkeeper could not afford to have her disrupt his operation again. Jonah was right. At least as far as Lilac Hall was concerned, she was a useless ornament. The thought was more painful than her blisters. Perhaps she had been spoiled. Perhaps it was only because she had attempted easier tasks in the past, but Lorraine was not accustomed to failure. And fail she had. Twice. When Mike returned, she would have nothing to tell him other than that she had tried and failed.

In the meantime, she had almost four weeks with nothing to do. She'd picked up the book that had seemed so fascinating when she'd started reading it on the train. Today she found herself unable to concentrate on the story. With nothing else to do in her room, she had headed downstairs. Perhaps there would be someone to talk to. But the rooms where guests normally gathered were empty.

As Lorraine wandered through the parlor, she remembered a piano practically hidden by a large potted palm. She slid onto the bench and opened the fall board, equally thankful that there was no one to care if she played and that her instructors had insisted she memorize her favorite pieces, for she'd found no music inside the bench. Seconds later, as she struck the first notes of Chopin's "Raindrop" prelude, Lorraine felt her spirits lighten. Congreve was right when he wrote, "Musick has Charms to soothe a savage Breast, / To soften Rocks, or bend a knotted Oak." Though she would not have described herself as savage, Lorraine found herself smiling by the time the last chords had died, signaling the end of the rainstorm.

"Bravo, my dear." Soft applause accompanied the words.

Lorraine turned, startled by the realization that she had not been alone. If she'd known she had an audience, she might have muted her playing. As it was, when she'd reached the thunderous chords that Chopin used to depict the height of the storm, she'd poured every ounce of her frustration into them, releasing her emotions as her fingers pounded the keys. And Mrs. Ferguson had heard her. Lorraine had been introduced to the heavyset gray-haired woman when she and her husband had arrived at the inn the previous day.

"That is just what this place needs," Mrs. Ferguson continued, "a little music."

Lorraine rose and took the few steps needed to reach the other guest's side. "Thank you, Mrs. Ferguson. I didn't know anyone was listening. Most people spend their mornings outside."

Mrs. Ferguson perched on the edge of a long padded bench, gesturing to the seat next to her. "It's a bit vexing. I thought I was going to enjoy it here, but the other guests don't appear too friendly, and there's not a lot to do. Harold doesn't want to play croquet, and we don't know how to play tennis."

"Would you like to learn?" Though she hadn't brought a racquet, Lorraine suspected Mr. Parker had a supply for the guests.

Mrs. Ferguson shook her head. "I don't think so, my dear. Harold and I came here to rest."

Only now she was bored, just as Lorraine had been. As a glimmer of an idea planted itself in her mind, Lorraine began to smile.

Mrs. Ferguson was the answer to her prayer. No wonder she'd been frustrated. She'd been traveling the wrong path, trying to put herself in first Mike's, then Betty's role, when all the while she should have been finding her own. She had been measuring herself against Mike and Betty and even Jonah, when she should have been using the talents God had given her, the ones that made her unique.

Lorraine might not be able to cook or to do laundry, but she could play the piano. More than that, she could bring the guests together. It was one of the talents that even Uncle Ambrose recognized, admitting that Lorraine was skilled at organizing both people and events.

Mike had brought new ideas to Lilac Hall, infusing it with more than money. Though Lorraine could not offer her inheritance, there were things she could do to make Mike's dream even better and, in doing that, perhaps make a place for herself. It might not be a permanent role—Lorraine wasn't certain she wanted to live here year-round, and she still needed to find a way to keep Cousin Alan from squandering her inheritance—but while she was here, she could provide activities that would make guests' holidays at Lilac Hall memorable.

"Do you play bridge, Mrs. Ferguson?"

The older woman's blue eyes sparkled with enthusiasm. "Yes. I love it. Why?"

Resolving to see if she could interest the other wives in an occasional game of bridge, Lorraine countered Mrs. Ferguson's question with another of her own. "Do you and your husband like to hike?"

"Oh, no, dear. That sounds awfully strenuous."

No hiking. At least not unless the other guests expressed a desire for it.

Mrs. Ferguson frowned. "Of course, Harold and I do walk around the arboretum at home. We enjoy seeing the different trees and plants there."

Not hikes, but guided walks. Those would be simpler to arrange and might appeal to guests of all ages and physical abilities. "There are many different trees here too," Lorraine said as she made another mental note. Though lilacs predominated close to the buildings, there were woods on all sides, and she had spotted at least a dozen different varieties of shrubs.

"Mr. Parker didn't mention that."

"There's also a pond that's big enough for rowboats."

Mrs. Ferguson's voice was wistful as she said, "I haven't been in a rowboat since I was a child."

"If I can find one, you and Harold can go for a row this afternoon. Would you like that?"

The older woman's smile was all the answer Lorraine needed. "We'll talk more at noon," Lorraine promised.

She had a plan. Now came the hard part: convincing Mr. Parker.

SEVEN

Mr. Parker wasn't there. Claudia, the head housekeeper, reported that he had gone to town for some sort of meeting and wouldn't be back until late afternoon. That was disappointing, but even worse for the proposed boating excursion, rain had begun soon after Lorraine's conversation with Mrs. Ferguson. Though she did not claim to be an expert on weather, Lorraine knew that the heavy, leaden sky meant the soaking rain would not subside anytime soon. The other guests appeared to share her gloomy forecast. As they assembled for the midday meal, they were grumpier than her cat had been the day Mike decided Muffin needed a bath.

Three other couples had arrived at the inn the day before, along with the Fergusons, bringing the total number of guests to fifteen. Right now, the majority of those guests appeared disgruntled. Though Lorraine greeted each of them as they entered the dining room, the replies were perfunctory at best.

Only Mrs. Ferguson wore a smile as she and her husband passed through the arched doorway. "I told Harold about the pond, and he said he'd take me boating." She gave her husband a look that proclaimed him her knight in shining armor. "All we need is a boat. Did you find one?"

Lorraine had not. Despite the rain, she had ventured to the work shed, hoping to uncover at least one rowboat there. Unfortunately, the shed held nothing more than lawn chairs, croquet mallets and balls, and assorted pieces of tennis gear. She had even searched the stables but had found no signs of a boat.

"We can't go out in this weather, anyway." Mrs. Ferguson tried to sound philosophical, though her expression mirrored disappointment. "It doesn't matter."

But it did matter. Guests traveled to a resort, expecting to have fun, not to sit around with nothing to do. "Rainy days are the worst," Lorraine said.

Though she had been thinking about outdoor activities for the guests, their reaction to the dismal weather made Lorraine realize that she should not delay in finding something for them to do indoors. Her mind began to whirl with possibilities. While it might be best to wait until Mr. Parker returned and she had his permission, Lorraine hated the thought of the guests wasting the afternoon, especially since so many of them were new arrivals. If Mike were here, he could compensate for the inclement weather by serving a special meal, but Mike was not here. What could she do?

"I hated rainy days, especially when I was a child." Mrs. Ferguson clutched her husband's arm as she spoke. "There was nothing to do."

"You must have been an only child. My brother and I used to drive our mother crazy, chasing each other around the house." Lorraine chuckled at the memory. Mike had never been one for sitting still, and rain had brought out his most mischievous side. It was the recollection of some of his antics that had given her ideas of activities to entertain the guests.

"A chase sounds like fun, but I'm afraid Harold and I are a bit too old for that."

Lorraine shook her head. "Maybe, maybe not. But you're definitely not too old for what I have planned."

"And what is that?" Mr. Ferguson spoke for the first time.

Lorraine smiled. "You'll have to wait."

She waited until the meal was served before she spoke. "Good afternoon," she said, hoping her voice would not betray her nervousness. Though Lorraine had played hostess dozens of times, it had always been in her own home, not in a public place with virtual strangers. There was no way of predicting how they'd react to her plan.

"I'm sure you've all noticed that the clouds are weeping. Days like this make me want to weep too." Lorraine felt a rush of pleasure when the guests laughed as she feigned wiping tears from her eyes. "I want to prove that rainy days don't have to be boring, so I hope you'll all join me in the parlor at two for an afternoon of fun and games."

There was a second of silence. As she'd feared, her invitation had surprised them. Then one man spoke up. "What kind of games?"

Lorraine shook her head slowly. "Now, sir, you must know that a lady never reveals her secrets. You'll simply have to come to the parlor to learn what's in store for you." The man grunted and murmured something to his wife.

Lorraine forced herself to eat the food Cheryl had prepared, though afterward, she could not recall what dishes had been placed in front of her. All through the meal and the hour between it and the designated rendezvous time she had wondered how many—if any—of the guests would come. To her delight, every one of them appeared in the parlor before the long clock chimed two. It seemed that curiosity was a powerful tool.

Unfortunately, that curiosity did not extend to each other. Lorraine was not surprised when each of the couples remained apart from the others. The lack of mingling was the first item she planned to address.

"I'm so glad you're here." That was an understatement, but she'd never admit how she'd worried that her latest idea would fail, just as her attempts at cooking and laundry had. "I have a number of things planned for us this afternoon, but first we need to get to know each other." Lorraine let her eyes move slowly around the room, acknowledging each of the guests. "Even though we've all been introduced, I doubt we know much more than everyone's names. Let's change that. I'm going to ask each of you to present someone else to the group and tell us three things about that person. You'll tell us the person's name, what he or she is most proud of, and the funniest thing that ever happened to him or her."

"How will we find out those things?" one of the women asked.

"You'll ask your partner."

As the couples started to turn to each other, Lorraine shook her head. "That would be much too easy. I want each of you ladies to choose a man who's not her husband to be her partner for this activity."

The woman who'd spoken before let out a small gasp, and for a second, Lorraine feared she would simply leave the room. It was, after all, a highly unusual request. Perhaps she should have let the women interview other women and paired men with men, but Lorraine wanted this to be a true adventure. She kept a smile firmly fixed on her face as the women looked at their husbands, their expressions reflecting both shock and curiosity.

Finally, Mrs. Ferguson rose and approached the youngest man in the room. "Mr. Talbot, I would be honored if you would be my partner." The ice was broken.

When the pairing was complete, Mrs. Ferguson spoke again. "It doesn't seem fair that you don't have a partner, Miss Caldwell. How will we learn about you?"

"I'll be her partner." The voice boomed from the doorway.

Lorraine spun around, startled by the sight of Jonah. Gone were the paint-spattered clothes. Though a few years out of date, his dark suit fit well enough to have been hand-tailored for him. His parents' farm must be a prosperous one if he could afford such fine clothing.

244

"Why are you here?" Lorraine asked, uncertain whether she was more startled by Jonah's suit or the fact that he was not working.

"I came in for lunch, and when I heard what you were doing, I had to satisfy my curiosity."

She nodded shortly. "All right, ladies and gentlemen. You have your instructions. I'd suggest you move your chairs so you're not disturbed by the other groups." When the men had rearranged the furniture, she continued. "Let's take fifteen minutes to learn what we can about our partners—at least enough to answer those three questions."

Since all the chairs were occupied, Lorraine led Jonah to the piano bench. Though her view of the rest of the parlor was partially blocked, she could hear the low murmur as the other guests began to talk.

Jonah tipped his head to one side, as if he were seeing her for the first time. "I already know your name, so tell me what you're most proud of."

She hadn't expected to have to answer that question. Lorraine thought for a moment. "That Mike is my brother," she said at last. "He has the courage I've always lacked, and he knows what God wants him to do. I'm still finding my way."

Jonah nodded. "You're fortunate to have a brother."

"Have you no siblings?"

"No. My parents were married almost twenty years before I was born. I think they'd just about given up hope of having children. At any rate, I'm their one and only." He wrinkled his nose, making Lorraine wonder about his relationship with his family. Perhaps one of the reasons Jonah needed to return to England was to care for them as they aged. "I always wished I had a brother or sister. It would have been nice to have someone to share my parents' attention."

"Mike did more than share attention. He demanded it. I suspect it was deliberate, the way he used to test our parents' patience."

"In what way?" Jonah sounded genuinely interested.

Lorraine clasped her hands together, smiling at the thought of her brother. "Mother tried her best to instill perfect manners in both of us. She was a real stickler on saying 'please' and 'thank you' for even the simplest of things. Mike thought that was absurd and refused, but a few nights without supper convinced him of the error of his ways. Sort of. He still refused to say 'please.' Instead, he'd say '*s'il vous plaît*' or '*bitte*' or '*por favor*.' He told me that he was reserving 'please' for really important things. That's why, when I received his letter asking me to *please* come here, I knew I had to."

Jonah's smile was wide enough to brighten even the gloomiest of afternoons, and his words warmed Lorraine's heart. "I'm glad you did."

"So am I." For so many reasons: her reunion with Mike, the opportunity to meet Jonah, and the chance to make a difference here. Lorraine rose to peer over the potted palm at the guests. "Look at them. *Listen* to them. They're laughing." The sound level had risen substantially, with occasional bursts of laughter punctuating what appeared to be intense conversations. Lilac Hall's guests were strangers no more.

"I'd say your experiment was a success." Jonah flashed Lorraine another smile, this one even warmer than the previous. "Congratulations." And then, before she knew what he was doing, he raised her hand to his lips and pressed a kiss on it.

$\mathcal{E}$IGHT

I tell you, young lady, you could have knocked me over with a feather when I found every one of my guests playing charades. Not just playing, but enjoying it." A sparkle lit Mr. Parker's gray eyes. "How did you convince them?"

Lorraine felt the tension that had been building from the moment the inn's owner had asked to speak with her drain away. She'd seen him enter the parlor during one of the more exuberant rounds of charades, when Mr. Ferguson had been flapping his arms as he pretended to be a windmill. Though Mr. Parker had said nothing, his eyes had betrayed his shock. Lorraine had expected a reprimand, but it seemed the innkeeper wasn't annoyed that she'd arranged afternoon activities without his approval. To the contrary, he appeared pleased.

"It wasn't difficult," she admitted. "People may say they want to relax on their holidays, but what they really want is a different kind of entertainment than they have at home. I simply provided it."

Mr. Parker leaned back in the chair, his expression thoughtful. His eyes moved slowly, as if cataloging the contents of the small office that was sandwiched between the parlor and the servants' quarters. When his gaze returned to Lorraine, he smiled. "Do you have other ideas?"

It was the opening she had sought. "Yes, sir. I want to organize a croquet tournament. I'd also like to find a boat so guests can enjoy the pond, and I might even try to convince you to buy a few bicycles."

Mr. Parker chuckled. "You're definitely Mike's sister. He's always brimming with ideas." The chuckle turned into laughter. "Sometimes I think my only purpose is to rein in his enthusiasm. I can see I'm going to have to do the same for you." A wink took the sting from his words. "Let's wait for the bicycles, but you can have the two boats that are in the cellar. They don't leak, but they need a new coat of paint. That's why I stashed them there. I didn't want anyone finding them and taking them out on the pond looking like that."

Two boats were more than she'd hoped for. "I can paint them," Lorraine said before Mr. Parker could change his mind. With two boats, she could expand what she had envisioned as a croquet tournament into a full-fledged athletic contest. She could even add footraces and tennis games to the competition, along with a rowing contest.

"Are you certain you want to paint?" Lorraine heard the wariness in Mr. Parker's voice. "Jonah can do that."

Lorraine gave the innkeeper her most persuasive smile. Perhaps it was foolish to protest, but just as Jonah wanted to do every bit of work on the carousel horses himself, Lorraine wanted the activities program to be completely hers. "I understand your skepticism, especially after my attempts at cooking and laundry, but I really do know how to paint. Besides, Jonah is busy finishing your merry-go-round."

Mr. Parker was silent for a moment, obviously considering her argument. At last he nodded. "All right, but you need to work in the carousel pavilion. I'll ask Jonah to keep an eye on you. I can't afford any more disasters."

"Thank you, Mr. Parker." Lorraine wouldn't argue, especially since Mr. Parker's stipulation would give her a chance to spend more time with Jonah.

Jonah. Lorraine was smiling as she left the office. Thoughts of Jonah did that to her. The man was more intriguing than anyone she had ever met. Just when she thought she understood him, he did something unexpected—like kissing her hand.

Lorraine paused, glancing down at the hand that grasped the railing. It looked the same as it always did, and yet it didn't feel the same. That was Jonah's fault. Other men had kissed her hand, but none of those kisses had felt the way Jonah's did. At the time he'd raised her hand to his lips, Lorraine's heart had skipped a beat at the gallant gesture. Even now, hours later, she could feel the pressure of his lips on her fingers. She was acting like a schoolgirl, but still . . . There was no denying it. Jonah was wonderful.

She was more like Mike than he'd realized. Though he was supposed to be concentrating on painting the lead horse, Jonah found himself sneaking glances at Lorraine more and more often. His first impression that she was a dilettante had been wrong. A dilettante wouldn't be sitting on the floor scraping paint from a rowboat. But Lorraine was not a dilettante. She was a dedicated, determined, and downright attractive woman. She hadn't complained when she'd broken a fingernail and scraped her knuckles removing old paint. Instead, she kept talking about how beautiful the boats would be when they were finished.

"You're enjoying this, aren't you?" Jonah laid down his paintbrush and stared at her, liking the way her eyes sparkled and her cheeks flushed. She seemed unaware that several locks of hair had come undone and were framing her face, making her look even more beautiful than normal. Unfairly beautiful, for though he ought to be working, Jonah couldn't keep his eyes off the bouncing tresses.

"I am enjoying it," Lorraine said with a soft chuckle. "I didn't expect to like this stage," she admitted, gesturing toward the chips of paint that littered the floor around her, "but it's fun, removing the layers of ugly old paint and knowing I'll have a clean surface for my paint." She flexed her fingers, then laughed. "Sometimes I feel as if my time here has been doing that to me, getting rid of the old paint."

Jonah blinked, amazed that she would be so honest. "What color paint is coming?"

"For me or for the boats?"

"Both."

"The boats are easy. One is going to be light purple on the outside with dark purple inside. I'm going to reverse the colors on the other." Lorraine paused and tipped her head to one side, obviously considering the second half of his question. "As for me, I'm not certain. I know what my parents would have wanted for me."

"Marriage." Though he hadn't expected it, the thought bothered Jonah.

"How'd you guess?" There was the faintest hint of sarcasm in Lorraine's voice.

He shrugged, pretending that he didn't find the image of her exchanging vows with another man distasteful. "It's what most parents want for their children." He knew from what Mike had said that the elder Caldwells had died a few years ago and that they'd been pillars of society. Though it didn't have the centuries of tradition the English aristocracy did, New York society had much in common with it, including the desire for appropriate marriages.

"Mine had high expectations." Lorraine wrinkled her nose. "Mother couldn't forget that one of her ancestors was a part of the English nobility, and she wanted me to live up to that. Father wanted me to be well cared for. That's why their will stipulated that I must marry someone who might be considered the American equivalent of a peer. My uncle has even chosen a man for me." Lorraine looked down at the boat, as if the simple lines fascinated her, but the rapid blinking of her eyes told Jonah she was fighting tears.

"What happens if you don't marry him?" Perhaps he shouldn't have asked the question, but Jonah wanted—no, he needed—to know everything about the woman who'd somehow managed to fascinate him. It had been little more than a week since she'd arrived, but that week had been the most memorable of Jonah's stay at Lilac Hall.

Lorraine looked up, her eyes moist with unshed tears. "I lose my inheritance."

"I see." That would be a major problem, because a woman reared the way Lorraine had been would have difficulty finding a way to support herself.

"No, you don't." She shook her head. "If I don't fulfill the terms of the will, the rest of the estate goes to my cousin. He's turning into a wastrel, and if the rumors are accurate, he'll use the money my father worked so hard to earn to build a string of gambling saloons." Lorraine blinked the tears away. "I hate the thought of that being my parents' legacy."

Though he wanted nothing more than to draw her into his arms, Jonah did not dare, not when she was so vulnerable. He couldn't mislead her into thinking he could offer anything more than friendship. Still, there had to be something he could say to comfort her. He took a deep breath as he composed his words. "That wouldn't be your parents' legacy. It would only be their money. You and Mike are their legacy."

Lorraine bit her lips, and Jonah had the horrible feeling that she was about to cry. Instead, she looked up at him, her expression pensive. "I never thought of it that way. That makes the idea of Alan and his dissolute life a bit easier to bear, but I still wish my parents hadn't tried to control my life. Do all parents do that?"

"I don't know."

Those lovely brown eyes seemed puzzled. "Maybe it's just ours.

I don't understand why your parents are insisting you become a farmer when it's clear that you're meant to be a carousel carver, but at least they're not forcing you into an arranged marriage."

Jonah decided not to contradict Lorraine's impression that his parents were farmers. There was no reason she needed to know that he was exactly the kind of man her parents would have chosen for her. That would only be cruel, when he wasn't free to marry her and keep her odious cousin from wasting the Caldwell fortune. But, though Jonah would not tell her everything, she needed to understand that he could not resolve her problem.

"Our situations aren't as different as you might think," he said slowly. "Like yours, my parents have expectations about my future bride. It's a family tradition that the eldest son of each generation marries a very distant relative. I have my choice of three: Jessica, Julianne, and Jocelyn." Jonah didn't have to close his eyes to picture the three sisters. Their images were burned into his memory, and if their blonde, blue-eyed prettiness couldn't compare to Lorraine's darker beauty, it wasn't their fault. "They're three lovely girls."

"Do you love them?"

Leave it to Lorraine to cut to the heart of the matter. Jonah refused to give her a direct answer. "I won't disappoint my parents."

But if he could choose, his wife would be a woman like Lorraine. Oh, why mince words? If the decision were his and his alone, he wouldn't settle for someone *like* Lorraine. Why accept an imitation when the real thing was so much better? If he could, Jonah Francis Edward William Stephen Manderley would ask Lorraine whatever-her-middle-name-was Caldwell to be his wife.

NINE

I heard your brother will be back in less than three weeks." Mrs. Ferguson gripped Lorraine's arm as they walked toward the pond to prepare for the first rowboat race. As Lorraine had hoped, the guests were enthusiastic about the athletic events she'd arranged, and a friendly rivalry had developed between the two teams. The fact that they were now tied meant that the rowing contest was garnering more than its share of attention. Every one of the guests planned to be there, whether as a participant or a spectator.

Lorraine had expected that. What she hadn't expected was that Mrs. Ferguson would want to arrive as early as Lorraine, but it seemed Mrs. Ferguson wanted to discuss Mike.

Though Lorraine suspected the older woman was as steady on her feet as Lorraine, she tightened her grip and inclined her head, as if she were about to reveal a secret.

"Harold and I are going to stay an extra week so we can taste Mike's food. According to the Boltons, no one makes trout the way he does." Mrs. Ferguson chuckled. "When the Boltons were here last year, Lydia tried to convince your brother to become her private chef. He refused, but she's not one to give up. I expect she'll try again."

The Boltons had arrived at Lilac Hall two days earlier, and, as soon as she'd learned that Lorraine was Mike's sister, Mrs. Bolton had waxed eloquent about his culinary skills.

"I doubt she'll be more successful this year." Knowing how much of himself Mike had poured into Lilac Hall, Lorraine could not imagine him leaving, unless Betty was unhappy here. "I suppose it's possible, though. Marriage may have changed Mike."

"Love can do that. Harold's love brought me more happiness than I dreamt possible, and it definitely changed me. Once we were married, I turned into a matchmaker, trying to bring that same kind of happiness to all my friends." Mrs. Ferguson gave a deep sigh, her lips curving into a smile. "Seeing you and Jonah together reminds me of the first few months of Harold's and my courtship."

Courtship? The thought startled Lorraine so much that her feet refused to move. She stopped and faced the woman whose company she'd enjoyed until she'd introduced that ridiculous subject. "I'm afraid you're mistaken, Mrs. Ferguson. Jonah's not courting me."

As two birds squabbled over possession of a branch, the older woman smiled. For a second, Lorraine thought her amusement was at the birds' antics, but Mrs. Ferguson's next words proved her wrong. "Perhaps he's not courting you yet, but he will. There's no hiding the kind of love you two share." She patted Lorraine's arm. "It's heartwarming to see a couple so much in love."

The woman was mistaken. Lorraine and Jonah weren't in love. They were . . . Lorraine wasn't certain how to describe their relationship, but it was not love. Of that she was certain.

"I don't want to disappoint you, but we're not in love."

Mrs. Ferguson's smile turned into laughter. "Oh, my dear, I may need spectacles to read, but these old eyes are still sharp. I know what I see. When you're in the room, as far as Jonah is concerned, there's no one else there. His gaze follows you everywhere, and you're not much better. You look at him every chance you get."

Lorraine couldn't stop herself from blushing. "I didn't realize it was so obvious." She hoped—oh, how she hoped—that no one else had noticed. Especially Jonah. It would be horribly embarrassing if he misunderstood.

Knowing she owed the other woman an explanation, Lorraine said, "It's true that I think about Jonah a lot, but that's only because he's different from the men I know. He argues with me. He challenges me. He . . ."

"Makes you feel alive." Mrs. Ferguson completed the sentence. There was no reason to deny it. "Yes, he does."

Her smile triumphant, Mrs. Ferguson patted Lorraine's arm again. "You're in love, my dear. Trust me on this. I know a bit about love."

Lorraine closed her eyes for a second, trying to absorb the impact of Mrs. Ferguson's declaration. Had the older woman seen something Lorraine had tried to ignore? Was it possible that what Lorraine felt for Jonah was in fact love? She forced her eyes open and gazed at the path she'd first walked with Jonah. The lilac buds were larger now, a few hinting at the glorious purple blossoms that would cover them within a week or two. There were more birds than there'd been that night, and sunlight had replaced the moon's pale glow. It was the same scene, yet different. Was she the same woman, only different? Was she a woman in love? It could be true. No other man had dominated her thoughts the way Jonah did. No other man had the starring role in her dreams. And no other man had made her feel the way Jonah did, simply by smiling at her. But none of that changed the fact that they had no future.

"He'll never court me." As she pronounced the words, Lorraine realized how much she wished it weren't true.

Mrs. Ferguson raised both eyebrows, as if she doubted Lorraine. "Why ever not?"

"Because his parents expect him to marry one of his distant relatives, and I . . ." Lorraine paused, unwilling to explain about Cousin Alan. She'd had a nightmare last night, picturing grown men sobbing as they left Alan's gambling den, their fortunes gone, their futures destroyed, and when she'd wakened, she'd wondered whether she could live with herself if she allowed that to happen. She wouldn't admit all that, and so she settled for saying, "I know what my parents would have wanted me to do."

Mrs. Ferguson's lips thinned, and for the first time since Lorraine had met her, she looked stern. "It's your life, Lorraine. Don't throw away your chance at happiness."

There had to be a way to stop this. Jonah frowned as he dipped his brush into the deep purple paint to put the final touches on the lead horse's garland. He ought to be concentrating on that, not thinking about Lorraine. It was ridiculous the way he couldn't get her out of his mind, even more absurd the way everything reminded her of him. When he heard guests laughing, Jonah remembered that Lorraine was responsible for that laughter. Walking toward the pond brought back memories of the evening he'd taken her there to bathe her blistered hands. And just this morning when he'd wiped the soap from his face with a slightly stiff towel, he'd recalled her laundry fiasco and the way she'd refused to let even that defeat her.

Jonah touched the tip of the brush to the horse, creating a lilac petal. This was what he was supposed to be doing, not trying to imagine where Lorraine was, not remembering how soft her hand had been the day he'd pressed his lips to her fingers. It was bad enough that he spent his daylight hours thinking of Lorraine, but now he even dreamt about her. Last night Jonah had dreamt that he was back at Traywood. That wasn't unusual, for he often dreamt of home, but last night had been different. Lorraine had been at his side, greeting guests. In his dream, she had been his viscountess. The tenants had seemed contented, Lorraine had been radiant, he had felt at peace. And then Jonah had wakened to an immense sense of loss. He could not marry Lorraine.

Jessica, Jocelyn, and Julianne would not be heartbroken if he did not choose one of them. They'd all find other matches. But Jonah's parents would be deeply disappointed. They'd raised him with the story of Manderleys marrying Manderleys, explaining that it was more than a tradition. It was a matter of honor, an unwritten contract that had been in place for centuries. No matter what his heart wanted, Jonah could not turn his back on generations of tradition. He could not dishonor his parents and the Manderley name. Not even for Lorraine.

"Good evening, Jonah." The object of his thoughts entered the carousel pavilion, the smile on her face telling him her thoughts had been more pleasant than his own. She hurried across the room, then slowed her pace, studying each side of the horse he was painting, even bending down to examine the horseshoe on the raised front leg. "This is absolutely magnificent. I didn't think it was possible, but it's even more beautiful than I'd expected." Lorraine's words were so filled with enthusiasm that Jonah knew she wasn't simply flattering him. She tipped her head to one side and squinted, as if scrutinizing the horse. "Did you paint your initials on it?"

Jonah nodded. It might be prideful, but he had wanted to leave his mark. "I did more than that. Look closely at the lilacs." He'd carved and then painted a garland of lilacs around the horse's neck, and in the midst of them, he'd added "J Mann" in small black letters. It didn't matter that that was not his true name. Jonah Manderley, the future Viscount Traywood, hadn't carved this carousel. This was the work of Jonah Mann.

"It's perfect." Lorraine gave him a radiant smile as she said, "Everything about this carousel is perfect."

Jonah could feel himself beaming with pleasure. Though he was dreading the end of his stay in America, he was happy that he'd be leaving part of himself here. He was even happier that Lorraine was so enthusiastic about his creation.

"The parts are scheduled to arrive in two weeks. From what I've been told, it should only take a day or two to assemble them." The platform and the rods were coming from one manufacturer, the steam engine that would power the merry-go-round from another. By the end of the month, the pavilion would house a working carousel.

"I'm sorry Mike and Betty won't be here for the unveiling. They'd love those horses."

Jonah heard the wistfulness in Lorraine's voice and wondered what had caused it. Surely she didn't consider it a tragedy that Mike and Betty would miss the merry-go-round's first few days.

"They'll have plenty of opportunities to ride when they return. Mr. Parker has agreed that the carousel will be open to the public every Sunday afternoon. That'll give everyone, including Lilac Hall's staff, a chance to enjoy it." Though Lorraine appeared pleased by that, Jonah felt no need to tell her it had been the one stipulation he'd made when he'd first discussed building the carousel. He'd wanted to ensure that everyone, regardless of their station in life, could ride his painted ponies.

Lorraine glanced around the room, counting. "Will all the horses be ready in two weeks?"

Jonah tried not to frown. He was behind schedule, and he suspected that Lorraine knew it. What she didn't know was that she was the reason. He'd spent far too much time daydreaming about her when he should have been carving. "It'll be close, but I should make it." He would, even if it meant forgoing sleep. "I have one pony left to carve."

"And this one needs paint." She gestured toward the small horse leaning against the far wall.

"That's the lead horse's companion," he said. "It has the same design, only everything is smaller because it's for the second row."

Lorraine laid a hand on the unpainted horse's back, almost as if she were planning to ride it. When she spoke, her voice was hesitant. "Would you let me paint the apprentice side? I'd really like to."

Though his instinct was to refuse, to remind her that he wanted this carousel to be 100 percent his work, Jonah found himself reluctant to pronounce the words that would dash her hopes. Instead, he felt warmth well up inside him at the thought that Lorraine might have a part in creating his carousel. She'd proven she wasn't a quitter, and if her painting wasn't as skilled as his own, chances were no one else would notice.

"Please, Jonah," she said, her eyes solemn. "I won't disappoint you."

Jonah sucked in a breath as her words registered. It wasn't coincidence that she had used the one word that had such special significance to her and Mike. This was important—vitally important—to Lorraine. Jonah's last reservation evaporated. "All right," he said, keeping his eyes fixed on her, "but on one condition."

"What is that?"

"You'll paint both sides. This will be your horse."

The happiness that lit her face left Jonah no doubt that he had made the right decision. "Really?" she asked.

"Really."

···ᏟᎬN···

She'd been painting for a week now, and for a week she'd remained hidden behind the screens. When he'd realized they would be working at the same time, Jonah had draped sheets over two tall screens to keep his carving dust from ruining her paint. It was practical, though a bit frustrating, for Lorraine had insisted he not look at the horse until she finished. The truth was, though he was curious about her progress, what Jonah missed most was the sight of Lorraine. It seemed strange, hearing her voice and smelling the sweet scent of her perfume mingling with the odors of paint and turpentine, but not knowing whether she was smiling or frowning or whether a tendril of that glossy brown hair was brushing her cheek.

"This is so much fun." Lorraine's voice came from behind the screens, slightly muffled yet still easily understood. "I don't know how you can give it up."

"Perhaps I won't. Perhaps I can find time to carve at home." But even as he pronounced the words, Jonah knew they were merely a dream. Traywood demanded a lot of time and attention. That was one of the reasons he had to return. His parents were aging, and although they did not complain, he knew they needed him to assume the responsibility of running the estate.

"I hope you can." Jonah heard the wistfulness in her voice and wished there were something he could do to reassure her, but he refused to lie. Chances were good that he'd never carve another horse. He wouldn't tell Lorraine that, just as he wouldn't tell her that the carousel was no longer as important as it had once been.

A month ago, Jonah had believed that when he left America, what he'd regret most was leaving his painted ponies. Now he knew that his greatest regret would be leaving Lorraine. He'd miss their conversations, her ready smile, the comfortable silences they shared. He'd miss hearing Lorraine playing the piano and watching her put guests at ease. Why deny it? He'd miss everything about her.

"Maybe you'll come back occasionally," Lorraine said, her voice once more filled with optimism. "I've been giving it a lot of thought, and I've decided I'm going to return every summer, even if it's only for a few days. I want to ride the carousel and remember how much I enjoyed being a tiny part of creating it."

She paused, and he wondered what she was thinking.

"Maybe we could arrange to be here at the same time," she said at last.

Never! For the first time, Jonah was grateful for the screen, because it kept her from seeing his reaction. He wouldn't return. It wasn't simply that Traywood would consume his time. The thought of watching Lorraine riding his carousel with her husband made Jonah's heart ache almost unbearably. If only . . .

He heard a soft giggle and wondered what had caught Lorraine's fancy. "Are you ready?" she asked.

To see her with her husband? Of course she didn't mean that. "Ready for what?"

"To see the horse."

"You've finished?" Jonah had thought it would take her another day or two.

"Yes. The paint is still wet, but it's ready for inspection."

He laid down his tools and approached the screens. As he did, Lorraine came out. Her fingers were spattered with paint, and a smudge marred one cheek, but what drew Jonah's attention was the uncertainty in her eyes. The woman who had sounded so confident of her abilities was now unsure.

"I hope you like it," she said softly. "I hope it's good enough." With trembling hands, Lorraine moved one of the screens aside.

Jonah stared, so astonished by the sight of her creation that words failed him. Never, not even for a moment, had he expected this. Second row horses were exactly that—secondary. Though their designs were similar to those of the outside row, they could not match the larger horses' beauty, simply because many of the details were painted rather than being carved. Somehow, Lorraine had overcome the challenge of working in only two dimensions, and the horse she'd painted rivaled his lead horse.

"You don't like it."

Jonah shook his head, regretting the silence that had been so easy to misinterpret. "You're wrong, Lorraine. I like it. Very much. So much that I was speechless. What you've done is beautiful." Slowly, he walked around the horse, careful not to touch the paint, though his fingers itched to do exactly that. The lilacs she had painted around the horse's neck looked so real that he wanted to rub them between his fingers to release the perfume.

"You really think it's beautiful?" Her voice held wonder, as if she couldn't believe his words.

"It's perfect." Jonah wanted to reassure her, but more than that, he wanted her to know that she was far more than the useless ornament he'd once called her. This was a woman who could do anything. Almost anything, he amended, recalling her attempts to cook and launder. "I couldn't have done better myself." He shook his head. "Why am I lying? The fact is, this is better than anything I've done. It truly is perfect."

Though he could tell she didn't fully believe him, Lorraine's face lit with pleasure. "I'm so glad you like it. I didn't want to disappoint you."

"You didn't. This is magnificent."

Jonah wasn't sure why he did it, but before he could stop himself, he had placed his hands on her waist and was spinning Lorraine around. Round and round they went, faster than the carousel would revolve, and with each revolution, he felt the excitement inside him build. This woman, this wonderful woman, was helping make his dream come true. The horse she'd created was magnificent, and so was she.

As he felt his head begin to spin, Jonah lowered Lorraine to the ground, and then, slowly and deliberately, he moved his lips toward hers.

Eleven

It was the most wonderful thing she had ever experienced. Lorraine's head was spinning, but not because Jonah had whirled her around. It was his nearness and the caring that nearness revealed that made her light-headed. Gone was the Jonah who'd kept her at arm's length—literally. In his place was the man she'd dreamt of, the man who loved her, the man she loved. Mrs. Ferguson had been right. Lorraine was in love.

As he wrapped his arms around her, Lorraine sighed with pleasure. This was what she had longed for all her life. This was what it was supposed to feel like when the man she loved touched her. Jonah's hands were warm and firm as they stroked her back, sending ripples of excitement through her body. The green and gold highlights in his eyes deepened as he lowered his head, but that was only the prelude. When his lips touched hers, she felt as if all the Independence Day fireworks she'd ever seen were exploding around her, creating bursts of color, each more beautiful, more powerful than the previous, leaving her dazzled and dizzy.

"Oh, Jonah," she murmured when he ended the kiss and allowed a few inches to separate them. "That was wonderful. You're wonderful."

"So are you." He released his hold on her and took a step backward, his expression changing from a warm smile to something else, something Lorraine could not identify. It looked almost like regret, but surely that was not possible.

Jonah took another step away and gestured toward the horse she had finished painting only minutes earlier. "I should never have doubted you when you said you could paint. If Mr. Looff saw your horse, he'd hire you in a minute."

It wasn't her imagination. The caring she had seen on Jonah's face, the tenderness she'd heard in his voice when he'd told her she was wonderful, were gone. What she saw now was the Jonah of two weeks ago, before she'd begun to work with him. It was as if the kiss had never happened.

It had. Lorraine could still feel the sweet sensations that his touch had wrought, but Jonah was chattering about painting. She didn't want to talk about carousel horses; she only wanted to remember how glorious it had felt, being held and kissed by Jonah. But Jonah had once again distanced himself from her.

Though she wanted nothing more than to run away and let the tears that stung her eyelids fall, Lorraine would not. Running away accomplished nothing. She would stay and see if she could make sense of Jonah's contradictions.

"Does that mean you'll let me paint the last horse?" she asked, proud that her voice did not reveal her distress.

He shook his head. "I have a better idea. I hadn't planned anything special for the rounding board, but if you want to paint scenes on it, it will make the carousel more special."

It was clear that Jonah expected them to return to the friendly camaraderie they'd had an hour ago, forgetting or at least not referring to the kiss. Though every fiber of her being shrieked that she wanted more, Lorraine did not know how to break down the barriers he had erected. All she could do was hope that spending more time together would help.

"What is a rounding board?" she asked.

In response, Jonah pulled out a scrap of paper and began to sketch the outline of a carousel. "The rounding board is designed to hide some of the mechanism," he explained, his voice as matter-of-fact as if the kiss had not occurred. "Let me show you why we need it." He continued sketching. "The top of a carousel looks a bit like an open umbrella. Here's the center pole. That's the most important one. The smaller ones radiating from it are called sweeps." Jonah added several vertical poles connecting the sweeps to the platform. "These are drop rods. They help support the canopy. They're also the poles that go through each of the horses." Returning to the top of the design, Jonah drew a circle around the sweeps. "This is the rounding board. As you can see, it helps block the view of the sweeps. It's usually painted, but it can be plain or fancy."

Lorraine studied the sketch, trying to determine how much work would be involved. "I'm not sure I have time to do anything too fancy." It was less than a week until the carousel was scheduled to be assembled. She closed her eyes as she attempted to recall her visits to Coney Island. "I can't remember anything about the rounding board on the merry-go-round I rode."

Jonah put down his pencil and smiled at her. It was a warm smile, a friendly smile. It was not the smile she longed for. "I'm not surprised. Most people focus on the animals first, but if they come often, they start to notice more details." He glanced at the sketch and then looked back at her. "What do you think? Do you want to try painting the rounding board?"

"Of course." It might be foolish, and she might be opening her heart to more pain, but Lorraine could not refuse.

Four days later, she was still mystified by Jonah's behavior. They had worked together every evening, and she'd made more progress on the rounding board than she had expected. As had been the case when she was painting the rowboats and then the carousel horse, she and Jonah had talked while they worked. They'd spoken of everything from the unusually cool weather, which was keeping the lilacs from opening fully, to the guests' potential reaction to the carousel. The one thing they did not discuss was the kiss. There was only one reason Lorraine could imagine: he regretted it.

"Come have a cup of tea with me." Mrs. Ferguson reached out to touch Lorraine's hand as she walked through the parlor. Though they would wait until Mike returned to institute high tea, Mr. Parker had agreed to keep pots of tea and coffee in the parlor each afternoon for guests who chose to remain indoors.

Lorraine sighed. When she'd spotted the woman sitting alone, she should have realized that Mrs. Ferguson would want company. Normally, Lorraine would have relished the time with the guest who had become her confidante, but she was in no mood for conversation today.

"I'm worried about you," Mrs. Ferguson said as she rose to pour a cup of tea for Lorraine. "You have circles under your eyes."

"I've been busy helping Jonah with the carousel." While that was true, it was not the reason for Lorraine's fatigue.

Mrs. Ferguson's look became appraising and more than a little skeptical. "It seems to me that ought to be putting a sparkle in your eyes, not making you look like Atlas, carrying the weight of the world on your shoulders. What's wrong, Lorraine?"

Lorraine took a sip of the hot liquid before she replied. Though she did not want to bother Mrs. Ferguson with her problems, the older woman had given her good advice in the past. Perhaps she would do so again. "Nothing's been the same since he kissed me."

Mrs. Ferguson set her cup on the table so hastily that tea splashed onto the saucer. "Did I hear correctly? Are you saying Jonah kissed you?"

"It's been five days now." Lorraine took another sip of tea, letting the delicate flavor soothe her throat. "I don't understand. All

I can think about is how wonderful it was, but he's acting like it never happened."

Furrows formed between the older woman's eyes. "Did he say anything right after he kissed you?"

"He told me I was wonderful."

"Good. Very good." Mrs. Ferguson picked up her cup again.

"But then he said I could get a job painting horses for one of the carousel makers." And, as flattering as that had been, it hadn't been what Lorraine had wanted to hear at that particular moment.

Mrs. Ferguson appeared to agree, because her face reddened. "What was the man thinking? That's not how you woo a woman."

"You were wrong, Mrs. Ferguson. Jonah doesn't love me, and he's not courting me. As far as he's concerned, the kiss was a mistake." Hours spent tossing and turning when she should have been sleeping had convinced Lorraine of that.

"I don't believe it." Once again, the older woman placed her cup on the table and leaned forward, laying her hand on Lorraine's. "If there was ever a man in love, it's Jonah Mann. He may be afraid—some men are—and he may be worried about the girl his parents want him to marry, but he loves you. I'd stake my reputation as a matchmaker on that."

Lorraine wished she were as certain. "I don't know what to do." The same sleepless nights that had convinced her that Jonah regretted their kiss had made Lorraine realize that both Mike and Mrs. Ferguson were right. She couldn't live her life trying to meet others' expectations. She needed to follow the path she believed God had set for her, and that did not include a loveless marriage.

"I love Jonah," she admitted. It was the first time she'd said the words, although they'd reverberated through her brain. "But I don't know what to do."

Mrs. Ferguson sipped her tea, her expression leaving no doubt that she was pondering Lorraine's situation. "I believe there's only one thing to do," she said at last. "You need to be bold. I know your mother probably told you that a woman should never take the first step, but you have to do that. Tell Jonah you love him."

Lorraine felt the blood drain from her face. "I can't." It was one thing to admit it to Mrs. Ferguson, quite another to declare her love to Jonah.

The older woman nodded solemnly. "You can do anything you set your mind to."

She was wrong. "You wouldn't say that if you'd eaten my food or had to use a starched towel."

"That's different." Mrs. Ferguson waved her hand, dismissing Lorraine's protest. "You didn't really set your mind to that. Did you figure out everything that was involved before you started to cook or do laundry?"

Lorraine shook her head. "No. I thought it was easy."

"And you were wrong. Convincing Jonah to admit his feelings may not be easy, but if you believe he's worth it, you have to try."

The problem was, Lorraine didn't know how to do that. She couldn't simply walk up to Jonah and announce that she loved him. But if she didn't, Jonah would leave Lilac Hall, never to return, and she would spend the rest of her life wondering whether he loved her. The thought of introducing such a delicate subject was frightening, the alternative even worse.

Lorraine closed her eyes, seeking strength. When she opened them, she gave a brisk nod. She'd do it. But first she had to clear the way. If she had learned one thing during her stay at Lilac Hall, it was that, no matter what happened with Jonah, she could not marry Robert. Even if it meant that Cousin Alan used her inheritance to lead people astray, she could not marry a man she did not love.

"Thank you, Mrs. Ferguson," Lorraine said as she rose and placed her empty cup on the tray. "I have a couple letters to write." Both Robert and her uncle needed to know she'd made a decision.

···ꝒWELVE···

ou've accomplished more than I thought possible," Jonah
said the next day. "The rounding board panels are beautiful."
Though her nerves were on edge, Lorraine managed a smile.
She had hoped that those who rode the merry-go-round would like
the rounding board paintings, but most of all, she wanted Jonah
to believe they were a fitting addition to his carousel. That was the
reason she had put her heart into them, creating a series of panels
featuring the lead horse and its companion.

In the first, a man stood next to the lead horse, smiling at his
wife and the infant she held in her arms as she rode. The second
showed the baby, now a young girl, riding it by herself, while a
girlfriend sat on the smaller companion horse. In the third, the
grown-up girl rode the lead horse's companion, her eyes locked on
her sweetheart, mounted on the lead horse. And then, because the
rounding board was a circle, spectators would see the girl with her
husband, holding their child. Round and round they'd go, forming
the circle of life.

"I wanted to tell the story of a girl's life," Lorraine said as
Jonah studied each of the panels. The primary panels would be
interspersed with simpler ones of lilac bushes, decorative hearts,
and scrolls. Later today they'd all be mounted onto the circular
board and lifted into position to hide the sweeps.

"Is she you?"

Lorraine shook her head. She'd deliberately made the girl a blonde and the love of her life dark-haired. And, though she'd been tempted, she had not given the man Jonah's features. "She's meant to represent every girl's dreams."

"Marriage and babies?"

"That's part of it, but there's more. The real dream is love." Lorraine's heart began to pound. This was the opening she had sought. Mustering every ounce of courage she possessed, she would do as Mrs. Ferguson had advised and tell Jonah of her love. "Jonah . . ."

Before she could complete the sentence, a man strode into the pavilion. "The last of the parts were just delivered, and the workers are here to assemble the carousel."

"Perfect. We're ready."

Her opportunity was lost.

The next few hours were bedlam, or so it seemed to Lorraine, as men hammered and pounded, turning pieces of wood and metal into a carousel, while others wheeled in the steam engine that would power the merry-go-round.

"Will you keep them outside?" Jonah asked when several of the guests, intrigued by the racket, tried to enter the pavilion. "Some of the magic is lost if they see the process."

And so Lorraine found herself standing guard outside the building where she'd spent so many hours, convincing the guests that anticipation was good, assuring them that they'd be able to ride the carousel in two days. Eventually they tired of waiting for a glimpse of the merry-go-round and returned to the inn.

As the sun began to set, the workers left, and Jonah came outside. Though fatigue lined his face, his eyes glowed with enthusiasm.

"Do you want to see it?" he asked.

"Of course!"

When Jonah opened the door and ushered her inside with a

flourish, Lorraine stopped short. Though she'd seen all the pieces, the finished carousel exceeded even her highest expectations.

"It's magnificent." She raised her voice to be heard over the chug of the steam engine and gazed at the painted ponies. They'd been beautiful, leaning against the pavilion walls, but now that they were mounted on the platform, standing proudly beneath the conical top and the rounding board she'd painted, they were nothing short of spectacular.

Jonah beamed with pleasure. "It's what I had hoped for. Still, it's hard to realize that it's finished." He smiled at her, his eyes radiating happiness. "Thank you for everything you did."

"It was only a small part."

"But an important one. I would have finished it without you, but it wouldn't have been as beautiful." He gestured toward the lead horse's companion and the rounding board. "Those are special. Thank you, Lorraine."

Jonah climbed onto the platform and pulled the lever, engaging the engine. Then, as the carousel began to move, he jumped off and stood at Lorraine's side, watching the horses revolve.

"I think we should share the first ride," he told her. When he was confident that everything was functioning properly, he set the brake and helped Lorraine climb onto the platform.

"Aren't you going to ride?" she asked when he started to help her mount the lead horse.

"I'll stand by your side."

Though, as she'd depicted in her panel with the couple and their baby, that was the position many men took, it felt wrong to Lorraine. "You should ride the lead horse," she insisted. "I'll ride mine." And for the few minutes of their ride, they would look like the young woman and her sweetheart in the third panel.

Jonah nodded and started the platform moving again, this time engaging the organ. Though the music was softer than normal so that guests would not be attracted to the pavilion, Lorraine had no trouble hearing it. As the horses revolved in the most glorious carousel ride of her life, she kept her eyes fixed on Jonah, and for the next three minutes, she scarcely breathed. This was what she wanted, being with the man she loved, sharing something they had worked together to create. This was the life she longed for. Whether they lived here or in England didn't matter. All that mattered was being together.

When at last the music faded, Jonah shut off the engine and helped Lorraine descend from the platform. He started to walk toward the door, but she laid her hand on his arm, stopping him. Though her hands were clammy with apprehension and her heart was beating so fast that it felt as if it would escape from her chest, she knew this might be her only chance.

"I wish the ride had never ended," she said softly.

Jonah nodded as if he understood. Perhaps he did, but there was more to be said. Much more. She could only hope her words would touch his heart and that he would not dismiss them as easily as he had their kiss.

Lorraine tried to smile as she looked up at the man she loved, but her lips refused to curve. It took all her of energy just to speak. "A month ago I didn't know what I wanted from my life. Now I do."

Though Jonah's eyes widened slightly, as if she'd surprised him, he said nothing. It was up to her to continue.

Lorraine took a deep breath, exhaling slowly as she formulated her words. "I know a woman's not supposed to say these things, but I can't let you go back to England without hearing them." She paused for a second before letting the words she'd kept deep in her heart flow. "I love you, Jonah. I want to be your wife."

For the briefest of instants, she saw happiness in his eyes, but all too soon it was replaced by sorrow. "What about the man you're supposed to marry and your inheritance?" he asked.

"I can't marry Robert. I don't love him. I've told both him and my uncle that." Lorraine kept her hand on Jonah's arm, as much to steady herself as to keep him from turning aside. "I realized the inheritance doesn't matter. You were right when you told me my parents' legacy wasn't money. I hope Cousin Alan doesn't squander it, but if he does, it's his decision. I can't live my life trying to protect him from himself."

"You'd be poor."

Lorraine shook her head. "You've shown me that what a person does is more important than the money he accumulates. I don't need new gowns or fancy jewelry. All I need is love." Lorraine looked into Jonah's eyes, willing him to understand. "All I need is you."

"Oh, Lorraine." Only two words, but they were so filled with emotion that they brought a lump to her throat. "I wish my situation were different, but it isn't." He laid his hand on top of hers, as if he were trying to comfort her. "I can't give you what you want. You know I have an obligation to my parents."

She had thought of little else. Though she had never met them, Lorraine could not believe that Jonah's parents would be so cruel as to deprive him of true love. "Surely they'll understand, if they know you love me."

His eyes were solemn as he gazed into hers. "It's not a matter of understanding. My family's honor is at stake. That's more important than you or me."

He sounded almost angry, and Lorraine wished she knew whether the anger was directed at his situation or at her for asking for more than he could give. Perhaps it was silly to pursue it when she knew there would be no happy outcome, but, though her heart ached so deeply that she feared it would never heal, Lorraine could not leave without knowing the truth.

"You don't love me." She made it a statement, not a question. Anguish filled Jonah's eyes. "I didn't say that."

"But it's what you meant. You're willing to throw away our

chance at happiness." Suddenly, sorrow turned to anger. "You're a fool, Jonah Mann, but I'm an even bigger one. I should have known better than to believe someone might love me."

She tugged her hand away from his and clenched her fists. "Goodbye, Jonah. I hope your honor brings you happiness."

··· ᴄ𝒯HIRTEEN ···

He was a fool, Jonah told himself as he walked around the carousel for what seemed like the hundredth time. When Lorraine had stormed out of the pavilion, he hadn't followed her. He couldn't, for fear that he would hurt her again. He clenched his fists so tightly his nails dug into his palms. That pain was nothing compared to what he'd inflicted on Lorraine. She hadn't deserved it. Beautiful, brave Lorraine deserved only love and happiness, two things he was unable to give her.

Jonah increased his pace until he was practically running, but there was no way to outrun his memories. Seeing Lorraine's distress and knowing he'd been responsible had been horrible. Her anger had been easier to bear, for not only had he deserved it, but though it would probably burn away by morning, at least while the anger blazed, it would keep Lorraine's pain at bay. If they were both fortunate, the light of dawn would help her see the truth: they did not belong together.

Hah! Jonah stopped abruptly at the realization that he was a hypocrite. How could he expect Lorraine to believe something that he did not? His gaze moved upward, focusing on the rounding board and the images of Lorraine's dreams. Though he hadn't admitted it when she'd shown the panels to him, those were his dreams too. He wanted a wife who would gaze at him the way the woman in Lorraine's painting looked at her sweetheart, the way Lorraine had looked at him as they'd ridden the carousel. Not one of the three Js, as he'd nicknamed the women who would meet his parents' expectations, would ever look at him that way. Jonah knew that as surely as he knew he'd never give any of them the kind of smiles that came so easily when he was with Lorraine.

With a disgusted grunt, he extinguished the lights and locked the door behind him. If he stayed, he'd only think about Lorraine. The carousel was supposed to be the embodiment of his lifelong dream, and yet when he looked at it, all he could recall were the moments he'd spent with her, the laughs they'd shared, the friendly arguments they'd had over things no more important than the correct shade of paint for the lead horse's saddle. Forgetting her would be easier once he was away from the carousel.

It wasn't. Too distraught to go indoors, Jonah walked around the grounds, wandering aimlessly. It was no use. No matter where he went, no matter what he saw, his thoughts revolved around Lorraine. The scent of the lilacs, the sound of last year's leaves rustling underfoot, the sensation of the breeze cooling his neck all evoked memories of Lorraine. And with each memory came the realization that he had destroyed something good. He'd torn out part of himself, and nothing would ever fill the empty spot that remained. Nothing but Lorraine.

An owl hooted. A rodent scurried for cover. It was an ordinary night for everyone except Jonah. He let out another groan as the magnitude of his idiocy weighed on him. How wrong he'd been when he'd thought Lorraine was a soft, spineless female. She was far stronger and braver than he could ever hope to be. Not only had she defied convention by declaring her love and asking him to marry her, but she was willing to give up everything she knew—a comfortable life in New York society, the companionship of long-time friends, the approval of her family—for him. And he'd been a fool, refusing the love of the most wonderful woman he'd ever met, all for the sake of family tradition.

Jonah stopped and stared at the sky, as if it would give him the answer he sought. It did not, but as he slowed his pace, his thoughts became less turbulent. The feud had been over for two centuries. It would not reignite if he failed to wed one of the Js. With that realization came another: it was time to start a new tradition—marrying for love. Jessica, Jocelyn, and Julianne wouldn't mind, for each had confided that she had a beau in the wings and that Jonah would be doing her a favor if he chose one of her sisters. That only left his parents. Jonah would not delude himself into believing that convincing them would be easy, but he also knew that the love he and Lorraine shared came once in a lifetime.

His decision made, Jonah headed back to Lilac Hall. It was time to make amends for his foolishness. As he reentered the house, he opened his watch and peered at the hands. Half past midnight. Too late. No matter how much he wanted to talk to Lorraine, he could not go to her now. He'd see her first thing in the morning, and when he did, he'd tell her she was right. Their love was worth more than anything. Somehow, someway he would make his parents understand, but even if they did not, even if they refused to accept Lorraine, Jonah would marry her, for she was his love, the other half of himself.

Feeling happier than he had since the moment he'd so stupidly refused Lorraine's offer of marriage, he climbed into bed. And though he hadn't expected to, Jonah fell asleep.

Lorraine settled into the seat as she tried to focus on the scenery that was rolling by. The gentle hills of the countryside were pretty, and on another day she would have enjoyed watching them. Today she could think of little more than the emptiness deep inside her. She had believed nothing could hurt more than her parents'

deaths, but she'd been wrong. Jonah's rejection was worse, for he'd destroyed her dreams.

She took a deep breath, thankful that the train was only half filled and that she was not forced to make casual conversation with another passenger. It had been less than a month since she'd headed for Plato Falls, convinced that Mike's letter was the answer to her prayers. On that trip, Lorraine had spoken to the middle-aged woman seated next to her, telling the woman of her certainty that being reunited with her brother was the first step toward an exciting new future. How wrong she'd been!

Though it had been exciting at times, her stay at Lilac Hall had been only an interlude, not the beginning of a new life. Now the future that had seemed so promising for a few fleeting moments looked bleak, her dreams of love and happiness gone as quickly as morning mist. In the space of a few weeks, Lorraine had met—and lost—the only man she would ever love. She knew that as surely as she knew her name.

As the train chugged its way toward New York, Lorraine tried to calm her nerves. It had been impulsive, leaving Lilac Hall this morning, but she could not bear the thought of seeing Jonah again. She had left her belongings in her room, telling Mr. Parker that she would return in a few weeks. Once Jonah had left for England, she would spend some time with Mike and Betty. She would establish an activities program for each season, and then she would leave. But first she had to heal.

"I haven't seen Lorraine this morning." Cheryl seemed annoyed that Jonah had interrupted her breakfast preparations with a question, but before he could apologize, she pursed her lips and added, "You might ask Mrs. Ferguson. They spend a lot of time together."

That meant waiting another half hour until the guests assembled for breakfast. Though he chafed at the delay, Jonah saw no alternative. Lorraine hadn't answered his knock on her door, and as far as he could tell, she was not on the resort's grounds. Mr. Parker might know her whereabouts, but Jonah hadn't been able to find him.

Jonah's spirits rose when the Fergusons were the first to enter the dining room. Not bothering with the social amenities, he covered the distance between himself and the older couple in a few long strides, then asked if either had seen Lorraine.

"She's gone."

It was what he had feared. He'd hurt Lorraine so deeply that she had left rather than having to face him again. If only he hadn't been so stupid! "Gone? Do you know where?" Though there was only one logical destination, Jonah needed to be certain.

"She took the early morning train to New York," Mrs. Ferguson said, her expression reminding him of a woman who'd eaten a sour lemon. "She didn't say why, but if I had to guess, I'd say it has something to do with you. What did you do?"

"I was a fool." Jonah wouldn't share the details of that foolishness with anyone, because that would mean exposing Lorraine to possible censure for being more forward than most well-bred women, but he wouldn't try to exonerate himself. Mrs. Ferguson was right. This was his fault.

The older woman nodded, as if she were not surprised. "You may have been a fool last night, but you're an even bigger one if you don't go after her."

That was exactly what Jonah planned to do. "I don't know where she lives." It wouldn't be too difficult to discover where the Caldwells lived once Jonah reached New York, but he didn't want to waste a minute. "Do you?"

"I do." Leaving her husband behind, Mrs. Ferguson walked into the parlor and seated herself at the small desk where guests composed letters. Pulling out a piece of paper, she scribbled an address. "That girl's one in a million," she said as she thrust the paper into Jonah's hand. "Don't let her slip through your fingers."

Though he feared he'd already done that, and that Lorraine would refuse to speak to him, Jonah nodded and thanked the older woman. Unable to do anything but worry about Lorraine, he found himself sitting at the depot an hour before the late morning train was scheduled to arrive. Four hours later, he was in a hansom cab, headed for Lorraine's home.

The three-story red brick town house wasn't as large as his parents' manor in England, but its classical lines were good, and the neighborhood spoke of wealth. It was the kind of house Jonah had envisioned from Mike's descriptions. Moving briskly, he mounted the front steps and rang the bell.

"I'm sorry, sir," the neatly dressed maid said when Jonah asked to see Lorraine. "Miss Lorraine is gone. I'm not sure when she'll return."

She must be out making calls. Though he hadn't expected that, this afternoon might be one of her friends' days to receive callers. "She came here today, didn't she?"

"No, sir." The girl shook her head. "We haven't seen Miss Lorraine in almost a month."

Jonah's lips twisted into a frown. He'd been certain that she would head here immediately, but once again, Lorraine had surprised him. Where was she? She wouldn't be calling on other women without having changed from her traveling clothes into ones suitable for paying visits. He started to hail another cab, then realized there was no reason to do that until he had a destination in mind.

He leaned against the Caldwells' iron gate and thought. Perhaps she had gone to see Mr. Looff about working for him. Jonah shook his head. That didn't feel right. Lorraine was somewhere in the city, but where? He closed his eyes, trying to blot out the sights and sounds of New York and focus on Lorraine. If he thought hard enough, he'd find the answer. Seconds later, Jonah's eyes flew open as he recalled the conversation he and Lorraine had had one morning.

He knew where she was.

$\mathscr{F}$OURTEEN

She had been wandering aimlessly for hours, stopping occasionally to eat and rest her legs. Though she'd entered a few shops, nothing had caught her fancy, and Lorraine could not recall what she had ordered for her midday meal. Now it was late afternoon, and she still felt like a rudderless boat, spinning in circles. Perhaps she should have gone directly home from the train station, but she had wanted to make some decisions before she did. Once she crossed the threshold, her uncle would want to know what Lorraine planned to do, now that she'd refused Robert's offer of marriage. So far, she had no answers.

Her thoughts continued to whirl, while her feet moved mechanically without a real destination. What was Jonah doing now? Was he in the pavilion, getting the carousel ready for its grand opening? Or was he relaxing, perhaps rowing on the pond? As the questions bombarded her, Lorraine's eyes widened in surprise. She might not know where Jonah was, but she knew exactly where she was. Her feet hadn't been moving aimlessly; they'd brought her where she needed to be: Battery Park.

For the first time since she'd disembarked from the train, Lorraine walked purposefully. There was no reason to meander when she knew that what she wanted was to stand at the edge of the park. That was where she'd find her answers.

Water lapped at the rocks; seagulls soared overhead, occasionally landing in hopes of finding a few bread crumbs; and in the distance stood Lady Liberty. Lorraine took a deep breath, trying to quell her disappointment as she gazed at the water. Everything looked the same, and yet it wasn't. This was the park she'd always considered special. Today it seemed ordinary. This was the statue that had always brought her a sense of peace. Today it did not. Nothing made sense. She stared at the massive green figure that symbolized hopes and dreams for so many, and as she did, Lorraine knew what was wrong. The statue had not changed, but she had. She was no longer the young woman who'd believed in a future of love and happiness. In her place stood a woman who knew such dreams were for others.

Children scampered through the park, shouting gleefully when they spotted a pigeon. Mothers smiled at their children's antics. A few couples walked, arm in arm, oblivious to everyone but themselves. In the past, Lorraine would have found pleasure in watching the other visitors. Today she could only think of the man who'd thrown away not just his chance at happiness but hers too.

She took another deep breath and straightened her shoulders. Those thoughts were accomplishing nothing. It was true that she would never forget Jonah. She didn't want to. But she needed to focus on the good things that had happened to her this month. Perhaps that way, she would find a path to the future.

She strolled along the perimeter of the park, corralling her memories. Being reunited with Mike. Meeting Jonah. Mike's obvious love for Betty. Helping Jonah paint his carousel horses. Organizing Lilac Hall's activities program. Falling in love with Jonah.

Gripping the iron railing, Lorraine looked at the lady with the torch. No matter what she did, no matter how she tried to banish the memories, her thoughts always came back to Jonah. He was the center of her life. But that was senseless, for he was gone. She closed her eyes, willing the tears not to fall.

"Lorraine!"

What a fool she was. Now she was imagining Jonah's voice. Lorraine kept her eyes closed, her hands on the railing.

"Lorraine!"

The voice was louder now, closer, and it still sounded like Jonah's. Despite her resolve, she opened her eyes and turned.

"Jonah?" she whispered, not believing her eyes. The man who was sprinting toward her looked like Jonah. He sounded like . . . "Jonah!" Tears clogged her throat, and the word came out as little more than a croak.

"I'm so glad I found you." He stopped only a few inches from her, his expression solemn.

Her heart beat faster. He was here. Jonah had been searching for her. As hope bubbled up inside her, Lorraine tamped it down. Just because he was here didn't mean he'd changed his mind. But he had come. Nothing could erase that.

"I wouldn't blame you if you told me to leave, but I hope you'll listen to me first."

He stood in front of her, his eyes ringed by dark circles, his expression filled with uncertainty. How could he believe she'd send him away? His presence meant they might have a second chance, for surely Jonah had not sought her only to repeat his refusal. The knot that rose to her throat kept Lorraine from speaking, and so she simply inclined her head, encouraging him to continue.

"You were right when you said I was foolish." He extended his hand as if to grip hers, then dropped it. "Only a fool would throw away one of God's gifts, but that's what I almost did. I almost threw away your love . . . and mine."

Lorraine took a shallow breath as her pulse began to race, and the hope that had lodged inside her when he pronounced the word "love" dislodged the knot in her throat. "You love me?"

Jonah nodded, the sparkle in his eyes underscoring his words.

"I love you more than I realized I could love anyone, but I need to tell you the truth."

Truth? That sounded ominous. As dread mingled with the hope that had set her heart to pounding, Lorraine said a silent prayer for peace and understanding. Jonah held out his hand, waiting for her to take it. When they were seated on one of the park benches, he turned to face her, keeping her hand firmly in his. "My name isn't really Jonah Mann."

Whatever Lorraine had imagined he might say, it wasn't that. "I don't understand."

"You know I'm from a town in England called Traywood. What I didn't tell you is that Traywood is my family's ancestral seat. When my father dies, I'll become Viscount Traywood."

A shiver made its way down Lorraine's spine at the thought that Jonah, the man she had once treated as a common laborer, was a member of England's aristocracy. What irony! Unwittingly, she had fallen in love with the perfect man. He would satisfy the terms of her parents' will at the same time that he fulfilled one of her mother's fondest wishes. But Jonah hadn't said he'd marry Lorraine. He'd only said he loved her.

"Is that why your family wants you to marry one of those distant relatives?" If there was a lot of money associated with the title, his parents might want to keep that money within the family.

"Partly." Jonah leaned forward, his eyes never leaving hers, his hand still clasping hers. "More than two centuries ago, there was a rift between two cousins. Each one claimed to be the rightful heir to Traywood."

"How could that be?" When she'd discussed her English ancestors, Mother had explained the laws of succession. They'd seemed straightforward. "I thought titles went to the oldest son."

Jonah nodded as he stroked the back of Lorraine's hand, sending shivers of delight up her arm. "They do. The problem is, those cousins' fathers were identical twins, and there was some confusion over which one was the firstborn. The midwife tied a string around the first boy's toe, but it came undone when both were in the cradle. After that, no one was ever sure which was the elder. The son who did not inherit was bitter."

"Understandably. He felt cheated." Though she did not like the terms of her parents' will, Mother and Father had given her a choice. The Traywood heir had been a victim of chance.

Jonah continued. "Their sons and their sons' sons carried on the feud until finally the matriarch decreed that the only way to resolve it was for the heir apparent to marry a woman from the other branch of the family. We've been doing that ever since. Even though we share no more than a drop of common blood now, it's what Manderleys have always done. I would be the first to break the tradition."

No wonder Jonah's parents had made the stipulation they had. Tradition was important, particularly when it was so well established. No wonder Jonah was expected to marry a Manderley—

Manderley?

"Did you say Manderley?"

"Yes." Jonah gave her a smile as warm as the summer sun. "I should have told you that before. My full name is Jonah Francis Edward William Stephen Manderley, future Viscount Traywood. I'm descended from Stephen Manderley. The other family are descendants of Maxwell Manderley."

"Oh, Jonah, I don't believe it."

His eyes narrowed, and he looked at her as if her words made no sense. "It's the truth. What part don't you believe?"

"Your name."

"It's a bit long, I'll admit, but that's another tradition. Each heir is named after earlier viscounts."

Her heart brimming with love, Lorraine laid her free hand on top of Jonah's. "My mother told me there was no such thing as coincidence, that what we call coincidence is really God's hand. Now I believe it."

"What do you mean?"

An older couple smiled as they walked by, and Lorraine heard the woman murmur, "They remind me of us when we were their age."

Lorraine was not smiling as she looked at Jonah. She would smile again only when she saw his reaction to her next words. "I'm a Manderley too."

His eyes widened, and the blood draining from his face underscored his shock. "Wh-what did you say?"

"It's true. One of my ancestors came from England. I never knew the name of the town. It might have been Traywood. All I know is that there was some kind of trouble, and my great-grandmother Manderley left England. Mother said the original Manderley was someone called Maxwell." Jonah's expression told Lorraine he understood the implications of her revelation. She gave him a playful smile. "You're not the only one whose family has naming traditions. My great-grandmother's female descendants have all had Manderley as their middle name."

Jonah chuckled. "So that's what the *M* stands for. I wondered about your initials, but I never asked. It seems I should have."

"It seems that I'm part of that other Manderley family."

"And my future title means I meet the terms of your parents' will." Jonah's eyes darkened, the love that shone from them so strong it took Lorraine's breath away. His lips curving in the sweetest of smiles, he said, "There's only one thing left."

He released Lorraine's hand, then stood. Bending one knee, Jonah reached for her hand again. "Will you marry me, Lorraine Manderley Caldwell?" He paused for a second before adding the one little word he knew would convince her. "Please."

$\mathcal{D}$ EAR $\mathcal{R}$ EADER,

I hope you enjoyed Lorraine and Jonah's story and all the carousel lore I included in it. If you were wondering why I chose to make Jonah a carousel carver, it's because I contracted a case of carousel fever fourteen years ago in what was, perhaps not coincidentally, the International Year of the Carousel. I happened to see a carousel horse in the tourist information area of an interstate rest area, and that was all it took. The very next day I was planning trips to historic merry-go-rounds and carousel museums.

Two years later, a woman who suffered from the same ailment told me I had carousel fever. Since I'd never heard of it, I decided to do some research. My dictionary didn't have a listing for *carousel fever*, but of course it had entries for both *carousel* and *fever*. Carousel was easy. Fever was a bit trickier. I didn't have an elevated body temperature, but there was some truth to the second definition: "contagious usually transient enthusiasm: a craze." There was no doubt that I was enthusiastic about merry-go-rounds and painted ponies, and there was also no doubt that it was contagious. I'd already infected my sister to the point where she was planning her trips around carousels. The problem was that the fever showed no sign of abating. If anything, it only increased. I've been known to convince my husband to drive hundreds of miles out of our way to visit an antique carousel, and when a museum in Idaho advertised a carousel exhibit, you can guess who planned to be the first through the door. I'm not alone. Thousands of people suffer from carousel fever, which is why there are several organizations devoted to carousels. There are also carousel-related magazines and conventions.

All of that made me wonder what it was about merry-go-rounds that caused such fascination. I believe there are three very special aspects to them. First is their beauty. With so much of what we buy now mass produced, the level of detail and the quality of craftsmanship in the early hand-carved and hand-painted horses is truly awe-inspiring. Secondly, for many people, merry-go-rounds trigger nostalgia for their childhood, which may have been the last time they rode a painted pony. And thirdly, there's the fun factor. Have you ever seen an unhappy person on a carousel? I haven't. The seats may not be comfortable; the music may be too loud; but there's something just plain fun about riding a carousel.

If you'd like to learn more, I've posted pictures and links on my web page, www.amandacabot.com. Go to the "books" tab, click on the cover for *Sincerely Yours*, and then click on the "Story Behind the Story" link.

In the meantime, I hope there's at least one merry-go-round ride in your immediate future and that you too develop carousel fever.

Sincerely yours,

AMANDA CABOT

Dreams have always been an important part of **Amanda Cabot's** life. For almost as long as she can remember, she dreamt of being an author. Fortunately for the world, her grade-school attempts as a playwright were not successful, and she turned her attention to writing novels. Her dream of selling a book before her thirtieth birthday came true, and she's been spinning tales ever since. She now has more than twenty-five novels to her credit under a variety of pseudonyms.

Her books have been finalists for the ACFW Carol award as well as the Bookseller's Best and have appeared on the CBA bestseller list.

A popular speaker, Amanda is a member of ACFW and a charter member of Romance Writers of America. She married her high school sweetheart, who shares her love of travel and who's driven thousands of miles to help her research her books. After years as Easterners, they fulfilled a longtime dream and are now living in the American West.

A Saving Grace

Jane Kirkpatrick

Dedicated to Jerry,
one more time

They shall not hunger nor thirst; . . . for he
that hath mercy on them shall lead them, even
by the springs of water shall he guide them.

Isaiah 49:10

·ₒ·ₒ·ₒ $\mathcal{O}$NE ·ₒ·ₒ·ₒ

*. . . My mama won't leave that place. Please make her come
home, Aunt Grace. I already lost my Papa.*

*Sincerely yours,
Caroline, age 8*

Grace Hathaway opened the letter while sitting on the wide,
covered porch of Oregon's Roaring Springs Ranch. She rocked
back and forth listening to the wind chimes and the low *awk-awk*
of chickens as they pecked on the lawn. She twisted a curl of her
chestnut hair as she read. Caroline's plea had not been what she
expected when the missive arrived at the remote Oregon ranch
just after breakfast. A second letter, signed by a lawyer, in the
same envelope explained that Grace's friend, Rebecca, mother of
Caroline, was hospitalized in a sanatorium-like facility in a town
called Olalla in Washington on Puget Sound.

*Following the drowning death of her husband, Caroline's
mother became quite despondent and felt she needed a place
of respite. She arranged for eight-year-old Caroline to be left
in the care of a friend in The Dalles, Oregon.*

The friend had visited Mrs. Holmes, the lawyer continued, and was alarmed by her condition.

Mrs. Holmes appears to be wasting away with the full support of the female doctor, Dr. Linda Hazzard, and her husband who operate the facility. It comes highly recommended for an unusual though apparently successful nutritional care approach involving fasting. The friend was unable to convince Caroline's mother to leave. Caroline is listed as your godchild and Caroline and the family friend asked that I send her letter along with my explanation. Please advise if you can come and offer comfort to Caroline, if not to her mother.

Very truly yours

. . . and it was signed by an attorney in The Dalles and dated in March, 1911.

Grace nibbled on a sugar cookie the cook had put out on the sideboard. She rested the letters on her linen skirt. *Little Caroline.* The child was her godchild and she was hurting deeply. Grace could afford to not teach piano on the circuit of ranches for a few weeks, though she didn't like reneging on an agreement with the ranching families. And a buckaroo she fancied might well find someone else to picnic with if she were out of the picture. Still, a child worried and her mother—an old friend of Grace's—suffered in her grief. She wasn't certain what she could do, but she was being asked to help and a Hathaway never turned aside a genuine request for such. Grace hoped the ranchers would permit her to leave her contract, knowing it was for the sake of a child.

Olalla. The name of the town rolled off her tongue like a lullaby, but what was happening to her friend there didn't sound like a soothing song; it rang a dissonant chord.

The stage ride north to The Dalles took three days through the mud and spring rains. Her small frame struck passengers on either side of her as they hit rocks and ruts, causing her to resettle the hatpins holding her straw hat. Nights at the stage stops, Grace longed for the feather mattress and hearty breakfasts of the Roaring Springs Ranch. Her employers had been kind about letting her go, and even her students acted like they'd miss her. The buckaroo tipped his hat but didn't seem the least bit chagrined that they wouldn't be meeting for cold meats and cheeses beneath the spreading cottonwood tree. Maybe the ease of saying goodbye was a good sign that going to help a friend was exactly what God wanted her to do and that her attraction for a cowboy was just a fleeting fancy.

With her arrival in the bustling town of The Dalles beside the Columbia River, Grace conferred first with the lawyer, then found the address where Caroline stayed. The child's small arms reached around Grace's neck as she lowered herself to the round tearstained face. She listened to the tale of Caroline missing her mother and her papa and rocked the child, the smell of lavender soap from Caroline's hair sweet to her nose.

"I was quite alarmed," the caretaker for Caroline told Grace after putting Caroline to bed. Jenny spoke frankly with Grace as the two women sat at Jenny's oak table. "First of all, Olalla itself is so isolated. Just a timber town. You have to take ferries and boats to get there and the sanatorium is even more remote, up on this hill in a rambling building where no one smiles and they look at a visitor as though they're someone bringing guns or knives inside." She took a long drink of cold milk. "What they check for is food: had I brought anything with me to eat or drink?" She leaned in to whisper to Grace. "They didn't even remove the pistol I carry in my reticule, just the piece of beef jerky I had left that helped sustain me on the dreadful trip." Jenny had a biscuit in her hand and she took a bite.

"What did Rebecca say? How did she look?"

Jenny brushed crumbs from her ample chest. "She said they were treating her very well, that she felt happier there than she'd been since Bertrand's death. Such a tragedy." Jenny shook her head. "You know he left her a handsome estate." Grace nodded. Jenny returned to her story. "But she's positively emaciated. She must have lost twenty pounds. I know she was stretching her corsets for a time. We all have a tendency to do that after a birth, and Rebecca never lost her baby weight."

Rebecca had always been a bit portly, so Grace hoped Jenny was exaggerating about looking emaciated. She watched the woman spread thick huckleberry jam over a glob of sweet butter on her second biscuit.

"What is the treatment, exactly? Did she tell you?"

"Some sort of special diet. Would you like some tea? Sugar?" Grace shook her head no. Jenny sighed. "The doctor wrote this book. I have it somewhere. It was all so . . . astonishing. Mostly female patients. And I would venture to say none that needed charity. The furnishings were quite lovely and the grounds well kept. Little cabins sort of off by themselves stuck beneath massive trees. I didn't see the inside of those. The husband is quite handsome. Sam Hazzard is his name. But the doctor . . ." Jenny said the word like she'd eaten cold mutton that had stuck to the roof of her mouth. "The doctor is the wife, and when she enters a room . . . well, she consumes it even though she's thin as chive. With a name like Hazzard . . . she *is* a hazard, but Rebecca wouldn't hear anything against her or Wilderness Heights, as the sanatorium is called." Jenny used what was left of her biscuit to point at Grace. "I didn't really describe all this to Caroline, of course. The child feels bereft. Who wouldn't with their mother choosing some wild place to lie in bed all day. Well, I think Rebecca's too weak to do much else, but to do that instead of be with her child? Surely her brain has been punctured like a pincushion and her mind is seeping out."

$\boxtimes$

Grace slipped into Caroline's bedroom. She'd be sharing the child's bed, but she didn't want to wake her. She lit a candle and began pulling combs from her chestnut bun, the light flickering in the oval mirror, her blue eyes looking dark in the candlelight. She really wondered whether she might be able to do more than what Jenny had attempted in rescuing her friend. She wasn't a great persuader. She didn't "consume" a room when she entered it. She was more shadow than light when it came to convincing someone of an action. Rebecca had always taken the lead in their friendship. Rebecca had married an Oregonian, and Grace had come to Oregon from Chicago because Rebecca insisted that Grace's life would be much more interesting in the West. She'd made her first trip when Caroline was baptized and returned six years later to find herself a traveling music teacher, an occupation she thoroughly loved and would never have found without Rebecca's invitation and her many contacts. When she learned of Rebecca's husband's death, Grace had rushed to be with her friend who, after a month, had seemed to be negotiating widowhood as well as could be expected. Grace returned to her work. Now, six months later, her friend was in real trouble and it concerned her that she hadn't reached out to Grace before isolating herself in a strange place called Olalla. *Give me guidance, Lord. I am apparently a flat note when it comes to helping grieving widows sing again.*

"I heard what she said."

"What?" Grace turned to Caroline's voice. "I thought you were asleep."

"I'm not. I evens-dropped."

Grace smiled at the child's creative word. "Did you? I'm sure it's not as bad as what Jenny described. I'm going to go there and—"

"Take me too!" Caroline sat up in bed, the candlelight reflecting against the satin blue ribbon of her nightdress. "Please, please, take me."

"Is Jenny good to you?"

"Yes, but I miss Mama. I miss Papa."

Grace sat beside her. "I know you do and she misses you too—and your papa, he'd be here if he could. But God loves you and looks after you." Caroline nodded, accepted the handkerchief Grace pulled from her pocket. "Hospitals don't usually allow children to visit and we'd both worry about you being left at a hotel all alone. It'll be better if you wait here with Jenny and pray, wouldn't it?"

"I guess. But she's not a pincushion. She's a good mama." Caroline began sobbing, the ache of separation a slice to Grace's own heart.

"No, no, she's not a pincushion." She stroked the child's arm. "Your mamma has had a terrible blow. I'll do my best to tend her wounds and bring her back."

"Promise? You promise you'll bring her back."

"I . . . I promise."

Caroline grabbed for Grace now as she sat on the side of the bed, hung on as though her little arms were ropes surrounding Grace's heart.

"How about if I sing you a lullaby, would you like that? It's time you got some sleep."

"Like Mamma used to?"

"Just like that." She held Caroline and began to sing "Rock-a-bye Baby," then "Hush, Little Baby." Her contralto voice soothed, and by the time Grace finished "All Through the Night," she could hear the child's even heartbeat against her own, watched as the eyelids fluttered shut, settling the child into sleep. Caroline's hair was soft as a flower petal, and Grace tucked the curls around her ear, then laid her gently onto the pillow. She cupped the candle flame and blew it out, then undressed in the dark and donned her nightdress before slipping beneath the quilt on her side of the bed. A breeze through the window blew across her face.

What had she gotten herself into, promising to bring Rebecca back? If it was true that Jenny had told Rebecca how much Caroline missed her and that still hadn't convinced Rebecca to come home, Grace wasn't at all sure she'd have any better luck. "This will have to be your doing, Lord." She finished her prayers, the words of the lullaby ringing in her ears: "Guardian angels God will send thee, all through the night."

She would count on that for the night and the light of day.

· · · *Two* · · ·

The steamship *Reliance* took Grace from The Dalles and its wide vista down the blue Columbia to Portland, a city of trees and stumps bustling like a would-be Chicago. The next morning, Grace boarded the North Coast Limited railway to Seattle where the train chugged north through tiny farms carved from the timber. She caught glimpses of Mount St. Helens and the magical Rainier and jagged snow-covered Cascades whose names she did not know. In the Seattle station, Grace stepped out to a magnificent arched building where women in straw hats handed out flyers reminding persons of her sex to vote. Imagine that!

With some effort, Grace found an automobile cab. As they drove through Seattle, she marveled at the bridges and sparkling lakes and tended gardens with pink blooming rhododendrons and lilacs ready to burst that lined the streets. What a different landscape from the now-distant ranches she'd worked on. Dropped off at the port, Grace bought tickets on the stern-wheeler *Virginia*, owned by the West Port Transportation company. Inside the ferry, she slipped exhausted onto the seat. She might enjoy the feel of sea spray on her face as the ferry glided between tree-covered islands with occasional glimpses of the open sea, but her feet hurt and she needed to finish a task she'd set for herself. When not gazing out the window at the lush landscape of the inland passage, watching light sparkle on her first view of the Pacific, or listening to the steamship's hum, Grace read Dr. Linda Burfield Hazzard's book *Fasting for the Cure of Disease*. She unwrapped the last cheese sandwich Jenny had sent with her and munched as she read. She had to know as much as she could about this doctor and her treatments if she was going to be successful in bringing Rebecca home. One thing was certain: the woman had opinions. She didn't like meat and claimed "overeating is the vice of the whole human race." Grace could think of other things more despicable than overeating, like allowing women to go without food and children to go without their mothers.

The ferry stopped at several little islands on Puget Sound. She was told to listen to the steward call out "Colvos Passage," for there she would find Olalla. She dozed, awoke, and finished the book Jenny had given her, putting it back inside her carpetbag. The doctor's book posed a remarkable theory that all illness from colds to tuberculosis to toothaches could be cured by improving the digestive channels and "purifying the blood" through fasting. Patients were encouraged to begin their fasts by eating only bits of cornmeal and broth followed by tomato and maybe orange juice until they felt better. "Elimination through clyster syringe is also required daily or more often if the digestive system resists." *Enemas?* Grace shivered. The woman wrote as though she knew all answers to all things, even quoting Milton's *Paradise Lost* to support her reasoning. This was such a strange matter. How on earth would Grace be able to challenge such a strong woman, especially if Rebecca was under her spell?

The ferry docked and Grace picked up her bag and walked down the wooden plank. The height of the fir trees forced her to bend backward to see the sky between the treetops. She held her hat and turned slowly. What a humbling place this was, full of timber and ferns. Dusk approached before long, but the small shops remained open to serve the ferry arrivals.

"May I take your bag, miss? Do you have others?"

"Oh, yes. Please." She handed her bag over to the man standing before a carriage with OLALLA HOTEL written on the side. A white horse with speckles let one leg bend in rest as it waited for the passengers to step up. Grace was the only one. A seagull swooped over her, landing to waddle toward the ferry. Grace had sent a letter making the reservation and was pleased with the hotel's efficiency in collecting her. She nodded toward the trunk set at the top of the gangplank and then watched as the man walked up the wooden ramp to pick up her trunk. He wasn't very tall, but his arms were thick as tree branches, and he tossed her trunk onto his back. When he returned to the carriage, loaded her trunk, and was about to help her step up, she said, "I'd like to visit the sanatorium. Is that on the way to the hotel?"

"The sanatorium?" He squinted, his eyes making a hummingbird-size glance over her slender frame. "Don't know as you need such a place, if I might say so, miss. And it's beyond the hotel. I operate the passenger boat what takes people there mornings and picks 'em up. Just returned before coming to get you." The rowing and handling of luggage must account for the man's upper-body strength. "You wouldn't want to go over there now. Visitors don't want to be there after dark. Fact is," he leaned toward her and whispered, "they don't like visitors to come there at all and I wouldn't think you'd need to be a patient, if I might say so."

"But friends help people heal. How odd that they wouldn't like family to help with their cure."

"Very strange goings-on there, miss. Some folks never leave— except for the autopsy."

"Autopsy! You mean they've died there? Of what?"

"More dying than I'd like to think. The doctor often does her own autopsies so no one knows for certain what kills them; but me,

I'd say they died of starvation. There's a very wary line between fasting—like the doctor claims—and starvation."

Grace's heart throbbed at her temples and she felt her hands grow damp inside her gloves.

"But still people come, and when their families try to take them home, they say they're being healed and won't go."

Just as Jennifer described her inability to convince Rebecca to leave.

Grace stepped up into the carriage and they left the dock. While she wanted to focus on Rebecca's situation, she couldn't set aside the beauty of this island place. They drove past goat farms and open fields of grasses with spots of standing water and black-and-white cows chewing their cuds. A wispy breeze brought a chill to Grace's shoulders and she pulled her shawl a little tighter around her shoulders. As they approached the village, she could see people weeding in their vegetable gardens, their planted flowers acting as colorful borders between carrots and the dark forests beyond. Olalla was really quite lovely. It reminded her of paintings of Scotland she'd viewed in art museums in New York. They passed a small church and then entered the village, where the carriage pulled up next to a two-story hotel that promised comfort.

A tall man—well, most men were tall against her five-foot-three-inch frame—came down the steps, took the reins, nodded to the driver, and tied the carriage at the hitching post. Then he helped the driver with her trunk, as adept with the luggage as her driver had been. Grace followed him inside as he slid the trunk from his shoulders, setting it down near the hotel desk. He tipped his hat at her.

"Thank you. The kindness of strangers is always welcome." Grace nodded to the man.

"Miss." He removed his hat then, holding it to his chest, just as a buckaroo would do. Not a dark Stetson—a homburg, instead—but a gesture as crisp as if it were a western style. The act and the gaze of his hazel eyes brought a humming sensation to her chest that surprised her and warmed her skin. A smile creased his wide face, not a handsome face exactly, but intriguing, with trimmed hair the color of roast beef and matching arched eyebrows that reminded her of Beethoven's in a portrait she'd seen. "Happy to be of service to you, Miss . . ."

"Hathaway. Grace Hathaway." Why was her heart fluttering? She could barely catch her breath.

"I'm . . . Claude Millikan. A pleasure to meet you." He had a voice like a cello, deep and soothing, and she thought his hesitation before giving his God-given name was sweet. "Please." He motioned for her to step up to the desk before him, and she told the clerk her name. She was aware he stood at her side, ran his hand through wavy hair before returning his hat to his head. She smelled a kind of musk, not unpleasant, emanating from him. She glanced at him when the clerk turned to reach for her key, and Mr. Claude Millikan was staring at her, one elbow leaned against the high desk. Admiration moved upon his face that brought her eyes back to the clerk. She hoped he couldn't see how her face warmed, and she was glad she wore a high collar. Her neck often blotched pink as a poached salmon when she was nervous or embarrassed.

"Here we are." The clerk handed her the key. "I'll have William take your trunk up for you."

"Thank you. And what time is dinner served in the dining room, please?"

"Six p.m. until eight o'clock. We have fresh sea bass for you this evening."

"I've never had such a thing."

"With a sauce of berries, the very namesake of Olalla."

"How enchanting."

"Perhaps you'd care to share a table with me, Miss Hathaway?" Mr. Millikan spoke, straightened, his hat back over his chest.

"I . . . well, I've only just arrived. I'm not sure."

"I like a late dinnertime myself."

"Yes. Well . . ."

"Shall we say seven thirty then?"

Why not? She was her own person. And he was quite pleasant to look at and obviously kind, as he'd helped the driver bring in her luggage, something he needn't have done. They'd be in a public place and it might in fact be more respectable for her to be in a restaurant with an escort rather than eating alone.

"Yes. Seven thirty will be fine. Thank you."

"I look forward to it."

William picked up her trunk then and began the climb of the stairs to the right of the desk. Grace followed him, conscious of Mr. Millikan's large presence still in the room, his eyes perhaps even following her. She was feeling quite delighted at having a dinner date as Mr. Millikan asked for his key.

"Certainly, Dr. Millikan," the clerk said.

Doctor? Grace halted. Why hadn't he said so? Grace turned, her hand gripped the stair railing. Perhaps she could confer with him about the fasting treatment of this Dr. Hazzard. This dinner might not only be entertaining but informative. She smiled as she took another step up, then gasped as she heard the clerk say, "And how are things at the sanatorium, Doctor? Are people still wasting their illnesses away?"

"Most definitely. But then no day is wasted under the care of Dr. Hazzard, as her patients would say."

⟡HREE

G race was glad William opened her door, as she wasn't sure her trembling hand could manage the long metal key. After setting her trunk at the foot of the four-poster bed, William pushed aside the drapes and opened the window, allowing a cool breeze off the Sound to flutter the white curtains.

"Oh, could you keep the window closed, please? I'm chilled, I'm afraid."

William complied and asked if she'd like a fire built in the coal brazier.

"No, I'll be fine." She handed him coins for his service. Her heart skipped a beat as she saw Dr. Millikan walk by her door just before William closed it. The man was attractive, but what should she make of his dismissive comments about the wasting treatment? Should she keep the dinner appointment? Maybe she should go down early or plead a headache. Jenny had said the only man at the sanatorium was Dr. Hazzard's husband, Sam. Was Dr. Hazzard branching out, hiring new torturers? What kind of a reputable doctor would pursue treatments the locals described as starvation? People did fast, after all. Religious people especially. But they didn't die of starvation.

She would use this dinner. She'd ask questions and try to find out what was going on at the hospital. It was a gift, her running into this doctor. She would glean from him what she could that would help her rescue Rebecca.

She unpacked and dabbed a wet cloth at the wrinkles on her dress. Then she napped without dreaming. Within an hour she was donning a yellow linen dress with a chaste scoop neck filled in with a cream lace inlay, the sort of dinner gown one might wear in Chicago or New York. Stylish but not provocative. Brown piping marked the neckline and, from bodice to waist, stripes of the same brown piping emphasized her twenty-four-inch waist. When she wore the slenderizing dress, she always felt taller, oddly, and more confident. She needed that tonight. She'd found herself slightly attracted to a man who might well be a cultist or charlatan at best, a destructive physician using his powers to harm rather than heal, at worst. She didn't know which he might be, but she would find out and be strong, corralling her emotions in the process.

She descended the stairs at 7:25 p.m., according to the gold watch encircling her narrow wrist. It was a Tiffany design her parents had sent to her for her twenty-fifth birthday in February, with a note saying they had planned to give her the watch when she wed, but they weren't sure they'd live that long. The less-than-subtle hint had not gone unnoticed.

She hoped to be a little early for dinner. Maybe she'd enter the dining room on her own, demonstrating her independence rather than have Claude Millikan escort her inside. But he already stood at the bottom of the steps, dressed in a dark brown suit with a yellow handkerchief that matched his yellow tie and perched like a flower out of his breast pocket. *Yellow and brown.* Good grief, it looked like they were . . . together, the exact same sunflower colors being worn by them both.

"You look lovely, Miss Hathaway."

"Thank you. I see you like yellow too, *Doctor* Millikan." She nodded as she walked toward the dining room. She rather liked the raised eyebrow of surprise on his face. She wasn't at all sure how she felt about his touching her elbow as they entered the room of white-covered tables. A purple iris in a slender vase sat on each one.

"I've only eaten here this week," Dr. Millikan said. "But I enjoy the evening light by that window table over there." He nodded toward the side table and, when she didn't resist, suggested those seats to the host. Claude continued his press against her elbow. She ought to have worn a dress with longer sleeves. Perhaps then his touch wouldn't have shivered her skin nor would she have felt so cool when he left her side as the host slid in her chair.

"As you've eaten here before, perhaps you can suggest something?"

"The sea bass is wonderful as the desk clerk mentioned. I've had it twice this week and not been disappointed. Thank you," Claude told the host as he accepted the large menu. "The berry sauce is perfect." He took out small glasses to read the menu, then returned them to his inside breast pocket.

"I understand the town itself is named for a kind of berry."

"That, and from a short story by the famed novelist and travel writer Robert Louis Stevenson. Are you familiar with his work, Miss Hathaway?"

Grace nodded. "But I've never heard of a work called *Olalla*."

"Published in 1885. Lovely short story of overlooking our flaws to find true happiness within each other. He's a Scot and this place has the look of Scotland if I do say so myself. The story even has a doctor as a principal character, always a fine addition to a tale." He smiled, those hazel eyes boring into hers.

"You failed to mention your profession when you introduced yourself earlier."

"Some are put off by the medical moniker and I didn't want to risk that with such a lovely new acquaintance."

Grace looked back at the menu, grateful it was so tall she couldn't see over it once she held it up to read.

A literary man, well-traveled it seemed, and one not uncomfortable discussing matters of the heart. This was not a good sign for a woman wanting to keep an emotional distance while interrogating him as subtly as she could.

They placed their dinner orders, and Grace said she understood he was employed at the sanatorium.

He choked at the water glass he'd just lifted to his mouth, apologized, and with his napkin, wiped his lips, generous lips on a smooth face with no whiskers. "You've done some detecting about me."

"Not really. I eavesdropped as I was removed to my room." She remembered Caroline's "evens-dropped" word and smiled.

"Ah."

"I'm quite intrigued. What do you do at the hospital, Dr. Millikan?"

"I . . . I'm doing research, actually. And please, call me Claude if you would."

"All right, Claude. What sort of research?"

"Extending my credentials by working with Dr. Hazzard. I . . . have an interest in digestive matters, as does the apothecary company I work for. Her patients come from all over the world. There are two British women there now, just arrived. And why are you in Olalla?"

"I've come to Olalla to . . ." She stopped herself. She'd planned to say to visit a friend, but perhaps there was a better way to get into the inner workings of the sanatorium and in so doing find a path to get Rebecca out. She coughed to cover her hesitancy, took a sip of her water. He'd changed the subject deftly from what he was doing there to what she was doing here. "I have a friend staying at the sanatorium. I'm bringing her greetings from her daughter. I've come to bring her a little assistance in her healing."

"You're a nurse?"

"No. A musician. It's my belief that music comforts the soul, opens it in fact when other methods falter. Music promotes healing. I would propose that music increases digestion which is, of course, what Dr. Hazzard's theory hopes to do through fasting, I believe. Fasting until one reaches health, am I not correct?"

"By all means."

Was he saying "by all means" one needs to fast or agreeing that "the end result is health . . . by all means"?

"What is your friend's ailment, if I might ask?"

"A broken heart. Her husband drowned some months back and she is grieving."

A frown, small as a horse shivering a fly from its flank, crossed Claude's face. "Dr. Hazzard is unlikely to have accepted someone for treatment who lacks a physical problem."

Grace hadn't considered that Rebecca might actually be ill.

"No one spoke of any ailment."

"Have you chanced to read Dr. Hazzard's book?"

"I have. She's quite outspoken, saying 'Appetite is Craving; Hunger is Desire' and that 'Craving is never satisfied; but Desire is relieved when want is supplied.' I think my friend is craving love and she is attempting to find it in this unusual way."

Claude sat back in his chair. "You've memorized a portion of her book."

"I don't hold with all she says." Grace decided to be neutral about Dr. Hazzard, not express her deepest worries based on Jenny's visit. She wanted Claude as an ally. "But I agree with her that eating without hunger can pander to appetite at the expense of good health. I'm not sure that it necessarily leads to desire or that fasting is the way to meet that desire. Health is what matters to me. I'm sure it's what matters to you as well, as a physician. Emotional and spiritual health count too."

"Most definitely. But your friend must have a physical need or how else would the doctor determine when the fasting is complete?"

"Yes . . . I see what you're saying."

Could Rebecca have developed some disease? Was that what had caused her to lose the weight Jenny had described? Perhaps a cancer.

How would she determine if Rebecca should leave and should she find another hospital for her, to treat what truly ailed her?

Grace unfurled the white linen napkin. "What are the procedures at the sanatorium, if I might ask?"

"They conform closely to Dr. Hazzard's writing. Reduced food intake. Massage treatments, hiking, extensive exercise, and other . . . activities." Claude looked past her as he spoke. "They're quite scheduled there." He looked back at her. "Have you made arrangements to visit?"

"I didn't think that was necessary. I just intend to arrive and see my friend. Surely there can be no problem with that."

Again that slight frown. "I would be happy to let your friend know that you wish to see her. Sometimes people don't want visitors. I could convey your concerns to her."

"That's kind, but I've come all this way so of course I'll see Rebecca myself. I have things to share with her. I—"

"It was only a suggestion." His voice crooned. "To save you discomfort."

"I don't need saving, sir." She sounded firmer than intended and was relieved when oysters on the half shell arrived, followed by a watercress salad with tiny red berries on top. When she looked at Claude again, he stared back with eyes full of curiosity beneath those arched eyebrows. It bothered her no end that she was pleased by the attention of someone condoning these obscure and possibly dangerous treatments.

They finished the main course and Claude was right about the sea bass. She'd never eaten such a flavorful dish. The sauce was tangy yet sweet. Then came the dessert, a frothy meringue tinted with lemon strips that ended the perfect meal, satisfying her food appetite. She wasn't so sure about her appetite for information. Every time she asked for more detail about Wilderness Heights or Linda Hazzard,

Claude answered with brief replies, then changed the subject. She found herself telling him about her life. Usually she could get men to talk about themselves, but this time he had her speaking of her time in New York at the Third Street Settlement House where she'd trained in music and worked serving lower eastside immigrants. "It was both a place to nurture neighborhoods through music but also create a kind of family for me by helping young children and their parents. I loved the work there," she told Claude.

"Why did you leave?"

"Oh, I like adventure too. I left New York for Minneapolis teaching music at a conservatory there. Then to Cincinnati and on to Chicago and finally to Oregon." Rebecca had urged her west. She hadn't told Claude that, only that a friend had asked her to bring her love of music and children and teaching west.

"And you came to Olalla from where?"

"The very high desert of Oregon," she told him. "I teach piano to the children of the vast ranches there." She sipped her coffee. Both had declined wine or after-dinner liquors.

"You don't stay long in one place then."

"A week at each ranch, then I return to the beginning of the circuit, you might say."

"No, I mean it sounds like you don't stay at any one venue for very long. New York. Minneapolis. Cincinnati. Chicago. The high desert . . ."

"Well, I . . . A year or so isn't exactly running away." But in a way it was. She'd always been restless, hungry for something but she wasn't sure what. Her parents lamented her difficulty in putting down roots, in not allowing a place or its people to satisfy her. His insight bothered her and his audacity at pointing it out with them having only just met made her want to tug at her corset where drops of perspiration had formed.

"And where did you come from?" She could change the subject too.

"California," he said, adding nothing beyond.

"Your entire life?"

"Most of it." He pushed shards of meringue around on his plate and didn't look at her. He certainly wasn't a braggart but a little more information would have been nice. She'd have to draw him out.

"Do you have any patients from California at the sanatorium?"

"I'm not sure where the patients are from." He motioned for the check. "And they aren't really my patients."

She didn't remind him that he'd told her there were British patients there. But maybe their accents gave them away and he really didn't have any idea of a patient's background.

"It would seem helpful to know something of patients' lives and families before coming for . . . improved health. One would think such knowledge would facilitate the treatments."

"One would think so," Claude said.

"Will you be returning to the sanatorium in the morning?" Grace asked as he escorted her to her room.

"Most definitely. Would you care to meet me early in the lobby? We could make the crossing together."

"Thank you. I would appreciate that." They climbed the stairs. "And might I impose upon you to make the introduction to Dr. Hazzard for me? I do so want to meet her and find out how she thinks Rebecca is doing."

"I'm not so . . . Certainly. It would be my pleasure." With that he opened her door, then stepped away, thanking her for a lovely dinner. Then he moved down the hall to his own room.

Inside Grace sat at the dressing table thinking of the evening. She opened Dr. Hazzard's book and reread the short section she'd quoted to Claude.

Appetite is Craving; Hunger is Desire. Craving is never Satisfied; but Desire is relieved when Want is Supplied. Eating without Hunger, or pandering to Appetite at the expense of Digestion, makes Disease inevitable.

Grace thought about the word "desire." She loved the Proverbs' definition of desire, coming from the words "Desire accomplished is sweet to the soul." She didn't think food hunger was the only way to look at desire. Everyone had desires, it was part of how we were created. It was a natural inclination to dream: to hunger, to reach. And when one accomplished one's goal, the result was sweet to the soul. That was satisfaction. But certainly desiring to "be well" by voluntarily refusing food until one actually became ill was not healthy even if it did remove corpulence. Surely Rebecca hadn't come all this way to eliminate a few pounds, and no one had said she had any physical ailments. She hungered for something else, something that couldn't be satisfied by food, and now the lack of food may well have touched her decision-making so she couldn't take food in, even if she wanted to.

Grace wanted more than anything to bring Rebecca home to relieve the suffering of her child and relieve Rebecca's suffering too. That was surely a desire worth pursuing. She only hoped Dr. Claude Millikan would be a help—and not get in her way.

· · · *F*OUR · · ·

I t was a wooden boat that carried them across the waterway
toward a bank of trees shrouded in mist. The clunk each time
William lifted the oars was a metronome to the swish of the wooden
blades cutting the water. A heron dragged its legs through the air
as it took off from the thick foliage. Grace clutched the sides of the
boat, conscious that Claude sat in front of her and slightly above.
When they approached the dock, Claude jumped on the deck-
ing, threw out the ropes to tie the boat, then held his hand out to
Grace. She accepted his help, embarrassed when the instability of
her move from boat to land caused her to brush against his chest.

"I'm sorry."

"Sea legs," Claude said. "Happens all the time." He steadied her,
then stepped back, as chaste as any man could be. He reached for
her carpetbag and his own black leather case. He seemed stiffer this
morning, distracted, not sharing his smile nor complimenting eyes.

"Be back at noon, Miss Hathaway," William said from the boat.

"Oh, I'll be here all day."

"Maybe," Claude commented as he tossed the ropes back to
William.

"Five o'clock sharp for the evening call. Before the bugs come
out." William waved before beginning his backward row.

319

"Most definitely." Claude tipped the brim of his hat.

Grace watched as William rowed away, unease growing as he disappeared across the water into the wispy fog. She was on her own now, walking up a path with a man behind her whom she didn't know, nor did she know if he was friend or foe. Still, he carried her carpetbag and right now that was a huge help given the slick trail.

Wilderness Heights, with its many rooms and two stories painted white, dominated the landscape as the sprigs of mist lifted to the towering trees above it. Grace could see small wooden structures like chicken coops nestled back among the firs. Maybe Rebecca had been moved to one of those, and if so, it might be easier then to talk with her, convince her to leave. "How many cottages are there?"

"I don't know. They were just opened. Here we are then." Claude huffed a bit as he set her bag on the steps of the veranda, placing his own medical bag beside it. She heard a clunk when he set hers down. "What do you have in there?"

"Just some of my 'tools of the trade.' I can carry it from here. Thank you though."

He opened the screen door for her, and her initial assessment of comfort offered by the fine high-back chairs, delicate needlepoint cushions, shining side tables, greenery, and elegant lamps gave way to concern as groans and cries ached out from the rooms beyond. The scent of camphor and a pungent disinfectant of some kind struck her nose. Her heart started to pound. A vicarious pain absorbed from the cries she heard?

"What is that?" She clutched Claude's arm.

"The smell?"

She shook her head.

"The sounds."

"Yes," Claude said. "Very troubling initially. Likely the massages. Dr. Hazzard performs them herself. Here's Sam then."

A man with military bearing approached them, hair as black as piano keys and a mustache so full it covered his upper lip. He

shook Claude's hand and put his dark eyes onto Grace as Claude
gave her the name of Sam Hazzard. "And you are?"

"Grace Hathaway. I'm a friend of Rebecca Holmes. I've come
to visit her and offer her comfort for a few days."

"That won't be necessary." He tugged at an ear in a disarming
way, but his eyes were endless black holes that sucked at her. "She's
only able to handle outsiders for a few minutes on good days. She's
making poor progress, I'm afraid. Oh, I ought not to be sharing
such things with you. Dr. Hazzard will have an update, if she feels
she can share it."

"You've revealed nothing sensitive, Sam," Claude defended. "But
perhaps Miss Hathaway could meet Dr. Hazzard and be allowed
at least those few minutes. William will be back at noontime and
she could return then."

"I'll return when I'm ready, and not a moment before," Grace
said. She hated that these men discussed her in front of her without
even noting that she had her own opinions.

"Yes," Sam said. He tugged at that ear again, like a small child,
thinking. "Well, let's see what you have in your bag then, shall we?"
He dragged out certain words, like a caress gone wrong. "We have
to be sure you've brought no food. Nothing to interfere with the
regime of the diet and a patient's journey toward health."

Grace opened her bag and Sam peered in, removing the ukulele
she'd brought along, and a harmonica. He held sheet music up
with a question on his somber face.

"You must have a piano here. Most sanatoriums do these days."

"Afraid not. This is a serious place of healing," Sam told her.
"Patients have no time for musical frivolity." He pawed through the
bag, unrolled a drawing of the Columbia River done by Caroline.

"Her daughter drew that for Rebecca."

Sam removed it and laid it on the side table. "It will distress
her," he said.

"But how could it? She loves that child and—"

"We know what is best for her. I hesitate to even let you bring these musical instruments to her. Dr. Hazzard would—"

"Surely they can do no harm," Claude said. "I've known music to soothe."

Grace smiled a thank-you at Claude before saying, "Dr. Millikan is quite right. Now if you've finished, I'd very much like to meet Dr. Hazzard since that is required before I can see my friend."

"And I must tend to my duties," Claude said. He tipped his hat at Grace and left the lobby–living area, as Grace thought of it. She wondered where his office was. She was sure she'd want to confer with him again before the day was out.

"Come with me then, Miss Hathaway. Quite the worldly name. I knew of Hathaways in Chicago. A well-regarded family. Are you from that line?"

"I might be. You're from the northwest then?" Grace followed him, carrying her carpetbag. She looked back at Caroline's drawing lying on the side table and vowed to pick it up on her way out. Like music, art infused encouragement to lost souls, and Caroline's art would do that for her mother.

"Dr. Hazzard began her work in Minneapolis." Grace hadn't heard of her when she'd lived in that city. "And we moved to Seattle after a time. Here we are." They'd walked down a short, narrow hall with closed doors on either side. At the end of the hall, on the right, Sam opened a door with glass labeled DR. LINDA BURFIELD HAZZARD, D.O.

A white-and-blue-striped uniformed nurse rose when Sam entered and Grace thought she blushed as she stammered her good morning. "Sam. I mean Mr. Hazzard. Your wife is with a patient." Her hands fluttered as she sat back down and Sam tugged at that ear with a lopsided smile.

"Of course she is. This is Miss Hathaway. She's here to visit Rebecca Holmes. But of course she must meet with Dr. Hazzard first. Will you take care of her until my wife returns?"

"Absolutely, Sam. Mr. Hazzard."

"Yes." He pushed himself to his full height from the counter where he'd lounged briefly, unsettling the nurse behind it. He winked at the woman, Grace was certain of it. "You're in good hands with Miss Johnson here. It's been a pleasure. I'm sure our paths will cross again."

Not if I can help it.

Grace looked at her watch. She'd arrived at 8:00 a.m. and was still sitting with Miss Johnson at 11:00 a.m. without seeing Dr. Hazzard or her Rebecca. She stood, paced, sat back down, then asked for a toilet. She was directed outside, which surprised her since the facility gave the appearance of modernity, and with sick people, bathrooms would surely be advised over privies.

"You'll have to leave your bag here," the nurse told her.

Grace nodded. She escaped the room and turned in the opposite direction back toward the lobby–living area. Caroline's picture still lay there and she picked it up. Then she pressed a door that opened onto another hall. The sounds of pain grew louder with the open door, and she debated about entering the hallway on her own. She decided against it as she really did have to use the water closet. After completing her duties in the hollyhock-bordered structure, she wandered to one of the cabins. Each had only one window and a single door off a small porch. She peered inside and saw a single bed, dresser, and chamber pot. At the porch door, she knocked but no one answered. She tried to push the door open, but it was locked. She went back to the window and saw two chairs, a long table, and various pieces of equipment—syringes and such. No hot plate for cooking; not even utensils for eating. Nothing on the wall to bring relief from the wooden walls not even whitewashed. At least no one was being left alone here. She stepped away from the cottage and bumped into a tall woman with a square face and eyes like a hawk's.

"What are you doing here? This is a private estate. You have no business—"

"You're absolutely right. I'm so sorry." The woman's eyes narrowed at Grace's fluster. Grace hid Caroline's drawing behind her skirts. In that moment she made a decision. "I was waiting to meet the famous Dr. Hazzard but had to . . . relieve myself. I have these . . . ailments that require frequent, well, eliminations." Grace actually blushed with the lie, hoping to appeal to Dr. Hazzard's healing desires and vanity with the subject. "After leaving the privy I noticed these little houses and thought perhaps if I were to be a patient here, would I be cared for in these cottages or in the sanatorium? But I never should have intruded."

"You should not have. But you are ill?"

"Yes, though I came here to meet the famous, well-regarded Dr. Hazzard about my ailment. But also to see my friend who is being made well here. Rebecca Holmes. Are you on staff here?" *Of course you are.* "Do you know Rebecca?"

"And you are . . . ?"

"Grace Hathaway. Of the Chicago Hathaways. And I don't have an appointment, but I was in Dr. Hazzard's office all morning and I know she's doing such good work and so busy and—"

"I am Dr. Linda Hazzard." The woman stuck her hand out like a man, to shake Grace's.

"You are!" Grace's hand flew to her lips, the other still clutching Caroline's drawing hidden by the folds of her skirt. "I'm so honored. That is," she grabbed Dr. Hazzard's hand and shook it like a giddy schoolgirl, "I'm so amazed that you are talking to me, little Grace Hathaway, right here at Wilderness Heights. I can't believe my good fortune."

The doctor smiled and sucked her hand free from Grace's grip, her voice changing to honey as she said, "I'm so sorry you were made to wait, Miss Hathaway. I never want any of my potential patients to wonder if they are always first in my heart. Shall we go now to my office, dear?"

Grace nodded and walked just a step behind the doctor, chattering about nothing. She knew she'd found a key to this woman's ways: toadying, obsequiousness; flatter and fawn. As they passed the lobby–living room table, Grace slipped Caroline's drawing back. She'd get it later or maybe ask Claude to retrieve it in case she didn't return to the hotel.

Because Grace was now a "potential patient," she was allowed to see Rebecca. "I just want to know if she's still progressing. It will help me decide if your treatment—should you accept me—is really right for me."

"Certainly. I'll take you to her room myself. But first, let's discuss your ailment. I assume from your earlier comments it is your bladder then?"

"Oh, yes. I can barely wait an hour between visits to the commode. Of course it wasn't always that way."

"No, we change as we grow older, but still, your age would not account for such a malady. I would need a specimen."

"And I can give you one. Within the hour no doubt." Grace sounded as cheerful as she could, hoping to disarm the woman into thinking she was addled-minded already and would be an easy pushover as a patient, so she could find out what really went on here, where the moans and groans of suffering truly came from. "And I am a musician. Your husband, whom I met when I first came, looked through my bag and found no problem with the instruments. Perhaps I could play a tune for my friend, as a reminder of how things will be when she is better, under your very wise care. Music soothes the suffering body, washes the soul of the dirt of daily living. A German proverb. Have you heard of it?"

"I've little time for music or proverbs. I'm English, not German. Can you provide that specimen now?"

"Oh, of course. I'll just dance to the privy."

Dr. Hazzard handed her a glass beaker and then told her of a small bathroom inside the hospital. "Down that first hall and to the left."

Grace did as she was told, glancing into patients' rooms but seeing little as curtains covered the open doorways, keeping eyes out but not the sounds of agony coming from many of them. She tended to her instructions in the bathroom, noting a second door from the room. She wondered where it went, but it was locked. She needed to know the hospital layout so she could get Rebecca out furtively if needed. She sauntered back to Dr. Hazzard's office, listening for Rebecca's tones among the sighs of discomfort.

"Now then, let us visit your friend. Mrs. Holmes, is that right?"

Grace nodded.

"She's having a difficult transition. Many emotional things affect her physical healing, but she accepts the massages well. The clyster syringe treatments have had to be extended to four times a day now, to compensate."

Four a day? Why, that could kill a person. And with no food in her, how could she have anything to . . . eliminate?

"Rebecca always did do things differently," Grace fawned. "My music might help."

"We'll see."

They walked down the black-and-white linoleum tile of the far wing with two rooms on each side. At the last room on the left, Dr. Hazzard walked into the open door and pushed back the curtain. Grace was grateful no moans had come from the room.

"Wait here," Dr. Hazzard told her as she stepped inside.

Grace looked past her to the bed and gasped at the skeleton of a woman lying there. "That . . . that's not Rebecca Holmes. It couldn't be!"

$\mathcal{F}$IVE

f course it's not Rebecca Holmes. We moved her to another room," Dr. Hazzard said. "I needed to check on one of the young sisters from England, They're orphans, poor things. I told you not to enter." She then crooned to the woman in the bed. "How are we today, Claire? Are we ready for our massage?"

"A little food. Would make . . . me . . . stronger." The whispered response still held a British accent, such as it was. The skeleton's eyes were bloodshot.

"Yes, but it will also make you ill. Your body is not ready for more food yet, Claire. You must trust me. You do trust me, do you not?" The woman barely moved her head. She looked as though she was sixty, her face sagging over bone, but Dr. Hazzard had called her "young."

Dr. Hazzard motioned for the nurse who had been sitting beside Claire to move as she looked at a chart attached to the bed. Grace's eyes met the nurse's, who looked away. *The nurse knows the woman is starving!* Claire made no eye contact but merely stared out the window as though a dark sky held her captive.

Before she could stop herself, Grace began to sing a lullaby. "Guardian angels God will send thee, all through the night."

The skeleton in the bed turned her eyes to Grace, searching for a moment before finding the source of the sound. A smile formed on her cracked lips. "My nanny sang that. Is my Margaret here?"

"No! Your nanny is not here." Dr. Hazzard glared at Grace. "I told you music was not a proper form of treatment. See how it distresses her."

Grace didn't think she looked distressed from the music—but she did look distressed. And emaciated. Starved.

"I'll be back shortly for your massage, Claire." Dr. Hazzard gave the nurse the chart, then trudged past Grace. "Come this way."

The room they entered was across the hall, one of the rooms farthest away from the two main doors. The woman sitting at the side of the bed, her head between her hands, shivered as she straightened to the sound of Dr. Hazzard's sing-song "Rebecca. This woman says she is your friend."

Rebecca gazed at Grace, the lack of recognition like a sword cutting Grace's heart. "It's me, Rebecca. Caroline sends her love."

"Grace? Grace Hathaway? Was that you singing? I thought it was angels."

"Yes, it's me, Grace." Grace dropped to her knees, her skirts swishing on the hardwood floor. She stared up at her friend, blinked back tears. Gently, she moved dry and flattened hair stuck to the side of Rebecca's face. "It's so good to see you. You look . . ." She stroked her friend's arm, touched her bony thighs beneath a faded nightdress. "You look like you've lost weight." Such a lame comment, but Grace hadn't known what to say about this thin woman with hollowed-out eyes and cheekbones. Her collarbones stuck out like a mountain ridge across a caved desert of pale skin.

Rebecca smiled. "Yes. I've lost my baby fat. Dr. Hazzard is helping me get well, though I am tired of tomato juice. I will never make another batch as long as I live." Despite her attention to Rebecca, Grace thought she saw Dr. Hazzard's shoulder sag in relief. Was she worried that Rebecca would condemn the doctor?

"Your friend," Dr. Hazzard crooned, "thinks we can help her as

well. Of course we'll do so, as we did with the Williamson sisters."
She turned to Grace. "They began their treatment in Seattle, in an
apartment I keep for patients there. The sisters have traveled the
world but chose my sanatorium to improve their health. But here,
we can treat you while you stay where you are in Olalla."

"Oh. Not in one of the little cottages?"

"All of them are spoken for. I think it best if you come in each
day until we see how the fasting affects you. If you need more support, then of course we'll bring you in to the facility. Meanwhile, I
think we have enough time now with your friend, don't you think
so, Rebecca?"

"Oh please." She reached toward Grace. "I'd love to have her
stay. She hasn't told me how Caroline is yet. Or how she came to
be here."

"Plenty of time for that. She can visit a few minutes each day she
comes for treatments. But now, see how your hand tremors. The
excitement is too much for you. It's time you rested and prepared
for your massage." That honey voice again.

Rebecca nodded agreement and Grace helped lift her legs and
swing her friend back to lie down. As she did so, the claw that
had been Rebecca's hand grabbed Grace's and she narrowed her
eyes, mouthing, "Thank you," before her eyelids fluttered and she
fell asleep.

Grace was returned by a nurse to Dr. Hazzard's office where
she was told to wait until her final admission information could be
reviewed. She wasn't sure what good it would do to be a patient if
she couldn't be here at the sanatorium. But it also meant that Dr.
Hazzard had patients in Seattle whom she must visit occasionally,
leaving the sanatorium without her dominating presence. Nurse
Johnson had told her the doctor took the two-hour ferry at least
twice a week. "Do you know where Dr. Millikan's office is?"

"Dr. Millikan?" Nurse Johnson looked puzzled. "Oh, you mean the apothecary representative. Yes, he's in the laboratory most of the time looking at the potions and pills that Dr. Hazzard provides to relieve discomfort and to assist with the elimination issues and speed the wasting process. He hasn't been here long." She whispered then, "I'm surprised the Hazzards allowed it. But then they need the money and his company pays them for allowing his research here."

Dr. Millikan paid to be a part of this? How despicable. Just to duplicate their potions and make money selling them to other unsuspecting patients. Grace's impression of Claude descended like a fallen soufflé. Yet the memory of his kind eyes shivered her flesh. What sort of woman was she with such contradictory responses?

Her stomach growled and she wished she'd tried to sneak in a sandwich, but Sam Hazzard would have found it anyway. The nurse smiled at her. "Beginning a fast is the most difficult. Be sure to drink lots of water." Grace excused herself for yet another "toilet moment" that Nurse Johnson was quite accustomed to by now, reminding her to use the outdoor privy as she wasn't yet a patient. Returning, Grace remembered Caroline's drawing, which she picked up, then decided to take it to Rebecca's room. She slipped down the hall, pushed back the curtain over the door marked 3, and whispered, "Rebecca?"

But the bed was empty. The room cleared of anything that suggested anyone had been in that room less than three hours before. What had they done with her?

Grace made her way back to the lobby–living area, then down the alternate wing where Dr. Hazzard had her office. She wondered where the laboratory was, then remembered seeing a sign near the stairs pointing to the second floor. Were their patients there too? Or only the laboratory and private residence of the Hazzards? She hesitated at the landing, then decided she'd explore it tomorrow. She didn't want to miss Dr. Hazzard's return. She stroked the smooth wood of the banister, wishing for just a moment that Claude Millikan would walk down those steps. At least she'd see him at the evening crossing. She wasn't sure how much she'd tell him or why she even thought of him.

"You wired my parents? Whatever for?" Grace felt invaded. "It'll just disturb them to think I'm ill."

"You are a single woman and we had to be certain you were your own guardian. After all, we wouldn't want to scrape against the law by treating without guardian consent. I assure you, my husband did not alarm them. He simply requested verification that you could make your own medical decisions and had the necessary resources to pay for such treatments."

"They'll be worried nonetheless. I'll have to wire them myself, reassure them."

"Of course. But meanwhile, we can begin the treatments. Starting now, you will eat only cornmeal and a broth we will prepare for you and send home with you. Where are you staying?"

"The Olalla Hotel."

"Ah, yes. You will have to endure the scent rising from the kitchens there. But it will be for your best health. I've analyzed your specimen and you do indeed have a parasite of some kind that makes you need to void frequently."

"I do? And you could find it so quickly."

"Yes. Have you traveled outside of America much? To Mexico or Europe?"

"I visited a Canadian province last year, a brief visit to Victoria." She'd gone with Rebecca and Caroline as a way to distract them from the loss of a husband and father, but they'd contracted no illness there, she was sure of it. There was nothing wrong with her, but the Hazzards had found something to cure. At least their discovery of a "disease" when there wasn't one made her feel better that Rebecca had no disease either. Taking her away wouldn't harm her; giving her food would bring back her health.

"British Columbia. Yes. The Williamson sisters also stayed there last year. Well, it's good we've found the source of this terrible epidemic and we know that with our approach you will be well in no time." She rustled some papers and then smiled a smile as toadying as anything Grace had yet seen in the woman. "Do we understand the needs here? I will weigh you before you leave and you'll be weighed each day. If I find you are unable to sustain the fast without support, we will arrange for a nurse for you at the hotel or, if space allows, bring you here. But of course it will be much less expensive if you can monitor the treatment on your own. Understood?"

"Oh yes. I'm so grateful that you've found what's wrong with me and that the cure is within reach, like a gold apple in a silver bowl."

Dr. Hazzard returned to her hawk's stare as she said, "You might start thinking of analogies that don't remind you of food. Fasting tends to brighten the mind for food and will only make you hunger more."

··· SIX ···

I didn't hear any of your music today, Miss Hathaway," Claude said.

They'd had a silent crossing in the boat with William and now walked up to the hotel where he expressed his first thoughts to her.

"Oh, I sang for a patient and she thanked me. Dr. Hazzard was right there with us."

He pushed his lower lip out in thought. "I'm surprised. But gratified she would allow it," he added.

"She wasn't exactly pleased," Grace confessed. "It brought memories of home to the woman—Claire Williamson, I think her name was—and she cried a bit, asking for her nanny, so Dr. Hazzard made me stop. I'm going to try the harmonica tomorrow for Rebecca. If I can find where they've moved her. After all, that's a cowboy's instrument and Rebecca should respond to that. She and her husband had a small hobby ranch for them to enjoy when Bertrand wasn't banking. But Rebecca loved going out on the range for the love of landscape and the grandeur of the cowboy life."

"You did enjoy your time teaching on the ranches," Claude said.

"I did. There is a music to the mountains and the sage." There she was again, spilling out information to him he didn't ask for nor need to know.

"You've arranged to return tomorrow, then."

"Every day in fact."

"I'm . . . surprised. You're quite the persuader, it seems. Perhaps we'll have lunch together one day."

"Or dinner tonight."

He grinned. "I admire a woman who knows the way to a man's heart is through his stomach. Shall we say 6:30 p.m.?"

"Most definitely," Grace said and felt her face grow warm at Claude's endearing smile.

When she reached her room, she realized she couldn't eat dinner with Claude. She'd have to show signs of wasting or Dr. Hazzard would think she was up to trickery. She sent a note to the kitchen asking them to heat the broth she'd provided and send it with a piece of corn bread that she would take at 9:00 p.m. To Claude she wrote that she wasn't ready for a big dinner after all, but that if he'd like to walk with her around the village and perhaps show her where she could send a wire, to please join her in the lobby at 6:00 p.m.

His reply was two words: "Most definitely."

The evening carried with it the scent of loamy earth and cedar. They heard small children stretching the day before being called in for rest. A dog barked and received a chorus of answers. Kerosene lamps already lit the door of the wire office where Claude knew the clerk by his first name. Grace sent an assuring note to her family that she was fine and simply gathering information for a friend who was ill and that the sanatorium staff had misunderstood. "Not to worry. Will write soon." She paid the clerk. Claude asked her to wait a moment while he too sent a wire "to my employer," he told her. She watched the setting sun while she waited. Her stomach growled again.

Finished, Claude slipped her arm through his elbow and patted her hand. He had long fingers, a pianist's fingers.

"Is your employer happy with your work?" Grace asked as they passed an apothecary shop. She wished she could ask him how he felt

334

about being paid to examine herbs and pills while patients groaned and moaned and what he intended to do with such information.

"They get what they're paying for," he said.

His answer carried a tone of distaste, and Grace frowned before asking him about the upper story and if there were other offices or patient rooms on the second floor or only the Hazzards' quarters.

"The lab and the Hazzard apartment take up most of the floor, but there are at least three patient rooms there as well. Perhaps for the more involved. It's very quiet in those rooms. The kitchen's on the main floor, as you may have noticed, along with just a few patient rooms. I'm not sure how they support the sanatorium with so few patients here at any given time."

"They have patients still in Seattle, you know."

"I wasn't certain."

Grace changed the subject then. She was giving him her information and she wanted his. "I don't know how involved my friend is, but she looked a far sight better than the woman from Britain. I don't see how that woman stays alive, do you?"

"There appears to be enough nutrition in the potions and the tomato juice. The human body can sustain on significantly much less than what we put into ourselves."

"Have you seen the woman? Claire?"

Claude shook his head. "No."

"If you do, you'll question whether there is enough nutrition in those potions, and remember, whatever they eat is later forced . . . out."

"Your friend. Is she looking forward to going home?"

"I had three minutes with her and none without Dr. Hazzard there. She doesn't talk about going home. She's way too thin. I've seen chickens with healthier thighs. And they've moved her from room 3 to somewhere else. I'll have to start all over tomorrow trying to find her."

"But surely they'll tell you where she is since they've agreed you can return each day," Claude said. "I'm impressed that Dr. Hazzard sees value in your visits."

"Yes." Grace couldn't very well tell him why she'd be going back daily. "I'm quite the persuader." She felt his elbow tighten on her arm and liked the firmness of it. His tone in responding to her question about his employers made her think he might be doing this job but not liking it.

"Would you like me to look for you? I could check the patient sheet and see where your friend is."

"Could you?" They stopped in front of a candy store that was, thankfully, closed, or Grace would never have been able to pass it by. "That would help so much. And Caroline's drawing, her daughter's gift. It's still on the lobby table where Sam removed it from my carpetbag. Might you bring that back to the hotel as well?"

"Consider it done. Now, there is a small pub that plays quite good music on a Wednesday evening. Would you care to stop in?"

"No. Thank you. I really do need to return. I must write to my parents to follow up on my cable."

He was perfectly compliant with her request, and at her room, Claude expressed a wish that she sleep well and added, "I look forward to the crossing in the morning. Will you join me for breakfast?"

"I'm so sorry. I have an apple and dried oatmeal in the room and will be content with that. I'll see you at 7:30 a.m. for the crossing though. Good night . . . Claude."

"Good evening, Miss Hathaway."

He turned toward his room and Grace raised her voice. "If we're to be seeing each other daily, I imagine it will be all right for you to call me Grace, if you'd like."

"Grace," he said, turning to her. He rolled her name around on his mouth like a caramel candy, firm and sweet. She nearly swooned at the look he gave her as he added, "I'd love to call you Grace."

⊠

"I'll meet you at the base of the stairs around noon," Claude told her as they walked up the path to the sanatorium. "And you could take the boat back at noon so you wouldn't have to spend the entire day here—unless you haven't been able to find your friend before then."

"Thank you. Yes. That would work."

They separated and Grace found Dr. Hazzard's office where she reported in and was weighed. "One hundred and five pounds. A half pound less than yesterday. Very good."

"I've done just as you've asked, Dr. Hazzard," Grace gushed. "I feel so much better already."

"Hmmm. We do need to discuss how payments will be arranged. Sam will handle that. You can meet with him at 10:00 a.m. in his office, upstairs."

Good, she had a reason to snoop around on the second floor.

"And my friend. Can I see her again? I want to play the harmonica for her."

Dr. Hazzard sniffed. "She had a bad night. I don't think playing the harmonica will improve her day." She tugged at a chin hair, yanking it and sloughing it onto the wastebasket beside her. She was thin as a finger but looked solid as steel. "Yes. Why don't you play for her. She had wanted to sign some papers she insisted we draw up and then yesterday after your visit she took a turn for the worse. Perhaps the music could soothe her nerves and we can proceed with what she wanted done with her estate."

Her estate? "However I can help." Grace swallowed. "You know I'm so grateful that you've found the parasite and that we'll starve it to death and I'll be well again."

"Indeed. Visit Sam and have him bring you back here and I'll take you to visit Rebecca Holmes."

"And what shall I do in the interim? I could sing for your Claire patient."

"No! Leave her be. Very distressing to have her reminded of her nanny. Her sister, too, was all a-bother last evening. You may walk the grounds. Exercise is excellent, meat is not. There are books to read on the lobby shelf. In fact that's where I'll ask Mr. Hazzard to find you at 10:00 a.m."

Shoot. She had no reason now to snoop the second floor. She decided not to try to find Rebecca, as she didn't want them suspicious of her. Instead she made her way to the lobby where she once again picked up the rolled drawing gathering dust on the table. She stuffed it into her carpetbag and would tell Claude later that she had it. She selected a book of poems, *Passion Flowers* by Julia Ward Howe, surprised that the sanatorium would shelve such a book. She took the poetry outside, checked her watch, and made sure she'd be back inside by 10:00 a.m. She would play along as a patient for as long as it moved her closer to Rebecca and to finding out what was really happening in this place. *Rebecca discussed her estate?*

The woman's dress hung from her as though she were nothing but a hanger. Faded and worn, it bore the history of something once elegant with lace at the sleeves and a ribbon of velvet around the neckline. It was a nightdress. The woman moved in a tattered pace as though her feet would not do as she asked. Grace stood at the bench she'd been sitting on beneath a spreading cedar tree not far from the front porch.

"May I help you?" She reached out her hand to the woman who swooned onto the bench, pulling Grace down with her.

"Please. Send this letter. My sister. Claire. She's dying, I know she's dying." The woman crushed an envelope into Grace's hand; her breath was foul like the bottom of a bird cage. "Send it. Today. Please. To our nanny. Margaret Conway. She's visiting in Australia. I need to get dear Claire out of here!" Her rheumy eyes watered. "I was the one who insisted we come. Now look at us." She gazed at the loose-hanging cloth that was her dress. "Just look at us!"

"Dora!" A nurse now jogged across the lawn toward them. "Dora, what are you doing out here. You'll catch your death of cold." She helped Dora stand. "Hello," the nurse said turning to Grace. "And you are?"

"Grace Hathaway. New patient." She waved her fingers making light of the encounter.

Dora jerked her head to look at Grace, the movement seeming to exhaust her.

"I come in daily for treatments. I live at the Olalla Hotel. Go home every night and get my mail," she chirped, hoping the words would bring comfort to the woman. She would mail her letter. She would.

Dora sank against the nurse then, mumbling, groaning.

"Was she bothering you?" the nurse said softly behind Dora's back.

"Oh, not at all. We were just chatting about what that bird was that flew off as you approached. But she's right, Dora, you don't want to catch a cold."

"No. No cold. Might die."

Grace now had two items of contraband in her carpetbag. She hoped Sam wouldn't go through the bag again. Finding Caroline's picture would be nothing to finding Dora's desperate letter to their nanny.

At 10:00 a.m. she was back in the lobby area waiting for Sam, who was prompt. "Please join me," he said as he led her to the stairs. "Ladies first."

She didn't like knowing he walked behind her, staring. Funny, she'd found Claude in that position to be quite flattering. Sam Hazzard made her queasy. At the top of the stairs he put his hand to the small of her back. "This way, dear." He leaned in front of her to open his office door, then guided her in with his hand, the size of a shovel. She felt like a melon being tested for ripeness.

The room was large, had plenty of light from floor-to-ceiling windows without curtains, as though inviting any and all to see that whatever transpired in this room was open to the world. Of course it was on the second floor where peering in would be difficult. Getting out would be difficult too. She was starting to see each setting here as a place she might have to escape from. It helped knowing that the wall bordered the laboratory and Claude would be in there doing whatever it was that he did. Still, she wasn't sure she could count on him just because she *didn't* know what he did.

"Now then. The fees are quite reasonable, but you are not getting the full benefit of the treatments so long as you are not a resident."

"Dr. Hazzard said there wasn't enough room here or I surely would have preferred to be where I would have immediate access to her. And to you, of course, should any problems arise."

"Yes." He dragged the word out. "We expect an opening within the week. Should that occur, we will definitely arrange for your admission. Meanwhile would you like us to draw directly from your account? And if so, what is your bank and accounting number?" He held a pen, ready to write.

"Is there another alternative? I don't think I brought my banking information along. I'd have to send a letter. I was only planning to visit until of course I met your exceptional wife and she identified the parasite that is taking me down. I'm so very grateful, but I don't have . . . those . . . numbers . . ."

He tapped the pen against the paper and looked up. *Lizard eyes.* "Do you have cash with you enough for an account here that can be drawn upon? While you await access through your solicitor?"

"Oh, of course. How much would you like?"

"A thousand dollars would make the start."

"A thousand dollars?" Did they think she was made of gold? "I, no, I don't have that kind of cash with me. I have one hundred fifty dollars."

"That will do to begin. Now let us look at these papers. They really don't need much of your review. They're standard. We'll deduct the expense of treatments and visits with Dr. Hazzard from the account while we await further infusion."

Infusion. That's a nice word for robbery by fraud. Grace did read the papers and drew a line through the words "indefinite withdrawal access by Wilderness Heights" and replaced it with the words "up to $150 dollars." "We'll negotiate how much more I'll need to add," Grace said, "when the account is close to the bottom. I find 'indefinite' is just such a gooey word, don't you think?"

Sam frowned and Grace fluttered her eyelashes at him.

"We can definitely negotiate arrangements," he said.

"Oh goody. Then can we visit Rebecca Holmes now?"

"Of course. Just let me get her file. There are pages for her to sign as well."

Grace picked up her carpetbag but Sam was already around the desk and had his hand on hers. "Let's leave that here. No sense in your having to carry such a heavy thing all the way to the end of the downstairs wing. You can retrieve it before you leave today. I'll make sure it's at the dock for you."

"I didn't bring any food with me, if that's what you're concerned about."

"Not at all. Not at all. Just too much to carry."

"Carrying it would be good exercise. Dr. Hazzard recommends exercise."

Sam took the carpetbag from her and took her arm in his and moved her toward the door. "We wouldn't want to tire you." How was she going to keep him from going through it while she was visiting Rebecca, and what about the music she wanted to bring to her friend? She'd have to sing.

They stepped out into the hall and Grace broke from his hold on her and put both hands to her mouth and giggled. "Oh, do you think I could see the laboratory while we're here? It's always good to know that the latest techniques and utilities are incorporated into treatments."

"Well—"

"It's just right here, isn't it?" She hated sounding like a fluffel-head, but it seemed to throw Sam off when she did. She skipped ahead of him and opened the door. Claude turned to look at her, eyes wide. He shook his head. She nearly gasped. "Oh, never mind," she said as she closed the door. She kept her voice loud. "I thought maybe Dr. Millikan would be here and he could bring my carpetbag to the dock, since he'll make the crossing with me. I'm sure that would be a help to you, wouldn't it? And I don't really need to see the laboratory to know that you're doing a fine, fine job here." Her voice sounded giddy even to her, and she hadn't even begun taking the potions Dr. Hazzard had prescribed she start.

"I'll ask him myself when we return," Sam Hazzard said. "Now let us find your Mrs. Holmes."

Grace went with him, eager to see how he would explain why Rebecca wasn't in her room—as her friend was in the laboratory with Claude.

·· · SEVEN ·· ·

Sam and Grace made their way down the stairs when Grace decided she must cause some distraction to allow time for Claude to return Rebecca to her room. Maybe he was being helpful, checking her vital signs or whatnot; or perhaps he wasn't. But whatever was happening, the look on his face told her he didn't want Sam Hazzard to know of it. "Oh, could you show me one of the cottages? I might like to stay there when I come here full time. They're just so cute, like a dollhouse almost."

"They are more expensive, of course. For the privacy."

"Oh, that won't be a problem. I just have to get those account numbers, you know." She giggled, then eased her way out the door at the back of the building.

Sam followed and used a key to open a cottage deep into the cedars and firs.

"There isn't much light in here," Grace said. "Even in the day like this. It might be quite dreary with the rainy season . . . why, I'd just waste away."

"Ah, but sleep comes easily during the day when the sky is shrouded with treetops, and as the treatment continues there are many days when one simply wishes to sleep. Try the bed if you like."

The last thing she needed was a panting Sam Hazzard hovering over her asking about the quality of the mattress. "Oh, that won't be necessary. I might like the hospital better after all. This seems so . . . sparse . . . for the additional expense."

"There is the single nurse, of course. You would have twenty-four-hour care."

"I see." A sick patient could be kept here as in a cell with no way to make her way to the mainland, no way to ever reach help if it was needed. She'd have to be certain she did not get relegated to the cottages. "So Rebecca isn't in one of these?"

"Not at all, though she has the resources. She's been so grateful to Doctor—" Sam stopped himself. "She prefers the hospital as well. Closer to the call of Dr. Hazzard who brings such comfort to so many."

They crossed back to the main sanatorium and Grace noted two patients she hadn't seen before were out taking the sunshine, with a keeper by their sides. A man and what looked like his son sat on a bench, and Grace could hear the man's sharp retort as they walked by. "I'm fine. They're doing me good. Now stop worrying. Never felt better in all my days. Tell your mother not to worry over me. I'm good here. Be home by June."

"You see how happy our patients are," Sam soothed into her ear.

"What? Oh, yes. I also see that each has someone to assist them. Might I be an assistant to a patient or two, while I'm doing so well and healing?"

"You would volunteer?"

"I would. Of course as I weaken in the transition before I become healthier and the parasite is destroyed for good, well, then I would need an assistant myself, wouldn't I? But until then, I could just help out while I was here."

"I'll speak to my wife," Sam said. "Here we are. A room with corner windows. Isn't that lovely?"

"And room enough for another bed. Why, I could move right in with Rebecca and be her assistant."

"As I said, I will speak to Dr. Hazzard. But here now is your friend." He pushed back the curtain around the bed. Rebecca lay quiet as snow and just as white. "I'll wait outside while you acquaint yourselves. Five minutes should do it, yes? And then we have papers for her to sign."

"How are you, Rebecca?" Grace whispered as she leaned over her friend.

Rebecca's eyes fluttered open though they looked right through her.

"Rebecca? Do you know who I am?"

"Grace?"

"Yes. It's me. I've come to take you home."

"But I'm not well yet. I . . . I have a parasite. And I'm still so fat! Oh Grace, Bertrand would be so upset with me for being so fat."

"Bertrand would love you if you were as big as Mount Hood. He wouldn't want you to be wasting away like this. He loved you and didn't want to leave, but that's what happens in life. It does, and, oh, dear, dear Rebecca—" Grace's words caught in her throat, the pain of seeing her friend like this. "There's no parasite, Rebecca. I'm sure of it. I have no symptoms and—"

"Time enough, ladies." Sam leaned into the door frame, then propelled himself toward the bed, papers in hand. "Now then, Rebecca. You wanted a codicil to your will, is that right? We've had it drawn up and the $5000 annually for the sanatorium is your bequest, is it not? And of course that's after you've paid for your care here."

"Five thousand dollars! That's ridiculous. She has a child to care for."

"There's enough, Grace." Rebecca gripped Grace's hand. "I've left some for you as well."

"But you're not dying, Rebecca. You aren't. You're going to get better. Tell her, Mr. Hazzard. Your treatments are meant to bring health, not death."

"Sometimes we are not as skilled as we would like. And it will comfort Mrs. Holmes to know all has been settled in her will."

"Don't sign it, please. Let me take it home and read it first, to be sure—"

Rebecca sighed. "I would like that. Yes." She sank back into her bed and dozed.

"See? She needs rest. I'll just take the papers home and read them tonight and then I can assist her in the morning."

Sam's eyes narrowed. "This is highly irregular."

"But she said she asked for it to be drawn up and now she just seeks another pair of eyes to review it. That's what friends are for, to be eyes for another. Sometimes a voice for another."

"Very well. Bring it back first thing in the morning and be prepared to help your friend see what it is she saw just a few days ago in wanting this codicil drawn up. It'll be a huge waste of money and a nuisance if she changes her mind."

"Oh I understand, I truly do. I'll bring it back when I bring the money for my own account. The one hundred and fifty dollars."

"See that you do." He turned on his heel and she could hear his boots clopping down the hall toward Dr. Hazzard's office.

"Rebecca," Grace whispered. Nothing. She began to sing then, "*Softly and tenderly Jesus is calling, calling for you and for me . . .* Rebecca. I'm leaving now, but you're not alone. Remember that. I'll be back tomorrow. Hang on, dear friend. Please hang on."

Grace breathed a sigh of relief when she saw Claude carrying her carpetbag toward the dock. William could be seen in the distance rowing his way.

"Thank you," she said. "Thanks so much for bringing this."

"I fetched it from Sam as soon as he returned. I take it you saw your friend."

"As did you. I wanted to ask what she was doing in your lab. I can only hope you were doing her no harm."

His shoulders dropped in relief. "I'm grateful you concluded that. But it's best if I don't tell you what I was doing exactly; just trust that I would never bring pain or suffering to any patient."

"I should hope not." She opened her carpetbag then and pushed around inside until she found the letter from Dora, Claire's sister. "Oh thank goodness." She clutched the letter to her breast. "Earlier today, when I was alone outside, a woman approached me. She was nearly a skeleton and she fell toward me, crushing this letter into my hands, mumbling things about her sister dying and her nanny needing to come. I must have not looked like staff nor a patient, but a visitor, so she sought me out."

"Which is what you are, a visitor."

Grace stepped over his comment. "She was so desperate, Claude. I ached for her and I've seen her sister. She is dying," Grace whispered. "And I fear Rebecca is too."

Claude pulled her into his arms then, a gesture as welcome as it was unanticipated. "Not if I can help it. Not if we can help it."

She was safe in his embrace, encouraged, his hands rubbing her back in comfort, his chin resting on her straw hat. His touch was so unlike Sam Hazzard's press against her waist with his sweaty palms earlier in the day.

"I've got to go to Seattle tomorrow," Grace said, pulling away from his safety and warmth, yet letting his arms linger on hers. What did she really know about this man and what he might be doing here?

"Seattle, why?"

"I want to read old newspapers. Sam said they came from Minneapolis. I want to see if there's anything about their diet treatment back there. I must mail Dora's letter so it will arrive in Australia where their nanny is visiting as soon as possible."

William arrived and they entered the boat, speaking not at all on the crossing. They docked near the hotel and heard the steam whistle of the ferry arriving from Seattle.

"Oh," Grace said, "I should go now!"

"Can you take a letter to the mailbag so it will go back with the Seattle ferry?" Claude asked William.

"Yes, Doctor. There's still time. I'll take it there myself."

"You won't delay?" Grace said. William nodded. "But I still won't get the other information I need—"

"Join me for dinner, Grace. I'll tell you all you'll want to know about the Hazzards' past."

Grace couldn't decide what to wear. Her heart beat faster than normal. From the potion given to her by Dr. Hazzard earlier in the day? Or maybe lack of healthy food. Or perhaps it was anticipating dinner with Claude. Except that she wouldn't have dinner. *Why did I agree to join him?* She called the desk clerk and asked if he'd send someone to deliver a note to Dr. Millikan, then she hastily wrote suggesting another change in dinner plans, pleading a headache. She did have a headache, but she also had to read the codicil. And she needed to know what Claude knew about the Hazzards. That knowledge would have to wait until morning. She folded the note to Claude as the bellman knocked at her door.

"Here—Oh." She gasped.

"Yes. I do hope I'm not disturbing you." Sam Hazzard dragged the words out. "I thought if I could assist you in reading the codicil, things would go more smoothly. I heard the bellman call and told the clerk I'd be happy to pick up the note for you. May I come inside?"

·... ℰIGHT ·...

Grace crumpled the note in her palm. "Oh silly me. I've changed my mind. And it would be unseemly to entertain a man in my room, even one so admirable as you, Colonel Hazzard. You must be a military man, your bearing is so regal. I really must have a word with the clerk for giving you my room number." She fluttered her eyes not to attract but to remind him of her fluffel-head ways. Her mind raced.

He stepped inside the door that remained open. "The clerk meant no harm."

"How did you—that is, William rows people and you weren't—"

"I told William I could take the mail to the ferry for him as I'll be heading that way myself soon enough, if that's what you're wondering."

He has the Williamson letter? "No, that is, William had already rowed us back and you weren't with Dr. Millikan and myself."

Sam smiled. "I wasn't. I have my own little boat."

I wonder where he keeps it.

"Oh. Well." She looked up and saw Claude coming down the hall. Relief like a balm entered her heart. "Here's Dr. Millikan. What a nice surprise." Thank goodness she hadn't let Sam close the door.

Sam touched the brim of his hat as he returned it to his head. "Dr. Millikan."

"Good to see you, Sam. Are you ready, Miss Hathaway? We're having dinner this evening."

Sam looked at her. "Are you? Eating? Your treatment . . . Well, it's certainly best if one doesn't waste away. And if you're wondering, William had already made his trek to the ferry, but he did say he had a letter from you to mail."

"My request for account numbers, don't you remember?"

"Ah yes. I do now. I didn't wish to bother you, Miss Hathaway. I only stopped by to make your legal reading easier." He sounded sincere for the very first time. Maybe he flirted with all the women he encountered. Some men were like that. "I'll be off then. Dr. Millikan. Until tomorrow, Miss Hathaway." He tipped his hat to her, then Claude, before descending the stairs.

"What was that all about?" Claude asked

"I—he—" Grace swallowed the lingering tension. "Rebecca apparently asked for a codicil to her will. She thinks she's dying, and Mr. Hazzard said she requested a codicil. She intends to leave five thousand dollars a year to the Hazzards. Indefinitely. Forever, if there's enough money, but that's so wrong. Why would she do that and risk Caroline's care? And he wanted to 'discuss' it with me. The man makes me feel like a fruit he intends to pluck." She shook her head. "It's all so astonishing."

"Bring the legal papers along and I'll have a look at them if you'd like."

"I'm not hungry now, I'm truly not." And she wasn't. She thought about food a lot, maybe because she wasn't to have any, but she wasn't experiencing physical hunger at all.

"Grace, join me while I look over the paper, then."

"All right. I do want to know what you know about the Hazzards."

She picked up the papers, passed the mirror with a grimace while Claude stood at the door. She was presentable enough. They descended the stairs and Grace breathed a sigh of relief that Sam wasn't waiting there. The host took them to the table they'd eaten at that first evening. A blue iris with a yellow center decorated the center of the table, a candle flickering beside it. "I'll just have hot tea. Thank you. You go ahead, Claude. Don't worry about me."

Claude ordered a steak with potatoes and a big leafy salad of fresh greens. "You really should take some protein. A dinner of cornmeal and broth is hardly enough."

"How did you know?"

"People tend to tell doctors things they ought to keep private. The cook told me. He was concerned that you might be ill. And now I see for myself. Are you fasting for a reason?"

"So I'll understand better what my friend is going through— even though it's not at the hands of the Hazzards." She crossed her fingers at the little fib. "So what do you know of them, from Minneapolis?"

"Dr. Linda Hazzard was tried for practicing medicine without a license after one of her patients died. But the jury found her innocent, as no one testified that the deceased ever asked to be relieved of the treatment. It was all voluntary. And she has a license of some kind so that charge didn't stick."

"But she puts her patients under her spell. It's like they're held hostage and are dependent on her. They don't want to upset her. And if they ask for food, she tells them they aren't well enough yet. They've given their will over to them, both of the Hazzards. That's what Rebecca has done as well, literally given them her will and allowed them to change it."

"Apparently Mr. Hazzard is quite a charmer." Claude took a forkful of a chocolate dessert. "This is quite delicious." He let his lips slide off the silver fork, smooth as a fingertip running along her arm. She shivered. "Care for a bite?"

"You're cruel, Mr. Millikan."

"You don't need to fast, Miss Hathaway. Your body is perfection as it is." He didn't grin but said it with such certainty she knew she blushed. Her napkin became quite fascinating with its tiny little stitches at the hem. "Shall I continue?" Grace looked up, nodded yes. "Sam was tried for bigamy and found guilty." Grace gasped. "He served three years in prison and then they both came west. Linda is the controller; Sam handles the finances and maybe some of the nursing staff as well, if you know what I mean."

"Bigamy and death! Oh Claude." She reached for his arm. "They're charlatans and dangerous ones at that. What will we do?"

"Let me look at the codicil and we'll decide from there."

Claude read over the papers, hmming and nodding his head at various times while Grace sipped her tea and watched this man whom she decided had to be on her side. His intuition at the dock, knowing she needed comfort yet being gallant, stirred her again, made her skin tingle to her toes with the memory. Yet he knew these terrible things about the Hazzards and still chose to pay them to let him be there, making money for some apothecary company. She mustn't let herself be swayed by those eyebrows, his quick intellect, and his episodes of kindness and warmth. If he was in any way assisting the Hazzards—and he was as he'd given them money—then he couldn't really be trusted. And he wouldn't tell her what he was doing with Rebecca, either. He said he wasn't doing anything to harm her, but what if he made up potions of his own in that lab and Rebecca was a guinea pig for his experiments! Why, he was no better than the Hazzards! She stuffed her linen napkin onto the table in a huff.

Claude looked up from his reading. "What's wrong?"

"Nothing."

"Do you think you can convince Rebecca to delay signing this?"

"Delay? She should never sign it."

"I agree. But if we can put it off for as long as we can, it will give us time."

He'd said *us*. "For what? I just have to get her to agree to come home with me."

Claude nodded. "But in the meantime?"

"What would I tell her to wait for?"

"Tell her to wait until she feels stronger."

"But she isn't getting stronger! That's what I'm trying to tell you. You didn't know her before. She must weigh less than I do and she's three inches taller. My friend is wasting away!"

"No, she isn't."

"How can you say that?"

"Because I'm feeding her. Every day."

Grace stared at him. Is that what he was doing in the laboratory with her? Was he feeding other patients as well? "What? But . . . I don't understand."

"It's best if you don't. Just don't do anything foolish like getting Dr. Hazzard to provide care for you as you fast."

She bristled.

"I'm serious. I know you want to help, but being a patient there is not wise. While I'm not yet certain of what's in Dr. Hazzard's reddish and purple potions, I can tell you that patients who take them regularly become very dependent on her and can't sort fact from fiction. I don't want that happening to you."

"I'm stronger than I appear, Claude Millikan."

"Perhaps, but this is not a trifling affair. You'll need all your strength to convince your friend to leave." He paused. " I don't want anything untoward to happen to Mrs. Holmes's best friend either."

Grace felt her face grow warm and she clutched at the high collar of her dress. She knew her neck was blotching as it did with just the memory of his having held her at the dock and given her comfort. Now he expressed genuine concern for her. At least she thought it was genuine. Oh, she didn't know what to think!

Grace waited until she heard Claude's door close, then slipped down to the hotel kitchen. "I'd like bread," she said. "And a little cooked rice if you have it. Actually, a lot of cooked rice."

"Yes, Miss Hathaway. I'll have it sent up immediately. Glad to see that you're feeling better."

"Oh, yes, just a little stomach upset. But I'll wait and save the bellman the trip if you don't mind."

She inhaled the scents of the evening's dining as she kept herself from the center of the kitchen activity. When the waiter walked by with plates of sea bass, she nearly swooned, it smelled so wonderful. But this was appetite calling and she must say no to it. Her body did not need that bass. She was in this kitchen because she had a plan to save her friend. If Claude Millikan could feed Rebecca, then she could too. Together they'd help her gain strength enough to leave.

NINE

She stayed up most of the night taking care of her plan. But the two hours of sleep she snatched before dawn revived her. That and the two pills from Dr. Hazzard's bottle. She did look them over before swallowing, remembering Claude's caution. But these were green. Probably tea or ground-up spinach, not the red or purple ones Claude referred to at all.

The April morning sang to her, and at the dock she greeted Claude, her voice sounding a little louder than intended, but then water heightened the velocity of one's voice. "Did you sleep well, Dr. Millikan?"

"I did indeed. And you? Did you have sweet dreams?"

How did the man know? "Dreams to add to my slumber."

Claude helped her into the boat, climbed in after her, and they rode in silence to the music of the oars and the water swishing against the wooden boat. "I wonder if Sam makes this same crossing." She spoke her thoughts out loud. "He says he has his own boat."

"There's a crossing farther up, miss." William pointed with his chin. "On Finney Creek. Keeps it as a private dock for staff to come and go. Can pick up the Seattle ferry from there too."

Grace looked at Claude. "You're staff."

"Apparently not in the same category as the Hazzards or the nurses."

That news pleased her. He was different than the Hazzards. Even they recognized it.

At the sanatorium, Claude went his separate way up to the laboratory and Grace headed to Dr. Hazzard's office. The woman waited for her. "Good morning, Miss Hathaway. So pleased to see you."

"Likewise," Grace said. She curtsied. Good heavens, she hadn't done that since she was Caroline's age.

"Let's check your valise."

Grace handed it to her with ease.

"Yes. Everything looks fine. Still hoping to find an occasion for the ukulele, I see."

"Only if it is deemed to be helpful. Sometimes if people are quite upset or very conscious of pain, music can alter their awareness and move them to a more restful place."

Dr. Hazzard grunted. "Let's get your weight then."

Grace stepped onto the big white scale. Nurse Johnson stood poised to write the number down. "You've gained four ounces." Dr. Hazzard clucked her tongue. "Did you have dinner last evening?"

"Only cornmeal and tea. That's allowed, isn't it?"

"Yes. But four ounces . . . that's not a good sign. You should be losing four ounces, not gaining. Did you take the pills?"

Grace nodded.

"Well, what are we to do then?"

"I think, if you had room, I would do better as a patient here, where you could monitor what I'm doing."

"I was trying to save you money by having you stay in the village."

"I know. You're so kind."

"I don't have a nurse available to be off site . . ."

"Perhaps, if I might be so bold. My friend, Mrs. Holmes, is in a large room now. There would be room for a single bed there and

I could possibly assist in having her feel better about signing the codicil to her will that Mr. Hazzard mentioned to me. Have you ever put more than one patient into a room?"

"Sometimes. Sisters. Until one's healing lags so far behind the other that the lack of progress might affect the other's health."

"That's why Claire is in a room alone?"

Dr. Hazzard narrowed her eyes. "That's no longer an issue. Claire Williamson passed on last night."

"She . . . she died?" Grace swooned, caught herself on the scale. "Her sister must be beside herself with grief. Perhaps I could sit with her, play music for her. How very terrible."

"It is terrible. She would not allow herself to heal."

Of course it would be the Hazzards' view that it was the patient's fault when they didn't improve. Poor Dora! She would have to find her, tell her that the letter went out. If she was able to get food to Rebecca, maybe she could get some to Dora as well.

"Let us return to your health, Miss Hathaway. I do believe it necessary for you to stay here now, to have better oversight of your care." She tugged at another face hair. "And I think it might be well to have you room with Mrs. Holmes. You have the same resistant parasite. Your weight gain attests to that. This could be well."

"I didn't bring a change of clothes with me."

"Not necessary. We can have your trunk brought here from the hotel."

"Or I could go back with William today at noon and pick up the trunk."

"That would be fine. But meanwhile, we have a sanatorium wrapper that is suitable and won't be a problem with the clyster treatments."

"Oh. Those."

"Should you show yet another weight gain tomorrow, we will begin those treatments. Today there'll be the massage. But first, we will admit you to Mrs. Holmes's room and arrange things so you can return at noon and then be back to officially become a patient here."

Her plan was taking shape.

"Rebecca? It's me, Grace." The two were alone at last. Grace had changed into the wrapper given her by the nurse, who had left when she thought that Grace had fallen asleep.

Rebecca opened her eyes with recognition this time. A frail smile formed at her lips. Her whole face looked as though the skin was but vellum stretched to cover cheekbones and chin, sunken eye sockets, a narrowing nose, her face as white as a piano key. "Who would have thought it would come to this?" Rebecca said. She looked right into Grace's eyes.

"It doesn't have to." She patted Rebecca's hand. "Here, I brought you some rice. Your body can't take much in, but rice will be comforting."

"I . . . can't. Dr. Hazzard will be upset. I mustn't upset her. She's done so much for me."

"She's put me in the room with you, to be your assistant. I'm sure she won't mind."

Rebecca blinked. A crust had formed at the corner of her eyes that Grace brushed away with her fingertips, careful not to scratch. She could see roads of blue veins at her temples.

"Are you sure she won't be upset with me?"

"I'm certain. Here." Grace took rice and pieces of bread from little cloth bags made from strips of her petticoat. She'd sewed them into the hem of her dress. They likely accounted for her extra weight, but it didn't matter now. This would work out perfectly. She'd stay a few days, feeding Rebecca, and when she looked strong enough, she would sneak her out.

She'd made the noon trip to the hotel, checking out and bringing her trunk back with her. William scowled the entire time.

"Don't worry," she told him. "I'm not staying long."

"That's what they all say, miss. But we don't call the place Starvation Heights for no reason."

"I'm in good hands. The Lord knows I'm here doing good things for my friend. And hopefully once we help her, we can help others too."

"You and the doctor doing this thing together, then?"

"No! Oh, no, and please don't tell him. I'll be fine."

"What do I say when he wonders why you're not making the evening crossing, miss? He's become attached to you, I'd say."

"He's very nice, I agree. Just tell him . . . I was called . . . away . . . and not to worry."

William grunted, docked the boat, and carried her trunk up to the sanatorium where Sam Hazzard met them.

"I'll check this for food," he said.

Grace gave William coins and smiled. She whispered to him, "I'll be fine."

Now, here she was with Rebecca with a sliver of cooked rice on her fingertips. She pushed it into the cheek pocket of her friend's mouth, closed the lips over it. She nearly cried with the feebleness of her friend's chew. With gentle fingers at Rebecca's jaw, Grace helped her keep her mouth closed so the rice wouldn't dribble out.

"Bless you, my friend," Grace whispered. "May you soon be well. May your appetite be satisfied with life, with your daughter and the memories of Bertrand. May you feel held in God's hands."

The effort tired Rebecca, but she swallowed three of the fingertips of rice before falling asleep. Grace finished the little bit of rice from the opened bag, then tucked the dress and remaining bags of rice and bread onto the hook with the hem showing not a trace of deception. The bread was of little value, given that it would take too much energy to chew it. She'd save it for herself. Still, she couldn't afford to gain weight. That would only increase the good doctor's interest in her care.

When the nurse did not return, Grace donned a simple dress. She didn't want anyone stopping her as she meandered around. Patients who could still walk were permitted to sit in the gardens and they didn't all wear wrappers. She could always say if asked that she sought her assistant. Or pretend to be one. The person she looked for was Dora. She wanted to comfort her over the loss of her sister and to tell her that the letter to her nanny had gone out. Her prayers were answered when she opened a door to one of the rooms. A nurse sat at the foot of the bed reading, but Grace recognized the formerly elegant nightdress now faded nearly as pale as Dora Williamson's face.

"I'm a new assistant," she said. "I was told you might wish a break. How is she handling the death of her sister?"

"We have not told her. Dr. Hazzard fears it will distress her and set her own progress back."

"I see. I can sit here if you'd like."

The nurse nodded and took her book with her. Once again, Grace was without a musical instrument except for the one she was born with, and she began to sing softly, this time a hymn that was also a prayer as most were. "Be thou my vision," Grace sang, the words bringing comfort to her own soul. She looked to see if Dora's eyes fluttered or if her fingers scratched at the sheets, any sign that she was still alive and might be hearing this prayer sung by a stranger. When she heard a small sound, she stood and, leaning over Dora's bed, she put new words to the tune she'd been singing. "You sent a letter, seeking kind help. I heard your cry and the letter went out. Now we await the most caring of souls; we pray for your healing, thanking heaven who knows."

Dora's eyes did not open but they fluttered. Grace touched her hand, then jerked as Dr. Hazzard barked, "What are you doing in here!"

"Dr. Hazzard. Just comforting Dora. The nurse—"

"Took a break. Yes, she told me you told her I'd sent you."

"I never assumed that." Grace pressed her hand to her heart. "I just said she might wish a break. I'm only trying to be helpful."

"Helpful is when you do as you are told. She'll return momentarily. Meanwhile, come with me. It's time for your massage."

Grace looked back to see if Dora moved, gave any indication she might have heard what Grace sang. All she saw was a tear that had leaked from Dora's eye, still closed to the dark sadness of this world the Hazzards now caged her in.

"Ow! Ouch! Must you pound so hard?"

Dr. Hazzard was using Grace's body like a mass of bread dough, pummeling it from shoulder to calves, then back up again, shouting, "Eliminate! Eliminate!" Each time she struck Grace with the side of her palms.

"Ouch! You must be bruising me."

"You won't bruise, if you've been taking the pills I gave you."

"I have. Ouch! Please. That's so painful."

"The parasite is resistant. It must be beaten from your body. Eliminate!" Dr. Hazzard kneaded her back now and shoulders, giving Grace slight relief before once again pummeling her like a pillow of old feathers needing harsh fluffing. "Finished!"

Grace eased into sitting, her body tingling at every cell, screaming for calm. However did Rebecca or any of the others so wizened ever survive this?

"It's time for Rebecca's massage. I'll be down shortly."

"Wait."

"What? Are you challenging me, Miss Hathaway?"

"I mean could we wait? She may be more likely to discuss the codicil if she's not aching from—oh, I know you only do this to eliminate the poisons in our bodies." Grace responded to the frown on Dr. Hazzard's face. "Perhaps put off the clyster syringe treatment for a few days as well?" She was sure that if Claude had been feeding Rebecca for a week or more and she was now adding rice that Dr. Hazzard might become suspicious about the . . . output of a clyster treatment.

"She already had her clyster treatment this morning." Dr. Hazzard hesitated. "We will delay the massage until tomorrow so you can assure her the codicil is exactly what she asked for."

Grace worked her way back to Rebecca's room and was rewarded by seeing her friend sitting up. "Grace." Her hand wave was like a descending leaf dropped onto her lap. "I dreamed you were here. That you fed me rice. I often dream of food."

"Do you dream of other things? Home? Caroline?"

She blinked back tears. "I do."

"Look, I brought you something from Caroline. We can't hang it up because the Hazzards thought it would upset you, bring bad memories." Grace unrolled the paper that Dr. Hazzard had overlooked as she sought only contraband food.

"It's the Columbia River. Oh Grace—" Her voice faltered. "I do want to go home, but I don't know that I'm ever going to be well enough. Dr. Hazzard says I'm not getting any better."

"You just need to eat more."

"But Dr. Hazzard—"

Grace put her fingers to Rebecca's lips. "Sh-h-h." She walked to the dress and removed a stitch, taking out another packet of rice. "It wasn't a dream, Rebecca. It's time we got you strong enough so you can leave."

TEN

Sam Hazzard arrived shortly after Rebecca had fallen back to sleep.

"Don't wake her. She really needs her rest," Grace said. "Isn't it good I'm here to help her?"

"Has she signed the codicil?"

"Not yet. I assumed you'd need to be a witness. Little old me could hardly act as such, especially when I'm a patient."

"Yes. That's right. How do you find your accommodations?"

"Lovely. I hope you don't mind. I've been playing my ukulele, just for myself, you understand."

"Keep it quiet. You don't want to disturb the other patients."

"I love the view out this window. Where does that path lead? To another cottage I can't see?"

He stood near her to look out the window, his hand dropping lightly on her shoulder. "Let's see. That path would take you to the staff boat. It's a good hike, but of course Dr. Hazzard and I believe in hikes, invigorating air, the scent of cedar and fir and the deep, earthy loam of the forest floor." He kneaded her shoulder as he spoke.

"I might just take a walk there later if it's so lovely."

"I'd be happy to show you."

"You would? Oh how grand. But first I'm due for my clyster syringe treatment. I'll see how I feel about hiking after that."

"Dr. Hazzard may not be able to perform that treatment today," Sam said. "She has an embalming and autopsy to attend to. But let's plan for tomorrow, shall we? Say at 10:00 a.m.? Oh, and here are the red pills Dr. Hazzard prescribed for you. I'll watch while you swallow. She requires a witness to pills taken here at the sanatorium. Good professional practices."

They had to leave this evening. She knew it. Waiting until tomorrow would only bring more pain for Rebecca. She knew where the path was now to the boat and hopefully, prayerfully, Rebecca would be strong enough to make the walk. She'd half carry her if need be. Dr. Hazzard was busy with the embalming and Sam had their "hike" in the morning to look forward to. Grace shivered in disgust. How different a touch could feel when one trusted and cared for the one doing the touching. And she did care for Claude. Maybe she should have told him where she was and that she'd become Dr. Hazzard's patient at the sanatorium. He'd find out soon enough if Rebecca told him when she was brought to the lab. Maybe she should just go tell him herself.

No! What was she thinking. Her heart raced and she could feel blood pounding at her temples. Her stomach fluttered inside and she drank more water that sloshed in her stomach, it was so empty. Sam had made her drink four large glasses of water to take the pills. He insisted she take the green ones as well. *What's in those things?* She didn't know. It didn't matter. What did matter is that he had also forced Rebecca awake and pushed the reddish pill down her throat as though she were a horse being treated by the vet at one of the ranches. She nearly gagged, but the water washed it down and she lay exhausted back on the bed.

"That should help her decide about the codicil," he said.

Grace wondered if Rebecca would even remember.

"Mrs. Holmes? It's time for your visit to the lab." This was a fair-haired nurse dressed in a blue-striped uniform wearing a white apron and cap.

Maybe I should get that kind of uniform. I could just walk Rebecca right out of here. Where would she find such attire?

"All right." Rebecca rose as the nurse helped her plop into a wheelchair. However would they get her upstairs? She had to be able to walk.

Grace started to follow her out, but the nurse stopped her. "Just Rebecca right now. I'm sure your turn will come if Dr. Hazzard has made the referral to Dr. Millikan."

Referral? What kind of a referral would be needed? Did she say referral or removal? Was Rebecca being removed to another room? Thoughts like hummingbirds lit and flitted away. She felt a humming in her chest as her heart raced, then slowed.

Uniform. She would find the kitchen. The staff rooms must be near there. She went down the hall trying to smell cooking. She couldn't. Well, of course there wouldn't be cooking smells. Oh, that bathroom door, the door she was going to check but didn't have time for. They likely locked the kitchen up so no patients would steal food. She walked back inside, trying to find the wing the bathroom had been in. Near Dr. Hazzard's office, wasn't it? She made her way, found the door, but Dr. Hazzard's door opened as well. She slipped inside the bathroom with just a crack open to hear what was happening in the hall.

"We'll keep the body until the sister passes, then bury them both. No sense stirring up trouble with the estate until both are gone."

"Yes. Perhaps we can hasten that?"

"If necessary. We'll decide when I get back from Seattle. We've two new patients coming in. I want to be ready."

They walked past the door Grace hid behind and she was certain now they could hear her heart beating. Instead of checking the door or seeking out the nurse's uniform, she rushed back to the room where she'd found Dora that morning.

"Dora! Dora! We've got to get you out of here. Tonight. You must be strong tonight!"

"I can't leave Claire. Nanny will come, save us. Have you seen Claire?" Her pathetic eyes begged for help, yet she was too weakened, too confused to accept it.

"Not today." Should she tell her? No, while Claire lived in her mind, Dora continued to cling to life herself, she still had hope. Grace would get Rebecca out and then with the authorities they would rescue Dora and bring justice to the Hazzards. It was all she could do. Getting one weakened woman into a boat would be all she could manage.

Stars lit the April evening, the air holding a chill like a wet shawl around them. Grace pushed the wheelchair slowly down the hall, grimacing with one squeaky wheel. *Bong!* Grace thought she'd jump out of her skin. The clock! Every sound felt magnified; every creak a potential threat.

Only soft moans broke the ticking of the large clock in the lobby–living area. Rebecca's head lolled to the side. She was even more tired after seeing Claude, wasn't she? Maybe it was the exertion of the stairs. Grace saw no evidence of an elevator like ones she'd seen in Chicago. That was probably it, fatigue from climbing the stairs. She'd managed to feed her a few more fingers full of rice and had consumed two of the bags herself. She noticed that her head felt light as a soufflé when she stood up too quickly. *The pills?* Or just weakness, lacking eggs or meat. Just a few more feet and they'd be outside. She stepped in front of the chair to open the door onto the back porch. The ramp extended from the right side; the path to the boat formed at the left. She'd have to push her across cobbled stones until reaching the path and then, if it was too slick or narrow, she would have to lift Rebecca and pull her along, praying she could hold her up until they reached the boat.

There might have been a moon, but the treetops were a guillotine to the light Grace desperately needed when she realized the chair would be a hindrance to their escape. They hadn't gotten far when Grace touched Rebecca's shoulder and whispered, "You have to stand now. Can you do that? I'll help you."

"Are you sure it's all right?"

"I'm certain. Come along. Your Caroline is waiting and all your friends who love you and want you back as the lovely woman you are. Come along now."

Rebecca stood, wobbled, sat back down. Grace pulled her up again.

Like a death march, Grace lifted her friend, then dragged Rebecca forward slow step by step. She caught a glimpse of the water, then it disappeared as they made their way around a rock outcropping, pushed back ferns licking at their arms. Her heart pounded with the effort, her breath a gasp.

"Are you sure Dr. Hazzard won't mind?"

"I am," Grace said. Oh how she wished she could comfort her friend.

"I'm not."

A man's voice. Sam! Grace's heart moved into her throat.

"Sam! What are you—"

"Going for a midnight walk, are we?"

"Yes. I—"

"You're going nowhere, little miss interfering friend, except with me. Both of you."

Grace started to flee, hoping she could get help, but he grabbed her arm, grabbed Rebecca's too, lifted Rebecca at the waist she was so slender.

"You are coming with me to a very special little room, just for patients who are out of control."

He dragged them back, his height and strength overpowering their feminine frames. Inside the sanatorium he pushed them into the bathroom with the unknown door. He pressed himself against Grace, the smell of sweat and alcohol strong. She couldn't move.

"Much as I'd like to stay here, little missy, I have work to do."

He threw her aside and she fell against Rebecca, who had collapsed against the bathroom tub. He opened the door with a key, and before Grace could right herself from the tangle of crinoline and skirt, he yanked her and threw her into the darkened room. Rebecca was tossed in beside her. He slammed the door shut and turned the key.

She never should have tried to do this on her own. She should have made sure the boat was there and that Sam wasn't. She should have told Claude, left a letter with William telling him what? Something, some sort of backup plan. What would Sam do with them? Had he gone to get Dr. Hazzard? Then Rebecca appeared to come awake. She couldn't see her friend's eyes but could hear her breathing as it quickened.

"It's so very dark. So small. Where are we? Who's with me?"

"It's me, Grace. I'm with you. You're not alone."

"It's so small. I can't breathe."

It was as black as the inside of a cow's stomach. She was hungry enough to eat an entire piece of tripe by herself. She laughed out loud. *So inappropriate!*

"Grace? Where are we? What are we doing here? Where's Dr. Hazzard? Grace?" She began clawing at Grace's arm, put a fist to Grace's chest. "What's happening! Have I died? It's so dark."

"It's going to be all right. We are not alone here. God knows where we are."

"Where is God? Why isn't he turning on lights? I can't stand the dark like this. I—" She clawed at Grace's hair.

"Here, let's see if we can find out how large the room is, if there is another door." Grace moved to pat the wall, count paces until the corner, but she only reached the first corner before she felt Rebecca fly at her from behind, yank her neck.

"Get me out! Get me out of here!"

Grace knew she had to calm her friend and her words were not doing it. She did what she knew to do: she began to sing, grasping Rebecca's hands in hers. First lullabies, then hymns, then little ditties from children's songs she knew. She held her friend now, arms clasped around her shoulders, and she sang softly, but then decided that was silly. Why not sing loudly. Why not wake up the entire sanatorium. Someone would find them, someone other than Sam Hazzard maybe. A nurse who would at least let them out and ask what they were doing there. The cook, up early to juice the tomatoes, maybe. She'd wonder what they were doing in a closet. An empty closet. Not even a broom to bash against the door. Anyone could find them. They'd be safe enough until Grace could escape and tell Claude to come with her, now that the Hazzards planned to hasten the death of Dora Williamson if need be. He simply had to remove himself from whatever it was he was doing. The lives of these patients came first.

She sang more loudly as Rebecca calmed and even joined her at one point, and then she heard the key turn and Sam Hazzard's face backlit in the single bulb hanging in the bathroom.

"Shut up!" he shouted. "Do you want to wake the entire hospital?"

"Yes!"

Her "yes" was a duet with Claude's "yes," his cello voice a burst of joy sent from heaven as Sam turned to face him.

"What are you doing here, Millikan? And who's that? The constable?"

"One might ask the same of you. I know of no treatment that puts innocent patients in a darkened room to scare them out of their wits."

"They were uncontrollable."

"I'll control them, then, right out of here. Come along, ladies. Constable, I think you can arrest for kidnapping to begin with."

The uniformed man grabbed Sam Hazzard.

"You can't take them. They have fees to pay. Dr. Hazzard will be back in the morning. We can discuss their release then."

"They are released, into my care."

"You're a mere pharmacist," Sam sneered.

"And a physician and a Pinkerton detective sent to gather evidence, my good man. These two are witnesses. I think we've just hit the mother lode. And you, sir, are under arrest."

$\mathcal{E}$LEVEN

hank goodness you thought to sing loudly or we might
never have found you."

"Oh Claude, I can't thank you enough, I can't." They carried
Rebecca between them toward William's boat.

"Will Dr. Hazzard be upset?" Rebecca spoke, breathless.

"Yes, Rebecca, she will be, but not from anything you did. You
just need to rest in the hotel. We'll get you well and then we'll go
home."

Grace wished she could see Claude's face in the moonlight, but
it was nearing dawn and it was always darkest then. She felt the
grip of his fingers against hers as they held Rebecca between them.
Strong hands. Caring hands.

William waited, rocking back and forth on his heels. "You got
them, Doc. Good for you!"

"Miss Hathaway did her part."

"I've no doubt of that, sir. None at all. Come then, let's get the
little lady in. You first, Miss Hathaway, then we'll hand—"

"Mrs. Holmes," Grace told him. "My very best friend."

"Here she be then. Light as Cook's biscuit."

"Yes, she is," Grace said. "But not for long!"

"Take care of them, William. And then come back."

"You're not coming with us?"

"I'm going back to look after Dora Williamson and the others, until we can make arrangements for all of their care." Claude kissed the top of Grace's head as she bobbed in the boat.

"Of course you are!" Grace said. "You're the nourishment to this long-hungering life of suffering. I'll come back to help as soon as I can."

The noon sun filtered between the trees, casting happy shadows on the hotel porch where Grace and Claude drank coffee. Rebecca was sound asleep in the room she'd share with Grace until she was well. Claude had returned after setting a new regimen for patients to ensure their survival, and the constable already had both Hazzards in custody.

"How did you know to come?" Grace said.

"You didn't make the evening crossing. Nor the morning one. I asked William about you. He was noncommittal, saying something about your having left, checked out of the hotel. When I got back, I learned you had indeed done so and I couldn't believe you'd have gone without saying goodbye." He looked like a small boy, his eyes downcast when he said next, "I guess it was a man's pride, to think you wouldn't leave without that goodbye. Something had moved between us, Grace Hathaway." He lifted her chin. "And I simply couldn't accept that I'd been all alone on my journey toward a shared heart."

"You weren't. I traveled there too, with bells on my toes and music on my lips."

He leaned to kiss her and she took the love he offered, wasting no time in kissing him back.

"It occurred to me," Claude said, holding her fingers in his, "that you just might be pretending to be a visitor but had somehow, in your beautiful addled brain, decided to become a patient, to get

372

closer to Rebecca." He whispered across her cheek into her ear. "I knew that if they gave you those potions, you might not be thinking well. William finally confessed and I decided around midnight that I couldn't wait until morning to find out if you were all right. Maybe that was crazy, but it turned out to be providential."

She loved the warmth of his breath, the brush of those eyebrows at her temple. She couldn't have been more satisfied than if she'd eaten a chocolate cake all by herself. "Love can addle a brain," Grace said.

"Most definitely," Claude said, then kissed her again.

Grace was totally filled up.

Epilogue

You actually read Dora's letter to her nanny?" Grace sat next to Claude on the ferry back from Kitsap's county seat. There, Claude had reported on behalf of a family member in California whose mother had died "at the hands of Dr. Hazzard."

"I did. Then sent it as a cable to Australia but with the letter too. So they'd see it was in Dora's handwriting, recognize Dora's words were written by her, but realize something was terribly wrong. I only wished I could have intervened before Claire's death."

"Why didn't you tell me you were a Pinkerton detective working for one of Dr. Hazzard's victims? You can't imagine all the terrible thoughts I had of you."

"Oh yes I can."

"Thank goodness Dora Williamson's nanny arrived and she and the British consulate are taking charge of the prosecution. What we have to share will only increase the likelihood that Linda Hazzard and her husband will be brought to justice."

Claude put his arm around Grace. They'd be at the hotel for a few more weeks until Rebecca was strong enough to travel. And

Claude would travel with them. A Pinkerton man could find work anywhere justice was in need of wisdom.

"Here we are, Rebecca. Home at last."

Caroline ran across the lawn to her mother, wrapped her little arms around her skirted legs. Lilacs bloomed and sent their fragrance across the banks of the Columbia in their own celebration of life.

"You're home, Mama. You're home. Aunt Grace brought you home."

"I only helped," Grace said. "As you did keeping your mamma in your prayers."

"This is Grace's friend," Rebecca said. "Well, mine too. Claude Millikan, doctor and detective."

Claude bent down to be at eye level with Caroline. "Is this the artist who drew that lovely river picture?" Caroline nodded. "It is as fine as any I've ever seen."

"Thank you, Mr. Claude. So you helped my mamma?"

"He did," her mother said. "And we will all be forever grateful, won't we, Caroline?"

"Oh yes, Mamma. And thank you, Aunt Grace. I'm so glad you answered my letter."

Grace stroked Caroline's hair, then looked up at Claude. "And I'm so glad you wrote it. Otherwise I might never have found the true music of my heart."

Grace wouldn't be returning to the Roaring Springs Ranch. Instead she'd join Claude in San Francisco, a city she'd always wanted to visit. He also had a sweet grape arbor where she could rest her eyes on green vistas. This time, she'd stay, marry the desire of her dreams, and be satisfied and busy teaching music to the Millikan children, once they all arrived. It was the truest way to satisfy the hunger of the soul.

DEAR READER,

Wilderness Heights, also known as Starvation Heights by locals, was operated by the Hazzards in Olalla, Washington, in 1911 when this story is set. There were two British sisters who took the cure along with many others following the Hazzards' wasting diet to cure them of all ills, many of which they did not suffer. Dora Williamson survived to participate in the prosecution over the death of her sister, Claire. While there was no Pinkerton detective operating at the sanatorium, the British sisters did suffer as described; treatments were as agonizing and harmful. Claire died before the nanny, the orphaned sisters' childhood nurse, left Australia. Margaret Conway arrived in Seattle exactly one week after receiving Dora's letter. No one knows who actually carried the life-saving letter out for Dora, but it may well have been someone like our Grace who wished to save the suffering. I took slight liberty with the setting of the sanatorium. It was not actually reached with a wooden boat rowed from the hotel. Instead one walked up a long narrow path into a dense forest. But there was a dock at Finney Creek used by the Hazzards to bring in patients secretly. I wanted to deepen the sense of isolation and bring Grace a way to have more time with her champion, Dr. Millikan.

The Hazzards were known to force signatures of wealthy patients who were dying, and Linda Hazzard even sold Claire's teeth following that sister's death. Yet she had many supporters. The

British consulate was involved in prosecuting Linda Burfield Hazzard in 1911–1912, the first such case where a foreign government prosecuted a case in an American court. Linda Hazzard was found guilty of manslaughter and served three years in the Walla Walla prison in Washington State. It did not stop her diet program. After her release, she went on to take advantage of many men and women hungry for healing and thinking they could find it by wasting away. Linda Hazzard died in 1938 after treating herself with her own fasting treatment that did not bring a cure.

The sanatorium no longer stands, having burned down in 1935. For more information about this unusual time in the Northwest, a look at the trial and fascinating events that followed, pick up Greg Olsen's award-winning book, *Starvation Heights* (Three Rivers Press, NY, 1997).

Meanwhile, stay well.

Sincerely yours,

JANE KIRKPATRICK

Jane Kirkpatrick's works of historical fiction have been CBA bestsellers for a decade, and one of her latest, a compilation with other authors, was a *New York Times* bestseller.

She is internationally recognized for her lively presentations and well-researched stories that encourage and inspire. Jane is the author of over 25 books, including historical novels. Many of her titles are based on the lives of real people or incidents set authentically in the American West. Her first novel, *A Sweetness to the Soul*, won the Wrangler Award from the Western Heritage Center. Her works have won or been finalists for the WILLA Literary Award, Christy, Spur, Wrangler, Oregon Book Award, and the Carol and Readers' Choice awards. Several of her titles have been Book of the Month and Literary Guild selections. She lives with her husband, Jerry, in Oregon.

Jane loves to hear from readers at http://www.jkbooks.com and http://Facebook.com/theauthorJaneKirkpatrick.

"She creates characters that tug at my heartstrings, storylines that make my heart smile, and spiritual lessons that do my heart good."

—Kim Vogel Sawyer, bestselling author of *My Heart Remembers*

"The Midwives series gets better with each book."

—RT Book Reviews

"Shorey includes surprises in all her books for her fans to discover, and what they find is never disappointing."

—*RT Book Reviews*

CPSIA information can be obtained at www.ICGtesting.com
Printed in the USA
LVOW08s1607160816

500618LV00008B/858/P